RITE OF THE REVOLUTION

By

Roquel Rodgers

"The history of our revolution will be one continued lie from one end to the other..."

- John Adams

CHAPTER I

ADAM WEISHAUPT
Ingolstadt, 1771

It opened up to his core - a pulsing petunia. It ate him in, and he went speeding ever faster down its blazing shaft and fell into a sky where a million mirrored spheres reflected the light of his soul into a soft and infinite luminescence. He heard the jingling of the universe in his ears. Time was of no essence here until he realized it, then the unthinkable happened and he was absorbed in the radiance...

He found himself again, regaining his shining unity on some other side of the cold, cold void. He wondered what had happened and realized it was very real and he was out of control. He was falling, falling, spinning, reeling head over heels. He pulled himself back together, remembering, remembering his old life, himself - the handsome fellow who fancied himself illuminated. And he was... He was...

"Who am I? Where am I?" He heard his own voice ask.

He rushed through an endless tunnel of purple spinning flowers – petunias, pansies, jacaranda blossoms, sweet peas...

"Ewige Blumenkraft!" He heard himself exclaim.

And he snapped back into his body, his silver cord coiling up at the base of his spine with a hiss. He reeled slightly in his crossed-legged pose and thanked God he had found his way back this time.

The tiny onion flower he had been contemplating lay wilted on his thigh in the light of the candle that was sinking into a pool of wax upon the floor.

"Blumenkraft," he whispered, twirling the stem between his fingers. It was so poignant... though he couldn't quite

1

remember why. It was on the tip of his thought, then it was gone in his next breath.

He scratched his stubbly chin, and took note of the blue vessels crawling over his muscular arms. He stroked the electric fuzz on his stomach and felt the comfort of his own body. He peered into his looking glass and confirmed his sparkling face in the candlelight. He was still there, still young, still winsome and handsome, and so brilliant inside those shining black pupils that seemed to melt upon the surface of the looking glass like two black-yolked eggs.

He raised an eyebrow and sniffed the half-drunk vial that sat on the table beside him. He almost took another drink before he remembered what it was – an elixir called kykeon made with the ergotine of meadow grass and spelt, fermented with elderberries over a fortnight and suspended in goat's milk. He peered down at the bit of liquid in the bottom. Though the recipe was written in a language only slightly resembling Greek, he had deciphered it and mastered the mind-altering potion in only a few tries. This evening's batch was exceptionally potent and glorious, perhaps the best yet, but it wouldn't do to have any more just now, for it was nearly dawn and he had a class to teach.

He opened his door against the night's snowfall and slipped the corked vial into an old tin box his brother had sent him, and tucked it outside beneath the stoop. The little stair was a stack of fieldstones, made long ago with the mortar falling out, and it had many holes for hiding things. Like his mind had many holes for hiding things. He'd been exploring them since the night of Eva Frank's wedding, four years ago when he had first discovered this other side of life.

It all seemed so unreal now, so very far away, but every fiber of him ached to be near her again. Even after so long a time, he was enraged, and his promise to possess her he renewed upon falling on his pillow each night and rising each morning.

In the days and nights since that fateful night, he had become a scholar, a lawyer, a doctor of theology, a formidable metaphysician, and a persuasive lecturer. He had risen to his prominent position through his cunning, his connections, and a fair bit of sorcery, and sat resting uneasily on his laurels at the ripe age of twenty-three.

On this particular morning, young Adam Weishaupt went to the University to give his canon law lecture, a series meant to supplement the Canon Law IV class. He had exhausted the topic in about twenty minutes and now in the lecture room, he fired-off a battery of occult and Eastern philosophies.

"The yin will be entirely black - a negative sucking hole, but only up to a point and then it will begin to be something else − yang, a positive protrusion on the other side - a daffodil, something created - and when that positive expands so positively the very fact that it *is*, creates a void. So there it is, you're on the brink of everything, when *voila*, there's nothing you recognize. For some kind of change is inevitable."

His students seemed dumbstruck as he unrolled Isaac Luria's original thirteenth century scroll of the Tree of Life and stuck it to the wall with pins. "Behold!" he said gesturing to it, "The Tree of Life!"

He stared at the symmetrical polygon of lines and spheres, at the ten sephiroh that took on their colors and swirled around in the air in front of the scroll, manifesting in ten dimensions. His voice was hoarse with the gravity of the information he was relaying. "Everything... is all right here. Contained within and without the ten luminous spheres. This is the microcosm of the entire Universe, the body of God, the soul of man, the breath of the breath..."

He became aware of his students fidgeting, and turned to see them all bewildered. A hand went up, "I don't think anyone understands what you're talking about, Professor."

Adam looked narrowly at the pudgy young man,   then went briskly around the room closing the windows tight. "As above, so below. This is the crux of Hermetic Thought. What is in the palm of your hand, radiates across the Universe."

"But what of Heaven's glory? And Hell's eternal fury?" asked another young man who sat in the front row.

"Oh they exist, too. Don't you worry," he said as clovers danced in and out of a kaleidoscopic mosaic of Arabian design. "As do all untruths, half-truths, whole truths, and outright lies. Everything you can dream of – exists!"

"But that is not what the scriptures say, or the canons," said a tall, dark-haired lad dubiously.

"You know what," began Weishaupt vaguely annoyed, "Augustine and Pelagius, and that insipid... Paul, they weren't privy to the kind of pharmacopoeia I have. Were they, the canons would be significantly different."

He pulled a hookah from the cabinet and filled its bowl with a pinch of hemp from his desk. He lit it, had a deep suck, ordered his students to partake, and continued his lecture, explaining what came after the Ain Soph Aur or the boundless light. "It begins to get dark again... Or not, but something happens, because there's always... something more." Smoke sputtered from his mouth. "Another great mystery beyond what we can fathom."

He saw some of them beginning to understand, squinting, nodding, making small noises of comprehension. Adam's mouth curved into a smile. Suddenly, the Bishop's boy ran into the room and handed him a slip of parchment.

Weishaupt snatched it up. "What is it now?"

"You are summoned to St. Michael's Cathedral in Munich to see the Archbishop," said the boy with a defiant air of authority.

Adam read the note, then wadded it up and threw it back at him. Were his teaching methods and curriculum under

4

scrutiny again? He had fought them off with their own retarded logic last time he was up against wall. Had they figured it out and seen through his defense, or were they now somehow watching or listening to him lecture with their diabolical Catholic sorcery? Did some of the eyeballs that covered every surface in the classroom belong to the Church? Indeed! Let them watch, let them stare, he thought. But for a few blood crimes against the Papacy, he had nothing to hide. He was the finest professor Ingolstadt University had ever seen. He was the genius premiere, intellectual beyond compare, the summum bonam genie, and by Job, they would soon realize it or be singed by his psychic fury.

Adam led his stout, white mare, out of the stable and saddled her. He felt cold and insubstantial, like ashes on the wind, as he rode the way to Munich, through the harvest fields full of farmers' sons and daughters busily mowing their wheat. He rode past the dairy farms, through the forest, and down the river lane.

He was halfway to Munich when he looked down and suddenly realized he did not have shoes. Had he remembered his breeches? Gratefully so.

He was still vibrating–He could still hear the faint song, the hum of the stew in which he was suspended, as his horse clopped into town and up the cobbled road to the Cathedral.

Niched in their own vignettes all over the façade of St. Michael's Cathedral, bronze statues of the Saints and various noble ancestors of the Wittelsbach family bantered and argued with each other. Only valiant St. Michael looked up from spearing the irascible Satan, to greet him as he approached. It seemed that the hemp he had smoked was bringing on another wave of the kykeon's colorful hallucinations. His meeting with the Archbishop would be all the more interesting.

Adam opened the door of the cathedral and stepped inside. The thick smell of frankincense brought an onslaught of memories. He gazed up at the ceiling that vaulted perilously above him, ornamental dizziness escalating to high hell, and he feasted on its surreal magnificence. He had entirely forgotten its effect on him.

He neared the gilded altar and looked up at its painting of St. Michael slaying a dragon. He remembered himself as a boy, a boy who yearned to be a priest. Now he was more than a priest, or rather he was what a priest was supposed to be, before the rituals of his Religion had become so misconstrued, profaned, and diluted by idiocy and greed.

Then suddenly he heard it - a muffled voice, cursing some unhappy expletives, though he couldn't quite make out the words. A tortured soul was calling out in misery. It seemed to be coming from the sanctuary behind the altar.

Curious. Who was it? What was it saying? Could it be the voice of his own mind calling out in agony for justice? For more hemp?

The voice wailed wretchedly. Adam stared at the altar.

He stepped into the sanctuary and looked all around it. He felt a wave of nausea as he leaned over, straining his heightened senses.

There was no one there.

He heard a cough at his back, and whirled around to find the narrow-templed, spectacled priest whom he remembered from so long ago – Brother Haster, the secretary of the Bishop.

"Thank you for answering our call, Doktor Weishaupt. The Archbishop requires your expertise," he said.

"In what manner?" said Weishaupt curtly, relaxing a bit. So he wasn't going to be disciplined after all.

"He shall explain," the priest widened one of his eyes as he looked up at Adam. As he did so, his yellowed face took on the visage of a weasel with soap bubbles for eyes. The weasel turned and led him through the transept.

6

Weishaupt followed him warily out of the church and down the hallway, staying a safe distance behind, for the bites of such creatures could be particularly nasty.

He wondered then how Brother Haster had escaped the Jesuit suppression and remained at St. Michael's when all the Jesuits in Bavaria had been ousted or forced to deny their faith and practices. Weishaupt reasoned that Brother Haster had probably been the first to deny their doctrines, so flimsy was his backbone. He had allowed Adam to be beaten, nearly to death, and for another boy to die here, and he had done nothing to stop it. Indeed, Brother Haster had probably won the right to stay on at the Cathedral for his role in betraying the rest of them, his Jesuit brothers, who, only a short time ago, were the rightful inhabitants of St. Michael's Cathedral.

Adam had not been inside St. Michael's since the day he ran away. He beheld the great dark hall, a place where he had had the good fortune not to be for many years. The place seemed to be made of fearful, tortured, purple-red spirits whose bodies formed the shapes of the walls and columns. He could see their rolling eyes looking back at him as he walked past. He had had the fantastic image as a boy, and so many years later it was still there and remarkably so in the glittery aftermath of the kykeon. The atmosphere clung to him like the rough tunic he had worn when he was at school here and he fell into a fit of itching, itching all over.

The weasel bounced lightly over the carpet. Weishaupt followed him through the impossible maze of hallways that seemed momentously, ominously familiar, then became new and confusing. When he thought himself completely lost, they came to a door.

The priest opened the door with a large ring of keys and they walked down another hallway that opened upon still another hallway. It seemed that a great joke was unfolding before him and he laughed hysterically. The weasel looked at him, "Are you quite all right?"

"I'm more than all right, I'm quite extraordinary," Adam assured him. He wondered if Haster remembered him.

"I remember you," said the weasel as if he could hear Adam's thoughts.

Suddenly the labyrinth turned into a dark and opulent chamber.

From a distance, Adam saw the Archbishop in his long robe, contemplating a book that lay open upon his lap. He sat upon a fabulous ebony chair and tapped his bejeweled scepter as they entered. Adam wondered if it was for luck or palsy.

"Your Eminence, may I present Doktor Weishaupt," said the weasel with a bow and a flourish.

Weishaupt knelt before him and gave his ring a smooch. He felt a hard sting of electricity come from the gold medallion to his lips. "Humbled. Truly I am."

The Archbishop, with his bumpy skin and bulging eyes, looked him over, and wrinkled his ugly nose, "No shoes?"

"I can't afford them on my meager income," Adam lied.

"How is your professorship this year?" asked the Archbishop.

"Very well. I have many promising pupils. I hate to be summoned away from them in the middle of lecture. What is it that you want?"

The Archbishop considered him icily,   then lurched forward in his face. "You are a good Catholic, Doktor Weishaupt, and as such, you are under the dominion of St. Michael Altar. Your very life is but a service to the Church, do not forget our Precepts."

"How could I ever? The Church is my life," he said piously making the sign of the cross.

"They speak of your prowess with demons," said the Archbishop in a low voice.

"Demons? Where?" Weishaupt looked around, terrified.

"Under the Cathedral, beneath the sanctuary floor, down

in the catacombs - there is a special vessel for discarding any befouled or uneaten sacraments after they have been blessed as the Body and Blood of our Lord. Though the situation rarely arises, it is strictly against our laws to discard any consecrated offerings with the rubbish or feed them to an animal. Any of the Host that may be wasted goes into this vessel."

"Yes, I *lecture* on the sacredness of divine offerings in first trimester Catholicism class," said Weishaupt.

The Archbishop went on with grave dismay. "How it could have spawned from so pure a source, I cannot fathom, but the contents of the vessel through putrefaction, have formed of a demon that is *most* profane. For three days now, it has shouted barbarous threats from the sanctuary during prayers and mass and caused fear among the congregation and priests alike."

Weishaupt was skeptical, yet intrigued. Anything was possible. Didn't he just say that? Someone did. "What kind of demon do you think it is?" He knew that the term 'demon' was catch-all term for a great many unpleasant things. And of course, one man's demon was another man's darling.

"It shall be your duty to discover its nature and remove from this holy place," replied the Archbishop.

So he hadn't been hallucinating the voice in the Cathedral. However, he was unsure about the Archbishop's assumption that it was a demon, but considering some of the personalities that shuffled over the floorboards above it, it could be far worse than a demon.

He began gathering his drifted faculties and dusting the sparkly dust off his consciousness. He may need every ounce of acumen to contend with this unwanted entity, or crazed squatter – more likely.

The afternoon sky darkened as they walked across the

ancient churchyard where Adam had played as a boy. He remembered the names on the headstones, the old oak tree, and the wild onion flowers growing beneath it. How sweet they had tasted.

"There," the Archbishop pointed at a weather-beaten, wooden hatch in the tall grass. "I cannot accompany you, of course. I am not allowed to touch what is unclean."

"No of course not," Weishaupt bit his tongue and opened the hatch.

The Archbishop added "My Holiness may agitate it and make it even more dangerous. May the Lord bless thee and deliver thee from the perils of Satan Lucifer, Doktor Weishaupt."

"Danke schoen," said Weishaupt as he climbed down the stone stairs into the darkness.

A shrilly cold draft penetrated his bed robe as soon as his bare feet touched the dank stone floor. He shuddered, biting his fingers.

The walls of the catacomb were lined with crypts, some of them open, the final resting place of several centuries' worth of dried-out, shriveled-up priests. He stepped out of sight of the Archbishop and performed the Cross with the lighted torch in his right hand, clearing the vectors running up through the floor out his crown chakra and across his chest through his heart, out his fingertips into the holy infinites. He closed his eyes and banished with the white-hot light, posted his guardians and commanded them to hold fast to the four quarters. "God help me," he said, aware that whatever he was about to confront would be all the more vivid and terrifying because of the kykeon and its amplification of his sensibilities.

He walked quickly forward through the carved-out tunnel, knocking away spider webs, averting his eyes from the mummified corpses shelved all around him.

St. Michael Altar housed forty some-odd *living* priests of the highest spiritual learning the Holy Roman Empire had to offer, and he, Adam Weishaupt, was how they would contend with this whatever-it-was beneath their own sacrosanct altar. He was certainly flattered, but what if this thing was dangerous? What if it attacked and possessed him? Was that why they had chosen him? Because he was expendable?

The passageway turned, and the cobwebs were thick and stuck to his face. He swiped at them with his torch, and broke off the ember against the wall. He watched helplessly as it fell and sizzled out on the wet ground.

"Sheisse," he said as the pitch-blackness consumed him. He could hear his heart beating, and he could feel the cold, greasy dirt beneath his bare feet. Thoughts of the decayed priests all around him made him shudder as he continued onward, feeling his way along their crypts.

He turned a corner once more. There at the end of the corridor, something shone a faint, aquamarine light.

Slowly, cautiously, he stepped closer and saw that it was a large, glass vessel of liquid, a milky film of debris inside, occluding its contents. It was the vessel of the uneaten Host.

He leaned forward, thinking the glowing thing beautiful and eerie, a combination that particularly fascinated him. Suddenly, pearly, white flesh like pickled herring stirred within it. He jumped back.

A tiny, glowing, white face peered out at him through a clean spot in the vessel. It blinked and focused its large yellow eyes on him.

"A golem!" Adam whispered, aghast.

A tiny pale creature a foot high, eagerly clawed away the filth on the inside of its glass and looked at him with huge eyes full of delight. "Adam Weishaupt," said the little glowing man in a voice that transcended both the vessel and his mind. "You've come!"

And before he could move, it locked him in its gaze and trapped him there as its huge golden eyes probed his.

11

CHAPTER II

Wurzberg, 1754

Young Adam returned to the house sometime after dawn and found it half-burned and empty. He was so cold in his nightdress he was shaking, and could not feel his fingers or his feet anymore. The warm char and embers felt good then painful as he walked through the ruins of the great room. It had been burned on the side toward the street, though the rest remained intact. He tried to put the front door back in place but it was so heavy he couldn't even lift it. Why had Father left it like this? No one had made a fire in the hearth and the cold damp had chilled the whole house. He called for them, but no one answered. He ran upstairs and threw open the door to their room. It was empty. The baby's gourd rattle lay on the floor.

He went into his own, little room and curled up on his bed. Hours passed. Adam was unaware how many.

When he awoke, a man stood beside him and looked at him kindly. His goatee and mustache were pointed and he wore a strange tie at his neck. Adam was startled and leapt from bed. "Who are you?"

"I am your uncle. I have come for you, to take you to school," the man said, his voice breaking. His clothes made him seem rich and foreign.

"I have no uncle," answered Adam looking him over.

"Yes, you do. I am here. Get your things together and let's go." He thumped the black top hat in his hand. "Your parents are gone and you cannot stay one more minute in Wurzberg."

Adam got dressed to go, then looked briefly around his parent's bedroom to see if they would protest, but they were not there. It was strange that Mother would leave the bed unmade. And wherever Father had gone, he'd left a book open on the floor. He picked it up and looked at the

Hebrew writing. It was open to the page that Father had helped him read the night before, the part where God was telling Moses to leave Egypt.

The man took the book from Adam's hand and tucked it in his satchel alongside another old book. He pointed at it and made a small sound.

"It's safe with me," his uncle assured him.

Was Father going to retrieve it wherever they were going, or was he, for some reason, no longer in need of it? A dreadful emptiness overcame him then.

"Shall we leave them a note?" The man tweaked Adam's chin, took a card from his pocket and left it on the side table. "There. They will know you are with me. Now, hurry."

Outside, he lifted Adam into his carriage and climbed in across from him. They were driven away by four black horses.

Adam looked out at the village for the last time and saw the tired, dour faces of the citizenry going about their daily drudgery. He hated them so venomously he could taste it, yet he could not quite remember why.

His uncle stuck his head out of the carriage and shouted to the driver. "Go another way. Go around the river, please!" Adam looked up then, and glimpsed them, silhouetted before the sun, two severed heads mounted at the gates of the town. Someone had painted a sign below that said "Sorcerers, Beware!"

"What's a sorcerer?" he asked his uncle.

"It's a person who practices sorcery," he said a bit breathlessly.

"What's sorcery?" the boy asked, feeling that he mispronounced it.

His uncle looked at him. "A way that is forbidden by the Church. It is not for you. Never for you! Do you understand?"

Adam nodded, and the two of them said nothing for a

long time. They crossed into Bavaria, in and out of snow-laden forests. As they rode over an icy bridge, his uncle began telling him a story. "In the Rhineland, where I am from, there is a legend…" And his uncle told him the story of the young hero called Siegfried and his many adventures. The tale was a long one, and seemed to be a fable against the love of money, for in this tale, a great hoard of elves' gold was stolen and whoever possessed it was turned into a monstrous dragon or snake. Adam listened with avid interest to his uncle describe the virtuous Siegfried, the only person pure enough to come into contact with the glittering hoard and not be tainted by the lust of it. Winning the golden treasure for his master, Siegfried slayed the dragon Fafnir whose blood drenched him, making him impervious to all harm, except for in one spot on his back where the blood did not touch. He triumphed again and again, rescuing the sleeping beauty Brunhilde, and would have lived a happy life had he not chosen to go to war. There he was slain by his own men who were jealous of his virtues.

"You and my father don't look very much alike," Adam said compulsively, after having scrutinized the man's face for many hours.

"That happens in some families," his uncle replied with a quick smile. "We were born beneath different stars."

At last, they entered Munich and the horses' feet clopped on the cobblestone. "We're here," said his uncle.

They drove through the streets in the bright sunshine. Several men stopped and inclined their heads to his uncle or to his horses, Adam was not sure which.

They drove up a small hill into a great cold shadow that was cast by a huge Cathedral with many statues ensconced all over its massive facade.

The driver opened the door for them and Adam jumped out, staring up at the shining bronze characters, so life-like and majestic.

14

"Come now, let's see about your enrollment," said his uncle, tapping his cane on the steps and taking Adam's hand.

They walked through the rectory and down a little corridor that twirled into a cozy staircase, his uncle navigating the way as if he lived there himself. Upstairs, he knocked at a door, and a gruff voice responded for them to enter.

In the small, candle-lit room, sat the pale, rotund Bishop at his desk. His uncle bowed respectfully. "Guten Tag, Your Excellency, I wish to enroll my nephew."

"Your nephew?" asked the Bishop, and inclined his head dismissively toward the door. "I'm sorry, Baron, the dormitory is full."

Adam stood, but his uncle reclined in the chair next to his. "I intend to pay all of his tuition right now," he patted the case he had been carrying the whole trip. His uncle opened it and withdrew a bag of gold coins and spilled them across the Bishop's desk.

The Bishop pursed his lips. "Is he Jesuit?"

"Is he Jesuit? Of course he is!"

"We cannot accept students who are not Catholic. And this one, well... He looks a bit *swarthy*," replied the Bishop.

"This is Weishaupt's boy. The Superior General wants him educated here, to be trained for the priesthood."

"Well why didn't you say so?" The Bishop scrutinized Adam. "How old is he?"

"Six," Adam answered off his uncle's inquisitive look.

In the hallway, his uncle bade him farewell and left him to his schooling. "I will return and visit you," he promised.

His uncle sent letters with money for shoes, and packages filled with hazelnuts, and little books about Jesus, but his visits were rare. He appeared at Christmas for the dinner at St. Michael's and brought Adam a new wool coat and some heavy boots. But in the summer, Adam was left at St. Michael's in the care of the monks while most of the other students went with their families on holiday or to visit relatives for the summer. He occupied himself doing chores for the priests and playing games of his own design. He always wondered if the man was really his uncle after all, and pondered still the whereabouts of his loving parents. Whenever he thought of them he felt a profound sadness, so he did not think of them often, and before long, he forgot them.

CHAPTER III

It was a warm, spring day when he first realized he could see things in water. Brother Ivor took the boys down to the river to catch minnows and study them. They were armed with nets they had made from sackcloth and wire, and were happy to be outside rather than confined in the classroom.

The river was clear and reflected the dark shapes of the overhanging trees as it swirled and pocked through the rocks and reeds. Adam stared at his own reflection. His eyes stared back, green, kind, but the face around them was older, handsome, and seemed very determined. Adam wondered how he had grown so quickly. He looked at his hands. They were the same – stubby, childlike, with bitten fingernails. He looked back in the water. Suddenly his face turned a way he did not. It seemed to be speaking but it was nothing Adam could understand. Then the man saw him, looked astonished, and lunged forward, swiping up at him from the river.

Frightened, Adam shouted, slipped down in the mud and fell into the water. The other boys laughed and jeered at him as he waded out, wiping his muddy hands in the grass.

He sat, pondering what he had just witnessed. Had it

been his imagination at work? That was the only explanation that made sense, and he marveled at the ability of his mind to generate such vivid images.

When they returned to the dormitory, he looked into the basin of water to admire the manly features he had spied that morning. But when he looked in, he saw that he was still the boy he had been yesterday. The face he had seen had most definitely *not* been his own reflection, and he wondered if it were not the spirit of the Isar River, or the ghost of someone who had drowned in it. Many people had succumbed to the swiftly flowing waters.

From then on, whenever Adam was around water, he bravely looked in to see what he could see. Soon he realized he could see pictures in the water like peering into the window of a house. He could watch people doing things in other places. They were unaware of him and he had no inkling of who they were. He wasn't entirely sure they weren't some figments of his imagination.

He broached the subject with another boy called Benno who was his same age. "There's a man in the water. Do you see him, too?" Adam pointed in the washbasin in the dormitory, touching the surface and rippling the scene as the military man rode upon his gallant white horse over hill and dale.

The other boy looked hard into the water, then back at Adam. "I see some dirt flecks in the bottom and a little black hair, is that what you mean?" he asked.

"No," said Adam. "Look harder. There he is, right there!" He could still see the man clearly in the water as he rode ever faster toward the rising sun.

"What are you talking about?" asked Benno. "Is this some kind of riddle like the man in the moon? What am I supposed to see?" And Benno looked sidelong at him and began telling him a harrowing story about an older brother of his who had gone mad and how he had eventually been turned out of his parents' house and run out of town. "It all began when he started to 'see' things that weren't really there."

"Never mind. I was only jesting," answered Adam with a laugh, and he resolved then that his visions would be his secret.

Two years passed and Adam's secret visions grew more vivid, more temporal and real. One day, he sat on the edge of the fountain in the middle of town, as he so often did, and looked at his own reflection – a pair of intense, green eyes, a prominent, long nose, and wavy dark hair above a thoughtful brow. Clouds drifted over his head above his dark reflection, and suddenly he saw himself standing in a field.

There were rolling acres of green crops for as far as the eye could see. He felt a warm breeze out of the south, but not at all like the Fohn wind that blew from the Alps. It was as if he was in a completely different land than Bavaria. But *where*? Where were these meadows of gold and green?

Adam blinked and looked back into the water. The scene had gone. A flock of geese flew in the sky above his head. He looked up at them as they flew over the spires of the Rathaus, Munich's government building, and out of sight.

He thought how he preferred lounging by his favorite fountain than tedious lessons at St. Michael's. What little he knew of outside life he had observed from these forays for the Bishop. There were normal people doing ordinary things outside the church walls. Butchers and bakers and farmers and women. He loved to watch them all. His favorites, though, were the women, and he lingered close to them whenever the opportunity arose, so that he could smell them and listen to their voices.

He had come to know the town and its nuances, its hiding places, and its secrets. Some weeks before, he had made a fabulous discovery. He had been petting a white

18

cat when a wagon startled it, and it went running down the alley. Adam followed it down the lane until the road became so narrow that only one person could pass. On the side of a building, a small door hung ajar and the cat slipped inside. Adam crept in after it.

The corridor was dark, but he could just make out the cat's white fur, and followed it down some winding, stone steps into the most amazing room.

Long, rectangular, and vaulted, it appeared to be a large crypt carved out of the bedrock. On the ceiling were the signs of the zodiac in the night sky. It glowed a heavenly blue, and the white stars around the signs of the zodiac luminesced enough for him to see. On either side, two long benches ran almost the entire length of the room. In the middle there was a long table upon which was a large bronze statue of a strong man spearing a bull.

The white cat jumped upon the table and began grooming itself. Adam picked up the cat and sat down with it on one of the benches, petting its soft fur and marveling at the underground temple and the finely wrought statue before him. Who was it depicting, he wondered? From what mythology did it come? He felt the silent sacredness of the place and concluded that it must be a place for worship though he was not sure to what deity it was consecrated. He lay down on the bench and admired the zodiacal animals above. Each of them was the work of a master artist. He wondered what materials had been used and concluded that the signs were a mosaic of translucent stones and glass pieces.

Alone under the man-made sky, he rested, letting his eyes close and sleep wash over him. Some noise from the upper world startled him from his nap, and he leapt up, remembering that he would be missed if he dallied much longer.

He squinted as the bright sunlight found him crawling from the small door into the narrow road. From down the street he could hear the church bells ringing, goading him on.

He ran past the front entrance of the church and looked up at all the statues of the Wittelsbach ancestors cast alongside the Catholic saints, each one in his own archway on the front façade. He often fantasized that these characters were God's playthings and the Cathedral was some great dollhouse, a mega version of the one in the window of the shop he so often ventured into on behalf of his masters.

He came into the church vestry by the side door and walked quickly down the long hall until it curled upward into the staircase that led him to the office of the Bishop. He reported to the Bishop's secretary, Brother Haster, a quiet, frail, young priest. He was shushed sternly and told to return to his lessons.

Adam walked back to the classroom where he sat quietly at one of the tables, and watched Brother Ivor write arithmetic problems on the slate board. Adam could do any numerical operation instantly in his head, and so he simply wrote the answers on his slate. This aggravated his teachers for they liked to see his labors. Brother Ivor had even accused him of cheating, of copying off someone else's slate, until the priests tested him, and saw for themselves that Adam could perform any calculation silently and quickly in his head.

After that, he'd been granted more liberties, given an iota more respect, and made a permanent messenger. Though he was not nearly the eldest of the students at St. Michael's, Adam was the most advanced in his learning, and therefore, they reasoned, could have the liberty to miss class on occasion. Adam was always at St. Michael's. No uncle ever came to gather him for picnics or holidays. He belonged to St. Michael's as much as any of the priests. He envied the other boys their holidays and afternoon visits by the river with their families, but was glad of this menial messenger job that allowed him to loaf at the fountain or wherever he pleased, on his way to and from delivering messages and fetching things for his masters.

There were nineteen other boys at the Jesuit school from age six to sixteen. Most of them were latter-born sons who had been turned over to the Church as part of their families' legacies and would become Jesuit priests. Adam was different. He was an orphan, his memories of his real parents a blur of goodnights and streaks of sunshine. The images bled together with those of the people he saw in the street and he longed to see the faces of his mother and father again in the waters of the fountain, but they would never come. And he did not want to remember what had happened. Think of other things, he told himself. Forget and forgive as Christ instructs.

Late in the afternoon, Adam was hunched over his scripture, transcribing the Latin onto the piece of parchment he was allotted for the day. He was careful with each and every letter as parchment was dear. The ink he had made was always perfect, unlike that of his classmates who often added too much water so that it ran and ruined the page. By the time Adam was out of school, he was to have copied the entire Holy Bible. He looked forward eagerly to the day it would be bound and he could hold the whole of it in his hand and read the Word of Lord that he, himself, had copied. It would be a precious thing indeed, for he had promised himself he would write each letter divinely. He would illuminate it, too, for he was a fair artist and enjoyed using colored washes. He practiced his artwork in a book of cloth paper he had found dropped in the road. He jotted down the visions he had, and illustrated them. His copy of the Bible stayed neatly stacked on the shelf in the classroom, but his colorful book of dreams - this he hid under his mattress. He was always worried that someone else would find it and see the pictures that he drew.

An older boy named Wilhelm passed behind   him, pushing his elbow and making him ruin his calligraphy. "Jew boy," Wilhelm called him.

Adam groaned in frustration for now there was a big black line across his perfect calligraphy.

"You smell like a Jew, you look like a Jew. You must be a Jew!" teased Wilhelm.

Adam gritted his teeth and looked at his ruined page, but restrained himself from fighting Wilhelm. He was so clearly outmatched that it would be not only futile but most certainly painful to engage him. And so what if he was a Jew? He wasn't, but what difference would it make? Jesus was Jew. Adam often wondered why there wasn't more emphasis on what Jesus, himself, had studied and learned that made him such an incredible person. How ever did he walk on water? By what means did he multiply the loaves and fish to feed the crowd of followers? And what had he been talking about with the Temple priests when he abandoned his parents in Jerusalem as a boy? Christianity? Adam knew that was not the answer.

The boys of St. Michael's were assigned various tasks for the general upkeep of the church and grounds, for the majority of the Jesuit priests who resided at St. Michael's spent their days roaming the countryside converting sinners and wayward souls to the Society of Jesus, and did not return until nightfall. In addition to cleaning, kitchen work, and the scrubbing of floors, Adam took his turn as altar boy once a month. He cleaned and polished all the metal plates, bowls and candlesticks in the Sacristy and swept the floors. He assisted the priests at prayers, and stood by with a candle snuffer or a ready flame for the lighting of the incense. Adam felt at home behind the altar, as if he was born to be a priest and that all the sacred objects were his by right. But the mass, however, the eating of the Body and Blood, he could never quite wrap his head around. Why would anyone want to eat the flesh and drink the blood of someone? Transubstantiation seemed barbaric and animalistic, even if the flesh did belong to the Blessed Savior. Adam feared that he alone had missed out on something and would be ridiculed for his ignorance. He worried that perhaps during one of his errands, they had belied the missing key that would answer why Jesus had died for Adam's sins and why His Body and Blood were to be eaten and drunk by the congregation. And if Jesus, and God, and the angels existed, why didn't they reveal themselves to the faithful? Why would they not return to put things right, when there was still suffering and violence in the world? He would become a priest one day, and God Himself would manifest when he called His Name, so pure and zealous was Adam's spirit. The other priests would look on in awe, and the faith of the masses would be renewed. God and His angels had appeared to the Saints, had spoken to the Apostles, and it was that hope of communing directly that kept Adam ever worshipful, ever pious, ever fervent in his prayers.

The underground temple became his favorite hiding place and he went there for a nap nearly every day. He knew how much time the priests would allow for each task, so he would hurriedly complete his errand, then slip into the little door and down the stairs into the cool darkness. Down in the temple, he would lie on the table, gazing up at the zodiacal figures – the ram, the twins, the crab, the lion, the virgin, all of them so marvelously rendered.

He closed his eyes, feeling himself sink into the table, with its solid cool strength pushing up against him from below. He had a pleasant dream about several lithe young girls whom he'd coaxed out of the river. They ran to him in their sheer, wet gowns and fawned over him, calling him "lovely." Their fingers caressed his bare skin and their teasing whispers tickled his ear.

He awoke then to find the white cat sniffing in his ear.

He rose, stiff and disoriented, and realized that he had been asleep on the table for quite some time.

It was then he saw a light moving down the stairs into the room. The shuffle of footsteps foretold of the impending use of the temple. He knew he was not its only regular visitor, for there was always water in the basin out of which the cat freely drank.

Adam quickly ducked beneath the bench. He lay upon the cold floor, still as a stone, daring not to even breathe. Soon, many pairs of gentlemen's shoes filed before his face. The owners of the shoes and their adjacent stockings took their seats above him in silent anticipation. The flickering torchlight cast their eerie shadows on the wall and Adam wondered who they were, for he could not see their faces at all, for the table in between the benches blocked his sight except for on the far end where the bench ended and there was an altar. Strange-smelling incense wafted into his nostrils and he heard the celebrant's voice intone a prayer in Latin. The men's deep voices responded, echoing around the stone chamber as if there were a thousand of them.

The musky incense that filled his lungs intoxicated him and made him think of the secretive animals of the night that crept behind the headstones of the Churchyard and yowled out in the darkness.

The slow beat of a drum began, and the men who filled the benches stood up. Adam strained to glimpse their faces from his narrow window of view. What came to his sight horrified him. The dried-out head of a ram with its long white tendrils of wool hanging about the robed shoulders of its bearer, stared with shriveled eyes from behind the altar. Its horns twisted round like those of a devil, it spoke unintelligibly, for its voice was muffled inside the ram's head. The others responded in unison in Latin, "Slay the doers of evil!"

As the ceremony progressed, a different animal played his role before the altar and spoke of his plans, virtues, and ideology. Adam saw that all the signs of the zodiac were represented in this bizarre ceremony as the men-come-animals, approached the altar in a procession and knelt before the ram-headed one who stood at the ready with a long spear. The effect was frightening and powerful and Adam dared not close his eyes or look away from this parade of creatures, so strange and terrible were they.

The thickly furred head of a hoary lion with its eyes cut out, passed through his window of sight. Through the sockets, the eyes of a man glistened in the candlelight, and for an instant, they connected with his own. He had been seen beneath the bench! He lay rigid with fear as the drumming continued with more fervency.

When all the characters had appeared at the altar, the bull-headed one rose and danced defiantly before the ram. Without warning, the ram-headed man sunk the spear into the bull-man and he collapsed on the floor. A great cheer rose up from the animals and onlookers.

"Mithra, Mithra, the Bull of Heaven is no match for the man-gods of earth!" said the ram-headed one in muffled Latin. "Behold the favorite weapon of the gods is dead, and now the age of the ram proceeds to your delight for the good of mankind."

Adam wondered if the bull-man had really been stabbed, but he was more concerned about the lion-headed one. Had he seen him beneath the bench? If so, would he betray him? He felt as if he should flee this place at once, but the feet and legs of the men who sat above blocked any hope of a clean escape.

Many years later would Adam realize he had witnessed

on this night, a rite as old as mankind itself, one that held the key to the mysteries of God on High. Not until he had tangled with the great Temptress herself, and listened to the ancient saga she revealed to him, would he understand the sublime significance of the age-old ritual before him now.

It was far into the night before the strange ceremony was over and Adam had an opportunity to leave the underground temple. Never in his life had he imagined such pagan rites still occurred in the world, particularly beneath the avenues of Jesuit Bavaria.

After all had departed, he waited half an hour for good measure, then hurried up the stairs. He checked the street before he emerged from the little door that opened into the narrow road. The town was quiet and he imagined it was well past midnight. His original errand had been to take money to the grocer and order the feast for the Bishop and the priests, for the cabbage and peas and parsnips grown on the grounds were far too simple for an occasion such as the Bishop's birthday.

He had completed his task hours ago. Now what would he tell them had delayed him? What would be his excuse for being absent these past nine hours? The sweat beneath his tunic was cooled by the night wind as he ran as fast as he could back to St. Michael's.

He wondered if anyone was awake to hear his story. He found Brother Haster at prayer in the priest's chapel and waited for him to finish. Haster turned and widened his eyes at him. "Where have you been?"

"I was chased by dogs and had to climb a tree. They wouldn't let me come down until their master called them home, only minutes ago."

"Were you bitten?" asked Haster, concerned.

"No, only delayed," answered Adam.

Haster believed him, thankfully, and Adam did not have to reveal what he had seen or where he had really been.

He continued to use the temple in the day, but never fell asleep there again. He thought often of what he had seen, and of the name *Mithra*.

In the Cathedral library he found a book of comparative religion and found *Mithra* indexed. It explained briefly that the Mithraic Rite was an ancient, pagan religion from Persia, and it described the underground temple, the *mithraeum*, perfectly. Apparently there were many of these subterranean temples built throughout Europe, the land that was once part of the Roman Empire, for Mithraism had been the official religion of the Roman army, before Constantine had adopted for all, the religion called Christianity.

Adam often wondered about the statue of the bronze bull; if the bull was the same as the golden calf fashioned in Moses' absence when he ascended Mount Sinai to receive the Ten Commandments. If this bull was the same, it was understandable that the strong man was spearing him. The bull was an idol and God hated idols. But if God hated idols, why did He allow crucifixes and statues of the Saints all over His Cathedrals? Adam's mind was always occupied by these contradictions, but he never spoke of them, for the priests said that such questions were a sign that an individual lacked faith, and was weak. And Adam was neither, and he would not allow himself to be perceived as such.

He had made the mistake of inquiring about the validity of the Immaculate Conception, and for that, he had been assigned the interminable penance of getting water from the well everyday at dawn, a job that was usually assigned to an older boy, but that boy had gone to the University to study, so the position just happened to be vacant.

He filled the basins in all the rooms, provided water for the cows and the chickens, monitored the cisterns, and brought in water for the holy font in the Cathedral.

The holy font was an uncanny bowl of water. Made of

violet-black marble it always had a knack for looking like night, and the things Adam saw there were of a very dark nature. Sometimes there was so much energy in the water, so many different pictures vying to take shape, he had trouble making out even one very clearly. The faces he saw seemed to belong mostly to the clergy of St. Michael's and their activities were not altogether recognizable to him. Before Father Lorenzo Ricci arrived, Adam had seen him in there, crowned by a throng of smaller, demonic faces that seemed to live in his hair and scream hideously all around him. It was a matter of days before the Secretary of the Society of Jesus, Lorenzo Ricci and his entourage from the Vatican arrived at St. Michael's to visit and monitor the activities of Bavaria's Jesuit stronghold. Adam was petrified when the face that he had seen in the water, turned and looked straight at him from the sanctuary of the Cathedral, during matins. The Bishop had been caught off-guard as well at the unannounced visit, and scrambled to make preparations to house and entertain the distinguished, Italian guests.

It was early one morning, and Adam was barely awake as he filled the font with water from the well. The stream of water he poured into the font wove itself together like a long, clear fishbone, then into a crystal braid, injecting the pool below with bubbles. The font drew him in as he leaned over it, and it whispered of things he never wanted to know. He tried not to look directly in, but poured water on the floor when he didn't. He was mopping up just such a spill when Father Lorenzo came in to give his blessing. Adam bowed and turned on his heel.

"Wait, young Weishaupt!" shouted Lorenzo. "You must stay and observe!"

Adam halted, surprised that someone of such importance knew his name. He stood aside with empty buckets and made the sign of the cross as the priest intoned the Latin words. The blessing for holy water was part exorcism – to remove whatever spirits may reside in it, and part consecration to God, but the former, he was almost certain, had no effect. The entire Cathedral, Adam had often noted, was inhabited by forms who were conglomerated together, like bodies from a mass grave, molded into the columns, walls, floors, and ornaments of the place. The lines of the marble attempted to delineate one from the other, though these forms were eternally, nonsensically fused. There were eyes, noses, fingers, arms, and legs that seemed to be frozen in the rock and in the burled wood of the place. Even when Adam was quite alone, there were always the eyes that watched from the black knots of the wood, and the flecks in the stone, so much like pupils, watching.

"Do you know why I have come?" Father Lorenzo asked.

Adam shook his head, for no one really knew the reason for the Secretary's visit.

"To find you, young Weishaupt," he smiled. Adam thought he looked positively sinister the way he forced his face into that unnatural expression.

"Why?" he asked.

"Because. You are a very special boy. I know what you can do. Do *you* know what you can do?"

"I'm quite good at figures. I'm learning geometry and trigonometry," Adam bragged.

"Are you? And you're ten years old. That is most impressive. But that's not what I mean. You can see things, can't you? And you can go places and do things."

Adam shook his head in bewilderment. Certainly he did see things, but no one knew that. And everyone went places and did things. Was he patronizing him?

"Go on, have a look in the water. What do you see?" Father Lorenzo pointed at the font. Adam looked in and saw the Pope, Benedict XIV.

"I see His Holiness, the Pope, himself," Adam said with no small amount of reservation.

"Very good! Come with me into the vestry and let's sit and have a talk."

Adam went with the Secretary of the Society of Jesus, who began explaining a strange way of visiting places, a way of walking away from one's body without moving oneself physically. And after he had explained it, he told him how it easy it would be for him to do. "Let's try it now. I want to test you. You're good at tests, aren't you? Lie down here in the window seat." Father Lorenzo pointed at the padded seat below the stained glass window. "I want you to tell yourself to visit the classroom. And there, you'll find your Bible, the one you're working on, and take it from the shelf and put it on the table where you do your schoolwork. Is that clear?"

Adam lay down on the window seat and closed his eyes.

"Now just think about how tired you are and when you're just about asleep, tell yourself to go to the classroom."

Adam listened to the sound of his breath. He had become quite adept at meditating, for the Jesuits insisted that all priests in training practice quiet reflection and meditation for at least one hour a day. Adam was a bit uncomfortable with Father Lorenzo watching him, but he obeyed and let himself relax. "Take me to the classroom," he whispered. He heard a whooshing sound in his ears, then a loud pop, and suddenly, much to his surprise, there he was in the classroom. He was floating, flying rather, just above the floor of the classroom. He flew up to the shelf where he put his bible. He took it down and lay it on the table. He heard another loud snap, and then he awoke on the window seat. He looked at Father Lorenzo in astonishment. "I did it!"

"We'll go and look right now," said Father Lorenzo helping him up.

They walked down to the classroom and looked in.

Brother Ivor was there at his own desk, and stood and bowed as the Secretary of the Society entered with Adam.

They looked at the table, but the bible wasn't there.

"It didn't work. It's not here where I put it! But I did put it here." Adam was disappointed.

"I just put your bible back on the shelf," said Ivor scolding him. "You must keep it put up or the younger boys may get hold of it. I would not like to see your hard work ruined."

Lorenzo patted Adam on the shoulder and whispered.

"See? You did do it," And he smiled his unnatural smile again.

They walked into the churchyard together where the other boys were playing. "You are a very useful little boy, Adam. You are an asset to our Society, and you must help us in our work. We have many important activities that require your skill. Many people can walk as you do, but none other that I know can effect real actions once there. You are very *very* special."

"Thank you, father," Adam replied proudly. "May I go and play now?"

"Just a minute. I will see you at evening prayers and give your next assignment. I have a special prize for you. You must tell no one about this. Do you understand?"

"Yes, Father. As you wish," said Adam enthusiastically, wondering what the prize would be.

Lorenzo grabbed his tunic as he started to run away.

Adam turned back in askance. "Tell no one of what you can do." Father Lorenzo reminded sternly once more.

That night, the boys filed into the Cathedral for evening prayers. Adam spied Father Lorenzo and his entourage behind the altar. Lorenzo gave him a benevolent look, and when they rose for communion, Lorenzo beckoned Adam with an outstretched finger, and took him aside as the others chanted.

"Tonight, when you lay down in your bed, I want you to visit the Pope in Rome. Can you do that?" whispered

Father Lorenzo.

"I'll try," said Adam.

"Very good. It is very important." And Father Lorenzo presented him with a small silver medal with a picture of St. Ignatius stamped into it, and put it over his head. "That's for you. For helping me."

That night, Adam lay in his bed in the dormitory. As the Secretary, Father Lorenzo had instructed him, he closed his eyes, and asked to be taken to the Pope. He heard a whooshing sound and then a loud pop, and he was in the Pope's own chamber. He marveled at the beauty of the room, its gilded bed and red velvet draperies. The walls were hung with elaborate tapestries and the marble floor shone with high polish. The Pope lay sleeping on his back, his head propped upon an embroidered pillow with pretty tassels all the way around it. Adam looked down at his own hand and could see nothing, for it was as if he wasn't there. He found the secret cupboard behind the angel tapestry that Father Lorenzo had described and removed the bottle that contained the Pope's medicine. "You must give the Pope his medicine, Adam. I am not there to give it to him, and he will be gravely ill if no one gives him his medicine." Father Lorenzo had instructed him. And Adam picked up the tiny bottle and poured it into the Pope's tankard that sat on his night table.

The Secretary and his entourage of priests left a few days later, but not before Father Lorenzo had given him a stern warning. "Tell no one of you can do. Tell them neither of your visions nor your ability to travel. The others do not understand and never will. They will deal harshly with you. They will whip you and throw you out of school, and then where will you go?"

Adam was confused by the threat, but accepted the Secretary's warning. The group from the Vatican had only been gone a few hours when one of the priests returned from his daily mission to report that Pope Benedict XIV had died. The boys were confined to prayer all day as the bells rang and the Congregation from town trickled in for mass that seemed to continue non-stop for a week.

Adam wondered if the Pope's medicine had done him no good. Perhaps he had been too ill to save as many elderly were, and he thought of the old ones whom he saw come in for mass one day, then carried in on pall the next. He wondered if Father Lorenzo was stricken with grief, and if he blamed him for the Pope's death. Perhaps Adam had used the wrong medicine!

Some weeks later, the Bishop read them the letter from Father Lorenzo, announcing his appointment to the position of Superior General, the head of the entire Jesuit sect, second in power only to the Pope himself. Adam listened nervously for some mention of himself as the one to blame for the old Pope's death, or some admonishment but there was none, only a cheerful thanks for the hospitality in Munich, and a benediction for the entire Jesuit community under the new dominion of Superior General Lorenzo Ricci and the newly instated Pope Clement XIII. Adam breathed a sigh of relief, but still wondered if he could not have done something more to save the old Pope.

CHAPTER IV

Life at St. Michael's Jesuit Academy went on as before, years passed, and Adam studied fervently, committing whole books of the Bible to memory, and excelling in mathematics. He continued to bear water to the font and the kitchen and the animals every day.

It was early one rainy morning that he poured water into the font. The only light in the Cathedral were votives lit for a dead man beneath a shroud. Adam had seen the dead laid out in this fashion many times, waiting while the undertaker's boy dug a grave in the Churchyard. He would undoubtedly be delayed for the rain, and Adam said a prayer of gratitude that he was bound to the priesthood rather than to a vocation like undertaking. Feeling fortunate, he peered deep into the dark, shining water of the marble basin. The water seemed clear and clean in its shiny blackness but for one speck of ash floating on the surface. Adam reached in.

In the water, rippled his own reflection. He admired his good looks and was caught suddenly by the realization that he was really growing up, growing into a young man. The face stared back, meeting his eye, and quizzically reaching out to touch him. Adam was then struck with the revelation that this was not a fanciful projection of himself, but in fact, a separate individual looking back at him, who seemed just as perplexed as he. Was it the same man he had seen in the waters of the river while catching minnows? He had seen him so many times since then, most times from afield, often on horseback, and surrounded by other men. He stared at the face, so similar to his own, but not his own. It was another Adam Weishaupt, co-existing and leading another life. Father Burton, his religion teacher, had made them study Thomas Aquinas' "Eternity of the World" in which he proposed the idea of simultaneous existences, that all moments in time were happening at the same time, in the same moment and that a body could leap from one possibility to the next if one had the will and means to do so. Was this Adam somewhere else? Or was this his future life he was prophesying?

Whoever it was in the water seemed very real and quite independent of him. The face was older than his own, a fraction longer, and the shoulders more rugged, broader, and stronger. Adam stared. *Could this be my father?*

"What do you see in the water, boy?" rasped a voice over his shoulder.

Adam looked up and was shocked to see a noseless leper hunching over him, his hot breath reeking from his toothless head, befouling the air. Adam stepped back, wondering how he had been let in. It was customary for the monks to chase off lepers and others with disease, but this one had gotten by and was now wanting some water from the font to go into his filthy canteen.

"Isn't that your brother in there?" The leper pierced him with his bug-eyes.

"Then you see him, too?" he whispered, astounded.

"He will help you regain what has been stolen, what has been lost to you. What is his name? Do you know it?" asked the Leper.

"I- I- don't know," Adam stammered, and backed away, hoping the leper's contagion would not take hold

That night, Adam dreamt of the man he had seen in the water and went to stand at his side. "Take me to the man I saw in the water," he said as he drifted off to sleep. He heard a whooshing sound like wind as he rose above his earthly self, slumbering in bed. There was a loud snap, and instantly he was standing before a large and stately house in the middle of an enormous farm. It was the same one he had seen so many times before in the water. Dawn was just breaking on the horizon, a splay of purple behind the black silhouette of forest.

Silently, he entered the house, and floated up the staircase into the room where the gentleman slept in his bed. He crept close and studied the man's face in the darkness, for he could see as well in the dark as he could in the light when walking this way. There were striking similarities to Adam's own face, like the dimpled chin and downward turn of the long nose, but the fair skin tone was not like his, and would never be. As he had suspected, the man was not his future self, but someone else altogether living in present time. But *who was* this man, then, if it wasn't himself? *Could this be my father? My brother?*

Adam saw a writing desk by the window. He picked up one of the letters and looked at the name of the addressee. His heart jumped in his chest, for the man had the very same given name as his own father. The man in the bed leapt up suddenly, calling out "Who's there?"

Adam shrank back and felt that he could be seen against the pale walls of the room. He flew out of there with all speed, and awash with the fast-blown distance covered, only an instant to the mind – he was back in his own bed in the dormitory.

He sat bolt upright then, and remembered what the leper had said. What had he meant? Had he meant that the strange man would help him find his family? But the words had come from a leper and anything he said should certainly be discounted. Shouldn't it?

What did Adam really know of his family? Where were they? Who were they? Why had they given him up to his uncle? He had no answers and no one to ask, for his uncle, the Baron von Ickstatt, had not visited or written in more than a year. For all Adam knew, it was possible that he had a family and that they were in Virginia Colony. There were many people from Bavaria and neighboring regions who had moved to the New World.

That night he wrote a letter, addressing it to the man he had visited in Virginia Colony. The chances that the letter would ever get to this person were questionable; Adam had never sent mail anywhere, much more to the New World. And the chances that this man would care to respond were doubtful at best. Adam kept the letter brief and cordial, not wanting to divulge too much of himself to someone who may not be sympathetic, much less, related to him. He mailed the letter on his next foray for the Bishop and prayed that it would arrive there safely.

It was the very day he mailed the letter that he lingered near the Isar river. Something told him it was the last day of summer this year, for it was an uncommonly gorgeous afternoon. In years past, he had noticed such days as this at the end of September and had taken them for granted, then the snow had come, and the summer was suddenly over. He removed his boots and stepped into the cool water and let it bathe his feet. He felt free and refreshed as the breeze blew through the rough fabric of his tunic. He sat down on a dry stone and watched the water flow by him. Suddenly beneath the water, he saw the face of Wilhelm, the older boy at the Academy who often called him "Jew boy." Now, beneath the blue haze of water, bubbles gushed from Wilhelm's mouth, and his eyes bulged. Adam could feel the suffocating burn of water up his nose and could hear it flooding into his lungs as it filled and forced open the back of his throat. He stumbled out of the river's shallows, choking.

Panting for breath, he sat on the bank, hurriedly putting on his boots. Hoping the horrific vision gone, he glanced at the water again and saw Wilhelm's body pale and afloat in the water. He blinked the vision away and ran from the river. As he ran back to the Cathedral, he began to realize that such a vision was an omen, a warning that Wilhelm would succumb to death by water.

He went in search of Wilhelm and found him in the kitchen helping one of the monks, Brother Salermo, clean a slaughtered hog.

"Wilhelm, you mustn't go swimming or play down by the river. I've had a vision," said Adam.

Wilhelm looked up at him, laughed, and tossed a handful of entrails at him, "Here, Jew, have a vision of swine!"

Assured of his nemesis' wellbeing, Adam returned to his chores, but could not dismiss what he had seen, so vivid and visceral had it been. He went to find Brother Haster to warn him, and found him with the Bishop in the hallway.

"Weishaupt, you look unwell," said the Bishop.

"Yes, your Excellency, I had... a terrible dream," replied Adam. "I saw one of the other boys drowned."

Brother Haster made a face and shook his head. "Which boy?"

"Wilhelm," replied Adam.

"We all have dreams, but rarely are their meanings as literal as they would appear. Go back to your chores and do not worry. Everything is as it should be," said the Bishop.

Adam breathed a sigh of relief at the Bishop's calm words, and worked until nightfall, scrubbing the red-stained floor in the kitchen where the hog had been butchered. His thoughts drifted to the letter he had written and his anticipation of receiving an answer from this possible relation. He dreamed of taking up residence in Virginia Colony with his long lost family, and of the joyous reunion with the doting parents and loving siblings with whom he belonged.

He washed in the basin outside, warmed himself by the kitchen fire, said his prayers in the chapel, and went to the dormitory to bed. He looked across the room at Wilhelm's bunk and saw that it was empty. He wondered briefly where he was, before sleep overtook him.

At dawn he was awakened by shouting, first from voices outside, then from all around him.

"Wilhelm's drowned!" someone shouted, and several of the boys went running out.

Was it true? A chill crept over him.

In the company of the others, he ventured across the misty churchyard in his bare feet. From far away, he saw them, Ivor, Haster, the Bishop, and several monks bent like vultures around their carrion, as they knelt beside Wilhelm's body, shockingly pale in the deep green grass in which it lay.

The other boys ran to see. Brother Ivor stood and prevented them from coming closer. "Please, Wilhelm Gumprecht has drowned. Go to the classroom and wait," Brother Ivor said with a heavy sigh. The priest wiped his eyes and turned back to the body.

Adam hung back, wary of the Bishop who turned and stared at him, his mouth agape.

He walked away with the others, keeping an eye on the Bishop whom he feared would come chasing after him, waving his cane.

"Who were his enemies?" Benno looked around, then focused on Adam.

"How do you know he didn't just drown?" asked a boy called Igor.

"Didn't you see his throat? It looked like something had bitten him," said another boy, wide-eyed.

"Maybe it was fish," suggested another. "In the water..."

"But why would he go swimming alone? We always go together," said Benno. "It's the rule."

"I don't know," stated Adam. "I told him not to go to the river. I warned him." He suddenly realized all the boys were looking at him, and he wished he had said nothing.

They returned to the classroom. Adam watched the others whisper and look sidelong at him. Brother Ivor came into the room. "One of our students has been called to his Father's house. Wilhelm Gumprecht has died sometime in the night. If any of you can answer as to why this tragedy has occurred, please come forward now."

The Bishop appeared at the door of the classroom with the monk, Brother Salermo, who had been with Wilhelm in the kitchen cleaning the hog. "Johann Adam Weishaupt. We must speak with you."

Adam rose and went with them to the Bishop's office.

"This boy came to the kitchen last night and told Gumprecht not to go down to the river!" accused the monk.

"What happened to Wilhelm Gumprecht?" questioned the Bishop.

Adam hesitated, then began explaining how he saw visions in water, how he was by the river when he saw

Wilhelm drown.

"And why didn't you pull him out of the water?" asked Brother Salermo. "Why didn't you save him?"

"It was just a vision. I didn't really see him drown." Adam answered.

The Bishop and Brother Salermo exchanged glances. "What do you know? Tell us what really happened by the river or you will be punished severely," said Salermo.

Adam bristled at the threat. "It was just a prophecy. I wasn't really there when he drown!"

"Where were you last night?" asked the Bishop.

"I was doing my chores. I cleaned the kitchen floor after Wilhelm and you butchered that hog..." he said, referring to Brother Salermo.

"It made you angry when he threw that handful of entrails at you, didn't it? And you picked a fight with him, a fight that ended badly," speculated Salermo.

"No. I said my prayers and went to bed," said Adam.

"After you and Wilhelm went down to the river to wash," announced Salermo.

"No, I washed in the dormitory, in the basin," declared Adam. "It's not me you're looking for. I didn't do anything!"

For nearly an hour, the two continued their interrogation of him until the Bishop and the monk became incensed at his arrogance and insolence, and resolved to whip him. Their line of logic made no sense to him, and the more he tried to reason, to explain, the angrier they became. The Bishop sat by, looking at Adam in disgust and disbelief as Brother Salermo railed against him, sweating profusely and proposing all manner of obscene and lurid scenarios. The words of Father Lorenzo came ringing back to his ears. *"Tell no one of what you can do, or they will beat you and throw you out of school."*

Hot with anger, Adam would stand for neither. He was furious that they would use their presumed authority over him to condemn him when he had done nothing but warn someone of danger. With all his might he wrested his arm out of Brother Salermo's grasp and flew down the hallway.

He ran breathlessly into the dormitory and gathered up all the things that belonged to him – his bibles, a ruler, his old cloth book, a green feather quill, a compass, three chalks, some coins, and some marbles. He threw it all into the pillowcase from his bed, and ran out the door. Brother Salermo ambushed him in the hallway and grappled for a purchase on him, but Adam was faster. He flew down the spiraling stairs and out the side door.

And thus his dreams of becoming a priest were dashed in moments. He could not stay at St. Michael's. He would not submit to being beaten. He would never become prey to the ignorant. He was better than that, and with everything in him, he would resist punishment, resist authority, resist capture. He had given them no right to rule over him. He had simply been turned over to the Academy and to the priesthood so that he could be educated, but he had never consented to their authority. They were all inferior - intellectually, spiritually, psychically, and he had long ago dismissed them as such, and the thin veil of humility he feigned he no longer found agreeable, not in the face of such abject stupidity. Now that they had threatened him and his physical integrity, he would be damned if he would submit to their counterfeit authority.

He dashed through the churchyard and found himself sprinting along the river where they'd found Wilhelm. He passed the matted grass where his body had lain, and he remembered his vision of him. Good riddance to St. Michael's, he thought. May he never set foot there again.

He ran straight to the center of town. He stopped and looked around, at a total loss for where to go, what to do next. There was his fountain sitting in the middle of the square. How he wished it were a person who could help him. It was a silly thought, but how fortunate he'd be if he'd made a friend in the outside world, one with whom he'd spent as much time, one who knew him as well as this fountain did. He'd had brushes with many of the townspeople who worshipped in the Cathedral but he'd neglected to forge any kind of friendship with any of them. He was shy, and his role as altar boy and messenger for the Bishop made all his interactions rather formal and terse. He wondered if anyone even realized he was anything other than a tentacle of the Church. Certainly they all thought he was an idiot or a narcissist the way he stared into the fountain all the time.

Now, he sat tentatively on the edge of the fountain
thinking about what to do next. He should write to his uncle and let him know what had transpired. But on whose side would his uncle be? The letter would take days to reach him. What would he do in the meantime? Perhaps some kind person would invite him in, he thought, but no one even looked at him. He was such a familiar sight at the fountain, and everyone was busy, on his way somewhere, burdened by something. The stark gray of winter loomed in the sky above the orange-leafed trees and the mindset of the townspeople was like rodents gathering stores for the cold winter months. They were all too busy, chopping, threshing, weaving, mending their roofs. Too bad he hadn't waited until spring to venture out on his own. He shivered and wished he'd thought to steal the blankets from his bed. Sleeping outside would be nearly impossible now.

He looked down the avenue and thought of the
shoemaker whom he had visited on so many occasions, for it had been his job to escort each of the younger boys to get new shoes. He had had more to do with the shoemaker than with anyone actually. Hopeful, he walked down the lane to the shoemaker's shop. He could be a cobbler's boy

and learn a trade. After tonight, he no longer had any desire to be a priest. Certainly there were other, better ways one could serve Christ. The world was wide open to him, now. He felt frightened, lost, and elated at the same time, as he pictured himself a cobbler. It would be as fine a trade as any.

When he got in front of the shoe shop, there was a note on the door.

> *God rest Herr Hoffer*
> *Funeral Mass at St. Michael's*
> *Friday at ten o'clock.*

Adam recalled the corpse beneath the shroud in the Cathedral and realized it had been the old cobbler. He was aggrieved to think of Herr Hoffer passed away and sadder still to think he could not ask him for his help. He wandered back to the fountain and sat contemplating his limitless lack of options. A light snow began to fall, dusting the skin on his face and hands and melting almost instantly into cool droplets.

It was then he heard a footstep from across the square. It was Brother Salermo. Fast as lightning, Adam ducked down behind the fountain and crawled around the perimeter of it as Brother Salermo scanned the place for him. His heart pounded in his chest and the tile was cold beneath his knees as he scrambled to stay out of sight. If Brother Salermo saw him, there would be a chase and if he caught him, he dreaded to even think how it would end.

A woman watched him from the alley where she sat plucking feathers from a headless chicken. He caught her eye but she did not give him away as he crawled past her, avoiding the monk's line of sight.

Finally Brother Salermo left the square. Adam peeked up to see him go, the monk's robes swishing about his feet as he took a side street to the river lane. Adam gave the silent woman a grateful look and fled from the square as fast as he could run. He would not linger out in the open again. He returned to the only other place he felt safe.

Down in the underground temple, Adam drew his vision of Wilhelm in his book, then lay upon the table and stared up at the signs of the zodiac until he was overcome by hunger. He climbed the stairs and ventured out into the street. He had several coins he had collected over the years, and hoped they would be enough to buy something to sustain him. He went to the grocer and found a loaf of bread that he could afford. He bought it and an apple and returned to the narrow alley. Night was falling. He bent over to pull open the door, but it was locked from within. He pressed his ear to it and thought he heard voices down below. He remembered then that he had left his pillowcase with all his things inside it, down in the temple. All his worldly possessions except for his book of visions that he had fortunately tucked into the top of his trousers, were as good as gone.

Having nowhere else to go, he spent the night crouched down on a stoop between two houses. He shivered all night and never fell asleep for fear of being found and ousted. The rabble that resided in this unsavory part of Munich kept odd hours and spoke loudly at one another. Through the long, chilly night, Adam's mind reeled about his predicament. When the sun rose, a patrolman approached him before he could get away.

"Where do you live?" he asked him.

"I've just moved here from Frankfurt," he lied. He did not want to be taken back to St. Michael's and prayed that his black trousers and white tunic did not belie their origins. "My parents are dead and I am looking for work," he angled for pity.

"What kind of work?" asked the patrolman.

"Anything," was Adam's answer.

"I saw a sign on Viertel Strasse for an errand boy."

"Danke schoen." Errand boy. Adam headed to Viertel Strasse. It was close by, in the same bad part of town. He found the sign in a window under a red lantern.

- Boy wanted for wood chopping and errands. 15 pfennig a week plus room and board -

He took a step back into the street and looked up at the building. The marquee read:

-The Frisky Cat-

He wondered what kind of shop it was as he knocked on the door beneath the red glass lantern. He could hear feminine voices and high-heeled footsteps within. Then, a painted lady in a lacey dress opened the door.

"Come in," she said. She smelled strongly of perfume and showed him into the parlor.

He looked around and saw that he was standing in a *Hurehaus*. He had only heard of such places and to suddenly be standing in one made his knees wobble. Lovely unclad women of various descriptions lounged about the room, reading, playing cards and napping on the sofas. Adam had never seen women like this, so many, so bare, and he marveled at the wonders that were ordinarily hidden beneath their clothing. They all looked up at him when he was led into the parlor.

"Well, who's this little boy?" asked a bare-breasted, dark-haired girl whose name was Lisette.

"I've come about the sign in the window," he gestured at it.

"Of course you have," the painted one purred. "What is your name?"

"Adam," he answered.

"Adorable, isn't he?" she asked the others, running her fingers through his hair. He was amazed at the nourishing, relaxing sensation of her touch and would gladly have taken such petting for hours. He had never been touched so tenderly, so expertly, or by a woman before.

The others looked at him and nodded approval.

"Very good, then. These are your mistresses. All of us require your obedience. Mainly you will keep the fires lit. There are *seven* hearths in this house. We get cold in here doing what we do, especially in winter. You and Marsa will do all the shopping for us. Most of us do not go out in public very frequently and never on mundane errands. I am the Madam of this house. If you have a problem, you come to me."

"Yes, Frau."

"Fraulein! Do you want this job?" she demanded.

"Ja, Fraulein," he answered desperately. The girls laughed.

"All right, little boy…" she said, shaking her finger at him, "Just so you know, I expect perfect obedience and respect. You'll take care of us, we'll take care of you. You will sleep in the room next to the kitchen." She turned and led him away through the house.

All the lamps on the walls were hung with crystal pieces, and there seemed to be dolls of all sizes and descriptions in cabinets wherever he looked. Red satin lined the walls of the hallway. Small paintings of nude women were hung neatly in gold frames all the way down to the kitchen.

There, a fat, old woman cleaned a blackened kettle with a wire brush. She looked over her shoulder at them with a grimace. "How long do you think this one will last?"

"He'll do better than the last. He's only half grown," Madam opened a small door beneath the stairs. She put the candle inside it. Adam looked into the musty-smelling, little room, barely three feet wide and eight feet long, but it was cozy and private and it would be interesting to live in this place with all women, after such a long time at St. Michael's. The irony was not lost on him and he wished he could tell the boys at St. Michael's of this new turn of fate. As always, he felt the Lord was looking out for him. He had only been out in the cold for a single night.

He followed the fat, old woman, Marsa, around the house, learning how to do his various tasks including keeping the fires lit, fetching water from the well and stocking the kindling bin and woodpiles with split wood.

He was supposed to feed the horse, the milk-cow, and the goats. The chickens were cared for by Marsa, and she did not appreciate anyone else gathering eggs or milking the cow.

Adam embraced his newfound freedom and new way of life. The prostitutes at the Frisky Cat Hotel were kind to him, though they teased and toyed with him incessantly, for it was obvious Adam loved their touches no matter how small or meaningless. When he had been proven trustworthy and obedient, and they believed he would not run away, Madam wrote a note for him, filled his pockets with bags of coins for each of the girls, and sent him to the Deutsche Bankhaus.

"Run so no one will rob you," she said and pushed him out the door.

He ran all the way down the street and around the corner. No one even gave him a passing glance.

The bank was large with ornate archways and a high, plaster ceiling. Clerks stood, keeping accounts at standing desks all over the floor. Adam approached the teller's window and handed him the note from Madam.

"Let's see what you have," said the small, old man, taking the notes. "Ah, you are from the Frisky Cat." He chuckled knowingly. "Business is good."

Adam watched him count each bag of coins, write down the amount in his ledger, and put it in the till. For each, he wrote the girl's name and a number on a slip of parchment, folded it, and gave it to Adam.

Madam and a girl named Serafina had the most money

by far. Serafina he recognized from mass at St. Michael's. Her large bosom and beautiful face had attracted the attention of every man, collared or lay, in the Cathedral. Wine had been spilt by the Bishop, men had stumbled on their way to receive communion, and prayer books fumbled. She was in her late teens and looked to be a gypsy. Her nose hooked slightly but her brown eyes were beautiful, bright, and heavily lashed. Her full lips curled devilishly and Adam had wondered what it would be like to kiss them. In the Cathedral she had kept her head covered, had spoken to no one, and had sat alone, but she seemed to know all the Latin prayers well, better than the Bavarian folk, and Adam surmised she must be Italian. He was astonished to find her in the Frisky Cat, for it was she whom the Virgin in the zodiac became when his eyes closed; it was the lovely Serafina of whom he dreamt in the underground temple. And now to be so close within her sphere sent a shiver down his spine.

He bumped into her outside his room one night. He felt the softness of her skin and the lace of her bodice against his arm. She looked up at him. There was a spark of recognition and she asked him how he fared in his new job. Adam felt his trousers tighten, and he trembled as she asked to see his room.

"You want to see it?" he stammered.

"I've never been in here before," she said. "I thought it was a dust closet or something."

"Well... Come in and see," he invited her.

She ducked inside and sat upon his straw mat. "I suppose it's better than some."

He turned up the lamp, and sensing that she might leave, grabbed his only possession that had not been in the pillowcase that he'd lost in the temple - his book of drawings - and opened it for her.

She smiled when she saw his unkind depictions of the priests of the Jesuit Church, of the other boys, of the creatures and spirits he had seen in the font, of all the images from the life he had left. He felt embarrassed as if he shouldn't be sharing his ridiculous sketches with anyone. She laughed at his drawing of the Beast of the Revelation, and again at the crazed look on John the Baptist's face in his picture of the Baptism of Christ.

"You're quite an artist," she said.

He loved her, he thought.

"Who's this? Is this a self-portrait?" she asked, pointing to a picture of the soldier he continually saw, posed next to a giant horse with a slain stag slung over its rump.

"No, that's someone else, someone who looks like me, but older. He's in the New World."

There was a rude knock at the door.

"What is it?" Serafina shrieked, annoyed.

"The fire's gone out!" It was Madam. "I expect you to pay more attention!"

Serafina opened the door. Adam cringed.

"What are you doing in here? Herr Turner is here, asking for you."

"He's a pig," she spat.

Serafina handed Adam back his book and crawled out.

Madam set her jaw. "This won't do," she scolded Adam. "I can find someone else, you know!"

Adam ducked out. "Sorry, Fraulein."

He was shocked when his bare feet hit the floor, sending icy picks of cold up his legs. He slipped on his boots and went around back to fetch some wood for the hearths and stoves that had gone out. It was so hot in his room with Serafina, he never suspected the fires had all died.

He filled each hearth with a stack of wood, and lit the kindling until the logs burned in each. Some of the rooms he entered were occupied by the girls and their patrons. He averted his eyes from their rollicking beds and quickly made the fires, though some things he saw out of the corner of his eye in the firelight, made him wonder.

In the weeks that followed, he began to obsess about Serafina. Though his body was busily employed in menial labor, his mind was completely unfettered and he dreamed of Serafina, of having her, of making love to her.

He was having just such a fantasy while stacking logs in the kitchen hearth for the supper fire when a great commotion came from the parlor.

"It's him! It's him! He's coming! Bar the door!" one of the girls screamed. They were all unusually loud anyway, but there was terror in Lisette's voice now. Adam jumped aside as Madam ran past him into the kitchen and grabbed a musket off the mantle shelf. Most of the girls dashed upstairs as Serafina struggled to bar the door.

"I'll do it!" shouted Adam and he took over trying to dislodge the rusty bar from its vertical position, but he was too late.

A huge man with long, greasy, gray hair forced open the front door and stood in the doorway, looking up the stairs at Serafina.

"Serafina!" he staggered toward her. "I told you I was coming back for you! You little whore!"

Madam pointed the musket at him. "You get out of here, now!"

He slapped the gun out of Madam's hands and grabbed her by the throat. He pinned her on the table and was squeezing the life from her.

Adam jumped up and grabbed onto the man's back like a giant spider. He choked him, his hands barely able to fit around his giant, bulging neck, and rode him out the door.

"Get off!" growled the intruder. He flung Adam off into the snow outside. The man was bigger and stronger, and knocked him silly with little more than a tap.

Adam grabbed the axe he'd left next to the door, and wheeling around, swung it at his head. The axe flew out of his hands and hit the gray haired man squarely in the temple. He fell in the ice with a muffled crunch. Adam stared at him, picked up the axe, and stood holding it above him, terrified, waiting for him to rise, as his dark blood seeped through the snow.

Serafina and the others watched him from the door. "My God, boy, did you *kill* him?" she asked in horror.

Adam looked down at the man's profile, turning pale, his eyes staring wide, a horrible grimace frozen on his face. Adam breathed in the frozen air, and looked up and down the empty street.

"Quickly!" yelled Madam, "Get him inside!"

They grabbed the man's hands and feet and dragged him in. His blood splattered on the wooden floor. Someone wound a sheet around his head. At Madam's frantic behest, they hauled him through the house, out the back door into the chicken house to be hidden beneath the straw. Marsa followed them out, protesting, until Madam ordered her to be quiet. There were other houses all around them. The last thing they needed was other witnesses.

Adam returned to the front step and quickly scooped up all the bloody snow in a bucket and brought it to the back garden. They threw it in the horse's muddy stall where it melted and lost its telltale redness upon the brown manure.

They barred the door, turned off the red lamp for the first and only time. They gathered around the kitchen table in pregnant silence. It was then that Adam realized that he had killed a man. The dread and guilt of the mortal sin sank in as he looked around him at the girls' stunned expressions. His hands and shirt were stained red and he searched Madam's face, quite in shock. Tears rolled down his cheeks and he began to cry openly. Guilt gripped him and he regretted deeply ever setting foot in the Frisky Cat.

Madam put an arm around him, "No, boy, no, don't cry." He looked at her face and saw that she was smiling. All of them were smiling.

"You did it." Serafina said to him. "You killed the

monster!"

"He was vicious with us and we could do nothing against him," said Lisette. "Now he is no more, and we are free."

Adam was kissed, praised, and thanked profusely with tears of joy. As they hugged him with gratitude and spoke painfully of a girl named Gisela whom he had strangled to death during an encounter one year ago, Adam realized he was being thanked for killing the man. He certainly hadn't meant to deliver a fatal blow, but he had, in that one blind moment when the axe found its mark.

"Gisela is avenged," whispered Lotte, her huge blue eyes running with tears.

"Indeed. But now, the question is, what shall we do with his corpse?" Madam tapped her long fingernails on the table.

"What if someone comes looking for him here?" asked Serafina, her eyes wild, his blood smeared all over her dress.

"Calm yourself. No one knows he was here except us," Madam assured her. "There was no one else here tonight. And these men, when they come here, they don't tell anyone where they are going."

It wasn't long before Astrid, a thin blonde with a gap between her teeth, remembered her cousin's pigsty in the next valley. "We can cut him up and feed him to the pigs. I will distract my cousin, and we will be done with him."

"Let's cut him up before he's frozen solid. Let's do it now in these clothes and burn them when we're done," Lisette stood.

Everyone who had blood on them rose and went out the door.

Adam thought that he would be made to do the dismembering but no one even offered him the axe at all. There were six of them who took the slippery axe and swung savagely at the gray-haired man's body until there were more than a dozen pieces of him. Adam watched in sickened disbelief as they flung his parts in the back of the wagon like pieces of firewood, and then heaped straw on top of them. Strings of meat and entrails remained on the ground out the kitchen door. Marsa gave Adam a hard look as she quickly pitched water on them and washed the bits beneath the blanket of snow. The ravens would find a meal in the spring thaw.

As the moon reflected off the snow, illuminating the way through the woods, Serafina and Astrid drove the wagon out of town. Adam rode in the back, wary of the stray arms and legs beneath the straw around him. Suddenly a raven cawed at them from an overhanging branch. Serafina screamed, spooking the horses that shot off at a run down the bumpy road. The wagon bounced roughly over the snowy road and the pieces of the gray-haired man were tossed about in the straw around Adam.

As they approached a farmhouse, he smelled the foul excrement of pigs on the chill night air. Serafina reined in the team and they quietly drove around the back of the barn. Snow fell on the horses' brown coats and glistened in their black manes. Astrid jumped down and waded through the drifts to the farmhouse.

Over the fence that rounded the barn, they could hear the pigs grunting, huffing in their warm little shelters. Quickly, Adam and Serafina pulled all the pieces of the gray-haired man from the hay and tossed them over into the pigsty.

The pigs awoke for the offering and began to eat. Adam and Serafina listened as the half-frozen flesh was chewed, as his bones were ground by the pigs' teeth. They talked to blot out the sound as they waited for Astrid to return.

"What is she doing with her cousin?" Serafina shivered with a giggle.

"We should be absolutely sure that all the remains are eaten. Do you have a flint?" Adam asked.

"If I had a flint, I'd build a fire," she replied, her teeth chattering.

Adam put his arm around her. She kissed him on the face, then put her cool-warm cheek against his. "You're such a good boy." He felt her soft hair against his face, smelled her sweet perfume, and savored the moment.

When they had returned to the Frisky Cat, Adam thought surely he would fall back into the lowly position he had previously held. But that was not to be the case. He had never known such appreciation, such admiration as that which was bestowed upon him by the prostitutes of the Frisky Cat. He was treated with all the reverence, honor, and respect due a hero. He was pampered, petted, loved, praised, and kissed affectionately at every opportunity. He was fed the best cuts of meat, baked for, and given fine clothes and soft, new bedding. A new spirit of freedom and happiness filled the house and it was because of him. He had set them free from their oppressor, removed their fear, and in return, he was treated like a prince. He still chopped all the wood, however, but he didn't mind.

Sometimes late at night when the house was quiet and Adam lay in his soft bed beneath the stairs, he still felt a twinge of sickness at the memory of the sound of the axe cracking the man's skull, and the vision of his pale face, as the blood released his earthly spirit into the ethers. He had broken the first of the Ten Commandments, and even though the gray-haired man most probably deserved his violent death, Adam felt a great bit of remorse for breaking God's law. But such morality grew further and further from his mind with every passing day, and he began to forget the rigid ways of St. Michael's Jesuit Academy.

One night when Serafina had come to lounge upon his new mattress of chicken feathers and chat with him, he asked her, "Will anyone ever find out about this, do you think?"

"I don't know... We can ask the cards." And she took a

deck of cards from her pocket and laid them before him.
He wondered how a deck of playing cards could speak an
answer. She saw the skepticism on his face and lit a new
candle. "The cards are a tool. They are a means by which
the spirits tell us what they see, for they are up higher than
we and can see the future."

Adam yearned to tell her how he could sometimes see
the future in a bowl of water, but she continued without
pausing, giving him the attention he craved, as she taught
him how each card had a variety of different correlations
depending on its position in a layout. He listened as well
as he could for he was distracted by her nearness, the
softness of her arm against his, the devilish curve of her
lips as she spoke.

"A card can indicate a person, a situation, force of
nature, energy, a time of the year, a day even, in the past,
present or future." She threw down seven cards in a circle
and turned them over one at a time. "You've run away
from home," she said looking at him, "but it wasn't really
your home, was it?'

"It was St. Michael's Jesuit academy," Adam confessed.
"I was to become a priest."

"A priest?" she scoffed. "A *Jesuit* priest?" And laughing,
she fell back upon his bed. "If you only knew...*If you only
knew...*"

"It's the highest calling there is." He stiffened, recalling
what the priests had always said about women, especially
lustful and unrepentant ones such as she who lay before
him, her breasts falling to the sides of her ribcage and
jiggling like two full skins of water as she laughed.

"Please forgive me. I do not understand how a normal
man could resist the love of a woman, even if it is for
God," she said leaning on one elbow. Her massive bosoms
stacked one on top of the other, creating a mile of smooth
cleavage that led like a road cut through a high field,
going over the horizon.

"To be pure enough to be in His service, one must be chaste, and abstain from the company of..." Adam stopped himself.

"Persons like myself?" she finished for him. "Or what? You might enjoy the pleasure of your own body in mine as you were created to do?" She waved her thick eyelashes dismissively.

He felt the forceful wave of lust enliven the serpent who lived between his legs and pull him long and straight toward Serafina. It was as if she'd willed it to happen.

"I'm not going to be a priest any more so it doesn't matter," he said impatiently, covering his lap with his book of visions.

"How old are you?" she asked him.

"Thirteen," Adam answered.

"You're a bit young yet," she said cautiously. "But not forbidden."

Adam stared at her. She smiled as she went through the suits and explained the significance of each, how hearts pertained to emotions, how spades meant the material world; how clubs meant action; how diamonds were pointed like swords and often meant destruction. She told him what each of the numbers meant and the subtleties of the meanings when the cards were in certain combinations. Adam listened and committed her words to memory as he did with all the information he encountered.

"And you must listen with your heart and train yourself to hear the voice that speaks the truth. It will tell you things, and sometimes the voice is the best indicator of the truth. Not the cards."

Adam never heard any voice in his head, but his own and those echoes of the priests warning him that these cards were a form of sorcery to be shunned and feared. Nonetheless, he learned to read the tarot with aplomb. Perhaps the priests were mistaken about such things.

Serafina's estranged husband practiced astrology, and

this art, too, she taught to Adam. "One cannot work the tarot effectively without the knowledge of astrology. You must know the signs of the zodiac and what they mean. They pertain to everything in a person's life," she said with a lofty air.

Adam thought of the underground temple and determined to bring Serafina there one day and show her the zodiac on the ceiling.

The lessons continued each night for several weeks during which time his affection for her deepened into something beyond boyish infatuation. The more he knew about her, the more he wanted to know. She told him she had fallen in love with a great man, a doctor and magician, but he had left her in Munich.

"Why would he just leave you here?" asked Adam unable to comprehend how any man would willingly leave the company of the beautiful Serafina.

"We had befriended some men in Rome who were not honest people and they involved us in a very dangerous plot that forced us to flee our home. Cagliostro and I had to go our separate ways or we would be recognized by those who sought us. My husband disguises himself very well. I, on the other hand, am not so well hidden from the eye, but hiding is not my forte. So I told him I would stay here and when things were quiet again, and there was no one looking for us, I would meet him in London."

"What happened that would make you have to run away from your home?" he asked. She was another refugee like himself.

"My husband has great powers. As a boy, he studied all over the East under a great master called Althotas, who taught him the ways of the gods. Cagliostro can heal the sick, he can predict the future, see the past; he can read a man or a woman for who they really are. He speaks with the spirits on high and can call up any sort of information that is requested. By those who know him, he is highly sought, for he knows all. And his eyes... Oh my god, his eyes, they see straight into a person's soul. There's not another like him in the world."

"How can he know all?" asked Adam dubiously, though he often dreamed of attaining such breadth of knowledge himself.

"Because. Anything that is, was, will ever be, is written in the stars, is waiting in the ethers, is already spoken by God, and if you know where to look or whom to ask, you can see what is to come. Everything you do is destiny. It is destiny that you and I have met here."

Adam sat silently for a while, trying to comprehend how everything he did could already be known and done before he had ever decided it. Finally, he asked. "Do you think you'll ever see him again? Do you think Cagliostro will really be in London like he said?" he asked, feeling a shiver of jealousy.

"Of course he will. He loves me."

"Does he know that you do this?" He said, referring to her prostitution.

"No," she said proudly, "And he will never know either, because I will never tell him."

"But if he truly has gifts of prophecy, won't he know already what you have been doing?"

"That is the funniest thing," she laughed, "He is blind to who I really am. His love for me makes him so. He has never been able to read me for anything I've done. I can tell him *anything* and he will believe me. Though I do not make such a habit of that, for he is my true love, too."

"Isn't there something else you could do besides... this?" Adam wondered.

"It's what I do best. And it's the only way I could make enough money to get to London safely and in style." She showed him her perfect, soft hand. "These hands do not do other people's washing, nor will they ever."

"If he's your husband, why doesn't he send you money

so you can meet him now?" he asked.

"He doesn't know exactly where I am, nor do I know where he is at this moment, and we have no mutual friends we can trust in either country. We have plans to go to the New World after we meet, and start our lives anew," she added. "We can be anyone we want to be, there. We can do anything in the New World."

It was then he suddenly remembered the letter he had sent off to Virginia colony before he had run away. If a reply had come, the letter would be coming to St. Michael's any day now, for it had been several months, ample time for a letter to cross the Atlantic and then arrive back in Bavaria.

"When will the letter from my brother be here?" he asked abruptly.

"The one from your... *family*?" she asked as if she didn't believe he had one. She shuffled the cards.

"Yes," he answered tentatively. That he would receive a letter back was mere fantasy.

With a deep breath, she turned over a card. "Well, your letter came today."

"Today?" He sat up straight and bumped his head on the slanted ceiling.

"But you mustn't go and get it. There is grave danger ahead of you," she added as she turned over a rough sequence of cards, but he knew that already. All he heard was that his letter had arrived.

CHAPTER V

As he gathered up an armload of kindling, he plotted how he could manage to return to that horrid academy and get his letter without being caught. As he fed the goats some hay, he stared into their trough of water and tried to see the letter. The water rippled and there appeared the courier carrying a small package to St. Michael's. His heart raced and the vision disappeared, perhaps because of his desire to see it. But the package was for him – he saw his name clearly on it.

He put on the white tunic and black trousers in which he had left so that he would not seem out of place there, at least from a distance. Since he'd been at the Frisky Cat, he'd been given quite a few items of haberdashery. He'd become accustomed to wearing colors and finer fabrics, not that his newfound clothes were well put together or even fit him, but they were certainly more attractive, and wearing something colorful and different made him feel good. Now, the old tunic and trousers scratched his skin. He'd forgotten how rough they felt, and he realized how much he hated them. No matter, he planned to slip into St. Michael's unnoticed, find the package, and run back to the Cat as fast as humanly possible.

It was dark by the river as he passed the little wood cross where Wilhelm had drowned. Thoughts of how much danger he was in crept to the forefront of his mind and he hesitated in his step, but fear of Wilhelm's tormented spirit accosting him prompted him onward into the churchyard.

He slipped among the headstones and saw that the light upstairs in the dormitory was still on. He saw the monks downstairs through the window of the rectory – Haster, Salermo, Ivor, taking their dinner at the table. A hard roll and some murky cabbage soup, no doubt. He did not miss the food at St. Michael's. Since he'd left, his body had begun to fill out considerably from all the meat and eggs he was fed at the brothel.

He regretted not scrying to see exactly where the letter lay. Now he would have to search for it. And there was no telling where it was. They could've sent it back already. He thought briefly of returning to the river to look into the water or even returning to the brothel to get a proper glimpse. But he was here now and the river was dark and he was afraid. Just get the letter and be done with this harrowing task, he thought. Tomorrow the letter may not be available.

He slinked past the statue of St. Peter and went silently into the Cathedral, going the back way through the transept to the priests' offices – undoubtedly that would be where the package lay. He walked silently down the hallway. He came to the first pair of doors. Cautiously he opened them. There was no one on the other side. He continued on till he found himself outside the office of the bishop.

The lamp was out and he wondered if there would be enough light to find what he was looking for. He reasoned that the Bishop was too important to be concerned with mail that was not addressed to him, so therefore it would be in Brother Haster's office. He was the one who handed out the students' mail.

He suddenly heard the monks chanting from the Cathedral. He had just missed them as they filed in from another doorway. Although the sound of them was beautiful, their voices were ridiculously self-righteous and needlessly oppressive, like the atmosphere of the whole place was needlessly oppressive. He pushed open Haster's office door. It was dark in there. How was he ever going to find his package? He took two steps forward in the pitch black and his toe met with some piece of furniture. Then he heard a rustle. Someone was in there, too. Suddenly a lamp came on. Brother Salermo's black eyes danced in the firelight. His expression was cruel, sardonic. "Looking for this?" He held up a paper-wrapped package with Adam's name on it. "Yes, I saw you sneak through the churchyard, you slick little Jew. What will you do to get it?" Salermo stared at him.

Adam snatched the package out of his hands, but Salermo grabbed him by the back of the tunic and pushed him to the floor.

"You're not leaving us again." He sat on Adam's back. Adam struggled to get out from under him, but he could not. Salermo was heavy and forced his head into the floor. Adam screamed.

"Shut up!" Salermo spat.

Adam screamed again. Salermo struck him in the face. Adam reached back and grabbed Salermo's crotch and pinched it mercilessly. Salermo grabbed the offending arm and twisted it excruciatingly behind Adam's back until it made a horrible, juicy, popping sound. Adam screamed again, overcome by the pain. Salermo grabbed his throat and began squeezing the life from him. Adam felt the blood pounding in his temples. He choked for breath, and prayed for Jesus to help him.

It was then that Brother Haster and Brother Ivor burst into the room. "What are you doing? Who is that?" asked Haster.

"It's the runaway. He's come back to steal from you, Brother Haster. I caught him in here," Salermo panted, letting go of Adam's throat.

"No, that's not true," Adam defended himself with half a voice. Salermo tweaked his arm again and Adam called out in pain.

"What is the penalty for runaways, Brother?" asked Salermo of Haster.

"Twenty lashes of the whip," answered Ivor.

Salermo held Adam by the back of the neck and steered him outside by his broken arm. Ivor and Haster followed. They tied him to a post in the courtyard. Adam looked at the windows surrounding the square and although he could not see their faces, he knew that everyone in the dormitory was watching. He thought and could not remember ever seeing anyone whipped before at St. Michael's.

When Adam was secured to the post, Salermo took the whip from Haster. "I'll do it," he said.

He heard the pop of the whip, felt its searing pain, and cried out. By the second or third lashing, Adam could hardly imagine how Salermo could deliver a more painful lash than what he was giving. He was sadistic. The pain seared him, making every muscle tense unbearably in anticipation of the next lash. The end of the whip wrapped around his body each time and the tail of it stung him somewhere on the chest. He felt his blood oozing down his back and his body shivered with mortal fear. His broken arm seemed a minor affliction in light of the pain he now endured.

His old bed was waiting for him in the darkened dormitory. Haster and Ivor helped him into it. "We hope you have learnt your lesson," Ivor scolded hollowly.

Adam said nothing.

There was no one asleep in the dormitory though it was well into the night. They did not speak but he could hear their breathing, their whispers.

Ivor had bound his arm in a muslin sling and wrapped more muslin around his body to keep his wounds from dripping blood on the floor. He lay on the bed on his good side and watched Ivor and Haster leave the room.

"Where were you all this time?" one of the boys asked him.

Adam dearly longed to brag that he had been employed in a brothel but telling his tale would be unwise. There was only one whorehouse in all of Munich and it would be easy to find him from that fact alone.

"I found an abandoned cottage in the woods," he lied. They all seemed convinced but begged for more details. How did he survive? What did he eat? Adam yawned and answered their questions in a low monotonous voice. Slowly one by one, they drifted off to sleep. Only one was still interested. "Where is this place? I want to go there! Will you take me there?"

"I can't," he told him, "the owners returned to claim it.

That's why I had to come back here. It was cold outside and I had nowhere else to go."

The other boy whimpered about not wanting to stay here, then turned his head on his pillow, and finally went to sleep, too.

Adam was more exhausted than he had ever been in his life, but his anger would not let him rest. With great pain, he got up and walked as quickly as he could to the lavatory. With every step he felt the wounds on his back crack open, smart, and ooze. His face hurt where Salermo had smashed his head into the floor. He touched it; it was swollen beyond belief.

In the lavatory, there was a row of   wash basins on the high table next to the window. Adam looked in them, but all of them had already been emptied. He thought of all the places where his package could've ended up, but it was unsafe for him to leave the company of the others.

With no water to scry in, he had no idea where to look for the letter. The only place other than the river that would certainly have water was the holy font. He was not about to roam St. Michael's unarmed. From a shelf, he took a candle snuff, detached the bell from the end and slipped the metal stick into his trousers.

The cathedral was dimly lit by the small lamps that that illuminated the portals. Adam stole in and approached the font. He stared in at his own reflection, felt his breath ricochet off the surface. "Where is my package?" he whispered.

The water rippled and showed the wrapped package. It sat on top of Brother Haster's desk, forgotten there by Salermo when they had been interrupted. Salermo's face suddenly appeared in the font. Adam blinked, and suddenly saw how Wilhelm had lost his life. He saw Brother Salermo chasing him into the river. Wilhelm had gotten his foot caught in something underwater and he had drown. Was that why Salermo had been so cruel? To hide his own guilt? And why had he chased Wilhelm into the water?

Suddenly Brother Salermo's face appeared in the water, but it was no apparition.

"I expect you did not come in here for worship," he said at Adam's back.

"I've seen your sins, Brother. I know what you did."

"I have no sins."

"What about Wilhelm?"

"He couldn't swim." Salermo grabbed him.

Adam shoved the   candle snuffer's end into Salermo's eye where it stuck. Oh! Oh! You little viper!" Salermo fell back into a pew, screaming in anguish.

Adam ran fast as he could back to Haster's office. He needed no light to see the whereabouts of his package. He snatched it off the desk, tucked it down into his muslin sling and ran out the side door through the churchyard and cemetery to the river. Dawn was threatening on the horizon.

Behind him he could hear the priests' voices shouting. They were coming after him. The pain of his broken arm and his beating slowed him somewhat but he kept on running and did not stop. He ran past the little wooden cross on the riverbank. "I got him for you," he said to it.

His shoes slipping on the icy tiles, he passed the fountain in the town square. The waters seemed to glimmer with a new light, and he took a circuitous way back to the Frisky Cat.

He ducked into the brothel just in time to encounter Madam coming down the stairs wearing a satin gown and smoking a pipe. She gasped at his muslin-wrapped arm and bruised face. "What happened to you?"

"I went back to St. Michael's," and he related his whole harrowing tale to her, showing her the lash marks on his back.

65

"Those filthy Jesuits! They come to my door, call me names and condemn me to hell. Thank God you're back here safe with us," she said as she helped him into a chair. He felt love from her and could not help his tears from flowing. "Now what is in this package that you would risk your life to go back and get?"

"It's from my brother, in the New World." His hand shook as he began to unwrap it. Madam held the package down for him as he tore it open with his good hand, revealing a letter tied to a tobacco tin with a peacock beautifully painted on it. He opened the letter with his teeth and read it.

Dear Adam,

Thank you for finding me. I, too, have seen the strange visions of which you speak and I cannot explain them, only that I feel our experiences are extraordinary. After much thought, I have concluded that we cannot possibly be natural brothers. So we will settle for 'brothers in spirit.' I look forward to our correspondence across, or In the water. Here are some of the spoils of my farm…

Not brothers? Adam felt a heaviness of heart, for he had so often imagined being invited to live at his long lost family's grand house in Virginia. Being made a gentleman or a soldier or placed neatly in some other mould in which he would fit. How fabulous life would be with a family. But it was not to be.

"Aren't you going to open the box?" asked Madam.

Nothing could be as valuable as finding a brother. He would not be in the box. He opened it anyway and found the small bundles of tobacco and hemp, a box of miniature fire cords, and a pipe inside. The pipe was exquisitely carved from alabaster, and originated in some exotic world Adam could hardly imagine.

Madam looked at the tobacco, sniffed it. "Is this a

66

Christmas present? May I have some?"

"It's for smoking I suppose," Adam shrugged. "Help yourself."

After Madam had packed her pipe, Adam sat back on his chair, put a tiny pinch of the green herb in the pipe's bowl and lit it. He coughed terribly for he had never smoked before, and wondered why people did such a thing. As Madam prepared another bowl to be lit, they examined the chubby, old face drawn in caricature on the box of cords – Dr. Franklin. Who was this jowly-faced man with the crazy smile and the bolt of lightning through his semi-bald head? He and Madam giggled at all the possibilities that came to mind and found themselves rolling with laughter.

The girls came to see. "What's that smell? It smells like a skunk!"

"Some tobacco from America," Adam said. His vision was getting blurry for some reason and the room seemed different somehow, the colors brighter, his pain dulled. The girls seemed different, too. He noticed things about them that he hadn't before – the mole on Lotte's chest and the feint mustache above Lisette's top lip. It was as if they were more real and alive now than they had been. What did they think of him, he wondered, and suddenly he worried that they did not approve of him. What sort of things did they say about him behind his back? Was he a man to them, or simply their boy? They said they loved him, but what exactly did they mean by that? His mind berated him with questions that he was too shy to ask.

"I want to try some," said Lisette.

Adam handed her the pipe and the box of fire cords. She giggled. Adam was relieved it was at Dr. Franklin's crazy picture on the box and not at him.

She put the pipe to her pink lips, brushed a long corkscrew curl from her face, and lit the pipe.

"This tobacco is not like my French tobacco," said Madam.

The girls all took a liking to the pungent smoke, and when it was gone, they coerced Adam into writing to his friend to send him more. "Please, for us?"

For Christmas, Adam sent him a beautifully knitted wool scarf and some wonderful spun rabbit fur socks Lotte had made. He enclosed a friendly letter and hoped that it did not sound too impolite.

Dearest Brother-in-Spirit,
The hemp and tobacco you so kindly sent were very popular with my friends. They present you with these fine items in hopes that you will send us more...

And it was not overly long until a large crate, weighing several stones, arrived, much to everyone's delight. For someone who was not a real relative, he was a fine and generous brother and Adam anticipated the day they would meet. Indeed they would, but not like he imagined.

He wrote a letter to his uncle and let him know he was no longer at school, but feared the man would come looking for him, so he never sent it. He often thought of what he was missing at Jesuit school and consoled himself he had already mastered the academic curriculum before he had left and there was little more, if anything, the priests could impart to him that was worth knowing. He had excelled at arithmetic, algebra, geometry, and trigonometry and mastered seven languages, all before his twelfth birthday. The Cathedral's library was limited only to those books directly related to Christian theology and Adam had long ago determined them all to be pedantic and repetitive. He resolved that he was missing nothing at school and never regretted his untimely departure.

CHAPTER VI

In the months that followed, Adam visited the underground temple frequently and discovered a chest of old books and cryptic charts. In the dim room, he read all of them, but could make little sense of the charts, for it seemed that some other basic knowledge was a prerequisite for understanding them.

He was terrified to discover that he was being watched from the shadows as a thin figure took shape and rose from the dusty corner. As it walked toward him, Adam dropped the book he was reading and made hastily for the stairs.

"Wait, boy!" said an unfamiliar voice. "I have your belongings."

"I'm sorry!" shouted Adam, frightened.

"I'm not going to beat you," said the man who appeared out of the shadows, thin and dusky-faced with dark eyes and long fingers, beckoning. "Won't you stay and discuss what you have been reading with me?" He coughed and Adam sensed that he was quite ill. He put Adam's lost pillowcase full of things on the table.

Adam took his pillowcase, glad to have regained it, for it contained the bibles he had so devotedly transcribed. "These books?" Adam asked, pointing to the chest. "Are they yours?"

"They belong to the temple. And to you. I put them here so that you would find them and read them." He answered. "My name is Barmoras. I knew we had a visitor. My cat told me," he said as the white cat rubbed itself around his thin waist.

"Thank you," said Adam.

"How did you find our temple?" he asked.

"Your cat led me to it."

"Ah, see, then you are meant to know about it. What is your name?"

"Adam," he replied, wondering if he should trust this man who undoubtedly practiced the strange animal rite he had witnessed.

"What do you want to know?" he said. "I am dying and I have taught no one my art. Out of jealousy, I have kept it all to myself all these years, and now when I die, it will be lost in this country. These charts are meaningless without the learning that my own master taught to me when I was a boy in Babylon."

"In Babylon?" asked Adam incredulous. "What then, are you doing *here*?"

"I came here because the stars sent me. When you begin practicing astrology, if you are good, you must follow where they lead you or go against what you know to be true."

And Barmoras took Adam as his apprentice and taught him the Mithraic religion, the art of Persian astrology, how to cast charts, predict the future, read the past, and intuit the best days for certain undertakings.

Barmoras was a strict master and insisted they begin lessons everyday at dawn, so Adam was forced to rise hours before sunrise to complete his set of morning tasks at the Frisky Cat. Barmoras had predicted his own death and had only a month to live. In that time, he filled Adam's head with the knowledge and lore of the stars, everything that the Magi who visited the Christ Child knew. Adam took copious notes, for not all of what Barmoras taught him could he so easily assimilate and integrate into his rational mind. The cycles of years of which he spoke were large and hard to fathom, the rulership of the strange gods and their strange names were none he had ever heard before. Their politics and wars, their lineages and entitlements, what stars were under whose dominion. It was a history that Adam had never before encountered, a history that pre-dated the Old Testament, and Adam asked if it was not mythology he was learning, for the characters had powers beyond the scope of any man, save for Jesus, and even He paled in the splendor of the deeds of Barmoras' pantheon.

"It is not myth. It is truth. These are the beings who began the world," replied the sage. "Beings who came from the stars."

Adam listened and learned but did not truly believe what Barmoras told him. He simply wrote down the information and humored the dying man by memorizing what he had to teach. Like Christians believe their stories are the truth, so did Barmoras believe that Mithraism was the truth. The strange ritual Adam had witnessed down in the temple was a Mithraic rite, and indeed Barmoras, beneath the lion's head, had spied him hiding under the bench.

Unlike Christianity, Mithraism taught that a man, if he was righteous, was obligated to right the wrongs of others, and that the ultimate end of creating a safe and peaceful world justified any means one had to employ. These means included putting all evil-doers to death, sometimes before their crimes could be committed. Rather than turning the other cheek and forgiving the transgressions of enemies, revenge and preventive measures were the manner by which all immoral, ill-intentioned men were to be dealt. The ancient philosophy was just the balm that Adam needed in order to forget and forgive himself for the slaying of the gray-haired man, and the maxim *Slay the Doers of Evil* became Adam's motto, though much more in word than in deed.

"And what of this man and the bull he is slaying?" asked Adam asked of the bronze statue upon the table.

"This is the god Mithra, a mighty king of divine lineage. He refused the attentions of the goddess of love and she and her father, the Lord of Heaven sent a great bull to kill him. But Mithra was mighty and prevailed, and killed the bull," Barmoras replied.

71

One morning Adam arrived at the underground temple and Barmoras was not there. Nor was he there the following day. On the third day, the white cat appeared, and he knew that the man had gone from this life.

In the spring, the streets of Munich were decked with the altars of the Virgin and Jesus for the Feast of the Annunciation, a celebration of the day of the Immaculate Conception and of the Crucifixion that were believed by many to fall on the same day in March. Adam had seen the procession go by every year, but had always been forbidden from going out on that day, for the priests at St. Michael's despised the people's celebration of faith that was independent of the Church. Anyone usurping their roles as God's appointed conduits was harshly condemned. In the past, the priests had gone so far as to dismantle the altars before the townsfolk could save their statues and relics, so now the people appointed armed guards at each altar so that no such thing could happen again.

Adam and Serafina visited the altars together for they were the only two Catholics at the Frisky Cat. Adam had always considered himself a priest in training, but now he was part of the laity and could partake of the things that ordinary people did. He felt as if he was a part of the community for once, as the townspeople greeted them along the path and offered them little painted crosses, and bread and wine. The music of a dulcimer and a lute enlivened the fair and the day was bright and warm.

The two of them knelt down on a bale of straw before the largest of the altars. Yellow flowers all around it, the Virgin statue was an old one, the paint worn off her mouth as if she'd been kissed too many times. Adam folded his hands and thanked God for watching over him. He prayed for the health and happiness of all the girls at the Frisky Cat who were so kind to him. His prayers were rather succinct so he muttered a few rosaries as he looked over at Serafina, murmuring fervently in Italian. He admired her devotion and wondered about the husband for whom she prayed, and of whom she so often spoke. As much as he wished he could simply erase Cagliostro from the world, he longed to be like him, to be possessed of great powers, for her description of him was nothing short of amazing. Cagliostro could not only find gold in its raw state in the ground, but could turn ordinary metal into solid gold. He had brought the dead back to life, and had parted floodwaters during a storm in Venice. He played with lightning between the palms of his hands, and knew how to call angels to his side. Adam was fascinated by the tales of the Great Cagliostro, but wanted to doubt that all that he had accomplished was true. He did not disbelieve Serafina, but thought that perhaps her perceptions were skewed by her love for him. If Adam could do all that Cagliostro could do, would she favor him, instead? He wondered and wished *he* were the Magnificent Cagliostro.

When they had visited all the altars, Adam thought of the underground temple close by, and took her by the hand.

"You have to see something," he said and led her down the alley.

"What is it?" she asked.

"Something beautiful," he replied.

They ducked into the small door and went carefully down the dark staircase. He felt the heat of her body behind him, her hands on the sides of his waist, and held them to him with his own.

When they had reached the bottom of the stairs, Serafina gasped at the ceiling. "It's so beautiful," she said. "What is this place?"

"It's a mithraeum," Adam replied, kissing her hands. "I have heard they're quite common in Italy and other places east of there."

"Well I have never seen one before," she said, sitting on

the stone table in front of him. He could smell her sweet olive skin. He brushed her neck with his lips and kissed her face. She looked up at him with her dark, soulful eyes.

"You're so beautiful," he said what he had felt so deeply for all these months, but had been afraid to confess. He stroked her cheek and kissed her. He felt confident, more confident than he ordinarily did, down in this sacred place, and let his hands roam over her white peasant blouse. She did not resist him. He found the string that untied it, and pinched the hot berries of her nipples and felt the ample softness of her enormous breasts around them as he kissed her. She pulled off his shirt and unfastened his breeches where the tip of his large, hard manhood was peeking out.

He laughed and gasped in disbelief as her hot wet mouth sheathed him. She stopped just before he was about to lose control. Excited beyond reckoning, he laid her down on the table and guided himself into her, feeling an amazing, burning sensation of bliss, as he stabbed her deeply, filling her small tight space with his cock. He felt her hot core squeezing him desperately as she cried out, wrapping her silky legs around his back and kissing him deeply with her tongue. He reveled in their mutual ecstasy for as long as he could, but suddenly lost control and grasped her in a passionate embrace, making her take all of him.

They lay entwined, skin to skin, and Adam thought he had never been so content. He let his fingertips trace the curves of her fine face and beautiful breasts. He laughed with delight and thought of taking her again.

Suddenly they were startled by the muffled thump of the door to the street above.

"Someone's coming," Serafina whispered, buttoning her blouse.

Adam gathered up his clothes and hurriedly pulled them on. He was suddenly remorseful, for they had defiled the beautiful temple and he had spilled his seed in the sacred place. He had not meant for it to happen, though he had wanted it, but he had never expected her to give in to him, not there. Now he would have to explain their presence there, and he knew it would be obvious to anyone what they had done, for she was a known prostitute. They crouched on the far side of the room, behind a low wall at the end of the bench and waited for many long minutes, but no one entered the room.

When no further sounds came, Adam reasoned that perhaps the wind had thrown open the door upstairs, or perhaps with all the travelers in the streets, one of them had simply opened it out of curiosity, opted not to explore it further then closed it back up. He felt strange and exposed because of what sin he and Serafina had just committed and he pondered silently what God's retribution would be for taking such pleasure in it. Adam had never confessed to masturbation, and would certainly not confess to fornication, and not confessing was an even worse sin. He consoled himself that he could confess all his sins on his deathbed. Until then, he would keep account of them but would not let them worry him. Guilt was a useless emotion, and he had watched how it had queered the personalities of the priests and the religious in detrimental ways, making them unable to accept themselves as human beings, and that made them seem somehow less than men. He would not live as they did, but enjoy the pleasures of the life that had been bestowed him.

At last, Adam stood, his legs aching from crouching so long. He pulled Serafina to her feet and they headed up the stairs. Adam pushed on the door with all his might, but it was locked. And try as he might, he could not force it to open. Any hinges that it had were on the outside of the door, and it was quite sealed and most probably locked from without.

"What do we do?" asked Serafina. "Is there another way out of here?"

"I don't think so," Adam replied. "I suppose we can look, but I've never seen one."

Despite his allegiance with Barmoras, it would be troublesome and certainly embarrassing to be found down in the temple uninvited. And the man was dead now, and who knew if he had ever spoken to anyone of Adam, his protégé? He would be an unwelcome stranger in any case, an intruder in their temple. Was this God's punishment delivered already?

When they had gone over every surface and could find no other way out, Adam looked at Serafina apologetically. "Someone will come and let us out eventually," he said.

She tossed her beautiful head and leaned upon the table, arching her back. "What do we do until then?"

CHAPTER VII

Adam turned sixteen on a cold February day. He had grown up strong and muscle-bound from all the wood chopping, and had become accustomed to the attentions and admiration of women. Even so, he was often lost in cerebral machinations, thinking on the mechanics of the smallest of minutia and the architecture of the greatest of the infinite.

When he wasn't busy with his wood chopping or other chores, he practiced his fortune telling techniques on the brothel's patrons and those in need of counsel who had heard of his great gifts. Whether he meant to or not, he fashioned himself after Serafina's husband, Cagliostro. Serafina had gone to London the year before and though he missed their love, he was glad not to have to hear about her damned husband or his occult prowess any longer. Adam secretly vowed to surpass Cagliostro's power and win Serafina for himself one golden day in the future.

As the months rolled by, Madam's business profited because of Adam's growing fame, and the brothel expanded to the building next door. He was given the use of a small, private alcove off the parlor that he closed off with a curtain and lit with candles for effect. He intuited resolutions and relied on the images he saw in his chalice of water that sat beside him on the table he had made. He cast charts the Persian way that Barmoras had taught him, when specific times were sought, and was often called to the houses of the wealthy nobility to read their fortunes in private. He charged a mark a reading and it nicely made up for his tiny income that had been raised to twenty-five cents a week for keeping the fires lit and providing security.

The Frisky Cat was not without its dangers and Adam frequently had to eject people from the property, though he tried reasoning with them before he attacked them now. Weeks after he and Serafina had fed the gray-haired man's parts to the pigs, the man's severed head rolled out of the straw when he unhitched the wagon. Horrified and cut down by the putrid stench, he put it in a burlap sack full of lime and stowed it beneath the tack room where he hoped it would never again see the light of day. He felt lucky they had never been caught and hoped that all would be able to keep their secret to the grave.

He tried to put the incident behind him, never mentioned it to anyone, and swore never to use an axe again for anything but its intended purpose. He now had a ring of metal knuckles that he kept in his pocket. It hurt most on the ear and Adam was not afraid to use it or the stick, a special piece of firewood he had saved for its length and integrity. He knew the constable, Bohrs, well enough that his word was taken over nearly anyone's. Bohrs had been the one who found him that morning after he had run away, and told him about the sign in the window of the Frisky Cat.

Although he had grown adept at and fond of this life, Adam knew his scholarly potential could not be ignored

77

forever. He was well-read and well-spoken, and had amazing gifts in several areas that he was occasionally inclined to use for gambling and devious intrigue. But the thought of leaving this good life seemed wrong also. He knew he should focus more seriously on his future, but he had no idea what vocation to pursue. He thought he would make a fine ladies' man for the right young widow, but the chance of finding such an employer outside of Paris or Rome was dubious. He remembered how he used to dream of becoming a priest. How foolish and innocent he had been. He had spent so many years preparing himself for that life, and now that it was not to be, he did not know what to do.

It was a still, warm night. The hemp had made his room unbearably smoky and he wandered outside to sip the night air. He stood on the corner, curls of pungent hemp smoke trailing up to heaven. A tall thin man in a black top hat and tailcoat passed by, smoking a cigar. They bid each other a "Guten Nacht."

Adam had seen these elegantly dressed men going to and from their strange temple up the street since he'd come to the Cat. The man came walking back. "What is that you're smoking?"

"Hemp," Adam said, holding it in.

"It's quite a perfume. Might I have a pinch?" The thin man gripped Weishaupt's hand in a strange grip. "Penske, Alfre."

The man took his pipe from his pocket and Adam put a pinch of the hemp into the pipe's bowl. Adam lit a stick in the lamp and lit the man's pipe, causing plumes of the delicious smoke to rise between them into the still night air.

"That's very good. Danke," said the man, glancing up at the Frisky Cat sign.

"Bitte," replied Adam.

He watched the man continue down the street and turn the corner.

He saw Penske again a week later, and he explained his formal attire. "I am on my way to Lodge Theodore. Perhaps you will be my guest one evening? You will bring some of your delicious hemp for my brothers?"

Adam agreed, and Penske came for him at seven thirty on a Friday evening.

Penske had brought him a top hat and tailcoat, "In case you don't have them, you can borrow these."

He did have a tailcoat that had been left at the brothel by a Russian violinist and it fit him pretty well. Penske's coat was somewhat finer, but Adam couldn't even get an arm in it. He borrowed his top hat and that fit tightly, but not uncomfortably so, and he admired himself in the looking glass. He looked like one of the men he saw at the Deutsche Bankhaus.

As they walked up the avenue, Penske stopped abruptly, "You do have the hemp, don't you?"

"*Naturlich*," said Adam. "Tell me again, where are we going?"

"Lodge Theodore of Good Counsel."

The way he said it made Adam worry. What if it wasn't just a men's club? What if it was something else? Or worse, what if it was boring?

As they entered the temple, Adam looked up and saw a pillar to each side of them. Crowning the hall was the insignia with the "G" between the compass and the square.

Penske introduced him to the lodge, and they took seats against the South wall.

"You must never repeat what is said within these confines, for members speak freely here, and some of our brothers' ideas dare to cross the limits of propriety. You may speak your heart as well, if it please you," said Penske.

Indeed, conversations and the exchange of ideas flowed

freely in Lodge Theodore because of the members' pledge of confidentiality. The venerable Right Worshipful Master, Weingarten, read a bit of Socrates to them and then everyone broke forth in a clamor of comments to each other. Much of the discussion was not always pertinent to the topic, but it was usually eye-opening, sometimes funny, and Adam learned much more than he had ever expected, about life, business, and philosophy.

Adam visited the lodge as Penske's guest twice a week for a month. He began to grasp that the ceremonies of the ancients were the core of the particular rite that was practiced there, and he burned to be initiated into the deeper mysteries. He went early with Penske to the temple to scrutinize and interpret for himself, the symbolism that had been painted and sculpted all over the lodge.

It was around this time that he received a letter from his brother in the New World who confessed to have contacted the masters at Lodge Theodore to go and bring him in.

For I have made such fine contacts in business at the lodge here that I would think it indispensable for a young man to be without such help...

So he had sent Penske to find him and bring him in. How divine to have a brother, even if just in spirit.

It was a Friday morning when he realized he didn't have any more hemp. He wondered then if he would still be welcome, for he had not been initiated, nor given any indication that he would be made a novice at all.

After the formal meeting that night, they adjourned to the mezzanine for port and cigars. He felt their eyes on him. Undoubtedly they were all expecting that a pipe would emerge from his coat pocket.

Finally the Lodge master said it. "Don't you have any of that good Indian herb tonight, boy?"

"It's all gone," Adam shrugged apologetically.

There were sighs and groans of disappointment. All of them appreciated the sultry flavor, wave of relaxation, and inspiring perspective that came from smoking hemp. Adam looked at Penske for help. He puffed his French cigar and handed one to Adam.

A gentleman with a hook for a hand asked when he would be getting more. "Perhaps you could procure some more from your brother?" They closed in on him, reaching into their pockets.

"Certainly, I could try. He's harvesting the new crop right now. Maybe our ritual will bring it along." His comment seemed to fall flat. "In praise of Demeter..."

It seemed a revelation to some of them. Adam supposed there were many reasons other than ritual that men joined the freemasons.

"Read a fortune, Adam. Who wants their fortune read?" offered Penske. Adam looked at him with surprise and wondered how and from whom he'd learned of his divination skills. "Go ahead. Show these gentlemen what you do so well."

Adam used a deck of playing cards and the gypsy square, and summarized the lives of several old men with stinging accuracy and got laughs from those who knew the "large wife," "the tendency to exaggerate the truth," and one man's "malcontented mistress." Adam begged out of giving advice, claiming he was too young to be of help in most of life's dilemmas simply because of his inexperience, though that was anything but the truth. He did not want to be caught up drawing charts all night, and he had learned from his readings of people at the Cat that to give advice made him seem partly responsible for their potentially rash or misguided actions.

"Are you going to do this as your profession, Adam?" one of them asked.

"It's just a hobby," Adam replied, but he knew that the

prophetic arts would figure prominently in whatever he did. How could he *not* use what means he had to predict otherwise unforeseeable outcomes?

"What is your station? Do you have employment?" one man asked of him.

"Yes."

"And what is it that you do?" asked an older man with a pointed mustache and goatee who seemed vaguely familiar.

Adam hesitated and did not meet their eyes. "I'm a courier and guard for some ladies."

"I assume they are kind mistresses."

"The kindest," answered Adam.

"How do they feel about having a *sorcerer* in their midst?" asked Weingarten.

"A sorcerer? I merely read prophecy. It's quite different."

"Soothsaying is a sin to the Church," declared the man with the hook for a hand.

"These are Christian ladies for whom you work?" angled the man with the pointed mustache.

He thought of Serafina writhing on him, seeming to glow red with the fires of Hell. "Of course they are," he answered, for she was indeed a good Catholic, albeit doing penance for the rest of her days.

When he had returned to the Cat that night, Adam wrote his brother a letter thanking him for the introduction, and enclosed all the money he had collected from the Lodge members. It seemed a lot of money to him, and he wondered if his brother would think it enough to bother with.

He was initiated unexpectedly one night shortly thereafter. Blindfolded, he was led to a secret room in the temple, sat at a desk, and given the elements to ponder. Later, when he was presented before the others in the lodge, and his blindfold removed, he stared up at the G in the keystone of the arch above the altar.

keystone of the arch above the altar.

"Whether it be God, Grace, Gravitas, or the Great Work of life that you hold dearest to your soul," the Lodge master pierced him with his hawk-like eyes. "Let your oath be unto that thing most sacred, and to your fellow man..." And Adam found himself a bona fide freemason, straddling the workaday world of sex at the Frisky Cat and the one of erudition, tradition, and privilege at Lodge Theodore.

He had grown into a man under the roof of the Frisky Cat, not a bad-looking one either, for he was taller than most, and his chest was broad. His face was handsome with a strong jaw and beautiful eyes, or so said his female admirers, and there were many. He often thought his had become the very image of the face of his brother in the New World, whom he had seen first so long ago in the water of the Isar River. His arms and legs were strong from the labor in which he was employed, and his intuition and second sensibilities keen and honed from the astrological readings he gave daily. He had become adept at the art of lovemaking from the hours spent with the skillful Serafina, and showed the new girls who sought employment at the Cat the exquisite joys that could be found in the mastery of their profession. There were more than a few who found Adam's heart irresistible and it pained him to watch them ascend the stairs to the bedroom with a gentleman on their arm. They would look back him with glistening eyes, and he wished they had chosen a nobler life.

It was early November and unseasonably warm when Penske and Adam traveled north to Hamburg to receive the shipment that came in fifteen large crates marked "HEMP – Hamburg." There, they loaded the crates into two hired wagons and drove them back to Bavaria. It was a long journey, but it made Adam more money than he had ever dreamed of having.

Now in his sixteenth year, Adam felt adrift as if he was waiting for something, something that may never come, and he thought of himself eighty years old, still putting logs on the fire for the girls who had themselves, become decrepit. He could not stay at the Cat for much longer; it was incongruous to his true nature, an intellectual self that began to reemerge as he hungered to learn new ideas and ancient traditions.

He scried into the basin in the kitchen and to his elation, saw himself surrounded by books.

"If you're so happy about the dishwater, wash the dishes," quipped Marsa seeing his expression. Adam obliged her as he always did, and scrubbed the supper plates and pans.

It was not long before his prophecy was fulfilled. As Adam walked out of the lodge one night soon after, the older man with the pointed mustache, one to whom he had rarely spoken, was waiting in the lane outside the Cat. Adam lifted his hat respectfully, and strode past.

"I am your uncle," he said at Adam's back.

Adam froze.

"Do you not remember me? The Baron von Ickstatt? It has been a few years, but neither of us has changed so much. You more than I, perhaps."

"Uncle?" Adam turned to face him, incredulous.

They had been at the same meetings several times over the past few months and this man had remained a curious stranger until now. Adam had thought he seemed familiar, but nothing more. He never expected to see his uncle at these clandestine affairs, and so did not recognize him in such company. Now as he scrutinized the man's face, he recalled the pointed mustache and goatee, the penetrating eyes and the large mole on his cheek.

"Uncle. Why have you not spoken to me before?" he asked.

"I wanted to keep my distance from one so seemingly gifted in the arts of prophecy. Your father was as well. It was his undoing," he said quietly.

"What do you mean?" Adam asked defensively.

"He should have been more discreet."

They exchanged a dark look.

"My brethren are sworn to secrecy. That is the first precept of our lodge. They would never tell what I do or say within those walls. It is a safe haven," said Adam.

"An oath is an oath... Or is it? I admire that you are bound by your word. It takes much more than words to bind most men."

"I want you to tell me everything you know about my family," Adam looked at him intently.

"They were killed by a violent mob in Wurzberg," was Ickstatt's answer.

"But why? What did they do?"

"Your father did exactly what you do. That is, tell the future," said Ickstatt with a guilty look. "And they were Jewish, though they had converted to Catholicism... Your father taught Ancient History and Canon Law at the University of Ingolstadt, where I am the dean. You were not aware? ...I suppose you were very young."

Adam sat breathlessly, trying to make sense of this information and the feint memories of his parents. "I don't understand. *Why* is it such a crime to be Jewish?"

"It's not a crime to be Jewish, but it is always risky to be different from the mad majority. And we as Christians, we believe it was the Jews, not the Romans, who were responsible for the crucifixion."

"Of course. My family is to blame for something someone else, long dead, did seventeen hundred years ago," Adam gritted his teeth. "What exactly did my father do to provoke them?"

"He predicted the death of someone very prominent.
When it happened, the people in the village accused your parents of sorcery. Your father was known for his mental abilities."

"What sort of mental abilities?" Adam wondered aloud,
but he already knew the answer to his own question. His own were formidable, and they had to have come from somewhere.

"I have never known anyone as brilliant as your father.
George could see the future. He could simply look at someone and tell him things in great detail. He was a scholar, a mystic, a healer, a clairvoyant."

For a moment, Adam thought he was hearing Serafina
describe Cagliostro. "I don't understand, what were we doing in Wurzberg if he taught in Ingolstadt? That's miles away."

"He was looking for a book," Ickstatt's eyes shifted to
his fine shoes. "His search took him to Wurzberg. He spent months there and when he had not found it, your mother grew impatient and packed up and moved you all to join him. In a letter he sent to me, he told me he was in great danger."

"In danger from whom?" asked Adam.

"I don't know," replied Ickstatt. "You mother should
have stayed in Ingolstadt and kept you safe. When I heard what had happened, I came as soon as I could, but it was too late."

"What book was he looking for?" demanded Adam.
What sort of literature had been worth their lives?

Ickstatt took a deep breath, and peered intently at him
from beneath his arching brows. "I have the book in my library in Ingolstadt. If you want it, I will give it to you. But you must come back to the University with me."

CHAPTER VIII

It was just after the New Year when the driver from the University came to pick him up. The girls and Madam stood out front of the Frisky Cat in their fur coats, and gave him kisses. Madam stuffed some money in his hand and kissed him on the cheek.

"You're my son," she whispered, a tear rolling over her red-painted cheek. "Come back to us if school doesn't suit you."

"I'll come back to visit you," he promised as he hugged her, and he had every intention of doing so, but this was the last time he would ever see her. He put his belongings into the back of the wagon, waved goodbye, and left them all behind, for the town of Ingolstadt and the University, a few hours' drive to the North.

Adam vowed silently to do his absolute best at the University. He would waste no time in idle thought or frivolous pursuit, and would learn as much as he possibly could. He literally could not wait to be in the library. For knowledge, he was famished.

Late in the afternoon, Ingolstadt was dusted in snow, and the clouds hung low to the ground, just grazing the tops of the stark, slate shingled houses. The color seemed to have been drained from the entire place, for no hue enlivened the grayish scene but those that Adam wore on his person. As he jumped down from the wagon seat in his long purple coat over his white, ruffled shirt, and red breeches, he felt conspicuous and eccentric, but terribly excited. He visited the library first and meandered down the tall aisles of books in wonder and amazement, stopping every step to pull another from the shelf.

The University housing reminded him of the dormitory at St. Michael's. It was a large hall on the third floor that he shared with two dozen other young men. There were other dormitories just like it and each had several floors of halls like the one to which he was assigned. He recognized several of the novices from St. Michael's but they barely acknowledged him. Even Benno, who was in his theology class, kept his distance. They had been close friends once, but now Benno seemed surprised to see him there and then largely ignored him whenever they passed. Adam reminded himself he was at the University to study and that it was a blessing not to be obligated socially by friends. But he was lonely now and wondered what had been said about him, for he sensed some sort of ill reputation had preceded him. He wondered if the two Jesuit priests who had come to save the souls of the inhabitants of the Frisky Cat that autumn morning had recognized him. Madam had sent them upstairs where several vixens were waiting to tempt them with carnal delights. The pair came hurriedly down the stairs and fled out the door, never to be seen again. How they all had laughed as they stood at the window, watching the priests run down the lane.

This University was as much controlled by the Jesuit Church as St. Michaels' school had been, and many of Adam's classmates were already bound to enter the priesthood. The courses were mostly standard and mandatory for everyone the first two years. Afterwards, one could elect to take courses more specific to one's intended profession. St. Michael's had well prepared him for the studies in religion that seemed to pervade his every course. Even his natural law class was full of divine laws and had its basis in Deuteronomy.

After four years at the Frisky Cat, Adam had learned the ways of man and woman, had seen more human nature in action than he ever desired, and now his mind was starving for meaningful knowledge. He welcomed the chance to learn, and to classify all he had experienced. He would not take this new opportunity for academic study lightly. The last thing he wanted to do with the rest of his life was to be employed in some form of menial labor like chopping wood or fetching water from a well. He had had enough of that and hoped to be able to hire out those tasks to someone of lesser means one day. Adam studied hard every day and spent most of his free time in the University's library, where it was relatively quiet and he could read without interruption.

One afternoon, Ickstatt summoned him to his office. Adam had been expecting his call. He entered the University building and climbed the wide, wooden staircase to the topmost floor. He found Ickstatt in his large book-lined office staring out the window. He turned when he heard Adam enter and offered him a chair.

"Are you enjoying your studies here?" he asked. "Your professors are exceedingly impressed with you."

"I am grateful for this opportunity, uncle," replied Adam. He knew why he had been summoned. "What do you wish to know?"

Ickstatt twirled the pointed tip of his beard. "There has been something brewing against us in Rome for quite some time," he said. "Our Jesuit priests have been arrested in Spain and Portugal, thrown out of the country. I fear it won't be long until this inquisition comes to Bavaria, to this Jesuit University."

Adam had heard that the Papacy had turned on its most fervently pious sect, but his disdain for St. Michael's, for the powers that controlled the Germanic lands, made him secretly hope that they would all engage and destroy each other, leaving everyone else free of them.

"I need to know who, who I should be aware of, who will come, and when. I know you can tell me everything I want to know. You're just like your father," he said almost accusingly.

"Where's my father's book?" asked Adam.

Ickstatt went to his wall of books and began searching through the titles on the shelves. At last, he pulled a small volume from the shelf. He blew the dust from it and handed it to Adam.

Adam took the book and tucked it in his coat pocket. "I must have water to see," he said. He pondered Ickstatt's contradiction – chastising him for using his prophetic gifts one day, then begging him to scry the next.

They walked downstairs and outside to the reflecting pool in the center of the sprawling campus courtyard. Adam looked into the water. A breeze stirred the surface of it. He saw the royal insignia, then the Monarch Prince Carl Theodore appeared in his stateroom. A man with black, thinning hair bowed before him.

"There is a man from the Vatican, an inquisitor of the Pope. He is having a conversation with the Monarch. They are talking about you," Adam heard their voices in the waves.

"What are they saying?" said Ickstatt.

"He is saying unflattering things about you, that you are a Jesuit, that the University will be dismantled unless it conforms. All Jesuits are to be expelled. Everyone is to be thrown out."

"This man you see, the inquisitor, what does he look like?" said Ickstatt twisting his chin whiskers.

Adam strained to see the man's face and described him as best he could to Ickstatt.

"When? How long do we have before they come to Ingolstadt?"

Adam looked past him, and cast a mental chart on the air and matched it with an approximate time, so adept had he become at astrology that he no longer needed quill or ink. "Just shy of three years," Adam replied.

Ickstatt sighed. "There is time, then. Perhaps I am overreacting, and this will all disintegrate before it comes to fruition here."

"Not likely, but I will keep you apprised," Adam stood, letting the wind swirl his clothes and hair. "Or I could do away with this inquisitor now."

Ickstatt looked incredulously at Adam's cool, green eyes. "For a price, of course."

"What?" asked Ickstatt, sure he had misheard.

"I want to be professor of Canon Law here, like my father," said Adam. Since he had come to the University, he had often thought of being a professor and enjoying the power to teach or taint any idea that he so chose, to influence hundreds, if not thousands of young minds, and make them see the folly of their religion. And more importantly, he would have a ready-made position to fall into when he graduated. His future would be secure.

"You are far too young to be teaching such a subject," said Ickstatt matter-of-factly.

"You had me study my whole life to be a priest. I know canon law as well as the Pope himself. Give me what I ask now, or you will not much longer have the power to grant such a request, will you?" Adam turned and began walking away.

"Wait!" said Ickstatt, starting after him. "All right, the position is yours, but you must graduate in time with your class or we will be suspect."

That night Adam lay in bed in the dormitory. He closed his eyes and relaxed deeply. He heard the familiar whooshing sound, like wind through a tunnel. He felt the tingling, numbing vibration of it in his chest. He felt himself rise up, floating above the room. When he reached the ceiling, he looked down and saw himself lying in bed with his eyes closed. Good God, he was handsome, he thought, with his dark intelligent brows and fine, sensual, well-formed features. Beneath his sheets, his body was splendidly muscular and well-proportioned. Had he been a woman, he would have made love to himself right there.

"Take me to the inquisitor," he said, remembering his mission.

There was a loud pop and instantly he found himself in a large and stately home. All was quiet as he glided down the hallway to a room at the end. He slipped through the closed door as if it weren't there, and emerged on the other side, in a bedchamber. A fire was burning in the hearth.

Hunched over a desk, writing by the light of a single candle, was the inquisitor. Deep in thought and murmuring to himself, he clutched his remaining black hairs with his hand, as if under great duress, and continued the next line of his letter. With such a habit, it was no wonder he had no hair left.

Adam leaned over his shoulder and read his letter. It was a letter to the Pope, defaming someone for his "despicable behavior and heathen ethics."

Adam glided up behind him, placed his invisible hands around his neck, and began squeezing. He could feel the man's blood trying to pass beneath his fingers. As his neck bones were breaking, the inquisitor wheezed and clawed at Adam's fingers, trying to pry them loose. He struggled in Adam's lethal grip, and with one last great effort to save his life, tore free of his clutches and stood pained and terrified next to the hearth.

"Who's there?" he screamed. Hands outstretched to defend himself, the inquisitor scanned the empty room as Adam glided up to his face, only a shadow before him. Adam grabbed his neck again and broke it with his hands. He let go, and the inquisitor fell upon the hearth stone.

Adam heard the distant bell, and then there was another loud pop, and he was back in his bed in the dormitory again, falling into a deep sleep.

CHAPTER IX

BENJAMIN FRANKLIN
London, 1773

"45" wanted to meet in an alehouse in the East End for
tea. It seemed a strange place to take tea but the patrons
there would probably not recognize him, so there would
never be any talk of their meeting. They had met
previously at a party of the secretive Order of St. Francis
led by Sir Francis Dashwood, a mutual friend who liked to
wear a turban and entertain his guests in the caves below
his estate in West Wycombe. Dashwood was the
postmaster general for England and had been merely a
professional acquaintance of Franklin's until the intriguing
invitation. They had all gotten to know each other rather
well, sharing liquor and women, and though Benjamin
was somewhat repulsed by the licentiousness of 45, he had
forged a true friendship with Dashwood. Benjamin
guessed that whatever 45 had, he did not want Dashwood
to know about, or he would have suggested they meet in
the caves.

It was windy and raining on the walk from the coach
down the alley to the inn. Benjamin wore his coat pulled
up over his nose and entered through the back. He found
the squinky-eyed bastard as he had said he'd be – at a
table in the back, a bottle of whiskey open, two glasses
poured.

"45" otherwise known as John Wilkes, was as much a
celebrity in Britain as Benjamin. He had been jailed and
relieved of his legislative position for inciting riots in the
name of rights for the common men and suggesting
independence for the colonies in the 1760's. For that, the
people looked past Wilkes' dangerous insanity that he
flared at those who crossed him, and idolized him. He was
a gigantic political troublemaker and Benjamin guessed
that what he had to tell him was socially if not politically

93

explosive. He vowed to himself that he would not be ruffled by the intelligence that Wilkes surely intended to divulge. But still he was curious. What could Wilkes have?

Benjamin sat down, his back to the room full of blinded, growling drunks. It was a dangerous place and he did not intend to stay long. "It's alwayſ a pleaſure, John," he shook Wilkes' sweaty hand. "How'ſ the little monkey?"

"A disaster. I'm going to have to give her to a Naturalist – someone without any common sense. Would you like a chimpanzee to call your own?" Wilkes passed him a package under the table.

"What iſ it?"

"Letters. Read them. You'll see what shit you are!"

"Thankſ, I do need to be reminded of that   ſometimeſ." Benjamin took the package quickly and deposited it into his satchel. "I thank you."

"You're most welcome. Don't you want a shot?"

"I muſt be going. There' ſ a ſtorm. And I've only got on my ſlipperſ." He lifted up a foot shod in a carpet shoe.

Wilkes grabbed him by the sleeve. "You can make one copy, but they must never be published or shown around. No one must know from whom they came. I could hang for this." Wilkes hissed, leering around with his teensy eyes.

Benjamin wondered whose letters these were. "Certainly. I do appreciate your looking out for my intereſtſ."

"I'm a messenger of truth and that's all I can be." Wilkes put a shot back.

Benjamin patted him on the shoulder and went back out into the pouring rain. He boarded the coach again. "Craven ſtreet," he told the driver.

He found a plate of his favorite cheesy biscuits and a hot teapot in a knitted cozy waiting for him on his table when he walked in the door to his quarters. It was the girl Polly, or perhaps her mother Peggy, or perhaps both who had conspired to treat him. What wonderful care they took of him. His books and things were dusted every day. His clothes were washed and ironed and hung meticulously in the wardrobe. He'd really married the wrong woman. Rather, he was wrong to marry in the first place under such constricting vows. The world had come to adore him and half the world was women. Oh, it was a shame.

He sat down and took the package Wilkes had given him out of his satchel. He opened it and found a stack of a dozen or so folded letters, their seals popped, addressed to Andrew Oliver. They were a bit damp and he wondered in what condition these letters were supposed to be kept. He took a bite of biscuit, and cheesy crumbs dropped on the parchment. He swiped them away but they'd already left greasy stains that then smeared. He looked at the date on the first letter. Over a year ago. The last of them was written a month ago. They'd been missing long enough, anyone could've dropped cheesy crumbs on them by now. Still, he chided himself for poor form.

There was a knock at the door. He looked up.

The girl, Polly, was standing there in her robe and bedcap. "Ye got everything ye need, Mr. Franklin? Anything we can bring ye before bed?"

Your sweet arse, his coy smile seemed to say. "Nothing, thank*f*. Good night."

"Noffing tall?" she said in a small voice.

"Not a thing, thank*f*." He gave her a wink.

The girl closed the door. She liked making conversation with him, obliging him to explain scientific theories to her in terms she could understand. He usually enjoyed it too, and for hours sometimes, but now he was eager to see these letters that Wilkes had wanted kept secret. Alone in his apartment, Franklin unfolded the letters and began to read. The handwriting of Massachusetts Governor Thomas Hutchinson was positively stuck-up. The tall majestic letters, so arrogantly drawn.

Residents of the Colonies should not be permitted to enjoy the same liberties as true Englishmen...

That was the statement that most perturbed him. That a man's rights could be abridged based on geography seemed particularly ridiculous. He knew, though, that the people of Boston had done much to enrage their English governor and his cronies who continually tried to take advantage of them. A mob of angry citizens had set fire to Governor Hutchinson's home a few years ago, and the Boston Massacre was a clear-cut case of an attack on British soldiers. He had always hoped he could resolve the troublesome relationship, but both sides only antagonized each other despite him.

When he had finished reading, he put down the letters and noticed that he had crumpled several of them along one side where he had held them in his plump, sweaty hand. He wiped his hand on his breeches and wrinkled his nose, considering just throwing them in the fireplace.

He took the first letter to his desk, hung it on a spring clip that he had invented for just such a purpose and removed his copy-pen from its case. He sat, and with ingenious accuracy, copied the hand-written script exactly, the second copy being drafted simultaneously by the pen in the jointed contraption that moved along gracefully with the slightest of his movements. He transcribed it verbatim, except for Hutchinson's grammatical mistake he was obligated to correct. "'Wa*f*' not 'were.' You ignorant jacka*ff*," he muttered.

When he was done reading and copying all the letters, he put one copy of each in a box on the mantle. He returned Hutchinson's letters to their envelope, reattached the waxen seals, then wrote a note to be delivered to Wilkes that he would like to return the originals the following

Friday. The second copy of the letters was put into another envelope. He considered mailing them to Joseph Warren. He was smart and would know how to take them. It would be disloyal to keep them secret from those whom they concerned.

He got up to get some hot water from the kitchen. He opened his door and ran into the girl's mother, Peggy Stevens, in the hallway.

"Mr. Franklin, you don't get much sleeping done, do you?" she smiled.

"I'm alway*f* occupied, my mind i *f* anyway, *f*o what'*f* the point of bedding down?" he tittered.

The woman of fifty laughed unctuously. She was attractive, the mature character-drawn version of the rosy-cheeked girl who had looked in on him some hours ago. He guessed she was starting the fire for the morning meal and washing and she was going about her business as usual. He had always retired before now or at least kept locked in and quiet inside his quarters, but now he had caught her, alone in the quiet of the dark house at four a.m. He could smell the witch hazel on her skin.

"I've read too much thi *f* evening and can't re *ft*. Forgive me for wandering through your hou*f*e," he whispered, his breath fluttering the candle's flame. He felt himself becoming aroused by her.

"Not at all," she smiled, the gay lines around her eyes crinkling. "Like some tea?"

He followed her into the kitchen, grazing the end of her long braid with the tip of his finger. He wondered if she had felt it, but he was too shy to grab it and throw her against the wall like he'd imagined. He could make out the delightful curves of her hips and waist beneath her dressing gown as she stepped before the fire. When she stoked the logs, her body was silhouetted before the hearth, nude to his eyes. She knew he was staring and turned around to strike a seductive pose. Like so many before her, she was caught in his magnetic pull – by his power and influence. It was the opportunity for which he had been waiting for so many long years. She wanted him, it was quite evident. He grabbed her long pigtail as he had always wanted to, and pulled her body against his.

"Dr. Franklin... I never expected this."

"Neither did I."

Though both of them had. The years of anticipation had simmered their passion for each other. She had worn no bloomers under her gown. Benjamin unfastened his breeches and sat her on his lap. Johnny was standing up and he pulled her down on top of him. She was tight and desperate as he penetrated her. Widows always were. He could feel her shiver on the verge of a spin with his first thrust. He stirred his hips into her and she spun on him over and over again until the expense of her love had run all over his lap.

"Oh, Dr. Franklin, yes..." she moaned.

Older women were responsive, so discreet, so grateful, and there was usually no fear of unwanted children resulting from such consensual copulation as this one. At least he hoped not.

When they were through, Peggy made him some eggs and tea, and they ate their breakfast together at the kitchen table in a haze of infatuation and morning light.

Benjamin had a wife in Philadelphia, Deborah, a plain dowdy hen of a wife. He had married her at a time in his life when beauty, wit, and sophistication mattered little to him. He was a poor candle maker's son, himself a printer's apprentice and copy writer who had only begun to realize his great potential.

His years of hard work and frugality had resulted in the fulfillment of most every one of his aspirations. He was famed, fortune'd, and hailed by some as the greatest man ever, alive or dead. Fat and blemished as he was, women found him irresistible and he was no stranger to extramarital affairs. He knew how to kindle a woman's deepest affection by paying her court over a long platonic period of time. It was his way of cultivating his prospects and it worked in spades for someone who was patient enough.

Patient or not, his philandering had caused a great scandal in Philadelphia and he thought better of putting Deborah through any further embarrassment, though he was not about to put himself in check to please her. He would not be one to deprive himself of God's greatest gifts. He took the first opportunity that arose to go back to the motherland in the guise of a political junket and sow his wild seeds. He found London particularly agreeable, and in London he had stayed.

But now, he had been insulted by Englishmen. There was no way not to take Hutchinson's letters personally. He had all but written names. If such things had only been said about them once, in one letter, but here were two years' worth of letters, back and forth between Hutchinson and Oliver, all of them belittling, mocking, and defaming the people of Boston. Franklin tried to distance himself from it; he was in England and that was where he belonged. What did he care what someone thought of someone else? He thought about it all morning and reasoned that Sam and Warren needed to know what had been said about them by their own governor. Perhaps it would encourage them to straighten up and mend fences.

CHAPTER X

HANCOCK
Boston, 1773

Dr. Joseph Warren, the good physician, received the letters in Boston, and promptly gave them to John Hancock to read with the stipulation: "Read them and pass them around, but no copies can be made, and they are never to be printed. And no telling anyone where they came from."

This, Hancock repeated to Sam Adams and his sidekick Sam Molitar, as the three of them sat at a table in the Green Dragon Tavern. Hancock felt something warm on his feet. He looked down beneath the table and saw Sam's St. Bernard cozied between his fine slippers and his owner's splitting shoes.

Hancock leaned on his elbows, and with some amusement, watched Sam's face turn a purple shade of red. He clenched his bony fists and began to shake. "Damnable serpents! They shall perish in their own Hellfire!"

He cringed as Sam Adams walked out the door with the letters in his hand. He sat awkwardly with Molitar, a short cat-faced man with whom he had little in common except the love of liquor, and waited at the table for Sam to return. He should have realized that he was taking the letters to the Boston Gazette. Later, he reasoned, that was why Warren had kept them from him in the first place.

"Where are the letters?" Hancock asked as Sam sat back down to his ale five minutes later.

"I'll give 'em back 'soon as I can, friend," Sam said, patting him on the back, now much calmer.

Hancock had been watching Sam for some years now, admiring how he inspired people to stand up and shout and burn things in the street. He brought them over to his point of view with his scary religious and political diatribes and encouraged them to take up for themselves, to take up arms. Hancock had always given him an open ear, but thought him rather too extreme, but now that his once very profitable shipping business was in danger, he wanted someone to *do* something. His own hands were tied. He had too much to lose if the vindictive British governor were to inflict further punishment on any instigator of protest. Hancock employed nearly a thousand of Boston's men in his company, their wives and children all dependent on him, and if he came under the axe, then so would they.

Sam Adams had nothing to lose. He had a job as a tax collector, but he collected no taxes. His can for collecting coin rattled like a tinny percussion instrument when he shook it at his audience to emphasize his arguments against being taxed. He could stir up Boston into a maddened frenzy. Hancock hoped at least he would make the British legislators rethink their stance.

He awoke early the next morning. His house girl set his breakfast, newspaper, and coffee on the fine linen tablecloth. He put his feet on the table and leaned back in his chair. There on the front page were printed several of the most inflammatory excerpts from the letters. Hancock gave a little laugh of delight and wiped his thin mouth on the lacy napkin.

He returned to the Green Dragon to find Sam at the bar with the South End gang, half of whom he employed.

"These are the times when God's people emerge from the sea of cowards, to fight for what the Lord hath given them that no mortal can taketh away: Liberty! Property! And the right to occupy oneself in whatever manner one so pleases himself and God!"

"Thinks everybody owes him something," gestured a crusty, burly carpenter with black thumbnails. "Thinks he's got more rights than us because he's more British."

"The Eye of God is looking down upon ye!" Adams slapped the rolled up newspaper in the palm of his hand. "Will we be the righteous, strong, and noble men created in His image or will we be trodden upon by Satan's guard, doomed to be the human kindling of hellfire on earth?"

There was a bit of snickering at the exaggeration.

Sam grew wild-eyed and stared vehemently at the snickerers. "No, friend. That's who the British be! Satan's own, whether they be on this new and sacred continent or

101

on the old and infernal one. They defile the land, corrupt the people, and suck dry the fat of the lamb and the ewe!"

Adams' dog was barking in accompaniment as he sucked down his ale and railed on. Thunder boomed and lighting flashed outside. Rain beat on the bubbled windowpanes. John Hancock sat quietly at a table by the door with his own bottle of rum. Sam Molitar put the package of letters down before him and tipped his hat. Hancock quickly tucked them into his satchel.

"God tests us, brother!" Adams got louder, "And so we are put to the wheel. These letters are Satan's testament, the Governor has shown his hate for us - God's chosen people, and their movements against us assail us like a plague of sores."

His colorful metaphors and damning analogies rattled the ear of one and all as the rain fell in sheets and windswept torrents, chasing in all the laborers whose work was rained-out, and drivers who'd had to pull off the road for fear of drowning their horses. By noon, the tavern was full of men drinking, snorting snuff, and smoking tobacco.

The South End gang became more and more drunk and angry as they listened to Sam read excerpts from the letters aloud. He derided each word of them as the most shocking and abhorrent thing ever.

A fellow stood and raised a finger. "I think we're all just blessed to be here and we should let the governor be."

"Complacency is the spittle that drops forth from the sinful smirk of the Devil's sneer! He's bored a hole in your heart, man! He eats away at your soul like a lamprey eel! Will your innocent babes be damned? Be damned because of something you were too lazy, too ignorant, too complacent to protest?" railed Sam.

"No, I guess not," answered the fellow.

"How bout too drunk to protest?" The bartender filled him a tankard of ale from the keg beneath the bar.

"Whatever your excuse, does not matter, friend. Damned

be damned!" Sam took a drink then shook a bible at the crowd in the tavern. "These are your rights as a human being that the Almighty God hath given you and every Christian man, His Laws, the laws of the righteous. Will you lay by the road and have them reneged by some cunning viper who dresses in the skin of man but serves the Dark One?" He gave them all a sinister leer.

The South End Gang, shuffled uncomfortably, grumbling, each his own particular mix of drunk and very angry.

"Who's he talking about – *Dark One*?" someone asked.

"Some Negro?" speculated another.

Sam was hidden in a thick cloud of cigar smoke. "Your rights have been stolen from you, your dignity stepped upon. Your beguiling governor, Thomas Hutchinson has lied to you, taxed you, and when you couldn't be taxed, robbed you, and for what public good? None, friend, none. But to fill his own purse! He's abused his powers and used your hard-earned money to make himself and his relations rich. How he badgers you to pay his hat whilst you and yours go without so much as a crust of bread. He pats his own back and feeds himself on the fruits of your labor, off the sweat of your backs! You owe the crown; you were *born owing*, weren't you? And he, the nobleman from England-your land, and your labor are his birthright! Taxes! Fines! Tariffs on your wares; the British stealing from each and every one of you!" Sam banged his government collection can against the scarred and stained, wooden bench.

"Let's burn his house down!" screamed O'Shannon, a skinny, hardened dockhand. Fiery laughter and cheers went up. Tankards were smashed together, and they all began to chant "Liberty! Property! Liberty! Property!"

The rowdy mob of drunken shipwrights and laborers poured out of the bar and went roiling down the wet street, shouting profanities. Someone hoisted a well-dressed scarecrow in a powdered wig and knickers and lit it on fire in the rain.

"Die, Hutchinson, die, you dirty raccoon!" screamed a woman.

Ashes of burning cloth and straw rained down on the mob.

John Hancock downed the rest of his rum and followed them out the door.

CHAPTER XI

Later that week, in the upstairs window of the Edes and Gill print shop, Hancock was maudlin in his long, sable coat over an impossibly ruffled blouse and pink satin knickers as he stared through a spyglass at the harbor below. He sighed, defeated, passing it to John Adams.

"Damn if we let that land and unload," said Hancock. "Everything, all for naught."

Looking out at the twilight sky and sea, Benjamin Church, Joseph Warren, and Sam Adams stood drinking the stiff punch they'd brought upstairs from the meeting in the main hall below that had just preceded this more private one. They all watched out the open window as the redcoats and the British Port Patrol commandeered the dock below and allowed the ship *Dartmouth* to moor in a slip.

According to O'Shannon, who had rowed out to it early in the week and coincidentally slipped a knife between boards of the hull, the ship was taking on water and had to dock for a caulk lest the already sick and scurvy-ridden crew drown.

"We'll dump it in the water," said Sam Adams.

"The tea?" asked John Adams.

"We can't do that!" exclaimed Church, "I mean, that's all Rotch's money tied up in that tea. He said he'd be bankrupt."

"Frig Rotch. Who's this Rotch fellow anyway? Bastard. There's principal at stake," cried Hancock. "We said no tea, no buying it, no selling it, no drinking it. If we can't enforce what we say is law then we should quit trying to lead the people of Boston and take up croquet or something we could actually do."

"It wasn't the law when Rotch set out for our harbor. It isn't fair to dump his tea," said John Adams.

"Fair? It isn't fair that I have all the money *and* all the good looks, but I do. That's what's not fair! You can cry about it all you want, but I don't go around putting unwanted tea in other people's harbors. I'm not about to let that foul perch unload his stinking tea if I can't unload mine. Hutchinson and his little, snively, coin-sucking brats can bang sand; they'll not see a penny more from me!"

"It looks like they're bringing in two more. Look," said Dr. Warren about the two other ships approaching the dock. A chill breeze blew into the room from the open window.

"I swear I'm going to go broke if Parliament keeps up this Tea Act much longer. They've already stolen one of my best ships," John Hancock continued, pacing.

"What?" asked John Adams. "They can't do that."

"They turned her back and I don't know what's become of her. She may have gone down for all I know. The captain had to sail her back to Belgium. If the cargo is intact it will be a miracle." He ladled some more rum punch into his cup. "More?"

"I heard that *The Porpoise* was full of tea," quipped John Adams.

"Tea? Who said I was bringing in illegal tea?" Hancock laughed bitterly. "What you heard was lies. It was a load of rare books. There were tablets and scrolls in that collection that hadn't been seen by anyone since Alexandria!"

"Who's Alexandria?" asked MacIntosh, the leader of the South End gang, all of which had just found their way upstairs to the long room.

"It was a library in Egypt," whispered John Adams.
"Sacked and burned long ago. Perhaps the greatest loss of recorded knowledge in history."

Tears flowed from Hancock's eyes as he continued.
"Here I am marching up and down in His Majesty's Guard, flashing my sash, doing a little tiptoe turn and waving my sword around – for what? To be robbed, humiliated, slandered, criminalized by these miscreants of the Crown." He took another gulp of his drink to stifle it down. He could've gone on and on about what esoteric knowledge had been aboard *The Porpoise*, what things were lost when those books were taken, he would never know. He had long dreamt of attaining the highest sort of learning, spiritual knowledge and power of mind that would allow him to lord over everyone else, outlive everyone else, out-do everyone else. Power to see beyond the veil of the mundane and know what others could not. How he *longed* for it, dreamed of using these forces against Hutchinson, the King, and the British Parliament who gave him such relentless grief and torment.

As soon as he had heard the collection was on auction, he had sent a private bid and won the library without contest. The owner's widow was in financial distress and was clearing out all of the contents of the ancestral castle so that it could be sold. John had heard of the infamous collection in his boyhood from his uncle, himself a book dealer and avid collector of esoteric materials, who often said he wished he could get at it and at least have copies made before the works were lost forever.

The books had been on their way, been en route to him from Sweden. And they were waylaid and somehow lost at sea. He had paid also for what the seller had sworn to him was an authentic piece of Christ's cross. It was a sore and heavy loss and Hancock's insurance was canceled. "Lord as my witness," he whispered dramatically, "I will wreak my vengeance!"

"To vengeance!" O'Shannon snarled and fell over.

"You'll help me get my vengeance, won't you Sam?" Hancock looked sorrowfully at his old friend. "Won't you?"

Sam Adams peered out from under his scraggly eagle-like brow. "Aye, my brother. Vengeance for the righteous is the reason for the Sons of Liberty."

To John, Sam seemed to have it all figured out – at least in his own mind, and that was really all that mattered as long as the material world corroborated it occasionally. John had hoped, too, the book collection would give him some power over his life, which despite all his money, always seemed to be reeling out of his control. John dreamt wistfully of learning the ancient, divine sciences whispered by the lips of God Almighty to his Chosen Men - secrets he could hardly fathom, and he had spent a large sum on the rare and ancient books. He had hoped they held the key to the missing pieces of his life, the parts of himself he could not reconcile with the world. He longed for some esoteric knowledge that would bring peace and enlightenment to an otherwise tortured life. That the books were unaccounted for was a terrible, grievous loss. He wondered what had become of them. There would be few if any that could read the languages of the books, much less comprehend them even on their most basic level. They might as well be at the bottom of the ocean.

John's hatred for the Crown grew, and his every idle thought was consumed with how to punish King George and Parliament for what they had done to his life and business. He seethed at the redcoats and imagined a pox and hell's fury on them all. He was beginning to feel the burning wrath about which Sam was always ranting.

"The Crown is but the architecture of Lucifer, and

George is its keystone!" shouted Sam to the room full of Sons of Liberty. "But his power is so overshadowed by the Almighty, and God is on our side, yea, we the people of Israel. Have faith in the Lord God and we shall banish the evil back into the dark isle from whence it came. The Devil Crown shall oppress us only if we allow it, brothers. Tempting us to buy his tea, then taxing us on it! Forbids us from growing it, then demands we drink! We'll drink it not!"

A roar erupted and   tea was cursed profanely by every mouth.

The full moon night was warm for December. The air was quiet and still over Boston.

Suddenly a great roar of savage voices shrieking and whooping and bellowing erupted from the Old South Church. The front doors burst open and a great, mad stampede of wild Indians went running and whooping down the road toward the harbor, waving hatchets and tomahawks.

They stormed the docks where the   *Dartmouth* and the *Eleanor* were moored, and jumped onto their decks. The crewmen onboard cowered in horror while the Indians overtook them. They hacked open the tea chests and dumped the tea over the sides of the ship into the dark water.

"Lord God," one of them said, "Save us from these savages!"

John Hancock let out a high-pitched   war-cry, then snarled at them like a heathen possessed, tipping a tea chest over the side. It was harder work than he had anticipated and he wished he hadn't drunk quite as much of Sam's stout before he had hit the rum punch. The red ochre on his skin stung as he sweated.

The captain of the *Eleanor* came out of the galley below "What the hell is this?"

O'Shannon, soot all over his face, drew a pistol and he and MacIntosh, shoe polish all over his, backed the Captain down into the galley. Moments later a shot was fired.

People hung out of every doorway all along the waterfront and a curious crowd gathered at the shore.

Across the water from the ship, the British Port Patrol turned on their beacon lamp and shone it on the savages as they unloaded the tea. "Savages, you! Halt in the name of the King!"

Hancock grunted and gestured rudely at them.

"Stop, Savages! In the name of His Majesty's Royal Navy! You are destroying private goods and you will be liable for the damages!"

The Indians picked up big fistfuls of tea and threw it at the Patrolmen.

The Patrolman squinted through his spyglass. "Lace? What sort of Indian wears *lace*? That's most peculiar."

Working feverishly aboard the *Eleanor*, John knew they had seen the demi-petticoat beneath his old brown coat. He had thought to take it off, but had gotten sidetracked somehow during wardrobe and makeup preparations at the print shop. Everyone would figure out that they weren't Indians sooner or later. It would be sooner, he supposed.

When they had dumped the last of the chests of tea, the Indians went running back into the town and scattered, disappearing down every alleyway in Boston.

John made it to his front gate. He caught himself on the post and had a vomit in the rose bushes.

CHAPTER XII

FRANKLIN

Spring blossomed, and as always, Benjamin was invited to a great number of social events. On this particular

Saturday afternoon, he and his niece, Sally, attended an Easter party at the home of Sir Francis Dashwood, the Lord le Despencer, one of the two postmasters general of England. His grand house, with its conspicuously circular garden and adjacent six-sided mausoleum was situated atop the highest of the green and rolling hills of West Wycombe. Heavy rain clouds were threatening on the northern horizon, but the party remained outside in hopes that the storm would veer off before it got to Wycombe.

Benjamin's niece, Sally, the daughter of his sister Lydia who also lived in London, was a rather plain and sullen girl. Her mother had asked him to introduce her to some young men who might prove to be more suitable husband material for her than her current beau who was an "artiste" of no means. Sally and Benjamin shared a table with Joseph Priestly and John Pringle, Benjamin's good friends from the Royal Society, His Majesty's and the world's foremost group of scientists.

"W-w-w-what do you have to say for your countrymen's activities – impersonating Indians and w-w-wasting all that good tea?" asked Priestly.

"It waſ a bold move," answered Benjamin.

"And not a very w-w-w-wise one."

Benjamin watched the eight children who had come to the party walk round and round the fountain rim till they were pulled off by their fathers and mothers and swatted for walking on the décor. They retreated to a row of chairs against the house and sulked for long minutes while the adults' conversation continued.

Benjamin pricked up his ears and eavesdropped upon what was being said at a table near them. "It's because of those letters of Oliver's that were published. They set the Americans off, got them all riled up," said a man at the next table.

The children one by one slipped away from their penitent chairs and went to organize under a crabapple tree, dividing themselves into two teams. One tall boy and the next biggest boy picked their teammates in turn till only the scrawniest little one was left.

"I ſee no point in oppo ſing the Crown. England is our mother country and we can do nothing about that, but make the beſt of it. Diplomatically, I would like to ſee a reconciliation, but that will take ſome forbearance on the partſ of both partieſ."

"Apparently, all the colonies are getting involved. Philadelphia, New York, they sent their blessings to the Adamses of Boston and shot off cannon to celebrate the tea heist," said Dr. Pringle, a portly man of Franklin's age.

"They've gone too far," said Benjamin pensively.

Sir Francis Dashwood, the Lord le Despencer suddenly appeared beside their table. He was clean-shaven, about Franklin's age with inscrutable eyes and a permanent smirk on his fat face. He wore a high silk cumberbun, perhaps to disguise his girth, and matching knee bands at the edges of his breeches. "Hello Benjamin, messieurs and mademoiselle, I'm so glad you could grace us this day."

"Why of cour ſe. Alwayſ glad to be invited. Let me introduce my niece ſally Johnſtone and you remember John Pringle, phyſician to His Majeſty, and Joſeph Prieſtly."

Three weeks last summer he'd spent at West Wycombe with Sir Francis Dashwood the Lord le Despencer and several others including John Wilkes, John Montagu the Earl of Sandwich, Lord Chatham, and some effeminate-looking Chevalier with a bunch of rings whose name he could not remember. They met at night in the caves beneath the property.

Some decades before, Despencer had engaged the unemployed local laborers to dig out generous tunnels between the natural caverns that existed beneath the property. What resulted was a long, interesting, series of underground rooms that sprawled for what seemed like miles – especially when one was intoxicated and groping one's way along with no lamp - in sort of a hook shape beneath the grounds. At the entrance of the cave, Despencer had built the façade of a grandiose gothic church. It was quite beautiful and certainly more inviting a foyer than what he had heard donned the entrance before. Reportedly, there used to be a rather gaping bear cave where primeval persons had scrawled nonsensical graffiti and left their archaic refuse all around.

Now Lord le Despencer and his cronies used the remodeled caves as their private meeting quarters, a place where wives were rarely, if ever, allowed. There was a banquet room, voluminous and impressive where a chandelier was suspended above the great round table, where they had been served delicious dinners of pheasants or boar they had shot on the property. There were more private rooms in the cave, deeper down the tunnel, however, where they had drunk wine and shared encounters with exotic and beautiful young ladies of the evening who wore masks and danced to the music of a blind, possessed, Negro fiddler. It had been a surreal encounter - one that Benjamin was sure, had resulted in Priestly's pathetic stutter.

Now Despencer eyeballed Sally. "Your niece, you say?"

"Yeſ, my ſiſter'ſ daughter."

"Righty-o, you naughty devil." He patted Benjamin on the shoulder and gave Sally a wink. "Bring her to the cave if you want."

"I don't think…" Benjamin began, squinting at Despencer.

"What cave?" asked Sally.

"A dirty old cave, of ſcientific intereſt to the Naturali ſt," Benjamin smiled wanly at le Despencer.

"Please define what *is* a Naturalist exactly?" Sally asked, resting her chin in her hand.

"A Naturaliſt if a philoſopher who believeſ that all cauſeſ

and effect*f*, beginning*f* and ending*f* are the part and par*f*el of nature."

"In the world of a Naturalist, there is nothing that science and material proofs cannot explain. There is no magic, no divine hand pulling the strings of life," continued Dr. Pringle.

"But does a Naturalist believe in God, uncle?" asked Sally.

"Does God believe in the Naturalist?" chuckled le Despencer.

Suddenly the Earl of Sandwich sat down, slopping his wine all over the linen tablecloth. He got right in Benjamin's ear with his acrid breath, "Whoever has stolen those letters ought to be hanged for inciting this vicious tea affair. Don't you agree?"

"Oh ye *f*, I heartily agree," Benjamin primly sipped his wine, wondering if some certain cheesy crumbs could somehow be traced back to him.

"I'm quite ready for it all to end," said Dr. Pringle. "What a perfect waste of fine tea, too!"

"And there's bound to be l-l-life l-l-lost if it continues," warned Reverend Priestly.

"Who do you *f*uppo*f*e *f*tole tho*f*e letter*f*?"

"They had to have been taken from both the homes of Oliver and Whately. Both staffs have been refreshed entirely and several couriers are now being examined. We, of course, as Postmasters, absolved ourselves of suspicion early on," Despencer said.

"Oh dear," said Benjamin hoping he hadn't harmed anyone, but fearing he had, and badly. The children were now running and screaming across the garden, pelting each other with crabapples.

"It's just all the w-w-worse for the colonies. They should be made to p-p-pay the ship owner for his l-l-l-l-l-l-loss," chimed in Priestly.

Whack! Despencer was suddenly hit in the head with a

crabapple. His eyes grew wide. He whipped his head around and boiled at every child in sight. "Who threw that apple? Who? Who did it?!" He got up and stalked menacingly after the children who screamed and went running off to hide.

Benjamin took a deep drink. He thought of the Adamses and Joseph Warren – how he had asked them to please not publish the letters. He guessed that it was Sam's impetuosity that was to blame and he had undoubtedly been the one to incite this 'tea party' leaving Franklin's arse to flap in the wind.

"Children should neither be seen nor heard. They should all be thrown down the well at birth. Really, it's most improper for them to run wild," Lord le Despencer grumbled, sitting his large rump back down in his chair.

"What would they do to this thief if they caught him, I wonder?" asked Sally.

"Likely hang him," answered the Earl of Sandwich.

"Oh no. Well, it would be too good for him, hm-hm," said Benjamin, swallowing any knowledge of the crime.

"The spies and thieves will fare better than the people of Boston. In our next agenda will be a vote on closing Boston Harbor. The king wants to starve them for a while." Despencer chortled.

"ſtarve them?"

"Yes, bring them to the brink of famine, then make them an offer they can't refuse. Something like that," smirked Sandwich.

"Well, I'm ſure they'll be pliant aſ ever."

CHAPTER XIII

Benjamin was invited to spend the summer at West Wycombe in the grand hospitality of Sir Francis Dashwood the Lord le Despencer. His invitation requested that he not bring anyone along. Benjamin had brought

Priestly with him the previous summer because he and Despencer were rewriting the Anglican Book of Common Prayer, a work that both felt was needlessly wordy. Benjamin thought the best way to do so was to enlist an Anglican priest to defend the text before he and Despencer ripped it apart. Joseph Priestly was an Anglican priest, albeit he spent more time now in his personal crusade to debunk the theory of phlogiston, the amorphous property declared by Becher to be in all combustible substances - than in ministry, but he had the theological background, and Benjamin had thought him easy-going enough to mix with Sir Francis.

Priestly was ever reverent with regard to the Book of Common Prayer and only thought a few redundancies be removed. Sir Francis, Benjamin began to suspect, had a more diabolical agenda, wanting to rewrite whole pages, renaming the Lord in some sections and making some rather questionable allusions. Sir Francis was not really a Christian as Benjamin soon confirmed.

The night when he brought them both down to the caves Benjamin watched in what can only be described as bemused horror as the Earl of Sandwich engaged the two prostitutes simultaneously. Poor Priestly had suffered a fainting spell and what must have been apoplexy, and begged Benjamin to lead him back out of the caves. Extremely drunk on Madeira, Benjamin obliged but failed to bring a lamp.

The following April, he had been delighted to find Priestly at the Despencer's for Easter and guessed that the night's events had either been forgiven or forgotten – at least by Priestly.

Now it was a blithe June day in the midst of his stay at Wycombe and Franklin took his tea with the Lord de le Despencer and his beautiful mistress, Miss Frances Barry, under the shady portico off the round garden just a stone's throw from the six-sided Mausoleum that housed some of the various remains of Despencer's close friends and his departed wife, Sarah Ellis, the Baroness le Despencer. The old lady had quickly been replaced by the alluring Miss Frances Barry who had large, beautiful, green eyes like a cat, a small mouth, and an unbelievably humongous bosom. Benjamin guessed her real hair color was a light brown or blonde, for the particular shade of periwinkle she donned was most unnatural, though not unattractive. She was much younger than Dashwood and was ever chatty and pleasant.

"We're so pleased you've chosen to summer with us again, Benjamin. I hope you will be staying longer than last year. A pity about your friend, the minister, what was his name?"

"Joſeph Prieſtly," answered Benjamin.

"Yes, well, what do you expect down in those horrid caves? Sir Francis has tried to entice me down there for years but I just won't be swayed to take life and limb in hand. And for God's sake, I told him, think of the spiders and the bats that must live and make excrement down in that foul cave. What if they become angry and attack me or some such thing? Wouldn't that be horrible? And we're so far from any medical person, it would likely be a deadly occurrence."

"I quite agree. The cave ſ aren't for the faint of heart," said Benjamin.

That evening, Benjamin watched out the upstairs window of his room as John Wilkes, then the Earl of Sandwich, and several others whom he did not recognize stepped out of their carriages and came into the house. He put on his coat and cravat and went downstairs to the drawing room. Wilkes and Sandwich hated each other and Benjamin was curious to see their interaction for it always proved amusing.

"Benjamin," said Sir Francis, as he walked into the room,

"we were just talking about you."

"I hope it wa ſ complimentary," said Benjamin. He worried much about how he was perceived by the British lords for it was up to them and their favor how his native Boston and his own dear colony of Pennsylvania would be treated. Out of pity, guilt over the letters, and allegiance to the colonies where he was born, Benjamin had agreed to continue in his role as Boston's London agent and to try and win back the favor of His Majesty and the Parliament. Keeping the company of le Despencer and his cronies was elementary to his political and social objectives.

Lord le Despencer pulled Benjamin aside then, "Please, you will excuse us this evening. We have much to discuss that does not concern you." He laughed a nasally and sinister laugh.

"I don't mind ſitting by and ſharing the wine if you don't mind," said Benjamin, drumming his fingertips on the Roman bas relief of Daedalus and Icarus.

"If you were to stay, it would be a breach of the confidences of the parties in this room. Frances would be glad to entertain you for dinner."

So, Benjamin was not invited to this gentlemen's meeting. He shot Wilkes a look. Wilkes smiled and rocked from toe to heel. He was the champion of the English common folk, after all, and Benjamin was discovering from his investigations, Wilkes held far more power than he had ever realized as the Lord Mayor of London. They had yet to discuss how the letters had seen the light of day, but Benjamin was sure Wilkes knew how the infraction had happened, and would not give either of them away, he hoped. Both their lives depended on his discretion. This meeting was undoubtedly to discuss the letters. It was just as well he not be present lest his honest face give him away.

As was requested of him, Benjamin took supper with Miss Barry upstairs in her quarters. He felt a bit strange eating dinner only steps from her boudoir. They spoke of the wonders of Paris and she listed her numerous distinguished friends and paramours from the theatre who lived there. Benjamin knew some of them personally and others only by reputation.

"You and I should take a pleasure coach to Paris next spring. Wouldn't that be wonderful? You could lecture and write, and I could paint. I've always wanted to paint."

"Why don't you paint then? It'   ƒa   ƒimple enough operation – to paint."

"Sir Francis won't let me," she pouted. "He hates my paintings and my drawings." And she told him of her artistic and marital oppression. She was a former actress and had been quite renown for her portrayal as Ophelia. She had been Dashwood's mistress since his wife the Baroness de le Spencer, had passed away four years ago, and had found her life and freedoms suddenly quite abridged.

He listened with sympathy and when they had finished their meal, she begged him to stay for an apéritif.

"Really, I ƒhould go back to my room and an   ƒwer ƒome correƒpondence tonight or my friendƒ and aƒƒociateƒ will think me baƒe and uncaring."

"No one would ever think that of such a kind and endearing soul as yourself, Dr. Franklin," she whispered, and put a hand on his arm. "I have some drawings that I've hidden from Sir Francis. Would you look at them?"

"Certainly. I'm quite an aficionado of art, hm-hm." He balked as she led him into her boudoir. She lifted her mattress and removed a small stack of parchment. She sat down on her bed and patted the place beside her, "Sit down."

The drawings were of a strange triangular object with orbs set along its sides. In one picture, a fairly well drawn self-portrait of Miss Barry stared up at the thing whose scale in the drawing indicated it was of a massive size.

"What is thi*f* you've drawn here?"

"I was hoping you would know. I saw it out back of the house one night about a month ago. Sir Francis and I had had an argument and I went out to the garden to get some air. It was about midnight. That's when I saw it. It was right over the house!"

Benjamin took his spectacles out of his pocket and inspected the drawings, all of which aspired to capture some hallucination he could hardly fathom. "What do *you* think it i*f*?" he asked her, wondering if it weren't a pictorial expression of an overhanging problem.

"It was a great, massive bird machine. I say it was a machine for it was black like gunmetal–I could see its material illuminated in its own lamps. It floated above and made a peculiar hum like the wings of a thousand humming birds... Do you think I'm mad?"

"No, no," he reassured her.

"Because I can assure you I am not. The horses went crazy. The ones in the paddock ran round from fence to fence. The ones in the stable kicked and whinnied. Oh, how I wish they could corroborate."

"Ye*f*, indeed. Well, you've got talent, and I think you *f*hould continue practicing your art."

"Oh thank you, do you really mean it? You like my drawings?"

"Ye*f*, they're quite... original. I think they'd be a good outlet for you. I'll *f*peak with *f*ir Franci*f* about your talent and let him know my opinion."

"You will?" She hugged Benjamin with great enthusiasm and bowled them over on the bed.

"Oh my goodne*ff*," he stammered.

She looked down at him, her giant bosom pressing down on his chest. She kissed him then and with much reluctance, slowly let him up.

"I mu*f*t be retiring now," Benjamin stood and took a deep breath. He bowed and kissed her hand, "I thank you for a plea*f*urable evening, my dear Miss Barry."

She curtsied. Franklin saw the lust in her eyes, her quiet desperation to be understood, and felt bad that his friend had so deprived her that she was hallucinating.

Safely back in his room, he drank a glass of milk and went to bed.

Sometime later, he was awakened by the feeling of a cloth being tied around his eyes. Rough hands pulled him up by the arms and forced him to stand. His hands were tied and a man's voice commanded him to "Say not a word or you will suffer the pain of the sword." A long heavy robe was dropped over his head and fell about him and Benjamin wondered if he was to be executed privately by Sir Francis and his cronies. Wilkes had told on him. Or was Dashwood seeking revenge for this evening's unexpected kiss from his mistress? He could hear the footsteps of at least three men as he was led roughly down the stairs in the pitch blackness.

He was shepherded out of doors, out the back, for he felt the damp night air on his cheeks and he recognized the cobblestone and grass of the circular garden beneath his slippers. They were going to take him to the tallest tree and string him up by the neck, he was sure of it. He was about to put up a fight when he remembered his initiation into the freemasons so long ago. He was blindfolded then, kidnapped from his print shop at a quarter to midnight, and taken to his initiation. Was he being taken to the caves now?

Benjamin had heard that Sir Francis still conducted meetings of the reputedly Satanic Hellfire Club, reformed now as the Order of St. Francis, down in the caves. From his prior evenings there, they had engaged in nothing more than social activities. Whiskey, hemp, and women of the night. There was nothing Satanic about a little debauchery, was there? Poor Richard, Benjamin's alter ego and writing persona who preached piety, purity, and penny-pinching, would think there was.

"Where are you taking me?" He whispered. He felt the cold tip of a sword on the side of his neck. They lead him by the arm in silence, over the grass, meandering a path, down a gently sloping hill.

He was stopped suddenly. He felt the sword tap his ankles, heard its blade strike stone. Up a few stairs. They were entering the caves. He could hear their footsteps on the hard flagstone floor of the faux church. The flagstone tile abruptly ended and Franklin stumbled into the cave. He could feel each of the chiseled-out bumps of the cave floor through his slippers.

He was led on in the darkness, his shoulder or knee occasionally brushing the cave wall. He sensed when they crossed through the banquet room for he could see the light from the chandelier through the handkerchief around his eyes. He was led again into the tunnel, through the poker room, for he smelled the rotten dank of old cigar, and on down the tunnel much further than he'd ever been.

At some length, he was halted. He could hear the soft trickling echo of underground water. The hands let him go. Despencer's voice commanded him to remove his blindfold.

Benjamin did so and found himself in the midst of a beautiful, candle-lit, primordial cavern. A river of spring water ran before his feet. It was a small stream but wide and looked quite slippery and unnavigable to him. Across the river, he saw their faces illumined from below, delineated from the darkness on the other side.

"Behold. This is the river Styx that you must cross to enter into the Abyss," intoned Sir Francis theatrically.

"Oh dear, you gave me quite a fright. I thought it might be you, but I wa∫n't entirely ∫ure," Benjamin looked behind him at the dark hole from whence he'd come. He wasn't sure which abyss was better. "Alright then," he said, "ſince there doesn't ſeem to be a ferry…" and began crossing the stream, stepping from stone to precarious stone. He was not without mishap and stumbled into the water up to his ankles just short of the shore. All hands reached out and helped him out onto dry ground.

They led him up into a small circular chamber where he had never been before. Candelabras lit a stone altar and a purple velvet chair set before it. He noticed then that the robes they all wore were a deep colored velvet. He looked down; the one they had put on him was just the same.

Benjamin was shown the chair and sat down in it. There was a strange design, a six-pointed star within a seven-pointed star, painted upon the floor. Despencer lorded over the altar, and the others – there were five or six surrounding them on all sides.

"Dr. Benjamin Franklin, you have been invited to number among the Order of St. Francis," spoke Despencer. "Join us in our ethereal wanderings through life eternal by the blood covenant." With that, Sir Francis slit his forearm open so that a stream of blood flowed into a heavy silver chalice upon the altar. Then each of the hooded members stepped up to the altar and cut his palm or his arm with a dagger and drained many drops of blood into the same chalice. Sandwich, Wilkes, the Chevalier, the ones he didn't know. When it was Benjamin's turn he let himself be cut and his blood poured into the chalice. If this ludicrous, heathen ritual would cause them never to betray him, it could only keep him and his interests safe from the hard slap of Parliament, the legislating body to which they all were tied. He was a little unnerved when they passed him the chalice again.

"Drink the blood of your brothers to bind us all unto each other," said Sir Francis.

Benjamin gritted his teeth and put the cup to his lips. The tiniest sip of the salty thick liquid, rolled over his tongue and down his throat. He sensed a hint of bile and of bourbon and stifled a gag. Each man drank a sip of blood. When it came back to Sir Francis he lifted the chalice and gulped down the rest of the contents with great zeal. He said a word Benjamin didn't recognize and threw a flammable powder onto a candle flame making a great burst of bright sparks. Benjamin's stomach lurched and churned the vile droplets as he watched a change begin to come over Sir Francis and the others.

"I'm *forry*," Benjamin gagged and puked beside his chair. He exited quickly, stepping however he could through the River Styx. By the time he'd made it half way out of the caves, he felt better. The taste of that hideous blood and the lack of air in the furthest cave had gotten to his head. Surely Despencer and Sandwich and the others would understand. But what had come over their faces in the moment before he'd lost it? Benjamin was certain he had seen a malign animus invigorate their eyes and the muscles in the faces. Or was it just the candlelight? Whatever the case, Benjamin was a blood brother to them now.

When he finally got out into the air that night, he sat down in the damp grass and caught his breath. The cut on his palm oozed and smarted and he wondered if he shouldn't tend to it sooner than later. He looked up at the stars, grateful to be beneath them rather than roots and rocks, and wondered how one would ever reach them.

The Order was dedicated to arousing the spirits of the aethyreal world and coaxing them to appear. Benjamin thought it all a bit ridiculous and staged, but some of the events that took place down in the caves that summer indeed made him unable to close his eyes at night.

By the time he returned to the bosom of Mrs. Stevenson on Craven Street, Benjamin was forever changed by his membership in the Order of St. Francis, and had a renewed appreciation for all that was simple, true, and good.

CHAPTER XIV

HANCOCK

They sat in the parlor, in the matching Elizabethan gilt chairs that John had bought from the monarchy before he had grown so disillusioned with the British Empire.

"You're making this a lot more difficult than it has to be. I have to make up excuses to see you. We've nothing left in common any more." Daniel Leonard looked at Hancock with despair.

"I have a lot of money and investments at stake, perhaps you don't understand. There's an end in sight to all this grandeur. If I don't protect it, it will be taken, taxed away, stolen by the Crown. Would you like me as much if I had nothing?" he answered quietly.

"Just stop talking about bloody taxes for one second? Please, John." Leonard's gray eyes stared at him, relentless. "If you simply remained loyal, you'd be rewarded, then you'd have nothing to worry about."

Hancock's housekeeper came in. "Mr. Hancock, sir, your Aunt Dorothy is here with Miss Quincy."

"Show them in," said Hancock. Leonard huffed at the intrusion and shot him a spiteful look.

The maid curtsied and the ladies walked into the room. Aunt Dorothy was about fifty and Miss Quincy half that. The latter was a plain girl, but pleasing and inarguably keen. They were absolutely dressed to the nines and John wondered what was the occasion, but thought better of asking, for he realized they had dressed up just for him.

"Have we caught you at a bad time, John?" asked Aunt Dorothy.

"No, lovelies. Come in and be seated. You know my friend, Daniel Leonard. Bess, bring us all some lemonade and something to eat."

"Pleased to meet you," Miss Quincy said in her soft

voice, and shook Leonard's wilting hand.

He regarded her icily and sniffed with disapproval.

"Yes, Daniel. How are things with the Cadet corps?" asked Aunt Dorothy.

"Not the same since that dreadful tea party," answered Leonard quickly.

"I'm so glad our family had nothing to do with that," said the old lady.

"Yes, a bunch of *heathens* are responsible for that. And how fortuitous of them to take up the American cause," said John, dangling his glass over the floor.

"It's a bit chilly in here, John," Miss Quincy shivered. "I don't believe I've worn enough clothing."

Leonard shot her a rude stare. "Lovely dress. Looks like a gigantic doily." He laughed and downed his lemonade.

"Shall we stoke up the fire, then?" said John, getting up from his chair and putting some logs on.

"This is all so transparent. You think you're going to get him just like that, sweetheart?" Leonard asked her with a snap and a sneer.

Miss Quincy and Aunt Dorothy exchanged an embarrassed look at the outburst. "Why no, we simply enjoy John's company, don't we, Dorothy?" said the younger.

"Yes we do," Aunt Dorothy patted her charge on the knee.

"Fiddlesticks!" spat Leonard.

The women gasped. Leonard stormed out. John followed him to the front door.

"He should be happy for John to have a female friend," declared Aunt Dorothy.

"Perhaps he has none of his own," said Miss Quincy.

When the visit was over and the ladies had gone, John Hancock went looking for Leonard. He rode his horse to the apartment they kept together, but he was not there. He knocked at the door and seeing no one around, used the key to come inside. The apartment was neat as ever, fresh flowers in the basin and a French cloth on the table. He checked all the rooms and called his name, but there was no answer.

He wondered where he could've gotten off to, and rode each of the four roads out of Boston a generous ways until he was sure Leonard was not anywhere close to town. He waited in a copse of trees in the avenue before Leonard's own grand home, and watched his Negro housekeepers shake out a carpet on the grass. He finally rode up to the front door, and inquired if Mr. Leonard was at home. The housekeepers could tell him nothing, but speculation. He declined asking Leonard's wife his whereabouts, and opted to simply investigate the stable. His horse was gone.

Late in the day, Hancock found himself at the wharf and peering in each tavern, looked for some sign of him. He sat and had several cups of punch in the Green Dragon.

It was six o'clock when John opened the latch to his own front gate and walked his horse into the garden. He looked forward to when his roses would bloom again. He missed their sweet smell.

He felt a hand on his waist and turned. It was Leonard. His eyes were full of tears as he laid his head on John's shoulder. John embraced him and held him as he cried on his coat. "What's the matter, Danny?" he asked.

"I want things to be the way they were. You're so preoccupied, you don't have time for me any more."

"I'll find time, I swear it. You are the most important person in the world to me, you know that."

"Where did you go? I've been waiting here in the garden all day. There's someone else, isn't there? Is it that girl? Just tell me."

"Don't be ridiculous. I've been looking for *you*. I rode all the roads in and out of town."

Leonard searched his face. "No you didn't. Please, I

don't believe you."

"I swear it. I did."

"Don't lie to me. Where have you been?" He said, his voice broken.

"Let's go inside."

"No! Don't touch me. I've had about enough of this!" Leonard stormed toward the gazebo.

"Please, Danny. It's freezing out here. Let's go in and sit by the fire. We'll have some supper. We can talk."

"There's nothing to talk about!"

"Where are you going?"

"For a walk."

John hung his head and sighed. The old pattern of their relationship, its uncomfortable coldness and crooks of heartbreak tore at him. But he'd rather have Leonard than any other. He wished there were a way. He watched him go, then walked after him.

CHAPTER XV

WEISHAUPT

Adam climbed the steep incline without stopping. The hill on the edge of town was perfectly round and flat on top and none except for a herd of goats ever went up it. He did not want to lose his composure in front of anyone, especially the other young men at the University, so he had come up here to read the book that had belonged to his father.

He looked at the world below, the sheep down in the sprawling pasture, the fat white clouds that hung about the green-dressed Alps jutting boldly up out of the Southern horizon. He took a deep breath and opened the book he had gotten from Ickstatt. It was written in his father's own hand, in Hebrew, a language that was undeniably familiar to him, but one that he could not remember studying.

127

Adam borrowed a Hebrew-Deutsch dictionary from the library so he could translate it accurately. As he began to read the swooshed calligraphy from back to front, he realized he already knew this language, and knew it well. He recognized the letters, long lost friends. He had only to look up a few phrases in the dictionary, for this language that he had learned in his early childhood suddenly came flooding back into his mind. He heard his father's voice as he scanned the title.

The author claimed to practice the "true magic" that Noah, David, and Solomon had gotten directly from God, and the text detailed the ways in which certain desired outcomes could be achieved. He claimed to have dispelled demons, saved the lives of monarchs, and even helped a king win a war by creating phantom soldiers for his army.

The practice of this lost art seemed a little severe, for the subject was to isolate himself in a cave or some such place away from all others for six months. Emphatic prayer, prescriptions for incense, and the assistance of a child, were required, and this was all to achieve the knowledge and conversation of one's Angel who, the author claimed, could be relied upon to aid the magician in his works. Adam inferred that after such an ascetic practice, one would certainly be hearing voices, but perhaps not from any angel. He continued reading, wondering how the author could advocate using the services of demons to produce his outcomes. It was a prospect that seemed foolish and dangerous. He put the book down reflexively when the author began spelling out the names of demons and illustrating the seals significant to each.

As he sat under the deep blue sky that was turning to dusk, he made the sign of the cross and wondered how his father had come by this book. Where exactly had it been when he'd found it? Why had he gone to Wurzberg for such a foolish thing? Had he really believed that the so-called 'sacred magic' would work? Or had he sought the book as a curiosity, a scholarly investigation? As he touched it to return it to his satchel, he felt intuitively that it had played no small part in the death of his parents. What was it that Ickstatt had said about why it had happened? "Your father predicted the death of someone very prominent." Who? Certainly Ickstatt knew. Was the book the means by which the prediction was made? Or was it the cause of death itself?

Adam suddenly looked up and there beside him were the shoes and legs of a man. "We've had no hemp since you left Munich," said a familiar voice. It was Penske, short of breath. He leaned over to keep from falling down.

"Well neither have I," retorted Adam.

"What are you reading?" asked Penske.

"A book," Adam answered simply.

Penske sighed. "Listen, I've got quite a bit of money for you if you'll send it to your brother, then we can all have something to smoke for the year. Will you do it, please?"

Adam could not refuse. Hemp would certainly taste fine right about now, and he took the large sum from Penske, and agreed to pen a letter to his friend in the New World that very afternoon.

As he sat in the University library reading the canons, and realizing he would be doing penance for the rest of his born days for the innumerable sins he'd committed at the brothel, Adam began to reason that he had nothing to fear from his father's book. God protected the faithful, didn't He? Curiosity burned at him, and he could not focus his attention of the dull fare that was assigned by his professor, especially with so gripping a book right inside his satchel, a book that literally called out to be read and understood. He put away his volume of canons, and reached into his satchel. He opened the book upon the table and undertook with a sincere mind to learn the techniques described therein. Where would such a practice lead? To Damnation? He recognized the controlling aspect of the Church, knew that it sought to keep men in low, common places, sought to have all spiritual power for itself. He quieted his mind and set to work.

Adam possessed the acumen and concentration necessary for the intense operations described and meditated for hours without a single deviation in his thoughts. What might take a normal man several hours to visualize, Adam conjured to mind immediately, vividly and without interference. The book advised the practitioner to isolate himself, but living in a dormitory, the best Adam could do was the top of the hill, to which he went and marked out his circle in rain, snow, or sun as his practice called him. Upon awaking from his trance, Adam found symbols of power traced in the sand by the invisible hands of his Guardians.

His practice, indeed, effected real results. Admittedly, he was not twenty-five years old, did not devote the six months' time, did not employ a child, for he despised them, and did not use the implements exactly as described in the book, for there was no way to obtain or make most of them without rousing suspicion among the citizens of Ingolstadt. Nonetheless, he had a great many strange, terrifying, and wonderful things occur to him just the same that spring on the lonely hilltop.

Of particular note were the sudden changes in the atmosphere. The wind would pick up out of nowhere sometimes, and with it came the voices of spirits whom Adam heard speaking magic words, and he worked feverishly to write them down and learn to employ them. Too, there seemed to be an unusual frequency of lightning, perhaps because it was spring, but he often wondered if its duration and intensity could be attributed to his activities. Adam had heard of people being struck by lightning and made sure to be off the hilltop when it seemed to loom close, though he often thought of how he might go about harnessing its might for his own use.

When he felt he was ready, from the ethers he called forth one at a time, the spirit personalities who claimed to have the ability to reveal hidden, lost and secret things. Outside his consecrated circle, within their own triangular confines, appeared misty spots of shadow that delineated themselves more or less in the forms of various ugly creatures. After scourging each one with his will, he interrogated it about the fate of his parents. Despite what his uncle had told him, he could never believe them to be dead. To his disappointment, none of the strange apparitions could tell him much more than Ickstatt had told him, and like his uncle, all of them claimed his parents to have passed from the world of the living. It was with grave disappointment that Adam concluded his evocations. He had expended tremendous effort, had scared himself to his very wit's end several times, and had gotten no satisfactory answers. One of the last ones he called forth, promised to "make an enquiry," but Adam thought him dubious.

When he was done with them he contained each spirit unhappily inside a small, brass bell he had gotten off a horse's belled yoke. The bells, he plugged with lead and wrapped neatly in a shred of cloth bearing the corresponding name. He kept them in a metal box, not unlike the tin box his brother had sent, and so reserved them for some future time. He had no real use for them or their legions at present, but looked forward to a day when such things would have untold value, and wondered when and under what circumstances he would ever use them. He knew innately to be extremely judicious about employing them, for their very natures made them dangerous and untrustworthy, and he was not entirely convinced that he could control them.

Some days later atop the hill, in the midst of an operation to bring a great library of books to himself, he sensed something amiss as a chill wind ruffled his hair. He opened his eyes, expecting to behold a misty apparition come to submit itself to him. But there, all around him were large, birdlike foot tracks in the ash with which he'd drawn his circle. He had been awake during this meditation, and had not sensed any bird of such enormity so close to him. He rose and looked around with alarm. He could not fathom what kind of bird had desecrated his circle and tracked the ash so far and wide. And even more disconcerting, he had not been aware of it at all. After closing his operations, he walked round the hilltop, following the bird prints. He faced west, and from there, in the smattering of footprints, saw a sinister depiction of a man being eaten by a large and gaping mouth. He stomped and smeared the image out with his foot and performed a fervent banishing.

It was not many days later that he awoke in the night in his dormitory bed with a strange feeling. Unlike St. Michael's dormitory, which was a vast open hall with rows of bunks, the University dormitory bunks were single and solitary. Curtains divided each man's bed and gave a foot or so of space on either side for a modicum of privacy. Although many of the young men stayed up, burning lamp oil till late in the evening, there was no one still awake on this night, save for Adam.

He lay under his covers and listened to the darkness, letting the heaviness of the day and of his tired body overcome him. He had just drifted off to sleep when he heard a scratching sound. He thought it sounded like an animal that was caught in a box and trying to escape. He at first tried to dismiss it. Someone had apparently procured a pet and was keeping the poor creature in a trunk or some other tight place. He could not tell exactly where the noise was coming from, but it mattered little, he thought, and closed his eyes again.

He awoke again later to the sound of claws trying desperately to dig their way out of the wall only inches away from him. He lit his lamp and stood at the foot of his bed, staring at the wall in the semi-darkness. No sounds came for a long time. He felt a cold and unsettling presence. He wondered if he should wake one of the other residents, but thought better of disturbing any of the others who slept peacefully all around him. They would certainly be groggy and irritable and ridicule him for his nervous suspicions of what was probably a rat making a nest in the wall.

Suddenly the noise came again, but now it was as if whatever it was, was using a metal tool to dig. He lifted his lamp and illuminated the wall several feet above his bed. To his shock, he found there, a great gaping hole in the plaster. He stared into the dark cavity.

Suddenly, there was shouting. "What is it? It's in my bed! Get it off me! Get it off me!" screamed a frantic voice in the corridor.

Adam pulled aside his curtain and saw the flash of a fleeing shadow. He ran after it, as the others were awakened by the young man's shouts.

At the landing of the stairs, he lost any sense of it. He banished cautiously and quickly. Wary of the darkness, he headed back to his bed. Most of the others were awake now. Dursmann, the man who slept directly opposite him, was standing in the hallway, in a sheer panic, speaking in breathless terror of the thing that had accosted him in his sleep.

"It was on me in my bed, weighing me down. I thought it was one of you trying to wake me, so I opened my eyes and I saw this creature with a monstrous beak, and great red eyes glaring down at me. It said, 'won't you come into my nest...'" he stammered.

Hysterical laughter broke out among the others.

Dursmann grimaced and wrung his hands. Adam looked at

him with concern. The young man was generally loud and boisterous, but now he seemed weak with terror. Adam thought of telling him he had been aware of the thing as well, but then reminded himself that it would make him seem like the culprit for causing it to appear in the first place. Adam knew he was already viewed as strange so he said nothing and went back to bed. He did not rest, but thought on what he had witnessed and how he might deal with it.

It was the next night when Adam was reading that Dursmann appeared at the foot of his bed. His eyes seemed unusually black and glistening, and he had a dank and putrid smell about him.

"I know who you are," said Dursmann in a hoarse voice.

"Yes, we've met. How goes it?" replied Weishaupt simply, feeling he should stand and defend himself from the intruder. He grabbed a stylus off his bedside table and held it before Dursmann, like a wand.

"It goes." And Dursmann whipped aside his curtains and was gone.

In the days that followed, Dursmann was involved in several fights with other students, was caught stealing and defecating in the flowerbed outside the office of one of his professors. He stalked Adam to and from his classes, and proceeded to act so loud and insane, that the constable was called to arrest him. Adam watched from beneath the archway of the library building as Dursmann was hauled away by two patrolmen. He felt a great amount of responsibility, for whatever had happened to him, had probably been because of the operations he had been performing. He did not know what to do or how to heal Dursmann of his psychic affliction, and for once sought the exegesis of the Church on how to deal with demonic possession, for since the night of the hole in the wall, Dursmann was a changed man.

A day later, Dursmann's wealthy father pried him out of

custody and he was returned to school conditionally. He breathed heavily now, apparently having been convinced that he needed to control himself or be expelled from the University. It was evident he was only superficially contained, and could go on a violent rampage at any moment. Adam did not want to involve Ickstatt in the matter. The dean was quite aware of Dursmann's condition, but completely ignorant of Adam's extracurricular rituals or his proximity to Dursmann.

Adam needed to get Dursmann alone, needed to have him medicinally subdued or at least bound and gagged to perform an exorcism, and that would be no easy task.

Adam quietly approached the young men who slept in the beds on either side of Dursmann's, and several others who Dursmann terrorized. He called a small meeting in the University's empty chapel, and laid out a plan of how they would ambush Dursmann and bring him to the botanical nursery on the perimeter of the campus. He did not particularly care to have an audience, but felt he might need the assistance of the others in case Dursmann tried to escape his confines.

The night came and Dursmann was slipped a large quantity of valerian root powder in his soup that evening in the dining hall. Adam and his conspirators sat together as Dursmann's eyelids fluttered and he almost nodded off. He trudged sluggishly back to his bed. Before he could mount the stairs, they turned him out the door and guided him across the campus. Dursmann threw them off of him several times, but never had the wherewithal to turn himself around and run away.

Adam had the nursery shed prepared and they sat Dursmann down on the floor as if they were going to sit and have a chat. Before their subject could react, they bound him with heavy twine and laid him out on the floor. No sooner had this been done than he began to resist.

Adam did not realize how difficult and taxing an

exorcism could prove to be. It was a trial of his own faith and psychic resources that took hours. He posted the others outside, each to a corner, facing out with a sword, to ward off any would-be intruders. He needed no audience to distract Dursmann's attention from the words he was speaking.

Alone in the shed with Dursmann, Adam intoned the prayers not once, but dozens of times in the face of the entity that inhabited him. It called itself the Morgizau and knew much about Adam, for he gleaned, it had originally intended to possess him, but finding him an unwilling body, had chosen Dursmann who was nearby and more easily penetrable.

"I killed your mother!" it screamed at Adam. Dursmann's pupils were wide, black, evil. "I cut off her screaming head!"

From the other demons he had summoned, he had been seeking the truth about what had happened to his parents. And here was the confessed killer, a demon called Morgizau appeared to satisfy his interrogations, most likely turned over by the others he had questioned.

Adam resisted lashing Dursmann as the instructions from the Church dictated, and tried to remain impervious to its grisly descriptions of his parents' last moments. He plugged his ears with little shreds of rags and vowed not to listen to it.

"*I* burned your house down!" it growled distortedly out of Dursmann's mouth. "Morgizau and Lorenzo! We led the mob against the devil Jews!"

Lorenzo? "Lorenzo Ricci?" Adam asked it.

"The Black Pope! He summoned Morgizau to kill them!"

"Why?" Adam shouted, trying to maintain his calm, but inside, he burned with questions and thoughts of revenge.

"Because George Weishaupt doesn't cooperate with Lorenzo! George Weishaupt is a traitor! George Weishaupt must die!"

He took a deep breath and resisted interrogating the thing further, for now that the truth was before him, it pained him to hear it. He put his mind back on task.

He stuffed a large rag inside Dursmann's mouth so that the Morgizau would have no way of interrupting his fervent prayers.

In the darkest part of the night, Dursmann's old personality began to reemerge, frightened and confused, alongside the grim guise of his possessor, who appeared as a supercountenance, contorting Dursmann's mouth and nose into a beak and making another pair of round, black eyes appear on the sides of his head. It squawked and shrieked terribly as Adam's powerful words struck it over again like bludgeons. Finally, it fell away from Dursmann and lay on the dirt floor, stunned like a bird that has run into a windmill. Large and hideous, its body verily was that of a feathered, beaked gargoyle, half-bird, half-bat, it seemed. Its gigantic feet twitched, its taloned toes opening and closing as it respired heavily as had Dursmann when it had inhabited him. Adam retrieved a brass bell, consecrated it and commanded the creature to go into the vessel.

The thing rose in the air, became a black blur of smoke, and obediently went into the bell. Saying prayers over it, he plugged the bell with lead.

It was dawn when Adam finally finished. He untied Dursmann who now slept peacefully, his entire countenance changed. The others who had fallen asleep outside, awoke and came in to see their old friend resting peacefully.

Adam took the brass bell with its wretched contents, and left Dursmann in the care of the others. He carried the bell into the light of the morning sun, and buried it in a remote place near a large, odd-looking rock.

The confessions of the Morgizau plagued Adam's mind

after that. He wondered if Superior General Lorenzo Ricci truly ordered the deaths of his parents as the Morgizau accused. Had his father been in the service of Father Lorenzo and somehow let him down or betrayed him? Was that why Lorenzo had sought Adam at school to see if he had his father's abilities? He soon regretted not taking the opportunity to question the thing when he had the chance. He could certainly liberate the Morgizau and command it to answer, but he had no desire to contend with it again at present. It evoked something so painful in him he did not ever want to confront it again. Not to mention, the entity was a stubborn one, and Adam dared not conjure back one so malign and difficult to control.

He remembered clearly, his meeting Father Lorenzo at St. Michael's as a young boy. The Secretary of the Superior General had come all the way from Rome, or so he said, to meet Johann Adam Weishaupt and teach him to astrally walk. Indeed, he must have known of his father's abilities, and thereby assumed that Adam had inherited those gifts. What a strange incident, he thought as he lay in his bed. How peculiar that Lorenzo had instructed him to administer the Pope's medicine. And the Pope had died, within days, hours even. Adam sat up suddenly, aghast with the realization that he had been used by Lorenzo Ricci to poison the Pope. His mind reeled and he felt at once sick and exhilarated. At the age of ten, he had unwittingly assassinated God's chosen manifestation, Christ on Earth, the Pope of the Holy Roman Catholic Church. There was no worse crime that he could have committed. Even sorcery seemed a trivial transgression in light of it. But he had done it because he was tricked by Lorenzo Ricci, not out of any malice or motivation of his own. But he had done it nonetheless.

And his parents... If Father Lorenzo   was so bold as to execute the Pope himself, would he not even think twice about ending the lives of a lowly, but gifted professor and his family? But why, particularly if he had found his father's talents useful?

He thought about the title 'Black Pope,' for that was the epithet given the Superior General, head of the Jesuits. He was second only in command to the Pope. If the Pope was Christ on earth, then was the Black Pope Satan on earth, conjuring things like the Morgizau to do his awful bidding? Father Lorenzo was a creature of Satan if there was such a thing, in league with the likes of the Morgizau, and undoubtedly others of the lower realms.

And though Adam had no evidence but the ravings of this subastral entity, Adam now believed Father Lorenzo had orchestrated the deaths of his parents. If it was true, he could not allow the man to go unpunished another day.

Adam returned to his dormitory and dug through his trunk. He found the silver medal of St. Ignatius that Father Lorenzo had given him as a reward for his unsuspecting obedience.

That night, he lay in his bed with the medal in his hand, and when he was on the verge of sleep, he told himself "Take me to Father Lorenzo." He heard the sound of the whooshing wind. There was a loud crack of thunder. And he was suddenly in a beautiful, candle-lit chapel in the Vatican. A black-clad figure knelt at the altar. Behind him in a formation, knelt six lesser priests.

Adam glided around the figure at the altar. Indeed, it was Father Lorenzo, his face older now, lined with care. He looked up, sensing a presence in the sanctuary. Adam remembered his sinister instructions to give the Pope his medicine. Now he kicked the man squarely in the face with all his might.

The Black Pope screamed and reeled backward. The other priests rushed to his aid, looking helplessly at the empty altar. Lorenzo lay bleeding from the nose and mouth, cursing and dazed. Adam laughed at the thought that it must have appeared that the Lord Himself kicked

Lorenzo in the face.

His laughter shook him from the realm of his travels and he snapped back to his body in the dormitory. He lay in his bed, still laughing. The other students who were passing by in the corridor gave him curious looks as his belly shook with hysterical amusement.

Of course, he was not in the least satisfied that revenge had been exacted, but he was bemused by the fact that he could inflict this level of torture on such a well-deserving subject. From then on, whenever Adam thought of it, he traveled to the Black Pope's side and assailed him in some way. Sometimes he assaulted him, giving him stigmata in unusual places, but other times he smashed holy objects, slammed doors, tore down curtains, and otherwise terrified the man before delivering some sort of injury. Once he had Lorenzo running down some stairs so fast, he tripped over his robes and tumbled perilously the rest of the way down. He was bloodied and terrified, but not killed.

The Pope, Clement XIV, came to inspect the stairs and the unusual phenomena that Lorenzo explained were the cause of his misfortunes of late. The Pope stared straight through Adam, and he realized that the Pope had no keener faculties than any normal, mortal man. He would think a true incarnation of Christ certainly would have been able to view some shred of his presence standing in the stairway. Instead, the Pope looked hard at Father Lorenzo and beseeched him to explain the source of his injuries.

Meanwhile, Adam brazenly continued his practice of sacred magic. He focused his energies on calling a great lot of books to himself. He unfettered the appropriate demon from his brass bell and instructed him in this errand. It had always been a dream of his to own his own library of special books, books that would enlighten his mind and make him as wise as King Solomon, books of definitive knowledge that would settle any argument with anyone. He had already exhausted Ickstatt's library of philosophy, history, canon law, and science, and committed many of the worthy volumes to memory.

That summer when the University was out, when he was not reading in the library or meditating atop the hill, he again supported himself by telling fortunes by the reflecting pool. There, he advised the troubled hearts of Ingolstadt, and told them of the events of their lives that would come to pass. For those who had the money, he cast their natal charts and interpreted the influence of the planets and the moon upon their blood, for as Barmoras had taught him, a man's blood was made of iron and the planets pulled upon him like great lodestones from heaven, and determined his disposition, fortunes, and actions.

This occupation did not last but a few weeks, for Baron von Ickstatt saw him out his office window one day, and was no sooner before him.

"What are you doing here?" he asked. "Are you doing what I think you're doing?"

"Probably," answered Adam who was consulting a young man who had recently graduated and found himself and his family deeply in debt.

"Come with me, now! Foolish boy!" Ickstatt glared at him with malice.

Quickly Adam spat out his advice to the young man as Ickstatt dragged him into the University building by his sleeve.

"Don't ever let anyone see you do such a thing! There are spies whose reports would land us all in the worst kind of exile! Have you forgotten the Inquisition!?"

Adam tried to explain, but Ickstatt hushed him. "You must *never let anyone see you do that*! Not now, *not ever*!"

141

So Adam unhappily secluded himself in the empty dormitory. As he had at St. Michael's, he had the run of the place to himself, and there he continued his practice of sacred magic in private for the rest of the summer. Ickstatt invited him to his house for dinner and gave him spending money so that he would not employ himself again as a soothsayer.

In the privacy of the empty dormitory, Adam continued the operations described in his father's book, but resisted calling wealth, fame, or women to himself. He had always compared himself to the steadfast and incorruptible Siegfried who was never tempted by the glittering hoard of the Nibelungen that brought everyone else to his demise. Adam was a devoted student, and was not at leisure to enjoy such things at present anyway. However, his lust and greed for knowledge was another matter altogether, and he waited every day for the lot of books to be delivered him by the minion. He studied its trigram and seal for an answer to where it may be in its mission, and was given an answer: "The sea." Many long months passed and the books never came. Sometimes he worried that the damnable thing had gone astray and had abandoned its task. Despite his doubts of the efficacy of some parts of the system, for he certainly was not practicing them perfectly, he felt that the practice of the rituals, themselves, was fortifying some inner part of himself. He was irrevocably aware of the enrichment of his soul, for when he intoned the prayers, he could feel a sublime exhilaration filling him deep inside, as if he was bringing immense energy and power into his body from above.

CHAPTER XVI

That August, fifteen crates of hemp buds and tobacco were loaded on a cargo ship bound for Hamburg. Adam received his brother's letter stating that the ship, *The Mercy* would be arriving near the middle of October, so he arranged to go to Hamburg by himself, for Penske was ill and could not stand to travel. Adam would quickly pick up the shipment that would last the freemasons of Lodge Theodore and their circles of friends, an entire year. He would make this journey as fast as possible and then return to school with all haste so as not to miss any classes.

Adam and Serafina had tried growing Indian hemp in the flowerbed at the brothel in Munich but had no success with it. The plants that managed to sprout were small and suffered much with the short growing season and high altitude. Indian hemp was a plant suited to a warm Southern climate, and though he still planted any seeds he had in the field behind the university, he continued to request American-grown hemp from his brother in Virginia, whom Penske had told him was very a high-ranking freemason.

"Your dear brother is very revered. He will merit the highest degrees while he is still young enough to enjoy them," Penske said.

"What secrets will be revealed to him then?" Adam asked delicately, hoping that Penske, in his weakened condition, would let slip the mysteries of the higher degrees.

"Ah, you will have to earn them for yourself and discover those greatest of secrets when your time comes," answered the gaunt Penske. "That is why you must stay up with the lodge. You and your uncle have not been back since you went off to school," he scolded.

Adam was not sure he wanted to continue to devote time to the freemasons. They were good enough people, but he felt that they, like the Church, only skimmed the surface of the sacred mysteries of the universe. Rather, they seemed more interested in making business and social

143

connections than truly pursuing the Heart of the world and the secrets of life itself, the things which Adam was discovering were his own raisons d'être. Moreover, he was unwilling to wait years to find out if their secrets were actually worth his time.

Adam looked at Penske's round, sunken eyes, and was about to speak, then thought better of it. His continued absence would convey his disinterest without his having to speak any criticism. He hated to disappoint his friend and would miss him, and he had while he had been in Ingolstadt, but it was a long way to the lodge in Munich just for one night of hobnobbing with gentlemen with whom he only had hemp in common. Adam had better things to do with himself. He wished that Penske would just divulge everything he knew about the freemasons to him and so save him having to waste any more time with them. How could he evaluate the worthiness of their ideology and truly know if he wanted to pursue masonry if he had no knowledge of what truths lay at its core? His uncle was of no help, either, for Ickstatt had been raised only lately, and had, himself, only been to a handful of meetings.

Adam climbed into Penske's wagon, threw his satchel in the back, and looked back at Penske as he leaned inside his doorway. Penske was not married and Adam worried that no one would be looking after him during his ailment, but he assured him that the lodge looked after their own.

"Take care, yourself. That is a long and dangerous journey," Penske warned Adam as he set off.

"I'll be fine. I know the way," he assured him, and he did, for they had made the trip together once before. All he had to do was head north and stay the course.

Indeed, Adam drove over the perilous road through night and day without a care, and happily without incident. He arrived in Hamburg on a Monday, expecting to find his crates of hemp already sitting on the dock.

It was raining, and he left Penske's wagon in the livery at the inn where he intended to stay that night before setting out for Bavaria in the morning.

He made his way down the grassy slope to the sea, and walked around the harbor under the heavy, gray sky searching for the vessel named *Mercy*. But there were none by that name.

At the last of the docks, he came upon a sailor heaping a bunch of wet refuse onto the dock. Adam looked down and realized that it was a huge mound of wet and disintegrating scrolls and books - old, foreign, and taking on the rain that now beat down upon them.

"Whose books are these?" Adam asked in horror.

"Yours. Take them," the sailor cackled. "I won't tell if you won't."

Adam gathered up an armload of them and headed back to his room in the inn. The first one he had picked was written in Italian, one of the many languages he had learned in Jesuit school. *Ways of Turning Earth into Gold* was a very old alchemy book that still smelled of the sulfur in someone's alchemy laboratory. He wondered then what else might be lying on the dock in the pouring rain. Was this the great lot of books for which he had asked? He put the book down on the table, grabbed the blanket off his bed, and flew out the door.

He gathered up two hundred pounds of wet literature in the blanket, and hoisting it over his shoulder, hefted it up the incline to the inn. He knew what two hundred pounds felt like having carried out as many and as heavy of intoxicated patrons from the Frisky Cat.

It had stopped raining, but the roofs and trees still shed drops that fell onto the muddy ground. Slipping up and down the slope, he made eight trips from the dock to his wagon, dumping the contents of the bedspread into it and filling it three feet high. Some of the books were ruined entirely, having the look of pasted meal, but others were in fair shape and salvageable. The collection turned out to be an exceedingly rare and precious occult library, uncannily waiting for him on a dock in the rain.

Adam felt a bolt of excitement. He sipped in the salt air, invigorated. He knew enough not to marvel at coincidence, for there was no such thing; there was only the Grace of God, and the mage's power of utilizing those implements He created for such purposes. These were indeed the books for which he had sent the minion, now delivered. He began to realize the kind of power that was at his disposal and the knowledge that lay at his fingertips, as the wee hours crept upon dawn and he read a book written in Hebrew about the Holy Qabalah. Most of the book, however, was quite confounding for it was not authored by anyone who spoke or actually wrote Hebrew. The author simply used the Hebrew language as a part of a code that he artfully organized into grids where correspondences could be inferred, and names and words spelled out, and other messages be interpreted.

As Adam read another about the Tree of Life, he noticed that Mercy was the name of the fourth sephiroh, or radiant sphere, and puzzled over its significance: In his world, the boat *Mercy* was missing. But yet - or rather instead, he had received all these books, and fate was dealing him the leisure time to read a good many of them while waiting around in Hamburg. He wished he had a pipe full of hemp to smoke while he studied them. Soon, he assured himself, the hemp would arrive.

He wondered what he would do when the ship arrived and he needed to load his crates of hemp in the wagon. He would figure something out. At least he had some time to sift through these books without fear of them ruining further and see which ones would be of later interest. Hopefully their true owner, whoever he may be, would never come looking for them.

The next day was clear. Adam rose at daybreak, taking

his spyglass, and went down to the harbor. He looked at every ship in sight and could not find any called *Mercy*. He saw an oarsman from a Portuguese freighter rowing a dinghy up to the shore and spoke to him in Spanish. "Have you seen a boat called *The Mercy*?"

The man shook his head.

For days, Adam waited in Hamburg, each day going out in the rain to look for the ship and coming back to the inn and reading for hours. He thought how he enjoyed reading much more when he had a taste of hemp, and it dawned on him to scry in the water and ask to be shown what had happened to it. He went down to the dock when the rain paused, and stood on top of a mooring and looked into the sea, but it was too gray and choppy and he could see nothing. He took his bowl and dipped some ocean water into it and held it until it smoothed over. He thought he saw George's face speaking to him, but it was simply his own reflection and he thought he needed to shave. The water showed nothing more.

He sat down under the tree and waited, one eye in a book, the other in the spyglass, watching tiny ships that moved across the horizon, until he got quite a headache. Soon he grew tired of the intermittent cold rain and resigned himself to staying in his room and going outside hourly to check if the ship had come.

He read at the little, round table beside the window for hours that turned into days. His mind danced with the vivid imagery of the angels described in the books, and he sat and meditated upon them. The letters of the Holy Qabalah took shape out of the air as he slept at night, and sacred words were spoken by the rain as it tapped on the roof, channeling pathways through his consciousness so that he could think of nothing in creation without it finding its way into a sephirotic or numerological classification. He saw correlations between the Qabalah and the tarot and every other thing he perceived, and he began to lose his sense of separateness from the forms of the world. Strange events began to happen, events that to Adam seemed real, though he felt they must be dreams.

While the rain poured outside, Adam sat up in his bed. He dreamed that he walked over to a book that was drying on the mantle, a grimoire called *The Book of Xxxxxxxxxxxxx*. He had opened it briefly and thought the illustrations too frightful to investigate. Delicately he touched the leather cover.

A voice that was as beautiful and sweet as the music of the fairies must be, spoke to him. "Come to me."

He felt a shining, white, light pervading him, burning him up through his fingertip. He opened the book and began to read. It was if he took a breath and inhaled the words inside it.

When he awoke, he sat up and looked over at the old book drying on the mantle, its pages still spread by straws. For hours, he tried to resist it while he read the other books, and delicately spread and blotted their damp pages with his clothes. But the book continued to call to him, and once in a while, he thought he saw it give off a flash of colored light, like sunlight through a prism, though the shutters were drawn and the room was dim but for the single candle that burned beside him on the table. As he perused the other books, he realized that sorcery was the crux of every one of them, and after reading the jaw-dropping formulas in a book entitled *Transformations of Men and Animals*, *The Book of Xxxxxxxxxxxxx* seemed rather harmless.

Contained in this library were the occult secrets of every civilization that had ever existed. Adam was certain that these books had been destined to find him and no one else, for who else would have had the inclination or aptitude to pursue these matters? He reasoned that whatever they contained, God had intended him to know. YVWH had created all these things, too, so how could they be evil?

And who was he to shun these arts now? For the past four years, he had earned half his living reading cards; he had "visions" in water, and he no longer believed that the moral restrictions put upon the followers of Christ were anything but political dogma designed to control the masses through shame. If there were real, tangible power to be pulled down from God Almighty, would the Church allow a man to do it? Certainly not. There was no Deity present in the rituals practiced by the Church. He had always wondered at their lack of substance, lack of effect, since he was a small boy at mass in Jesuit school. There was no Lord present for the prayers, the liturgies, the communions. The Lord did not come because He wasn't being properly summoned. If anything, He was being mocked. These books, however, like the one that his father had found in Wurzberg, contained precise methods to make contact with other powers, and if the force did not show itself, did not cooperate, it was sent away promptly.

At last, he picked up the book and began reading. He said the Lord's Prayer and asked that Jesus protect him from the evil spirits that may be provoked by the practice of this ancient art, and then prayed for his Guardian Angel to manifest.

His room was on the second floor at the very end of the building. It had three windows looking out, but trees made it secluded and private from the road. He stood beholding the eastern window and saw the cloudy figure of a woman appear, calling to him in a song. When he looked harder, the morning sun rose behind her and he thought for an instant as the first rays of sun broke over the horizon, that he could see a face, strange and exquisite. "Come to me... in Magan," beckoned the apparition.

But when Adam rose to do so, she broke apart into a hundred thousand fine points of dust that floated in the air and glimmered in the light of the new day.

As the dust pervaded him and he breathed it down his

dry throat, he coughed and realized then he had been for several days without much food.

Famished and weak, he went to the innkeeper to inquire if there was anything to be had. The innkeeper, a sour-faced old man, gave him half a sausage, a loaf of bread and some ale.

When he returned to his room with the plate of food, he looked at the knife the innkeeper had lent him. It was a beautiful thing with an inscription in Hebrew on the handle: *With this Knife, I bring Elohim*. He wondered who had made it, and why the innkeeper would lend such an instrument to a random guest.

He took the knife down to the harbor and washed it in the salty water. It gleamed in the daylight and was certainly not the kind of cutlery that was meant for slicing sausage. Such a dagger had been called for in some of the rituals, and now he had one in his possession. He did his best to wash it of any residual energy it might have picked up from vulgar kitchen use, and went to the innkeeper to give him some silver for it, but the innkeeper refused, saying it was not his and that he had never seen it before. Adam shrugged and gladly accepted the dagger from wherever it had come. It was a beautiful and effective instrument and Adam used it often in the days that followed, losing himself in study, ritual, and meditation.

Before he realized it, two more weeks had passed and the hemp had not arrived. Adam's anxiety was mounting, for he had been away from Ingolstadt for so long. University classes had begun three days after he had left, and that was now over a month ago. It was still another six days' drive back to Ingolstadt after he left Hamburg and the weather was beginning to change. He knew his uncle was already furious with him for his absence from school. He could feel it. But the thought of returning to Lodge Theodore without the hemp was not something he cared to do. He did not want to explain that he and his generous brother had failed them all and there would be no hemp for the Lodge. But what else could he do?

The brethren at Lodge Theodore would be disappointed, but the University was in session and he was missing his classes. The harbormaster promised to watch for the ship and Adam gave him a letter of authority to collect the shipment on his behalf and the last of his money to store it in a warehouse. He would have to return to Hamburg when it finally arrived, whenever that may be.

Adam covered the books in the wagon with the tarp he had brought to cover the hemp to protect it from rain, and set out for Bavaria. He read the books while driving through the countryside. He would study all of them lest he miss some important piece of knowledge. He glanced back at the huge pile under the tarp. What would he do with them when he got back to the dormitory? He had thought overmuch about having a great lot of books, but never even considered where he would keep them.

The weather outside of Hamburg was as fair as any, and though it had rained nearly every day while he was there, the fields and roads he traveled outside of town were dry. It was midday when he began to sense that he was being followed. He stopped his team to have a listen to his surroundings. He strained to see into the thick woods. Unnerved, he continued onward, whipping the horses to a faster pace. As he rounded a bend, another coach yielded and let his by. He wondered if the sounds of the oncoming coach were what he had sensed, for birds and other animals take flight as drivers pass. Perhaps he had simply heard the footsteps of a deer or some other, startled grazing animals whose footpaths crisscrossed the road in so many places.

As the hours passed, Adam's mind wandered back to his books, and he picked up another and read the afternoon away as the horses walked the dusty road.

As the sun set, he came to the bottom of a hill and

considered camping there in the grove of trees for the night, but thought he would go a little further in the light of the half moon, and make camp when it set and he absolutely could see no more. He looked up at the stars, tiny white fires in the deep blue sky. What were they? Who were they? Where were they? And what was this earth upon which he stood, really? It was all the Grace of YVWH, His creation for His people, the Jews. He was one of them, he could not deny it for he felt the power of Him as he pronounced His Name inside his head, much more than any of those whose barbarous names he had spoken aloud. And though his Jesuit Christian beliefs had shaped much of his life, he could not deny the blood that coursed through his veins was that of Solomon, David, Moses and Abram.

Adam bowed his head and prayed for forgiveness for engaging in sorcery and hoped that He would understand that he only wanted to be closer to Him and that sacred magic was his means of doing so. His mind was thus occupied in its internal conflict when a group of robbers surrounded him. He cracked his whip, but one of the robbers grabbed onto his horses' bridles and held them fast. The others, holding knives, clutched the wagon on both sides of him.

"Give us your wares!" said the leader of them whose lips had been cut off, giving him a false and permanent grin.

Adam dropped the reins, and put up his hands. "I've got nothing but books, books written in foreign languages."

The lipless leader held up his lantern and looked at him suspiciously, then back at the books. "We'll burn them to keep warm then! Get down from there! Take off those boots!"

Adam took off his boots and jumped down. One of the thieves poked him in the ribs with a knife while the other searched roughly through his pockets. Adam held his arms out to the sides, wondering if he would be stabbed. Was this how his precious life would end? He loved himself and took a sweet breath in. He smelled the stench of liquor, urine, and old sweat on them and was revolted. Adam's pockets turned out empty, for he was completely without money or food, having stayed so long at the inn.

"He's got nothing," said the one with the knife. He pushed Adam down and spat on him. "Should we kill him?" he asked.

"Might as well," smiled No Lips.

The one with the knife made a downward thrust, but Adam rolled beneath the wagon and scrambled up a tree to safety. The thieves looked up and laughed at him. They ripped back the tarp on the wagon. He listened as they dug through the misshapen, old books and fragile scrolls he had tucked together inside several crates. He cringed at their rough handling of the collection.

"Books! Ha! That'll make a hot fire," said the leader as he jumped in the seat of the wagon, and the others sprawled on top of the books in the back. Adam watched as they rattled away down the road and were quickly lost in the darkness.

"Thanks for the horses!" one of them called back.

As easily as the books had come to him, they were taken away. He was sickened to think they would be used to fuel the thieves' fire. Beneath the silent moon, he stumbled his way down the dark road. When his bare feet began to hurt and he could walk no more, he stopped and fell asleep next to a great rock.

When he awoke in the early morning in the pile of cool, dewy grass, he was disoriented, and aggrieved to realize that the night's events had not been a bad dream. His feet were chilled and cut on the bottoms. He was penniless, famished, and stranded. Munich was more than four days' journey away. He thought of returning the shorter distance to Hamburg, selling some of the hemp when it finally arrived, and then returning home at least on horseback.

But he thought he would be better off to continue homeward where he could explain the problem to his financiers. They were undoubtedly waiting for him and concerned at his whereabouts, for he had written to no one the entire time he had been away, and now he had no way to do so.

As he walked southward through the forest, he tried to remember everything he had read, and wished he had a quill and his cloth book to write down what he recalled. He was certain to forget the descriptions, the rituals, and especially the nuances of the practices the books described. All would be lost, and he would most likely never encounter such books again, not without a great amount of effort and a greater amount of money. Distressed, he walked on, through the tall grass, stepping over the wheel ruts molded and dried in the road.

Before long, he heard the sound of carriage bells coming up behind him. He turned to see a magnificent white coach detailed with gilded rosettes. It was pulled by four, beautiful, bay horses. The carriage came up alongside him. The man inside leaned out. He was young, dark, and well manicured. His nose was round as his chin and cheeks. His features smiled without his face meaning them to. "Where are you going?" he asked in low German.

"Bavaria. I was robbed," Adam sighed in disbelief. "And now I'm walking back to Munich."

"Munich?" the man scoffed. "Would you like a ride?" His dark hair was curled in a strange fashion at his temples.

"I would be grateful. They took my boots, too," said Adam.

"My name is Mayer Bauer... of Frankfurt. I'm on my way to Ingolstadt."

"I go to the University," said Adam.

"Well then, please, accompany me and we shall talk along the way. How does that sound?" The driver got down and opened the door for Adam. Adam got in and took the soft, silk bench across from Mayer, who was finely dressed in a black goatskin suit with a white ruffled shirt. Adam surmised Mayer was at least a head, maybe two, shorter than he, so small was his stature.

Adam told him of the details of the robbery, of the grisly appearance of the leader of the thieves, and how he had nearly lost his life.

Mayer opened a compartment beneath the bench and pulled out a crystal decanter and two balloons. "Brandy?" he asked. "It always calms my nerves."

"Please," answered Adam, for he had not eaten or drunk anything since the day before leaving Hamburg. "I have a brother in Virginia," said Adam with pride. "He was supposed to have sent a shipment of Indian hemp to Hamburg for me. I waited there for many days, and while I did so, I came upon a great load of abandoned books."

"Books?" asked Mayer.

"An entire library of the most... enthralling of works." Adam told him of the scrolls and books that he had had in his possession, works in Greek, Italian, Hebrew, and Aramaic. He hinted at the occult nature of the books, but did not trust this new acquaintance well enough to disclose too many details.

They stopped at an inn in the woods. They sat at a table beneath a tree and ate bowls of venison soup, and then cocoa cakes with sour cherries, and talked of the fashion of coffee and how both of them much preferred it to tea.

"The Prince hates coffee. He says it gives him the worst bad breath," said Mayer.

"I'm surprised he could smell it over his politics," laughed Weishaupt. "As long as he doesn't outlaw the coffee. It's so ridiculous when they outlaw things they don't have a taste for. Especially when it's not doing anyone any harm."

"Kings are capricious and governments easily

corruptible," said Mayer.

"We should do away with them all. They have done nothing for the state of mankind that we couldn't have done better for ourselves. They're nothing but fancily dressed tax collectors. They simply have enough money to gouge *more money* from the people. Had they no cooperation from their minions and adversity from the common people, they would have no gold, and therefore no power, and they would fall, and we would all be free of them and their ridiculous laws."

"I couldn't be more in agreement, but please don't ever say that I said that," said Mayer, twisting the gold ring on his little finger.

They rode along through the forest, listening to the songs of the birds that rang out through the trees. Adam could identify most of their calls because of his lessons with Brother Ivor, and taught their names to Mayer.

They were riding along in this manner when suddenly Mayer looked with horror out the window and exclaimed "Oy!"

Adam saw it, too. It was a wagon on the side of the road. Draped over the side of the drivers' bench was one of the thieves. Where his face had been, appeared to be a pile of chopped, raw meat. The others lay strewn all around it, dead, their faces mutilated like the first, their eyes pecked out. Ravens scattered from the scene as Mayer's coach drew near.

"My wagon..." whispered Adam, in shock, as the carriage came to a stop. Cautiously both men climbed out.

"This is your wagon?" asked Mayer incredulous. "And these are the men who stole it?"

"Yes," he breathed.

The horses danced nervously in their yokes. They, the wagon itself, and its contents seemed unscathed as Adam went around, inspecting the animals for injuries. He guessed that whatever had happened, had befallen these thieves only a short time ago.

Upon the bench in a pool of blood lay the strange knife given him by the innkeeper.

His eyes darted around as Mayer clutched the back of Adam's shirt, "Leave it all and let's be on our way! Quickly, man! Whatever, whomever has done this may still be lingering."

Adam stood, searching the depths of the forest that concealed the mystery of their murders in its dark thickets. No birds sang, and all was eerily silent.

"I have to take the wagon," Adam said. "It belongs to a friend, one of my brothers at Lodge Theodore. I can't leave it. I'll follow you."

Whatever had happened to the robbers, they undoubtedly deserved it, and Adam was too happy to have regained the lost books. He felt a bit strange to take the dead man's seat as he shoved his corpse over the side. He climbed onto the bench and wiped the blood from the knife and dropped into his satchel. He grasped the reigns and maneuvered the horses around the bodies and back onto the road.

They quickly left the cursed place and the robbers to the scavengers of the woods. Adam thought better of claiming his boots off the dead man's feet. He stared over his shoulder as they took off down the road, for fear of something following him, and fought off the horrid images of razor-clawed monsters that came roiling to mind from *The Book of Xxxxxxxxxxxxx.* He shuddered and tried not to think of what had befallen them as he drove away from the grisly scene, grateful to be in the company of Mayer's carriage.

When he got back to the dormitory in Ingolstadt, he found a letter from his brother waiting for him, explaining that the British had delayed all exports for inspection and that the promised shipment of hemp had been sitting in port in Virginia, unbeknownst to him. Adam was disappointed, but kissed fate for the load of sacred books into which he dove headfirst. He had collected more than he imagined, and many of them were in decent shape. He spent weeks restoring them, carefully separating their fragile pages and unrolling the scrolls and drying them all over Ickstatt's office.

At the very bottom of the pile, there was a simple box carved out of a single piece of dark wood. Weishaupt picked it up and examined it. Something rattled inside. He found the knife he had gotten from the inn in Hamburg and gingerly loosened the only seams of the box. A lid slid off and inside was another very old sliver of wood. He didn't know what to make of it. He brought the box to the window and scanned it. The only mark it bore was a small cross with four tiny hash marks coming out from its center.

Ickstatt's clock chimed and Adam realized he would be late for the viewing of the animal dissection. He was to take careful notes and make drawings for Ickstatt's records. The Baron had other plans this evening and would not be attending as usual, so Adam was to go and have his front row seat and record the procedures.

The University of Ingolstadt had only recently installed Europe's foremost observation theatre, a three story high stand of seating overlooking a ground-floor demonstration stage. The venue was large enough to seat several hundred spectators.

Every Friday since its inception, Dr. Gunstein, the head of the medical arts department, demonstrated some facet of bodily systems with a live or deceased subject. The medical students were required to attend, and any others who found such graphic displays of animal functions intriguing also attended. Adam sat in the Dean's seat, feeling a bit conspicuous as he took copious notes and artfully diagrammed the scene.

Dr. Gunstein had already begun his dissection of the

stiff, white corpse of a young man who had died of the wasting. He had completely removed the skin on one of his legs and was now connecting a clip and wire to the muscles just below his kneecap. Dr. Gunstein wound a crank and sent a current of electricity into the corpse's leg, making it jump. He changed the placement of the wires to a different muscle in the front of the tibia, and made the corpse's toes curl forward. After seven or eight unnerving shows of bodily contortion of the corpse, Adam felt that he had adequately captured the gist of the experiment, and didn't think he could stomach anymore. He reached in his satchel and found a copy of a book called *Sephir Yetzirah* and began to read.

He felt eyes on him and looked over. Sitting across the mezzanine from him was Mayer Bauer, the man in whose coach he had ridden after he had been robbed.

After the laboratory demonstration was concluded, Adam shook Mayer's hand, and the two of them went to the biergarten to have a drink.

"I couldn't help but notice you were reading that book," said Mayer, pointing at it in Adam's satchel. "...in Hebrew."

Adam got it out, flipped through it. "Yes, it's quite interesting. The Qabala, I don't know if it's a veritable-"

"Of course it is. Have you heard of *The Zohar*?"

"I believe I have that in my collection. Is it something I should read?"

"Most definitely, my friend. *The Zohar* speaks of the divine marriage, the sacred acts that bring us closer to God. It is the ancient wisdom of a Rabbi and his son. They were confined to a cave for ten years and there they heard the voice of God explaining the Torah to them."

They discussed the Pentateuch, metaphysics, and modern philosophy, and Mayer invited Adam to come back home to Frankfurt with him when the University let out for midyear, so that they could continue their discussion of Jewish mysticism.

CHAPTER XVII

It was there at the Bauers' mansion in Frankfurt am Main that Adam first met her. Her eyes were a deep violet, like the sky above the sea before dawn. Her fine skin was sheer perfection and her beautiful face was sweeter than any he had ever beheld. Her long blonde hair was crowned with jewels, and cascaded over her bare arms. She was strong and healthy as if she engaged in some daily athletic activity. Adam wondered what it could be, as he sat across the table from her at dinner and made polite conversation with her in Czech about rabbits, an innuendo that brought a smirk to her delicious mouth. Princess Eva was her name and she was barely fifteen.

According to Mayer, her mother was Catherine the Great and her father was Jacob Frank a Jewish mystic, and veritable messiah, who had been jailed and exiled for heresy over his interpretation of *The Zohar*.

"He is the reincarnation of King David, and Rabbi Sabbatei Tzvi, the true Messiah," said Mayer of Eva's father. "My family has taken it upon themselves to preserve Yakob's line through Eva."

Adam had never heard of Frank or Sabbatei Tzvi and looked at Eva for verification. She blushed scarlet at the mention of her exiled father. They politely dropped the subject for fear of embarrassing the girl further and Mayer gave Adam a look that intimated they would speak of it privately at some later time.

"She's magnificent," he sighed to Mayer when she was out of earshot.

She had barely whispered a word back to Adam. But there was something in her strange eyes the way she looked at him, that ate at him. He knew that although she did find him an attractive and desirable partner, she could never act on it. Adam was so far below her class, his even being at the same table as she was a surreal encounter for them both. Adam gathered that Mayer's wealthy parents had taken in young Eva after Jacob Frank had been imprisoned, promising to find her a husband of wealth who could overlook her father's unusual personality and predicament.

One night, he found her watching him from a balcony overlooking the garden, and held her gaze. He relished the seconds that it lasted and traveled back there in his mind countless times. How she had looked at him... He began to fantasize about her and made no excuses to Mayer for wanting to come and visit him in Frankfurt whenever possible.

At the University, his mind often wandered to thoughts of her. What was she doing at this moment? Was she thinking of him, of being with him? She was but a girl, too young for such thoughts. It would be years before she would consider a husband, he told himself. But he was grievously mistaken.

The next Christmas, her engagement was announced. It was toasted over braised pheasants by Mayer's father, that Princess Eva would marry the Comte Valois-Kolmstecht. Adam was devastated, and as he gazed upon her incomparable beauty, he could not hide his disappointment. The arrangement obviously had been made for her, by the elder Herr Bauer who was her guardian these many long years while her father was in exile in Brno.

Adam sat in the garden cursing fate and the myriad of restrictive social customs, and smoking the Indian hemp that Mayer had sent for from the islands of the Far East. It was a different strain than George's for it had a reddish purple hue and was quite a bit more heady. The smoke brushed his face and filled his nose and he thought back to

161

the brief span of time before tonight when the possibility of his having Eva still existed. Marriage was so final, so cruel. He thought of all the ways he could change this sorry fate, and resolved to take some sort of action, though he knew not what.

It was nearly midnight and everyone else had gone to bed. Christmas Eve was tomorrow, though it mattered little in a house belonging to Jews. Still, it was a magical time for Adam, and he felt the festive charge of the season in the air.

Eva appeared behind him, silent as a ghost in a winter fox robe, and sat down next to him. "Why do you sit here so sad?" she whispered.

"Because you will never be mine," he replied at last.

She touched his hand. They gazed at each other for a long moment, then he pressed her hand between his and kissed it sorrowfully. How he longed for her, longed to be this near and nearer to her. He knew that they were being watched by dutiful servants, but it was not his reputation that would be harmed by their indiscretion.

"Come with me," she said as her lips brushed his ear. He looked at her beautiful face in exhilaration and disbelief.

She led him by the hand through the sleeping house. It was silent, and their whispers and footsteps were muffled by the thick carpets and tapestries.

Her chamber was dark and warm. As soon as the door was bolted, he kissed her and his hands slid over her smooth skin. Her fur robe fell away revealing her nubile body that was unbelievably velvety and exquisite. She let him stare at her, her chin turned so that it rested in the hollow above her collarbone. She was divine, with wisps of blond hair at her neck. He felt a charge of electricity and a hot inescapable magnetic pull as he kissed her and touched her. As she whispered in his ear of how they would be joined in a sacred union, he penetrated her and knew that he had neither felt nor imagined a greater pleasure. She moved to complement him and seized upon his member in an endless procession of joyous explosions. For one so young, Eva seemed experienced beyond his reckoning as she introduced him to pleasures he never imagined possible. She looked heavenward and murmured a prayer in Hebrew that conjured a strange, tangible ball of ecstatic electricity between their hearts. Adam's fascination only heightened his arousal, for she was verily a mystic, herself.

Of the many highly-seasoned prostitutes he had enjoyed, none had ever made him feel like she did, for she endeared herself to him in so many countless ways. She rode on him in ways he had never before fathomed and that for hours. He found her legs wrapped around his back as she raised and lowered herself on him. His release was held in check by the strange power she held over him, for she had captured him and controlled him. He cupped her breasts, teasing her hard nipples, as he thrust into her. She cried out in her beautiful voice, so like the voice of the angel he had heard in the inn in Hamburg. And when he finally joined her, he was overcome with a tingling jubilant lightness, as his heart, mind and pelvis sang out like a chorus of angels as he imbued her with his power. They were suspended in ecstasy for many long minutes, kissing and murmuring divine words to each other.

When they had made love eleven times, Adam lay next to her in her satin bed, shaking. She kissed him on his mouth and down his nose, then pushed aside his locks of hair and whispered, "I was made for you."

"When will I see you again?" he asked.

She whispered in his ear for him not to worry about her marriage, that it meant little more than a social contract, and with that open-ended promise, they reveled in each other until daybreak.

Eva was in love with *him* and he with her. And it was like nothing he had ever felt before. Smirking he glided all

163

the way back to his dormitory in Ingolstadt. His feet barely touched the ground, for he knew that she was truly his, no matter to whom she was married.

Many a night, he lay awake in bed, willing his astral body to find her, to be transported to her, but his desire for her was too great, too physical, and prevented him from leaving his body, else he would have found her and made love to her every night.

The invitation to her wedding came, detailed in gold and sealed with a faceted amethyst in the wax. He returned the card that confirmed he would be present and enclosed a special note to her.

My Dearest Eva,

Your horse is broken now and stands ready for you to mount. Please accept him as a wedding gift from your dear friend. You would be wise to forsake all other beasts in light of this one who dreams of you, the rider for whom he was made.

Respectfully yours,
Johann Joseph Adam Weishaupt

He hoped that she would read it and not the groom's mother. He ached to speak with her again, but all his letters went unanswered. He had no occasion to see her, not till her wedding day, and desperately counted the days until it came. Mayer would be there, and several others he knew. He fantasized that his friends would help them escape when she left her despicable groom at the altar.

Adam took a coach with Mayer through the Black Forest. They drank four bottles of wine on the way, and merrily discussed Judaism and Catholicism. Adam confessed that he had been born into a Jewish family.

"That's why I'm your friend," said Mayer matter-of-factly. "I could tell you were one of us."

"Please don't tell anyone," said Adam. He did not wish to jeopardize his career, for there was and had always been much prejudice against Jews, especially among the Jesuits. He hoped that Mayer did not take offense, for none was intended.

Mayer laughed, lifted a scolding finger and was about to reprimand him, then suddenly something outside the coach caught his eye. "Stop! Stop the coach!" He cried, peering through the curtains and jumping out the door before it had even come to a stop.

Adam looked and there in a tiny clearing, a single blessed ray of sunshine fell upon a fairy ring of purple-tinged mushrooms. Adam got out of the coach and beheld the magical sight.

"Do you know what these are?" asked Mayer crouching down and pointing to them with a silly grin.

"They're mushrooms," Adam replied.

"Yes, but have you ever eaten them before?"

"Of course I've had mushrooms. They've a delicious taste, a chewy texture," Adam assured him.

Mayer laughed. "No, no, no. This kind is not delicious. Come, help me pick them. You'll be amazed, my friend, amazed. Give the cap a little tap-tap before you pull them up," Mayer handed him the driver's hat to fill, and the two of them picked all the mushrooms, tapping caps and pulling them up by the roots. When they had filled three hats and emptied them on the roof of the coach to dry, they got back inside and continued on their way.

At last, a fantastic, white palace appeared through the trees. Colorful silken banners flew from every turret, and fabulous coaches lined the drive.

Servants dressed in finer clothing than any Adam had

ever seen showed him and Mayer out of the coach.
Weishaupt felt a lump in his throat, he was so overcome
by the splendor and sheer scale of the place. Fountains of
marble more ornately carved than anything he had ever
seen lined the walkway, creating an arching canopy of
water overhead.

"Mayer, look at that!" exclaimed Adam, pointing to
some pilasters, each carved with an illustrated chapter of
Homer's Odyssey.

"Kitsch," tut-tutted Mayer.

They came to another magnificent, gold gate that was
raised for them. Diaphanous silks hemmed with jewels
hung from the lintels above, and fluttered softly in the
gentle breeze. Orchids had been planted on either side of
the grassy path. Adam estimated how much money the
smallest detail cost and saw that in his whole existence, he
had not spent or even seen so much money. And it all
belonged to Eva, or rather, to her new husband. Adam
could never compete with such wealth and grandeur. How
could he even have dared to dream?

He sighed bitterly at the tragedy that was playing out
with him as the helpless central figure. Fate seemed to be
calling him to act, but what was he supposed to do? Why
had he done nothing to stop this wedding from taking
place when the woman he loved was to be taken away
from him?

As he looked around at the lavish palace, he felt the icy,
hard slap of high society, how exclusive and malevolent it
was with its trappings and affectations and fineries. A
sickness overcame him at the thought of her marrying this
man who was so far above his own station. He felt sweat
beading on his brow.

"The groom's father is the most powerful man in the
Rhineland and he will inherit his title in a few years. Eva
is making a very good match," said Mayer, seeming to
read his mind. *"There's nothing you can do about it,"* he

said with finality.

Adam put his head in his hand as he walked, unable to hide his emotions that had been so stirred up by the wine and the breathtaking beauty of the palace.

They came into the main garden, surrounded by crystal clear pools, reflecting the wonderland of rare flora that was planted all around the array of pagan statues. They were led to the left side of the aisle and seated behind the Wittelsbachs, the dignitaries of the Valuderberg Republic and the Bavarian court.

"At least we've got good seats," Adam said, aware of the many guests filling in the rows behind them.

"Of course we do," said Mayer. "You're with me."

From what Adam had gleaned, the Bauers had pockets as deep and as vast as the ocean itself. He reminded himself hollowly that there were different kinds of wealth, not just the monetary kind. Mayer was a remarkable fellow and a good friend, but he would never have the looks, the physical prowess, or the rapier mind that Adam took for granted. Let him have his gold.

Adam looked around the garden in amazement. Each aisle was marked with a cherubim carved of clear crystal, and the long benches on which they sat were crafted of the finest hardwood and inlaid with pearl and topaz. He had never witnessed such grandeur, and he was so in awe of it, he began to weep.

Mayer looked worriedly at him and handed him a handkerchief. "This is a happy occasion. Please…"

Adam regained his composure, but lost it again when Eva appeared at the end of the garden on Moses Bauer's arm, in a splendorous gown of gold brocade, adorned with diamonds and pink rubies that sparkled like stars in the afternoon sun. Its train trailed for yards behind her as she walked unbearably slowly toward her intended at the altar. Adam looked at her fine face, just visible beneath her veil and thought her beautiful as ever, but hypnotized, fixated on that which lay before her. Burning with jealous rage, he scrutinized her groom and wondered what lines had crossed to make him; why was *he* the one to have her? Adam swiped away his tears. Why hadn't he done away with this man before now?

Through her veil, Eva glanced at him as she passed his row. He looked sidelong at her. Never had he seen such magnificence, and to think - for one night she had given herself completely to him. She had been his, and if he was not so stupid, so inept, so poor, he could have her still. This could be his own wedding instead of that despicable rat waiting for her at the altar.

"Damn it," he cursed aloud and put his head in his hand. Mayer kicked him gently.

He watched bitterly as she pledged herself away in the Lutheran wedding ceremony. He fortified himself against her, thinking viscerally of her, and focused his energies on strangling her smug-faced, velvet-covered groom, yet only succeeded in making him cough. What a whore she was. How she had betrayed him. It was in these moments that he felt something in himself irrevocably turn. The youth he had been only moments before, was killed by the cruelty of his fate. The sacrament of marriage became to him the most loathsome act of betrayal of the self, and he scorned the tradition, customs, and necessity of the entire institution. Marriage was a joke, a mockery of what was supposed to be divine love between a man and woman, and in this case, as in most, it was nothing but an insensible financial contract wrought for the rights of breeding and transference of estates.

Finally the charade was at its end. The celebrant presented the couple, and a thousand snow-white doves were let loose into the sky. Applause rang out as the couple exchanged kisses. Adam felt a cold sweat run down his back and he wanted to vomit. He did not clap with the others, but stared so hard at Eva that he drew her gaze to him. She stared back at him as the guests applauded their union.

"I love you," he mouthed at her brazenly.

She looked away, to happier faces for congratulations.

Adam and Mayer trailed the other guests into an alcove designed after an Indian temple, where a virtual sea of powdered, white wigs floated above an extravagant buffet, chatting merrily and filling their plates with sumptuous food. Roasted chops of lamb, crustaceans and butter, the finest cuts of roast beef, candied vegetables, cherries soaked in liqueur, Persian honey cakes. Some of it was so strange and exotic, he couldn't guess what it was. It was a shame he felt too sad to eat. A jaunty, young organist, who could have been no more than twelve, accompanied by three violinists played joyous music for dancing, music that mocked his grave misfortune with its brilliance and frivolity.

They found the wine and a group of people Mayer knew from summer in the South of France. They spoke of "bateaux" and when Weishaupt could no longer feign interest, he sat down on the edge of a fountain. He leaned over to glance at his reflection and saw his handsome face, his long, aristocratic nose and deep-set eyes. His fine, curvaceous mouth turned down at the corners, and as hard as he tried, he could not lift it into anything close to a pleasant expression. The water rippled, but his own sadness was all the fountain would reveal. Perhaps he would be sad forever. Did this girl really matter to him? There was something magical about her. There was no denying it. He had felt her presence was of a higher resonance, more perfect than others, from the moment he met her. There would never be another one like her and now she was gone, married to someone else and out of his reach, forever.

Grief chewed at him, making his stomach feel taut and

hollow as the guests' laughter and voices crackled above the mirthful music. He drank to make the cold emptiness go away while he watched the richest nobility on earth rub elbows. He was embittered that the occasion made him unable to be his gregarious self and take advantage of the chance to fraternize with so elite a crowd. The chance might never come again. Weishaupt drank more wine and pictured Eva turning to him during the ceremony, declaring her love for him, and marrying him instead of that toad. He pictured setting loose a legion of demons upon the wedded couple, demons who would annihilate Lothar and deliver Eva back to him. Barely able to keep his balance, Adam downed the most delicious wine he had ever tasted and resolved to make off with as many bottles as Mayer's carriage could hold.

Mayer was suddenly in his ear, "We're staying here tonight. I forgot to tell you about my invitation."

Weishaupt hadn't thought about it. "I was just going to lie down in the hedge over there. Do you think anyone will mind?"

"Yes," replied Mayer. "Don't embarrass me, please."

Eva and Lothar reappeared to applause and congratulations and Adam wondered if they had consummated the marriage. He remembered the laces down the back of the bridal gown and doubted that they had had time enough to get the bride's dress off, copulate, and get dressed again in a single hour. The thought was comforting.

Mayer and Weishaupt joined the queue to congratulate them. When it was his turn, he bowed to them both and said, "May you find true bliss."

"Danke," she whispered, offering her hand to be kissed. Weishaupt took it and kissed it a little too ardently under Lothar's suspicious eye. He heard her soft, feminine sigh of pity and remorse as his lips touched her skin, and he stood looking at her until she turned from him.

When the guests were gone and the party ended, Mayer and Weishaupt were shown to their rooms in the palace.

"Look in the armoire," Mayer said, pointing a gilded monstrosity with pearl-inlaid doors as big as two rowboats. "There should be a bathing suit to fit you. We're going swimming in the pool. It's heated from the bottom like a real Roman bath."

Weishaupt swiped at the armoire, then sat down on the satin canopy bed and fell back, letting the room spin as it may. He dozed for a few minutes and awoke in a somewhat better condition than that in which he'd fallen, though he was not willing to be cajoled.

Mayer came into his room and roused him. "Come on! The pool!"

A full moon reflected in the steaming water of the swimming pool. It was huge, oval, and made of pink marble with a fish-shaped fountain at the far end.

Mayer sat down, laughing giddily and splashing his feet in the water. He was hirsute, with thick black fur on his calves and on top of his shoulders.

"You look like an orangutan," Adam said bitterly.

Mayer jumped up and chased him around the pool, laughing and cursing at him. Weishaupt finally dove into the water and swam across the pool. The water was sobering and soothing, and when he surfaced, he saw the bare feet of Eva and her bridesmaids standing beside the water. Weishaupt looked up at her.

"Did you have a good time at my wedding?" she asked, swirling the water with her toe.

"No," he said. "I loathed every minute of it."

Her red lips curved into a smile. Weishaupt watched as her maids dropped their robes on the ground.

"Where is your new husband?" he asked her.

"Sleeping off the wedding wine," she replied as she stepped down into the water. Her long blonde hair hid her breasts. Her body was sleek and her skin tawny olive and smooth.

Weishaupt caught his breath as she slipped into the water next to him, brushed close then swam away, stirring his desire anew.

"Why do you and Mayer insist on wearing those ridiculous suits? Are you too modest, or are you hiding something?" she asked.

Her bridesmaids giggled. Adam peeled off his wet bathing suit and flung it into some foliage nearby. Mayer looked at the water.

"Take yours off, too," she plied Mayer.

"I need to wear a bathing suit. Otherwise I get cold," said Mayer. "All this hair is for aesthetics, not warmth."

The bridesmaids swam over to him and pulled him into the water, attempting to remove his bathing suit. Mayer fought them and jumped out of the pool saying he'd return in a moment.

Weishaupt was locked in Eva's sphere as she drew him across the water toward her. He said a silent prayer that her husband would sleep peacefully all night.

"So what do you do now that you're married?" he asked solemnly, keeping a prudent distance from her.

"I'm going to go places I haven't been in a long time."

"Like where?"

"Where do you want to meet me?" she said in a low voice, her soft eyes shining.

Weishaupt looked around to see who heard. A servant turned and walked inside. "Anywhere," he whispered. "I'd give anything to be with you again."

Mayer returned then, holding something behind his back. "Guess what I have?" And he presented a hat full of mushrooms. "Mushrooms! Did you forget?" and he popped one into the mouth of one of the brides' maidens. The girl made a horrible face and spat it out.

He handed some to Adam and Eva. She put several into her mouth and washed them down with a drink of champagne. "Ugh, that's revolting."

Adam followed suit. The mushrooms tasted sickeningly musty, but he ate them and several more. "What is this supposed to do?"

"It's magic," said Mayer as he climbed back into the water with the bridesmaids. "Magic mushrooms."

The vile taste of the mushrooms turned Adam's tender stomach and he wondered why they had all eaten them. It was then they were distracted by the sweet sound of a violin. A dark-haired man who had sat in front of them at the wedding ceremony appeared playing a Stradivarius. He was thin and wore an unusual suit of clothes, none like Adam had ever seen, and seemed himself, powdery pale and strange. As he played, a fine white powder puffed up from the insides of the violin, dusting his eyebrows that arched wickedly. His nose had a decided sneer.

"Uncle!" exclaimed Eva. "What do you have in your violin?"

He plucked at the violin, making more of the powder puff up, "Coca, my darling."

"I knew it! I love you!" Eva leapt out of the water and kissed her uncle on the lips. He let his hands caress her bare backside. "My uncle is the Count de St. Germain, of Paris," she looked back at Adam.

"Is that so?" Adam asked, wishing this "uncle" would depart.

Adam extended his hand to shake, and to his surprise felt the familiar grip of the freemason. The Count's eyes twinkled. They were disarmingly pale and blue like some strange dog's. His black pupils seemed to flicker in the middle of them as if they were slipping in his head.

"Indeed," replied Adam, suddenly noticing the purples, greens and pinks in the flesh of his face. Adam had heard of the age-old immortal, Count de St. Germain, from Serafina, but this gentleman was not at all the type of person he had expected. Adam watched him closely, said

173

nothing, but suspected if there was such a fellow, this was not he.

While Eva sniffed coca through a reed from the insides of the Count's violin, Adam stared around him at the world that had suddenly taken on the strange quality of being made up of millions of tiny inlaid pieces, each in itself a perfect jewel.

The Count smiled at him and offered him the reed. "Drugs were given to man by the gods so he could see and understand the myriad of life and witness the underpinnings of the fabric of his own existence..: Sniff, so that we all may lead deeper, more meaningful lives."

"Is that so?" Adam knew he'd recently read something that corroborated that in one of his books, but he could no longer pronounce the words to communicate the quote, so he simply took the reed and sniffed the bitter powder from the violin. He felt immediately invigorated, strangely, eagerly awake while the mushrooms continued to awaken and amplify his senses with beautiful hallucinations.

As the Count continued to play his violin, and shoot him strange grimaces, Adam looked to the heavens and was catapulted to a place where his cares were of no consequence, a world where only love and bliss existed. And he was there with Eva, smitten, his loins on fire, heart open and bleeding out for her. The water in the pool was warm and seemed to embrace them and unite them in a sea of feeling. Where one ended and the other began, it was not possible for Adam to tell, as he felt her sweet breath above the water. She loved him, and he her.

He saw God in those violet eyes and marveled at the feminine magnificence she epitomized, the incarnation of some goddess she was, and she was before him, staring into his soul and holding him there.

"You know I can never resist you, Adam Weishaupt." When she spoke, she talked into him, each of her words reverberated and lived a life of its own, as it floated through the air and twinkled, becoming part of this crescendo of love like he had never felt before - though he had absolutely no idea what she was saying.

He turned then and became aware of Mayer and the others watching them. Mayer tut-tutted disapprovingly, and the bridesmaids turned away.

Adam literally couldn't resist Eva. He pulled her to him and kissed her luscious mouth, and then down her fragrant neck.

"Not here," she whispered and took him by the hand and led him up the steps out of the pool. "Come," she said to him.

She pulled him through the maze of silken tapestries that fluttered in the nighttime breeze. He ripped one down and covered their nakedness, drawing it around their shoulders. They came to the garden wall. Eva pulled an iron latch in the wall, and a hidden panel opened. Adam marveled as they entered and climbed the spiraling stairs.

At the top was an airy spot for a tryst with large, open windows on either side. A canopied bed and a spectacular bowl of fruit on a table beside it, awaited them.

The room, with its gilded walls and sparkling draperies, seemed to Adam to be the most fabulous and magical place he'd ever witnessed. He looked at her perfect face and tasted the salty sweetness of life. Their skin was hot and generated such intense electricity with its friction that his hair stood on end.

She lay down on the bed, her damp tresses spilling across the crimson pillows. He was in awe of her body, being given to him on her wedding night. But this was how it was supposed to be. This was what fate had intended, what the stars had commanded. He knew it. He ached to join her and no sooner was he inside her, filling her. She spun immediately, holding his body close and kissing him deeply. He swallowed the sweet juice of her mouth and thrust into her slowly, her body enveloping him so divinely. He looked up at the ceiling medallions and tapestries and saw them come alive, growing, undulating. He felt his excruciating release into her. A soft, angelic voice sang as he ascended up into the dome of a Heavenly Cathedral made of gilt and jewels.

Then a voice spoke to him "Hush, you are in the Abode of the Lord," it said, and he felt himself filled with the ecstasy of love. He marveled at the wonder of this place to which he had been transported, for never had he seen anything so beautiful and splendorous. The palace had come close, but this heavenly place was made entirely of gold and many-colored jewels, more pure and precious than any that he had ever seen. His vision lasted only a few seconds, and then he fell back to earth, opened his eyes, and she was there beneath him, soft and hot, and desirous of more love.

They lay together utterly engaged, in a state of electric bliss. He felt her soft breath on his shoulder and wanted to devour her, drink her, take her as a part of himself once more.

"Eva!" came a man's voice.

"It's Lothar!" she said, her eyes wide with horror. "We can't let him find us together!"

Adam put his hand to her face, and with the other, he held her fast by the arm. "I'll kill him and take you as my own. Be mine, Eva. Please."

"Don't be stupid, Adam," she pulled away and said. "We're only lovers!"

"What?" he asked. Her words struck him cold. He heard the sound of Lothar running up the stairs. He looked down. He was naked. There was an open window, the starry sky and a gentle breeze. He climbed up on the sill...

The next thing he felt was the hard jolt of the ground meeting him and the wet grass prickling his palms and face. The wind was knocked from him for it had been at least twenty feet that he had jumped from the window. He couldn't quite remember now what had just happened, though it had been only a moment ago.

He found himself outside the palace wall at the edge of the Black Forest. A dragon or a bird swooped at him from above. He fought it as it covered him. He pulled it off and found it to be a silk robe that had fluttered down upon him. The cool wind reminded him of his unclothed state and he hurriedly put on this gift from above. Where were his boots? Where was Mayer? Adam wondered briefly if his carriage was here waiting for them. Perhaps he could go get in the carriage. But it was inside the gates of the castle and he doubted he could get back inside without alarming anyone.

He stood, breathed deeply, felt the zeal of the night enter into him. Something was different suddenly, new, uncharted. The Schwarzwald seemed to rustle with breath. The white rocks of the road sparkled, leading him into the Black Forest, the place of enchantment and danger. He was not afraid and his energy seemed limitless. There was no one, no beast so angry and full of wrath and power as he that he could not bring down, and he swaggered into the mysterious unseeable blackness of the wood.

Blind in the darkness he was led by some power he trusted but didn't understand. Thoughts of exacting revenge on Lothar and all the ways that he could kill him, undo him, clamored in his head. He wanted to lie down and tell himself to find Lothar, but he could not relax. His heart raced. His feet seemed to leave the road, carrying him through a field, then cresting a hill. On and on he walked by the light of the stars, for miles, consumed by his hatred, his thoughts of murder, his heartbreak over losing Eva. He did love her, and most unequivocally so. And he had been spurned by life again. What had she to gain by uniting herself in this way with someone who was not meant for her?

He felt the tickle of long grasses against his legs. He

looked up and found himself in a field of barley.

A sphere on a post floated at the end of the row and struck something deep inside him. He stood, aghast, unprepared, and immobile as the horrible memory came flooding back before his eyes.

CHAPTER XIII

He was awakened by the loud crash of the front door falling in downstairs. From his dark little room, he heard his father and mother awaken and the baby start to cry. The sound of heavy boots running up the stairs... Adam shrank beneath his blankets as the footsteps clomped on the landing. He heard his mother scream. His father shouted no, please, they didn't understand.

Adam's door fell open, too. They caught him before he had the chance to hide. Hard hands gripped his arm cruelly and he was dragged from his bed, down the staircase out into the cold darkness by a thick, bearded man whose cruel grip on his shoulder rendered him immobile.

What was the reason for this? Adam looked desperately around for something that made sense. He saw their things come outside, too. Father's books, the big copper kettle, a box of coins, some quilts and shoes. They were tossed from one person to the next and lost in the crowd. There was a mob of people, armed with sticks aflame. He heard the chickens clucking as they too were taken from the coop. The men's eyes shone in the torchlight as they beat and kicked his father on the ground. "Sorcerer! Devil Jew!"

His mother screamed and pleaded that they were not. The circle of men around his father closed in and he heard him begging for all their lives. "Please let us live... Whatever you want, I'll give it to you."

Adam bit the man's arm, tasted his blood.

178

"Little fiend!" the man cursed and let him go.

Adam tore away and ran to see his parents. "Mother! Mother!" he shouted.

He saw her face, helpless, horrified. "My baby! Run away, Adam!" she screamed at him.

Adam ran to the top of the street. He heard his father scream, a horrible, sickening noise, then suddenly stop. A roar of laughter and jeers arose from the crowd.

It was then that he looked back and saw their heads raised up on poles, cut-off at the neck, and bouncing like some macabre, dancing puppets, their house blazing on fire behind them. And he curled into a ball beneath a bench outside a shop and closed his eyes.

Now, so many years later, beneath the cool, starry sky, he walked barefooted toward the sphere at the end of the row of barley. Overcome with emotion, he reached out and touched it, and realized it was a gourd. A tatter of cloth hung about it. Someone had made a scarecrow. He felt the lumpy flesh of the gourd as the hot tears rolled down his face. Burning behind his eyes, he cried out for the terrible loss of the people who loved him. He saw their heads bobbing on the ends of two poles in his mind's eye, and remembered them in life – his mother and his father. He saw them clearly now, his mother so dark and beautiful and kind; his father, lighter with the same wise green eyes as his own. His father patted his head and showed him the stars. He felt their love all around him.

He lay down on the soft earth and cried for them, for the grave injustice that had been done to them. And what had happened to the baby? The thought of the fate of the little one, his little brother, laid him out on the ground, and he hugged the earth in desperation for understanding.

After some time, he rolled over onto his back and made out the constellations. He was coming back to his senses somewhat. He felt himself. He was there. He had himself, if no one else in the world. And he was good, even if he had been born a Jew. He wondered what would happen if he meditated on something pleasant. He regained control of his faculties and counted his blessings – YVWH, Christ, Eva, Mayer, Ickstatt, his brother in Virginia, the University, his books, and his abilities. He would find his way back home, back to school where he belonged. He pictured himself vividly - a scholar, a professor of canon law, making his way up through the intellectual community and social strata to a status that would be worthy of the woman he loved, to a position that would enable him to avenge the family that had been stolen from him.

He returned to the comfort and simplicity of the University and threw himself into his studies. Baron Ickstatt noticed the change in him and sat him down in his office.

"Since the summer, you have been different," he said to Adam.

"I remembered what happened when my parents died," Adam said, looking out the window at a faraway mountain.

"I am sorry," said Ickstatt.

"I'm a Jew," said Adam simply.

Ickstatt sat on the edge of his desk and took a deep breath. "Do you know the history of our Jesuit Church? Do you know about St. Ignatius and how he started the Society of Jesus?"

"Only what they taught me at St. Michael's. Dates and facts and things, I suppose I do. Why is that important?"

"St. Ignatius was a Jew, a Jew who was persecuted for being a heretic. To keep himself, his family, and the other Jews in his community from being killed, he began the Jesuit Order and converted all the Jews who were in similar danger to the Christian faith through the Sacrament of Baptism. The Jesuits have always kept the faith of their ancestors. Christianity, for many of them, was only their cloak of protection. The early Jesuits and many of us, to this day, believe mainly in the old books of the law, in the Talmud."

"So you're telling me that our Jesuit community is actually a hotbed of closeted Judaism?"

"Now most are truly believers in Christ, as I am," Ickstatt said. "But that is not how we began. The Jesuit Order is and has always been a safe haven for practicing Jews." His voice was a cautious whisper now. "You are not alone if you doubt Christ and the exegesis of the Church. But listen to me, Adam, it is not safe or wise to be openly Jewish. I know you fraternize with the Moses Bauers. They're a very distinguished and wealthy family, and those with money are safe to do as they please. Intellectuals of no means, such as yourself, however, must practice discretion, especially if you are to stay at this University and take over your father's position."

"I see," said Adam, glancing around at the great lot of books he had left in Ickstatt's office, many of which were in Hebrew.

Ickstatt looked at the books, too. "You have quite an esoteric library here."

"It's foolish to keep these books here where others will see them, isn't it?" asked Adam. "Can we bury them on the grounds?"

"Nonsense. They'll ruin in the ground. There is a quite a large space beneath the floorboards," and Ickstatt pried up a long slat in the floor with a letter opener, revealing a large dark space below.

When they had tucked all the books in the space, Adam retrieved two of them and put them in his satchel to study. He thanked his uncle and returned to the library.

So often his mind wandered to thoughts of Eva, but he

would not let himself revel in his angst. He scried on her often to see if she thought of him, if she regretted her fate. Usually he could stamp out thoughts of her and distract himself with a book, but sometimes he could not help recalling their nights together, their unparalleled lovemaking, and the sacred perfection he felt with her.

One evening in October, he could not seem to exorcise thoughts of her from his head. She had been on his mind all day that day, and wherever he looked, he was reminded of her. He read five hundred pages of St. Augustine's discourse on Paul's epistles and when he tried to summarize it for the paper he was writing, he realized that not a word of it stuck in his brain. Eva, Eva, *Eva* was all that he had read.

CHAPTER XIX

Boston, 1774

Sam was up at dawn to say his prayers. When he had finished, his thin and regal wife, Elizabeth, had a bowl of gruel waiting for him on the table. She poured him a cup of coffee and stood over him with the pot.

"What are we going to do with all these soldiers afoot? I don't even want to go to market for them looking at me." Her blue eyes had a way of scalding him when she was upset.

"We'll oust them yet. Back to the hellfire that broiled them forth," he answered.

"*We* and what army?" she asked. "They're here to stay."

Sam spent most of the morning at the table drafting compelling letters to the allies of the Sons of Liberty up and down the coast and on the Continent, asking that the letters be continually forwarded "to any God-fearing man." They had many correspondents and hopefully they would all remain sympathetic to Boston's cause. Sam was careful to illustrate in no uncertain terms that the war being waged now was betwixt Good and Evil. Clearly this conflict between the Colony of Boston and the English Parliament was no ordinary strife, but a struggle waged on earth embodied by human souls fighting in the spirits of God and Satan. The last blood that had been shed was that of the Boston Massacre several years before, but Sam could feel the hatred brewing again, the torrid wrath of men of the Lord, and he knew that it wouldn't be long before more of the red stuff was spilt.

He sealed and stamped his letters and carried the bundle of them to the postmaster's office. On the way, he passed the Boston Common and sneered at the hundred redcoats camped there. On a usual day, there would have been merchants and lesser tradesmen, those too poor to own shops, out with their carts, sharpening knives, selling tobacco and house wares. Stray children could have been found idling in and under trees, but there were none of them anymore. All of Boston's usuals had been ordered to clear off. Now instead, there were British army tents, cooking fires, and a menagerie of canon, waiting, threatening.

Sam walked slowly across the square, inspecting them bodily and circumspectly. Ugly, foul-smelling, unwashed, Brits with their big yellow teeth and close-set eyes. Disgusting! One crawled from his tent just as Sam passed by. A hideous maggot of a man, teeth astray in his mouth, large protruding blue eyes, but over six and a half feet tall as he stood up next to Sam.

"Sleep well, pretty?" Sam asked him.

"I was cold in this wet damp and I shivered all night," the ugly redcoat replied.

"Maybe you should get back to England, ye infernal beast!" Sam hissed and walked on.

He had not heard from Franklin, Boston's London agent in three months and was becoming concerned. Without

Franklin in position, there would be no one to deliver to Parliament the ultimatums he had in mind.

But the King had beaten him to the punch with ultimatums. Posted everywhere, on every tree by redcoats, he found copies of the Port Act.

The site of the Tea Party became the scene of a mob that afternoon. The closing of the Port of Boston put several thousand of Boston's rowdiest out of work, out of money, and out of their minds. The gates to the docks were barricaded and forty redcoat British soldiers stood in formation in front of them, flanked by cannon.

The shipwrights and dockworkers and their women and families screamed out in protest, burning copies of the Port Act.

Sam stood upon a crate and read the Acts aloud to the mob. "The Port of Boston is hereby closed. All activity upon these waters is strictly prohibited by His Majesty and such will be enforced."

The crowd threw rocks at the soldiers standing guard. "Miserable piss-rats!" someone screamed.

John Hancock blew his whistle. "Gentlemen, this is precisely how the Massacre started! We will have a civilized and peaceful protest or we shall have none at all." The Massacre was an emotional chord and he saw several of the burliest tear up. The grumbling subsided and the crowd came to order, their rage simmering.

Sam continued. "'The Boston Legislature is hereby dissolved. A legislature of Massachusetts delegates shall be allowed one meeting in Salem, but only for purposes of selecting council members... Article three: Soldiers will be quartered in private homes until permanent barracks can be constructed.' You redcoats can go to sleep in my house, but you will not wake up in the morning!"

The crowd laughed, then got loud and crazy and started throwing rocks at the redcoats guarding the dock.

O'Shannon threw a knife and it whizzed past a redcoat and stuck in a mooring. The soldiers fixed their bayonets and advanced on the Boston mob, running them away from the Harbor. Adams jumped down from his soapbox and fled along with them.

Aloof from the mob, Hancock walked back to his own house, dejected. His fellow Bostonians were a bunch of drunks who didn't have anything to lose. He had money gone out and not come in, many times over. His ships could not enter the harbor. His business totally disrupted, and without cash flow, Hancock was digging into the family money – money he'd sworn never to touch - to pay his debts.

More than anything, however, he dreaded housing redcoats. His house was his pride and joy and he hated the thought of two-dozen filthy British soldiers mucking everything up. It would take months to clean up after them. In fact, he thought, he should just get used to the idea that he would have to redecorate completely. But that would be contingent on whether or not he survived this invasion, and if they would ever leave. He had the fortune, and now misfortune of having the loveliest home in Boston, and feared that he would be called upon to entertain General Gage if quarters were to be selected in accordance with rank.

That afternoon General Gage and his personal attendants and footmen arrived in five carriages. Hancock greeted them at the doorstep, "I had a feeling you'd be imposing yourself on me."

"Did you?" Gage walked past Hancock into his house. Gage's men followed.

"Please take your boots off at the door and leave them outside?" Hancock called.

He lingered outside, but when none returned to remove his boots, he took after them up the staircase.

Gage rubbed his greasy face on a tapestry and inspected
a vase on a two hundred year-old credenza.

"Stop touching my things, please," said John with a
stamp of his foot. He should've hidden that in the barn
cellar with the silver and crystal.

That evening dinner was prepared with all care. A soldier
watched over the cooks' work to make sure there was no
poison put in the food.

Hancock invited Daniel Leonard to join them for dinner.
He hoped that the sight of two men in love would perturb
Gage and his officers enough that they would leave. Gage
scrutinized them as they ate in near silence. Hancock
made a number of blatant homosexual overtures at
Leonard, blotting the butter from the corner of his mouth,
and covering his hand tenderly with his own. He dropped
his napkin once and put his face in Leonard's lap as he
pretended to grope the floor to find it. Gage did become
uneasy, and quickly picked up the dropped napkin and
handed it back to John. John tried to engage Leonard and
Gage in conversation about ladies' fashions, but to no
avail. Leonard was clearly uneasy around the uniforms
and clammed up. As soon as they were finished, Leonard
patted Hancock on the shoulder and left.

It wasn't too many weeks before Hancock had had
enough. He stormed down onto the veranda where he had
everyday enjoyed his breakfast until the intrusion. There,
Gage and some of his favorites were drinking tea and
having eggs.

"What has happened to my curtains? Who took them?"

No one answered. Hancock screamed shrilly that enough
was enough. "You will lose this war *and* this colony, and
then you will all suffer untold pain!" With that, he
retreated to the garden where he was met by more redcoats
who had decided to camp there. He ran to the barn,
saddled his own horse and went for a long ride.

He rode for hours in a fit of anger and frustration. Rather

than going home, John went to see Leonard and instead found red coats in their apartment near the Wharf.

"Where's Daniel Leonard?" he asked them on the stair.

"He went out," a redcoat replied, slurring his words.

"Out where?" queried Hancock.

"How am I supposed to know?"

"Are you quartered here? It's a bit tight, don't you think?" John went out before he could answer.

He waited across the street at the Green Dragon Tavern where he could see the apartment clearly and drink off his anger. He took a seat by the door and ordered a bottle of rum and a small beer. He drank and waited.

Late in the afternoon, a beggar in an old cloak came in. John Hancock did not like being pestered for money, so he put up his hand. To his surprise, the beggar pushed back his hood—It was Sam. "Those bastards are going to arrest us."

"What? What for?" asked John.

"The Devil needs no reason for his Damnation, brother."

"No. I suppose not. Is John Adams is in as deep?"

"Aye, they want him, too. We've got a coach packed. Come with us now. We must make haste."

Hancock looked around nervously. "Where?"

"Salem."

"I'll catch up with you there."

"Don't delay."

John waited around all afternoon in hopes of finding Leonard. At six o'clock, a hired coach returned and deposited Leonard across the street at his front door. Hancock tapped Leonard's shoulder. "Where have you been all day?"

"None of your business!" Leonard was surprised to see him and fidgeted with his keys.

John grabbed Leonard's collar and shoved him inside and up the stairs to the second floor. The redcoats were playing cards and turned too late to see them. One of them got up and followed them up the staircase. John shoved Leonard into the upstairs bedroom and locked and barred the door.

"Is that Daniel Leonard in there?" asked one of the redcoats at the door.

"Yes it is," answered Hancock in a perfect imitation. "Please let me alone to sleep."

Leonard registered alarm. John clapped a hand over his mouth before he could say anything. "I've had about enough of your capricious ways. I've waited months to be intimate with you. I don't know if you're worth it anymore!" he growled.

Leonard looked hurt and tried to speak. John removed his cupped hand from Leonard's mouth. Before he could answer, John ripped his shirt, exposing his smooth, white skin, his tiny, pink nipple. Leonard writhed with excitement as John tore down Leonard's pants and caressed him. John put his mouth on him and let the juice run down between Leonard's buttocks. He roughly flipped him over and pulled down his breeches exposing his ready arse. John was hard and he was big. Holding him by the hips, he carefully penetrated him. He felt wonderful. John found Leonard with his hands and stroked him and thrust into him with his own. He brought him to his knees and took him slowly, savoring each hanging beat of his muscles. Leonard began to arch and buck in a frenzy, and John could not resist him.

Both of them lay spent on the bed, John's fingertips teasing the last drops from his lover. His skin felt hot and wet against his chest. He stroked him ever so gently as Leonard began begging for more, tears running down his face. He grew hard and long again in John's skillful hands. John suckled him, torturing, teasing him, squeezing him and preventing him over and over again, until he, himself, was hard with desire. He took him again and made him beg, bending him over the chaise longue and thrusting into him mercilessly until he knew he was completely, utterly his, under his control, and then he let both of them climax together.

Still damp from their passion, they escaped in one of John's carriages and were on their way to Salem by midnight. Leonard slept on John's shoulder. John wondered why he had been put off for so long when such pure delight had awaited them.

What they enjoyed was certainly not condoned by society, the Church, or anyone, and it was indeed rare to find a willing partner at all in Boston, though Leonard was not John's first or even his third lover of the same gender.

John Hancock fantasized of a country where men who loved men could be free from shame and persecution, where they could be openly in love before the skies and God and all. If this place in which they found themselves now, this colony, this country, could be that, then all John's fortune, all his life would be well spent.

They arrived at Salem in the morning and went immediately to a hotel and checked in under Leonard's name.

They convened with the Adamses for lunch, and acted as if they had merely bumped into each other along the road and had decided to join company. Sam had already called a meeting of the Massachusetts legislature for three days hence, June seventh, and he and John Adams were hopeful that a great number of patriots would join them.

That evening, John left Leonard in the hotel while he left to discuss what they would do in the meeting. Leonard begged John to accompany him.

"No," John answered. "These men will suspect us if we continue to keep such close company. They know me too well and will see how deeply I care for you. We mustn't..." He sighed, "I'm sorry."

"Well, I don't intend to sit forsaken in this room during

the meeting of the Legislature. I've as much right to attend as anyone," said Leonard.

"Of course," John agreed. After all, Leonard was a prominent lawyer in Boston, a Tory, but well-respected in most circles, and politically minded as well.

For the next three days Hancock and both Adamses wrote letters about the recent events in Boston, to all their Sons of Liberty contacts, to all the presses in operation, and to any sole sympathizers in their correspondence who may not have gotten the word, or their version of it. They would need as much support as they could get. At night and at midday when they rested, John returned to the hotel where Leonard waited for him in the cool sheets, his nude body warm and anticipating John's.

June seventh came with the look of morning rain, and the Massachusetts Legislature adjourned without askance of the Crown. Massachusetts delegates had arrived in Salem to voice their opinions which had become heated over the financial strains under which many of them had been put by the Port Act.

The Tory side had congregated and formulated a   plan as had the Adamses and Hancock during the days since the Port Act came into effect. They had no choice but to dominate and manipulate the circumstances on all levels. The time for action had arrived.

The gentlemen found their places, assigned seating, an arrangement John had devised so that representatives loyal to the Crown could not congregate together in the rows, but were strategically broken up and surrounded by larger groups of Yankees – people the Adamses and Hancock were sure were on their side.

Sam Adams entered and found a Tory trying to take his designated chair as Clerk of the Assembly. Sam sidled up to him, then spoke loudly to Thomas Cushing. "Mr. Speaker, where is the place for your clerk to sit?" And scowled down at the man sitting there, a short swarthy-faced man, Ethan Owen.

Cushing gestured to the place where Owen was sitting. "Right there, Mr. Adams."

Sam sat down on Owen's lap, much to his dismay and dipped his pen into some ink to begin recording.

"Will you remove yourself? Please!" Owen blustered.

Sam turned around and regarded him. "Oh my! What are you doing there? I hope my company is not making you uncomfortable."

The delegates laughed.

Owen got up and Sam sat down in the clerk's place.

Hancock looked out at the delegates and saw them either laughing or scowling at Sam's antics. He watched Leonard in the back row, hand on his chin, staring voluptuously at him, then with a look of cold dismissal, he looked down his nose at him. *Was that what he was doing or was it just his way of teasing?*

Thomas Cushing opened the meeting with a sidebar about confidentiality. "What is said in this meeting until it is passed into law is not for outside discussion with those not part of the legislature. Is that understood?"

Hancock hoped the throngs of people that they had called to the meeting would indeed tilt the scale in the Yankees' favor. The assembly got right to business. John took the floor and described the dire situation in Boston and the precarious position of his own business, concluding that if he were sunk, so would be the eight hundred families in the area who were employed by him. "Without some sort of retribution, without the ability to import or export, the people of Boston will not survive this blockade. There is no way for any of us to make a living unless we change this ridiculous law."

"What do you propose we do then?" asked Cushing.

"I propose we divert taxes into our own account. Cease paying the Crown anything and use the revenue to form a new government, a government run by people who live in the Colony."

"But we'll have to defend our authority. Who's going to do that?"

"Everyone. Everyone who lives here who cares about his freedom and his right to live a good life without having to work every day of the week just to put a bean on the table. We had a militia for the French and Indian War and we took care of ourselves. There's nothing new about it. Our men are still ready."

"But we don't want armed conflict with the British army. That would be suicidal..." someone spoke.

And a heated discussion began. Someone among them was having a coughing fit. John looked up to see Leonard choking into his hands. He pled with the guards at the door and they let him outside. They had made a rule that none of the assembly would be allowed out until the meeting had adjourned, but Leonard seemed desperate for some air. They had been up late the night before smoking tobacco and hemp. Leonard smoked too much, John had warned him.

Hancock returned to the Inn around seven o'clock that evening. On the table, a stack of parchments and a well of ink had been left out. He wondered to whom Leonard had written. He opened the door to the bedchamber and found his lover waiting in bed for him. Candles were lit and Leonard pretended to sleep.

John slipped into bed with him, asking after his health.

He found Leonard passionate but cruel and wondered what was the matter. He seemed to beg for punishment and John was not hesitant to dole it out. He poured hot candle wax on Leonard's chest and forced him to lie perfectly still as he dribbled hot wax closer and closer to his manhood. When Leonard was long and ready, he blew out the candle, dipped it in some oil, and pleasured him slowly with it as he suckled him.

192

The next morning the delegates had just assembled in the meetinghouse. They were sworn in, and after a quick recap of the findings and proposed resolutions, there was a vote. The resolutions to divert money and raise the militia were formally decided. No later than ten seconds after the resolution was passed, there was a loud banging at the door.

Leonard unbolted the door and stood aside at perfect attention as twelve redcoats and a page marched inside. The page read a proclamation to the assembly. "By order of General Gage, this meeting is adjourned on suspicion of sedition and treachery to His Majesty's Crown. Please disperse immediately or you will be arrested."

John Adams jumped to their defense. "This is a private meeting of citizens and no concern of the Crown."

Hancock stepped forward. "By His Majesty's own edict, we are allowed to meet in Salem and that is where we are and that is what we are doing!"

"Disperse!" shouted the captain of the redcoats.

Sam Adams looked around for any indication as to who had reported them. Whose face would betray him? He saw the man who had opened the door quietly slip out. All the others looked genuinely shocked and worried at the prospect of arrest. Everyone was equally surprised, even the Tories who searched among themselves for the same.

Hancock returned to the Inn and quickly began gathering up his things. "Daniel?" he called into the bedroom. "Let us make haste." But when he entered there was no one there, not a trace of Leonard. He had taken his clothes from the wardrobe and gone.

John turned back to the table on which the parchment and ink still lay, and picked up the blank piece of paper. He made out the impressions of Leonard's writing by holding it close to the lamp. He took a pinch of ash from the fireplace, dropped it on the page and gently agitated it over the parchment. It filled in the impressions of the letter that had been written on top. He could read enough of the correspondence to realize that what had been on top of it was a letter to General Gage.

John felt sick, then. He lay down on the bed and scrutinized the letter over and over. It said in cold terms that the "rebels meeting in Salem plan to divert HMR revenues into a private account." Leonard was a spy.

John felt the cold blanket beneath him, and the loneliness he loathed enfolded him again. He found some whiskey in his satchel and poured himself a drink. He sat pensive and sullen for a long moment until he heard the sounds of the redcoats marching outside. He slipped down the stairs and out the back of the inn, as they came in the front. He found the Adamses waiting outside and stepped up into the carriage with them, and they were gone into the night.

CHAPTER XX

FRANKLIN

The trimmings were set with great invention around a huge, roasted wild boar. There were pheasant and puddings galore. It was the Royal Society's Annual Christmas Feast. Benjamin found his name card and took his seat as the others sauntered into the dining room behind him. He was glad to move on to dinner.

In the drawing room, there had been another hour's worth of talk about who had stolen and published the letters that incited the Tea Party. "I couldn't imagine who would do *f*uch a thing," Benjamin said for the fortieth time. Was there nothing else to talk about? He had tried to change the subject dozens of times, "Have you heard of thi*f* new theory of animal magneti*f*m?" "That remind*f* me of a letter I received from a friend in China," but the Royal Society and their guests were all up in arms about the American conspiracy and would not let it drop. Benjamin filled a second glass of Christmas wine and wished he were in different company.

"I've heard there are two young men in Philadelphia who say they're going to duel over the letters," said Crutchfield, a dark-haired new inductee who had done a remarkable study on plant cycles, "One man believes they were stolen by the English. Another believes they were stolen by an American. And they're going to shoot each other over it!" He laughed.

"What beastly conduct," said the Princess of Bulgaria.

"S-s-sad they h-h-have nothing better to do than k-k-kill each other," said Priestly.

"Where was this, did you say?" asked Lord Duthermeyer.

"Philadelphia," answered the young Crutchfield.

"That's where Benjamin hails from." Dr. Pringle pointed at him.

All eyes suddenly turned on Benjamin. "What do you make of the letters, Dr. Franklin?"

He felt his stomach tightening and his throat clenching - the feeling he got when he had unresolved guilt, guilt that he couldn't quash with a fair dose of scientific reason or some trickery of logic. What if the truth that he had sent the letters were to come out? The Bostonians all knew from whom they came. How long would it be before one of those drunks let slip? Who's to say his name had not already been leaked? He would be cornered like a dog, when they found him out - a Royal Postmaster stealing mail. He and his affairs would be delved into and there were *many* loose ends that would surely surface were he not to guide the curious to the answers they sought. Better to be out with it in the open air and let the pieces fall where they may, and let none of his good associates think that he had acted to deceive them.

"I did it. I publi ʃhed them!" he heard himself confess. "I

ſtole them, and I publiſhed them in the Boſton Gazette."

Silence fell upon the table.

"Iſ that what you expected? I'm ſure it waſ not," he said taking a sip of wine and wiping his mouth with his napkin.

The twenty some-odd guests stared at him for some seconds, then hardly a word was spoken for the rest of the meal.

Then Lord Duthermeyer whispered to Franklin "You should take care that your papers aren't seized, yes, you should take care." He nodded at the candle's flame.

"Thank you," said Benjamin, remembering some unseemly circulars that had come through Duthermeyer.

"Didn't Lord North say they'd throw the thief into the Tower?" joked Dr. Pringle, wiping the pork grease from chin, and trying to lighten the mood.

"Newgate," said Duthermeyer in a grave tone.

Benjamin excused himself immediately after his last bite of squash and last gulp of wine. Pringle got up, too, and they both bid the host and his guests a Happy Christmas.

"I can't believe it, Benjamin. Why would you do such a thing?" queried Pringle in Franklin's private carriage home. "Do you realize what sort of trouble you've started in the colonies? They're practically in open rebellion."

"I am juſt a meſſenger of truth, and that' ſ all I can be." He heard himself quote Wilkes. He was hardly expecting what was to come.

Benjamin woke up early Saturday morning and walked to a coffeehouse to have a meal. He had barely sat down when he saw the headline of the London paper:

Benjamin Franklin Confeſſeſ: "I ſtole the Letterſ!"

As he nibbled a boiled egg and some berry tart, it seemed that people all around him were whispering. When he looked at them, some averted their eyes, but others stared right at him, and kept on gossiping.

It was the same on the walk home. Franklin walked quickly to get his exercise and was ever glad he was able to kick up a fast pace.

"There he is! There's Benjamin Franklin!" said a woman.

"Why you go into other people's mail like that?" asked a man in a cap.

Benjamin kept his head down and said nothing. The man followed, accosting him as he strode down the avenue with an escalating series of "Eh? Eh? EH?!"

"Pleaſe leave me alone," he begged.

But there were more people just like these. Every time he set foot out of Peggy Stevenson's house, he was abused.

"It's that old doublesnake!" hissed an old woman.

"Two-face!" a boy shouted.

"Snake-face!" called a fat girl.

A horseshoe flew past his head and clanged on the road in front of him. Benjamin spun around looking for his assailant. Had it struck him it very well could've killed him. There was more than one malcontented face staring at him from the dark doorways along the avenue. Any of them could've thrown it. He felt his blood boil and realized he could be the target of an angry mob at any moment. He hurried on and vowed to stay out of public sight. He briefly considered laying blame where it belonged – on Wilkes, but then if he gave that explanation, he would be confessing to being in John Wilkes' confidence. As hard as it was to bear seeing people turn against him, he decided he would rather take full blame for the letters than confess to being a comrade of Wilkes.'

Benjamin's niece Sally was ever helpful and he was glad that he had helped her make so many friends in London. His sister hoped that she would marry soon, and Franklin was initially glad when one of her gentleman acquaintances began courting her. He wondered if her boyfriend, Piers, wasn't a British agent sent to spy on him under the auspices of seeing Sally. He watched the boy closely and was not entirely convinced of his sincerity with her.

New Year's Eve came and Benjamin agreed to accompany Sally to a ball at Piers' family's home. He knew of the family by name and reputation and was a little reassured that at least Piers' identity wasn't a fake. But one could certainly be who one said one was, and still be a spy.

The snow fell in pillows and the smoke in the air was thick as their carriage pulled away from Craven Street. Franklin brought along a cane he had purchased that concealed a sword within it. It could be unsheathed cleverly with the push of a button, and Benjamin wondered if he might be called on to use it at some time in the evening.

They arrived at Piers' house on one of London's most expensive lanes in the West End. The party was grand and Franklin found himself the oldest person at the fete other than Piers' great-grandmother who had been wheeled out early to look at the guests and was now being wheeled back to her room at a quarter to nine. Franklin guessed the party was in part, for Piers, a reception of sorts, as he had just returned from his stint in the military. His mother spoke with him while Piers and Sally danced. "We are flattered you're spending your New Year's with us, Dr. Franklin. It *is Doctor* Franklin, is it not?"

"Ye*f*," said Benjamin, and he informed her of the latest fascinations of the Philosophical Society. She introduced him to various young women, many of them he thought far too beautiful and well mannered to be eligible for Piers. Sally, he began to think, was a good match for Piers as long as his heart was in the matter. Clearly she had seen this long before he, and he thought to congratulate her, but she spent most of the evening in Piers' company, leaving Benjamin quite free to mingle with the other young ladies.

At the stroke of midnight, Benjamin gave kisses to at least two-dozen women in his proximity. "I've never had a better New Year'ƒ," he said, his face wet. He saw Sally and Piers quite content and was glad they had come to this party rather than to one of Franklin's own friends.' His old friends had suddenly become quite standoffish these days anyway. Fortunately, Benjamin had not been called upon once in this company to make excuses or amends for the letters and the ensuing controversy. He wondered if they were aware of his role in the affair, or if they were simply too well-bred to make mention of it.

At half past twelve, the other guests began leaving the party, and Franklin and Sally joined the queue to bid Piers and his parents a Happy New Year. Piers' mother leaned in to Franklin's ear and said something he couldn't hear above the din, something about an "announcement soon" at another party. She clasped his wrists and kissed him on both cheeks.

Franklin smiled and thanked her. Was there going to be an engagement then? He looked back at their stately home. Sally could certainly do worse.

She was beaming when they got into the carriage. "Isn't he just the most wonderful man?" she asked.

"He'ƒ wonderful, ƒally," Benjamin got in, too, only to find a rather stout figure taking up more than half of his bench. "Good Jeƒuƒ!" gasped Benjamin and opened his cane into a sword.

"There's a man in our carriage!" exclaimed Sally.

"Forty-five. No need for alarm. I saw your carriage and thought I'd accompany you home," said an unfamiliar English voice. John Wilkes' bulbous nose and squinty eyes came into light.

"Wilkƒ! You horrid owl! What are you doing? Thi   ƒ i ƒ a

private carriage!"

"You act as if I am unwelcome," Wilkes said affecting hurt.

"Uncle, do you know him?" asked Sally.

"Ye∫," said Benjamin after a long hesitation. "I do."

"You may never know where you will find a friend. …Or an enemy." said Wilkes.

"Oh I have ∫ome idea∫, but there' ∫ not much difference the∫e day∫ between them."

"Well I am a friend. There are those who would do you harm on this night. Allow me to cloak you in my influence until we arrive at your residence."

"Plea∫e, that really won't be nece∫∫ary, thank you."

"Au contraire."

Benjamin really didn't care to argue with Wilkes in front of Sally, fearing that too memorable a conversation in her presence would lead to too many questions. He did not care to describe the character of Wilkes to her either, or answer as to how he was acquainted with him in the first place. He smiled agreeably. "I thank you, ∫ir. ∫hall we take the young lady home fir∫t then? Then your∫elf?"

"Good by me," Wilkes replied.

Benjamin had hoped that acquiescing to Wilkes' suggestions would placate him enough to keep his mouth shut, but of course, he could not.

"I'm sorry mademoiselle, we have not been introduced." He picked up Sally's hand and kissed it wolfishly. "John Wilkes, I'm a member of the Lodge to which your uncle belongs."

"Yes, I think we've met already. Once," said Sally tentatively. "At Easter."

"Oh yes…" he smiled. "You loveliness is quite familiar to me," he said.

Franklin had never seen such a rake in action. Maybe himself, but he was much lighter-handed about it. Wilkes was Pan, employing every trick of the façade and tongue to seduce. Benjamin was proud when Sally parried most all of Wilkes' advances. He tried to think of something to say that would shut him down.

When they arrived at Craven Street, Franklin begged Wilkes' pardon and got out of the carriage with Sally. "Too much wine. I must go in. My driver will take you home."

"You'd better hear what I have to say. I may not get another chance," said Wilkes.

"Juſt a moment." And he walked Sally inside and came back out to the carriage. He mounted and rapped on the doorframe with his cane. The driver started off.

"What iſ it that you feel you muſt ambuſh me and keep me up till all hourſ?"

"There's a plot against you, the most sinister of plots. People say you abused your positions as Deputy Postmaster and Massachusetts' London agent for your own gain."

"Yeſ, I'm aware."

"You should leave here and go back to your own country at once so you can prepare."

"Prepare for what?" asked Benjamin impatiently.

"For what's to come. If you stay here, you may be caught in a trap, and we may not be able to get you out!"

"Really. I can quite handle myſelf and my own affairſ, thankſ."

Wilkes was insulting. The very idea that Benjamin couldn't handle himself and needed protection of any sort was ludicrous.

CHAPTER XXI

Benjamin spent much of the next two weeks in his room reading. He had Sally go to the library for him and fetch him certain books, but she was busy every day, spending more and more time with Piers' family. He asked Peggy if she wouldn't mind running his errands now, but even from her he was beginning to feel shut out.

Polly had gone to care for an elderly aunt, though she still wrote to him almost daily, proposing all sorts of her own scientific theories which Benjamin felt obliged to stamp out in light of more reasonable ones that he had gleaned from the members of the Royal Society. In one letter, Polly asked about the sun's heat; if it was on fire actually, and if so, what made it burn. Benjamin was obliged to inform her that the sun was not on fire, but full of heat from its natural composition that made it like a molten ember.

It was a Tuesday when the royal summons came for him to appear in Parliament on January twenty-fifth. Benjamin was reading a history of vitriol when Peggy called up the stairs that there was a messenger at the front door. Benjamin lumbered downstairs and found one of His Majesty's Royal Pages waiting to personally hand him a royal summons.

Franklin signed his name on the register, tucked the summons under his arm, and stole silently upstairs to read it. In his apartment, he looked at the rolled parchment and wondered what preparations he should make in case of the worst outcome.

He spent the rest of the day writing letters to several people instructing them what to say, what code was going to be used, where to find such and such, and how to dispense with it. He burned most of his questionable correspondence in the fireplace. He decided to have Sally take the mail outside of London proper so that his letters would not be looked at. Benjamin was beginning to suspect that his mail was being read somewhere in transit. The last letter from the friend who had taken over his old printing business had indicated that his letters had all been opened and re-sealed. The printer had made a reference to the wine Franklin sent him being opened already and spoilt by unknown hands. There had been no wine of course, only letters.

He went downstairs to get some hot water from the kitchen. Peggy and the maid were talking. As soon as Benjamin stepped into the kitchen, the women stopped.

"What can we get for you?" Peggy did not meet his eye, something she had always done when they spoke.

The maid ducked outside to feed the chickens some vegetable peelings.

"I *fufpect* you think ill of me now." He laid a hand on her shoulder.

"I don't think ill of you, Benjamin. I'm just disappointed in you. I didn't think you were a turncoat."

"I'm not. There'*f* more to thi *f fituation* than it appear *f*. You mu*ft* believe me."

"I'm not in the business of politics, so I don't much care. It's just that you stole."

"Li*ft*en, really I didn't."

"Then how came you by those letters?"

"I have many friend *f* and when I received them I did not know what they were."

"But then you read them and you had them published in America where they would incite a vicious revolt."

"I did no *fuch* thing."

"Well the Times says you did."

Benjamin sighed. A man could say whatever he wanted, but the newspaper always seemed to have the last word, no matter what the truth. Just as well as the press had worked for him in the past, it now worked against him. And later, he found out, the two men who had intended to duel had only said so, with the design that the person who had stolen the letters would come forward. He had been tricked by some Tories.

Several nights later, Mrs. Howe looked at him over the chessboard and sighed. Her wig was parted straight down the middle, and curled up into cornucopia-like horns on either side of her head. It gave her a decidedly goatish look and made her wide nose look even more prominent. Her intelligence, beautiful porcelain skin, and shrewd no-nonsense assessments of most everything they discussed excited Benjamin. Her husband was almost always away on business leaving her alone sometimes for years on end, and Benjamin often fantasized that he would bed her during one of his late night supper visits. Though she said nothing of the letters, he could tell she was uncomfortable now in his company. He made a few science jokes to lighten the mood, but she only sniffed.

The letters and the subsequent scandal had brought about his demise in London. He could go nowhere without a piteous or hateful glance from those who had admired him, even worshipped him, only a month before. The London paper had trounced him soundly, made him out to be the lowest kind of criminal – a mail thief, a violator of private parcels, and an instigator of rebellions for causes of greed. What had he to gain, really, in the first place? Absolutely nothing. He had lived in perfect harmony in London for decades, his only intrigues being science, married women, and the interesting discoveries of his fellows at the Royal Society.

He thought of Wilkes and his role in this fiasco and wondered how far Wilkes really could've foreseen. Didn't Wilkes warn him to show them to no one? How had Wilkes procured those letters, by what forces, and who else knew to whom they had gone? Never mind Wilkes, it was Cushing and Sam Adams and Dr. Warren whose fault this breach of confidence was. Hotheads - all of them.

"Your move, Dr. Franklin," said Mrs. Howe impatiently.

"Oh ye *f*." He made an absent and quickly calculated move, and Mrs. Howe put him in checkmate. "Oh dear." He hadn't seen that coming.

She had become a fine opponent under his tutelage these

past few years, after having had the audacity of challenging him to a match. She stood, politely yawning. "I shall be retiring shortly," she curtsied, offering her hand.

His kissed it, savoring her skin. Their relationship had become stressed since the incident of the letters as her brother was Lord Howe. Benjamin imagined he had more than a few things to say about his sister's friend.

"Thank you for the delicou ʃ dinner and your kind hoʃpitality."

"A pleasure. And do take care on your way."

He knew what she meant. There was cause for concern in the realm of his safety. There were those in the government and those crazies astray from the government who sought a target for their ire and Benjamin was well in the sights of both. He had ducked a horseshoe already. Who could tell what would be thrown at him next? He left out the back door under an umbrella and the carriage took him to Seven Craven Street.

When he arrived, Peggy opened the door for him. She looked tired and worried.

"Iʃ there ʃomething wrong?" he asked.

"Oh Dr. Franklin…" she began and her grievances went on for an hour. They drank chamomile tea and she asked if he wouldn't leave. There had been four different gentlemen come to the door, asking of his whereabouts and she told them nothing of course, but the aggressive nature and unseemly appearance of these gentlemen were quite unsettling to her.

"Who were they?" he asked.

"I haven't the foggiest. One seemed to be concealing a weapon in his coat," she added.

"Oh good heaven ʃ," said Benjamin exasperated. Where would all this end?

On January twenty-fifth, Franklin's carriage pulled up

outside Whitehall to a bloodthirsty crowd. His menservants, Peter and King so expertly maneuvered him to the gate, that the throng barely noticed him until he was inside. Then came the rocks and abuse.

"He reads other people's mail!" someone shouted and a rock struck him in the back.

Franklin felt he had gotten away easily, though coming back through might be disastrously different.

He entered the foyer and there was no one in sight. The last few times he had appeared to plead the case of Boston, there had been a virtual social club in this area. He was to appear before the Privy Council so perhaps not very many of the members of Parliament would be present, he reasoned.

But they were *all* there to watch, and had already taken their seats in anticipation of his arrival. Lords and Dukes and Earls filled every named seat, and the clerk murmured there had never been a more full house for anything. Benjamin was led to the cockpit, the isolated seat he was to occupy throughout the proceedings. All around him, rumps and tail feathers were adjusted with a great huffing and puffing.

"Punish him," said an anonymous voice, vocalizing for all the indignant minds that seemed to bear over him from all around. He felt their eyes searing into him as he sat on the hard wooden seat, wearing his blue velvet coat and fur cap. He looked around him. There was the Earl of Sandwich sneering down his nose at him; Lord le Despencer staring coldly through him; Lord Dartmouth and Lord Hillsborough who had always hated him, and the gamut of them, English with power, all incensed at him. No blood brother boys club was going to come to his aid. Rather, the Order of St. Francis seemed to have turned against him. The Prime Minister, Lord North, was on the bench, his wig crooked and his vestments misbuttoned and crumpled. Benjamin thought he seemed hung-over and a bit bug-eyed and miserable.

He looked at where his own barrister, John Dunning, was supposed to be sitting and to his horror, saw that his place was unoccupied. Where was his lawyer? What if Dunning had decided to leave him high and dry, undefended? He wouldn't. *Would he?* The doors were closed by pages in powdered wigs, and Lord North called the Privy Council to order. Just then, Dunning pushed his way through the doors, and went to take his place near Benjamin.

"Thank goodne*ff* you're here," he murmured, relieved.

"I beg the pardon of the council," Dunning addressed the Prime Minister, but Benjamin could barely hear his voice Dunning was so laryngitic.

During the long and formal opening, Dunning began an hysterical coughing fit that did not subside. Benjamin got out his own handkerchief but could not reach Dunning nor summon a page to hand it to him. Dunning sounded as if he would suffocate as he tried to stifle his cough into his sleeve. His attempts to curtail the cough only made it worse and Benjamin thought Dunning would surely drown in his own phlegm right before his very eyes. He watched drool escape from Dunning's mouth onto the pleading.

The Prime Minister Lord North paused in his invocations, "Wouldn't you like to be excused until further time when you can control yourself, Mr. Dunning?"

Choking, Dunning swallowed his cough, waved, and managed to whisper "No, no, I'm fine. Let's let's begin." He swallowed the cough until he could stand it no longer and then he vomited up everything he'd been suppressing and some extra onto the podium before him.

Solicitor Wedderburn, the prosecutor, turned to Franklin and smiled. "State your name for the Lords of the House."

"Benjamin Franklin."

"*The* Benjamin Franklin who for the past twenty years has been living in London for the express purpose of gaining notoriety for himself and monetary compensation for his fellow colonists?"

"I don't think that'∫a fair ∫tatement..." Benjamin tried to finish, but Wedderburn kept on.

"You've been at Parliament, pestering for favors, reimbursements, land grants, posts, secrets, and money. Like a leach on His Majesty's coffers! You sir, are a parasite of the meanest kind."

"A para∫ite i∫a mean–"

"A self-aggrandizing writer of sappy contrivances and faulty speculations. *Poor Richard*! What kind of heathen trash would read such pitiful rot? Oh! That's easy – Americans! Too ignorant and poor to know good literature or poetry. Too stupid to know the difference between pig swill and pearls! Your only competition among your feeble-minded readers is the Holy Bible, not that anyone understands it or they'd behave like proper citizens. You know Mr. Franklin... It's *Mister* Franklin, isn't it? You're not a doctor, you're not studied, you have no degrees but for those kissed up at you at your drunken meetings of pretentious minds and body snatchers. I've read many of your studies, your anecdotes and 'wisdoms' and am doubtful that any of them are true. You have and do deal in lies, in fabrications. Whatever of yours that *is* of merit, is undoubtedly stolen. Like those letters. Let's get on to the letters, sir. Do you know of these letters?"

"Ye∫, I do."

"Do you know who wrote them?"

"I believe they were   ∫igned by the Ma   ∫∫achu∫ett∫ Governor Hutchin∫on."

"That's very astute of you. Perhaps the Royal Society will bequeath you with another medal for your good guesswork. I'd like to bestow you with some sort of honor for mispronunciation. Huffinfon? Ffuh-fhuf-fuh," Wedderburn made a ridiculous face that bore a great resemblance to Benjamin's.

A great bout of laughter erupted from Parliament and lasted several minutes.

"You know, I hate to put a damper on your achievements, Mr. Franklin," Wedderburn continued, "but the lightning rod has been in use by the Greeks for thousands of years. If you'd had the aptitude to study abroad like the rest of us, you'd know that. Brilliant of you to come up with it on your own, though. Next he'll think he invented the carriage wheel!"

Another roar of laughter from the Council. Even the Prime Minister was chuckling.

"Oh, we've all been admiring your coat," he continued.

"Thank you," Benjamin looked down at it, pleased with its fine hand stitch and wise color.

"Did your Quaker granny make it for you?"

The lords laughed for a good five minutes until Lord North called them back to order. "Keep to the matter at hand, solicitor," Lord North adjusted his wig and scolded Wedderburn.

"I think the question that is burning in all of our minds is where those letters came from."

"I *f*tole them." Franklin said.

"You f-tole them? The great 'doctor' Franklin, postmaster general, appointee of His Majesty, a petty thief and common pilferer?"

"Thi*f* i*f* a political i*ff*ue–"

"It is indeed a political issue, Mr. Franklin, and you are on the wrong side of your politics. And of the law. I think we all had higher expectations of you. Your face is on the fire cords! I say, truly if you can't trust the likeness on a box of fire cords, who can you trust?" Wedderburn showed a box of fire cords made by a company to which Franklin had allowed a ridiculous caricature of himself to be used in exchange for a few quid. Now he wished he hadn't.

Wedderburn lit a cord,   then waved it out. "Smells like

sedition."

The lords laughed and laughed.

Dunning stood up to make his rebuttal but his voice was lost in the room. Franklin hoped he would have the opportunity to make the points that he knew Dunning wanted to make.

"If I may put ſome thing ff traight..." Franklin tried to answer on his own behalf, but Lord North shut him down.

"You are not allowed to speak out of turn!"

"May I pleaſe addreſſ the Council?"

"No."

And the proceeding spiraled downward from there. Wedderburn summed up his case: "From now onward, mister Franklin, you will forever be recalled as a 'man of letters.' *Homo trium litteratum!*"

When the lords' laughter finally subsided, Lord North struck the gavel. "Benjamin Franklin, you are dismissed from your duties as His Majesty's Royal Postmaster and hereby sentenced to ten years in Newgate Prison."

Newgate? Franklin was shocked. They were sending him to prison?

Dunning looked at him helplessly and hacked up some phlegm into his handkerchief. "This is not a... excuse me.... a criminal trial. This isn't the proper avenue to prosecute," Dunning pled with Lord North.

"This is His Majesty's Privy Council and we are the highest judiciary in the land, sir. We can do what we deem right and just."

A page ushered Franklin and Dunning through a side door. Another led them down a long hallway to another building. Dunning kept at his side as Benjamin's watch and valuables were taken from his pockets by the bailiffs, and they clapped his arms and legs in irons.

"They can't do this to you. I don't understand. This wasn't a criminal trial," stammered Dunning, his voice having completely returned. "We'll get you out, don't worry."

"How?" asked Benjamin and he was whisked away by guards.

CHAPTER XXII

Benjamin had never even visited anyone in prison and had little idea of what a squalorous and horrible place it was. He had been there some five weeks and already had heard as many prisoners executed below and twice as many die of a sickness that was going around. It was dark, putrid-smelling, and full of dangerous and insane characters whose angry babbling and cursing he could hear through the walls. Fortunately, he was in a private cell – no bigger around than a steamer trunk, but he was all by his lonesome. There was nothing in there save a pan that was slid back and forth through the slot in the door for food. Food consisted of a ladle-full of slop, no better than what pigs were fed and he abhorred the thought of where it had originated.

Benjamin lost weight, and had never felt dirtier in his life. The itching blisters on his back, stomach and arms had returned and he was afraid to take his air bath for fear of lice, etcetera on his skin. He was humiliated to be incarcerated and prayed that his reputation and legacy would survive this dismal episode. Where were his friends from the Royal Society? Where was Pringle? Where was Lord Chatham? Where was Sally? Where was Priestly? No one, not one of them had come to visit nor even sent a letter of condolences or encouragement.

His ten-year sentence would put his release at age eighty – if he survived. Life had just begun to be fun for him. He had spent all the good years of his young life engaged in industry, piety, and frugality, in the service of his fellow man. And for what? To die a pauper in a foreign jail. Perhaps Poor Richard had been all wrong. Perhaps one should live fat every day and forsake work altogether. Look at where prudence and honesty had gotten him.

But the real reason he was in here was because he had gone against the Crown. Wilkes had used him as a pawn to incite trouble. He had been set up and knocked down by the Order of St. Francis; they had not stood by him as they had promised. They were not about to stick their necks out for him, the thief of the letters that had caused the single most memorable incident of their time, the Boston Tea Party. He remembered Wilkes' warning – "We may not be able to get you out." Wilkes knew they would not help him before Parliament, had known all along. And Benjamin had joined their ridiculous group, drank their blood for God's sake, and it was for nothing, for jail. If only he had someone, anyone, to talk to, to help put it all in perspective, some paper on which to write a letter, but there was no luxury of quill and ink in this vile place. The walls and floor were stained with the blood and excrement of those who had rotted away before him in this very cell, and they had written upon the walls in it. He could smell their decay. It was now his own.

He lost count of the days and sank into a deep depression. He had nearly given up asking the guards to see Dunning who had done nothing at all to try and exonerate him. The man was completely useless. Why he had chosen a calm and reasonable barrister he lived to regret. One needed a spitfire, a man on the verge of mania to defend him in court. He should've chosen someone loud and unreasonable, a man others would be afraid to question or cross. But it was too late now.

When he grew tired of brooding and remorse, he occupied himself by fantasizing inventions, of flying machines, of many wheeled devices for household uses, of electrical applications, of lightning and its causes, of the cause of colds, of the origins of waves, of his estranged family. Perhaps his abandoning his family was the reason

RITE OF THE REVOLUTION

for this blackest of fates. He had indeed left them all high and dry, only sending a small bit of money back to his wife every six months. She had died of a broken heart, he knew. Had he cared? Now he had time to feel the guilt he had so long evaded. When he had received word from William that she had died, Debbie had been gone nearly six weeks. And the idea of his returning to be at her graveside did not seem a good enough reason to make so long a voyage. If he did not wish to be at her side in life, why would he make such an effort to return when she was dead? He had confidence in William's managerial skills to settle any affairs she had outstanding. There was plenty of money in their name and he trusted that William would give her a proper and respectful burial in his absence.

Spending time with his wife had been no more interesting to him than spending time with a chicken. She was so despicably simple, so nit-picky, so humorless, and she saw no mystery in life, no need for fascination, for exploration, for investigation. She was most content with her pointless embroidery, and he wondered how someone could justify her time spent in such a needless and insipid pursuit when the world held such wonderful things that called out to be discovered. What he had seen in her at age twenty was gone. The plump, sensual lass whose smell drove him mad, turned into a dowdy, old frump who made pasties with no spices but salt, and her company was equally flavorless. He felt sorry that she did not seek out the company of other men as he did women, but he feared what sort of demented, old codger would have found her company worthwhile.

He had long grown tired of her, but now it seemed he was being punished for abandoning her. He had vowed to take care of her all her life, but he had run off for the last half of it and slept with countless other women. It was the dead of night and his mind reeled with guilty thoughts. Could she look down from heaven and see him suffering?

213

He would die alone as she had. It was the ironic, poetic justice that seemed always to bite everyone in the end. How sorry a fate. For the first time in his life, he regretted his philandering ways.

As he was recalling these affairs, recalling some that he had long forgotten, he heard a noise outside his cell. A footstep, then a whisper of a woman. "Dr. Franklin, are you in there?"

The door opened and there stood a Sister of Mercy. She was young, beautiful, with laughing eyes and lips the color of wine. She held a single white candle.

"I'm not a Catholic..." he looked up at her.

"Come with me. The sisters wish to help you." She pulled Benjamin up from his seat on the floor. "Please do not speak," she whispered. "Or we will be heard and then you will have to stay here."

Benjamin raised his eyebrows and followed her. He had not taken so many steps in one direction in weeks and his legs felt wobbly. They walked through the prison by the candle's light and he heard the soft snoring of the other prisoners.

She took him through a small door at the end of the hallway. It opened into a dark place and they walked into it. It was wet beneath his feet and Benjamin realized they were going into the sewer. "What exactly if our deftination?" he asked in a whisper.

She didn't answer.

The sewer turned and split and he followed on her heel. This nun seemed to know it well and picked out their way easily in the dark. There were deep holes to step in and Benjamin found them all. "No one'f going to come after uf, are they?"

"Not through here," she whispered back at him.

For over an hour, they traveled this way through the dark, watery filth. Benjamin had never dreamed of going in such a place, but was exhilarated to be escaping from prison and happier still to be in the company of a woman, albeit a nun.

At last they came to a set of narrow, stone stairs that ascended steeply up to the surface. He could smell the smoky night wind above the sewer's stench and was glad of it. The nun beckoned him up after her and he followed. He found himself on a residential street in London. The nun bade him follow, and he did so. He recognized the street and wanted to make a run for it, but hesitated. "Where are you taking me?" he asked.

"This way," she beckoned.

Why was this sister out so late at night, he wondered? And why was she breaking him out of prison? He'd never been much for Roman Catholicism even with so many Jacobite friends, but now he felt indebted to the Papacy and vowed to audit a Catholic mass when the next opportunity arose.

They came to a large and beautiful mansion not far from Piers' house. It was brick and covered with morning glory vines. He had passed by it many times and thought it quite lovely. She opened the wrought iron gate. The garden was deathly quiet, and the light, wet snow that they had missed while underground, now sublimed on the ground.

"This is the home of my mistress," she said and rapped on the door.

Two housemaids came outside with buckets of warm water and brushes. They stripped him and scrubbed the sewer's filth from him in the courtyard. Benjamin looked down at his tattered blue velvet trousers and dirty shirt as the maids peeled the tattered rags from his skin. He had forgotten the blue coat in jail, having used it as a pillow, but it had been in rough shape as well. These had been his very best clothes and he vowed to have another suit made just the same.

When he was rinsed and wrapped in a blanket, a tall woman with long, dark hair appeared. She was dressed in a strange, red dress with a large, emerald brooch at her throat. "*The* Benjamin Franklin. The famous. The dashing. How lucky we are to have you." Her voice was deep, almost vibrato.

"It i*f* I who am lucky, I *fuppofe*." He smiled at her, taking both of her hands in his. "If it i*f* you to whom I owe my liberation, thank you."

She inclined her head. "This is our home. My name is Belilah. You must stay with us for as long as you will. I expect you would like to be bathed after such an ordeal."

"Ye*f*, ye *f* I would. I am still quite filthy. Quite." He stared into her eyes. She was lovely, mysterious, alluring. She was either Greek or Italian, both breeds he particularly loved.

"Restore yourself and we will convene on the morrow. Tabitha will take you to the bath."

He followed the maid through the house that was quite opulent and spacious, to a tiled bathing room, arched and made of green stone. The water in the tub was steaming already. Franklin felt the smooth marble beneath his feet and anticipated the warm water on his skin. Before he realized what was happening two beautiful young women surfaced in the water. Giggling, they took him by the hands and eased him into the bath.

"Oh my goodne *ff*," stammered Benjamin, embarrassed. Johnny grew long and began to rise as they soaped and scrubbed every inch of him, making light conversation with him about his inventions, his travels, and his celebrity. The brunette went behind him and wrapped her arms around him, pulling him back into the water as the blonde scrubbed his belly with a lavender scented soap and brush. The brunette scrubbed his head and the blonde poured a pitcher of warm water over him. When he was clean, they kissed him. He let his hands wander through the water till he found their soft, bare skin and glided his hands over them. They giggled and chided him teasingly.

He began to wonder if he hadn't died in prison and was now in some fabulous level of heaven.

"If thif a convent?"

"No." The pair laughed and led him out of the water. They patted him dry with the softest towels he had ever felt.

"To what do I owe thif pampering?"

"To your genius, Dr. Franklin," said the brunette at his knee.

"To your good works," said the blonde.

"Very good, very good," smiled Benjamin nervously as the blonde buffed his backside dry. They helped him to lie down on a long, padded chaise. They applied a scented tingling crème to his skin and massaged it in with their hands until he fell asleep.

They woke him later with gentle whispers, wrapped him in a downy robe and slipped fine, new slippers on his feet. He blinked his eyes open again and did not know where he was. This wasn't Newgate, nor was it the Craven Street apartment.

Then he realized what had happened was real, when the maid, Tabitha, appeared. "Come, I'll show you to your room," she said.

She led him upstairs and down a carpeted hallway to a suite at the end. She opened the doors on the most lovely of rooms. It was pale blue with small stuffed ornamental birds everywhere. The bed had a grand canopy of blue silk with beaded tassels, and was large enough to sleep six. The pillows were silk and the shade of them reminded him of his lost blue coat.

"Sleep well," her voice was soft as his sheets. No sooner had she gone out than Franklin slipped between them and fell deeply asleep.

When he awoke, he drew back the curtain and realized it was late in the day. He felt a little lost and wondered if the jailers of Newgate had the hounds out for him. He looked out the window and saw business as usual on the streets below, people walking past and carriages driving by. He wondered what day it was.

There was a knock at the door. He opened it and a French maid curtsied. "Bon jour, Monsieur Franklin. The mistress asks you get dressed and join her for tea."

Benjamin's stomach rumbled at the thought. "Of cour *ſe*. But what *ſ*hall I put on? I believe the clothe*ſ* I arrived here in are ruined."

"Look in the armoire and you'll find something to suit you," she said, and set a basin of steaming water on the dressing table.

He did as he was told and found some strange robes of a dark blue silk that when he put them on made him look like a sultan. He thought of Dashwood and his ridiculous turban. The pants that accompanied them were loose like the legs of an elephant, but they felt cool and soft on his skin. He combed his hair, had a shave, and patted his face with the toilet water that was sitting on the dressing table.

Out on the veranda, the table was set for tea and Belilah was waiting for him, an enormous white cat purring in her lap. The bodice of her dress was tight and so low he could see the tops of her aureoles. Her skirt cascaded all around her chair. Franklin marveled at her magnificence and bowed extravagantly in the role of the sultan. "Mistre*ff*... I have come for tea." He was giddy.

She smiled, amused. "You are such a charming soul, Dr. Franklin. We are so fortunate to have had the opportunity to acquire you."

"A*ſ* I am glad to be acquired." He dug into the refreshments with both hands.

The garden below was large and lavish, and a pretty, young woman in a riding coat and jodhpurs walked four large dogs on leashes some distance away. Benjamin recognized the nun by her red lips. "The *ſ*i*ſ*ter of Mercy –

if ſhe off duty?"

"She's not a nun. That was but a costume in case she was caught. Only women clergy are allowed on the Newgate grounds."

"What am I doing here?" he asked, smiling, feeling impertinent.

"We have acquired you for our own uses – which we hope you won't find too taxing. Now it is my duty to make you as comfortable here as possible. We hope you will be happy in our care."

"I don't believe I quite underſtand."

"It is rather unorthodox, but let's just say money can do a great number of things that would seem otherwise impossible."

"ſo you paid my bail? I thought there waſ none."

"No, no, no. Not bail. We bought you from the English government. You belong to our lodge now."

"How very extraordinary," Benjamin didn't quite know what to make of the situation. It seemed good – there was no problem *not being in jail,* however it had transpired. "Your lodge?" he asked.

"This house, this property is the sacred lodge of the London Dog Star Sisterhood of the Memphis Rite. Come, you've not heard of us?"

"No…" Franklin racked his memory. "No, I can't ſay as I have."

"Formerly we were the sister lodge of the London Lodge, but they were not interested in pursuing genuine knowledge of sacred rites. They would rather drink brandy and congratulate themselves."

"I ſee." He wondered whether he should ask for more details, but guessed that it was Wilkes' group of freemasons who had estranged themselves from this sister lodge. "I have been warned that I ſhould return to my home country, that I am not ſafe here in London. Iſ Parliament aware of my liberation?"

"Certainly."

He wondered if he shouldn't send   Dunning a note to let him know his whereabouts. "I*f* there any paper record of my acqui*f*ition?"

"No. It was a private deal brokered by unnamed parties. The official record will reflect that you only had a hearing by the Privy Council and were let go the same day... into the custody of our facility."

"Thank you. My reputation I think ha *f f*uffered more than I." He looked her in the eye. "Though I hate to think what would have become of me bodily, mentally, and *f*piritually after *f*uch a long *f*tint in jail."

"Yes, we couldn't stand by and allow it, not when so many of us are such... ardent admirers of yours."

"And here I thought all my admirer *f* had turned again *f*t me. When will I meet the other*f*? I will want to thank them per*f*onally. Hm-hm."

"They would have it no other way. We all understand that politics change, but people do not."

Not in his wildest imagination could Benjamin have foreseen what the sisterhood had in mind for him. The twenty-eight members met nightly, he was told, but never on the new or full moon.

Benjamin was ritually bathed by the blonde and the brunette again, perfumed, robed in black satin, blind-folded, and hung with amulets. He was led out of the house, in a procession. He felt gentle fingertips guiding him and he sensed a number of women before and after him. The night air cooled his skin as it fluttered beneath his satin robe. Then he heard the crackle of a fire and felt the blaze heat the satin on his skin. He became nervous and excited. He heard the women's voices reciting invocations, in Latin of all things. The Pater Noster... then his blindfold was removed.

He found himself in the middle of the garden, the high

shrub all around, a fire burning in a bird bath-come-pyre. He stared around at the circle of London's wealthiest women, nude from head to toe but for their high white wigs and jewelry. Some of them he recognized despite their heavy Egyptian eye make-up. He smiled and gave a little familiar nod to Madame Howe, and Miss Barry, and wondered if they weren't the ones who were the instigators of his purchase. The other women he thought he recognized vaguely but could not name, though he was quite sure he had seen them about socially before. He could tell by their fine skin and beautifully ornate wigs they were of the upper crust of London society. Something told him that perhaps some of these women had been involved with the Medmenham Monks, Dashwood's now-disbanded group of elite who used to practice ancient sex rites in a renovated monastery next to the Thames. Their group had been rumored to make use of the most beautiful wives and mistresses of the ruling class.

They formed a circle around him and holding hands, they sang

"Come oh Libra, come oh weightless ones,
into the circle for your time is nigh..."

Three women left the circle and presented themselves to him in the middle of the ring. They disrobed him, kissing him, caressing him. He was quite nervous and thought about running away, scaling the high wall and going back to Craven Street, but something else made him stay and show his appreciation.

The Libra women laid him down on the dais that had been prepared with pillows and satin sheets. They kissed him all over his body, dividing him in thrice. The most beautiful kissed him full on the mouth and peered down at him with her laughing eyes, as the one in the middle caressed his chest and abdomen, paying careful attention

221

to his nipples. Another titillated his thighs and testicles with her soft fingertips. Johnny had been erect since his bath and he longed for her mouth to kiss it. It was no sooner that his wish was fulfilled.

The first woman kissed him deeply, as the third one sucked his Johnny, preparing it for penetration. The second girl pinched his nipples as the third one sat upon his Johnny and had a ride. He held back his release for he knew not how many of these women he might have to pleasure. The three each rode him and squealed with delight at his Johnny thrusting into them. He preferred the second girl, the one who had abused his nipples, and she rode him for a second time. Her put her nipple in his mouth and held her tightly.

He was virtually unaware of the actions of the women in the outer ring, though he caught the voluptuous eyes of Belilah whom he had not recognized before, in her white wig. How different and pale and ethereal she looked with white hair, and sapphires hanging from her ears and neck.

The second girl was probably thirty and small and reminded him of someone whom he couldn't recall, but with whom he was familiar in the sexual sense. Her body seemed to know his. She had countless orgasms in his lap. Through his excitement, he became aware of the chanting, the masturbation, the voyeurism of the other women all around them, and his arousal grew irrefutable. With a tremendous shaking, he ejaculated, holding her close to him while the other two cosseted around them. As he rolled over and lay spent upon the satin pillows, he was vaguely aware of Belilah's voice blessing the ceremony and paying tribute to the mother Isis, in whose name all these rites were performed.

"Prai*se* I*sis*!" Benjamin said with a weak punch to the air.

Late that night, he lay quivering alone in his canopied bed, wondering if such a thing would ever in his life happen again. What a bizarre yet wonderful experience; it answered the burning questions he had always had about women. *Is that all they do?* Look after children and manage the household? Certainly some women, but this group of London's elite apparently had far more intriguing avocations than the norm.

He wondered briefly about their husbands and laughed smugly about le Despencer. He had abandoned him in his moment of need. When speaking up for him would have done him untold good, Sir Francis Dashwood, the Lord le Despencer, sat silent and smug. Now Benjamin felt a surge of power and applauded his mistress and caged bird, Miss Frances Barry. He wondered about her mental instability and how such a ritual may affect a demented person. He remembered the odd drawing, the heavy triangular object hanging above her head in so many of her illustrations. It certainly didn't bode well for her state of mind. Still, he wondered how she would feel against him; how it would feel to be inside her. He had always thought her beautiful, but too young for him, but could not put their kiss out of his mind. He marveled at the miracle and wonder of his own blessed life and fell asleep with a feeling of glee for the future.

All the next day, he was fed pomegranates, fresh seaweed, scones and jam, liver, greens, milk, and oysters. He guessed it was to restore what vitality had been spent the previous night. So they were going to continue making him their love slave?

Belilah joined him for the oysters and some champagne and confirmed as much. "Did you enjoy yourself last night?" she asked with a seductive smile.

"Oh ye*f*, very much. I can't *f*ay I've ever done anything like it before."

"We were all very pleased that your genius extends to the boudoir."

Benjamin blushed. "The plea*f*ure was all mine."

"No," she said simply, and to his astonishment, informed him he would be expected to perform the same services each night until the moon was full.

That night proceeded like the previous.   He was bathed again by the blonde and the brunette, whom he was disappointed to learn, were forbidden from joining the fray. "Mistress would be very upset if you waste yourself on us," said the blonde.

"I'll have the two of you yet," Benjamin promised as they toweled him off.

He let himself be robed, blindfolded and led out to the garden by the procession of priestesses. On this night he was obliged to honor the Scorpion. There were only two of them but they were an intense pair. One confessed her love for him and demanded he return the sentiment. "Say you lovest me, too," she growled in his ear. "Say it!"

"I love you," he said. And he felt her clench, her nipples harden, and she bit him on the shoulder. When they were through, he felt a bit suffocated as they collapsed on him, still ardent in their desire, staring at him with such emotion.

He got acquainted with Miss Barry several nights later. She was quite reserved in her affections at first. She was soft as a whisper, then he brought her to ecstasy quickly. He watched as she stayed in that state for many moments then fell upon him, whispering his name and laughing. The two other Aquarians were sensual and skillful and toyed with him until he was excruciatingly aroused. Then Miss Barry sat down on johnny again. When each had gotten her share, they were quite through with him, though polite enough to finish him off and then help him up and ask after his wellbeing.

He had never investigated the workings of natal astrology in depth and indeed thought it a bunk avenue of science, but now he wasn't so sure. Verily there was something to the typing of the personalities, at least in the bedroom. He observed that the women who shared the same sign did have remarkable similarities to each other, both physically and with regard to personality.

As much as he liked Aquarius, he suspected there was something deeply depraved lurking beneath the cordial facade. Capricorn was nigh as painful as Scorpio, enjoying a long, laborious copulation. By the time he had relieved the two rather hefty Capricorns of their internal tensions, he was sweating and could barely catch his breath. He lay staring up at the stars and Belilah laid a hand on him to make sure he was still alive. The Sagittarians had been easily pleased and tender. The Pisceans were a bit cold and a little self-serving, he thought. Belilah was one of them, and he enjoyed her, though he felt she was slightly condescending, and did not appreciate his fat.

He wondered when he would enjoy the sensual company of the indomitably horned Mrs. Howe, and wagered that she was an Aries. He had often dreamed of being with her, of touching that porcelain skin, of seeing her unclothed. He certainly never thought he would actually have the opportunity. He wondered how her husband allowed her to be out every night and then he remembered he had not been at home with her in many months. Perhaps all of these women were without spousal supervision, these wives of the lords who had more important places to be than at home.

He stood in the window of the library and looked down into the garden. It looked innocuous enough in the morning light - the lovely flowers, the high circle of shrubbery, the bird fountain, its scorched bowl now full of water and sparrows. Never would an unindoctrinated visitor guess that such unorthodox activities transpired down there. Beyond the garden wall, the West Enders bustled by. He could see the tops of their hats and their carriages through the break in the trees above the wall.

How he longed to take a stroll, to sit in a coffeehouse and

have a conversation with a friend, to write a letter, to see what the rest of the world was up to. He was hesitant, however, for the last few times he had been out in public, he had been accosted and threatened, prosecuted and jailed. He wondered if he could get hold of a newspaper so he could at least read about what everyone was doing. His thoughts wandered back to the Adamses of Boston. What trouble were they making now? He began to long for his colony, for its safe simplicity of life. How strange, after all these years to suddenly be getting homesick. For the past twelve years he had considered London his home, but now he was no longer a welcome part of things as he had once been. And despite these women's affection for him he was a secret now. He was fringe. And if there was one thing he was not, it was an outsider. He had always prided himself on his being in the midst of things, the center of everyone's attention. Where were his friends? He wanted to pen them all angry guilt-inducing letters for abandoning him. But could he? What confidentiality was he bound to now that he had been 'acquired?' Could he tell anyone his whereabouts without being whisked back to Newgate? Was he verily a prisoner here, now?

The next few nights proceeded like the last as he was introduced to the delights of the rest of the zodiac. By the time it was Taurus' turn, he wanted a vacation at a monastery. He enjoyed being the center of the ritualized affections, but he was getting a little ragged. From what he knew of astrology, he had five signs to go, four more nights of sex acts to perform. He was seventy years old, he had to admit. He wasn't sure he could hold up to it but he did not want to disappoint. He ate the food they served him and rested all day every day, and to his surprise, he was able to finish off the zodiac with flying colors.

Alone in his room, he wondered if he shouldn't beg his hostesses' pardon and go back to America. From the newspaper he had stolen from the kitchen, Boston was in turmoil, occupied by redcoats, and its port was closed. He was supposed to be acting on Boston's behalf as the Massachusetts agent in London, but he dared not show his face again in Parliament or he would be arrested. He had no correspondents now in his new home, not even Polly, and no one outside this bizarre sister lodge knew where he was. He was beginning to wonder whose clothes he was wearing. The sultan clothes smelled faintly of pipe smoke as if they had been worn by someone before him. These women had undoubtedly had other captives, and he wondered what had become of them. Had they escaped to tell the tale or had they met their fates in the circle beneath the starry sky?

He sent a card to Madame Howe that he would like to see her privately. She sent a coach to pick him up that night, for it was a full moon and there would be no ritual. When he had arrived at her house for dinner, she greeted him cordially and acted as if the previous weeks' events had never happened. They sat in the drawing room and drank claret. She was a Virgo and had had the last of him, which hadn't been too bad, but admittedly by the time he had gotten to her sign, he was rather used up. She seemed to understand, and knew that her charms appealed to him as they always had. He remembered well a wedding ten years before when he had first seen her, and how he had whispered in her ear while they were dancing that had they not both had spouses he would take her right there.

"Do you know if there if any help left for me in London? I am quite concerned that Boſton if on courſe with diſaſter."

"My brother and Lord Chatham, both, have sympathy for the problem in the Colonies. Why not have them plead on your behalf in Parliament?"

"That'ſ ſomething I ſhould do myſelf."

"You're under our supervision and you cannot go out in

public any more. Would you care for a game of chess?"
She smiled.

Benjamin was tired of playing the captive and worried
much about his homeland and his responsibilities as a
diplomat. He had to go home. He knew that Sally or
Peggy or Priestly would undoubtedly help him out of this
tight spot. If only he could get back to Craven Street.

He continued to drink with Mrs. Howe, making a game
of it, the loser of the chess piece having to take a swallow
of gin, until they both became quite drunk. She made a
few lewd comments about their copulation and in the
midst of an hysterical fit of laughter, passed out cold upon
the chessboard. As the room rocked sideways, he picked
her up and staggered to the chaise and laid her down upon
it. He kissed her fondly on the breast and snuck out of the
back door of her house. The coachwomen who had driven
him over would surely have stopped him leaving had he
gone out the front.

He showed up at Seven Craven Street at two in the
morning. He knew where there was a key hidden beneath
the cement toad that sat in the garden by the kitchen door.
Silently he crept into the house and stole up the stairs to
his old apartment.

He knocked softly and opened the door. Upon the desk
lay a figure beneath a sheet, the toes of a man sticking up.
"I beg your pardon. Are you sleeping?"

There was no answer. The whole room smelled of rotten
meat as if a plate had been left out too long. He lit a
candle and noticed that his own things were packed in
crates and cleared from the shelves and closets. He began
searching for some of his own clothing to wear. He had
grown tired of the satin robes and Bedouin pants. The
person asleep on his old desk must be the new tenant. It
seemed strange that he did not use the available bed
beneath the window. It was then he noticed the copper
dish containing what appeared to be a torn scrap of

parchment. Slowly, he walked round to the head-end of the sleeping tenant and pulled the sheet from his face. It was a cadaver. Benjamin reeled in horror. "Good Jeſuſ!" There were instruments of dissection, mutilation in the open drawer of his beloved desk. "Who iſ thiſ?" he said aloud.

Quickly he grabbed a suit of clothes and went out the door, coming face-to-face with Peggy on the landing. "What are you doing here?"

"Oh my goodneſs, you gave me quite a fright!"

She glared at him. Her lips were pursed tightly. "We thought you were in jail."

"No, no, not in jail," he tittered. "That waſ all a big miſunderſtanding. I had to perform ſome volutary ſerviceſ, then I waſ releaſed and here I am."

"Then what are you doing lurking about at this time of night? You smell of liquor!"

"Occupational hazardſ, you know me."

"I thought I did," she spat.

"Peggy, pleaſe. I wiſh I could tell you what'ſ happened theſe paſt few weekſ, but-"

"Save your breath. Why are you dressed like a sul-tan?"

"Who'ſ thiſ unfortunate perſon on my deſk?"

"It belongs to Polly's new husband. He's a *real* doctor."

"Obviouſly not a very good one."

"He's a scientist. And don't say what you've seen in there. I'm not sure if it's quite legal."

"I ſhould ſay not!"

"I had rates to pay, and he needed a private office."

"All right, fine. I'll be out of here ſoon enough. Where'ſ ſally?" he asked, changing the subject.

"When you were dishonored, Piers' family recommended he break things off with Sally. You know how it looks to be a relation of a traitor? Well, perhaps you don't. It doesn't look good."

"ſo the engagement iſ off?"

"Yes, the poor heart-broken dear. We tried to console her, Polly and I, but there was no doing that. If only you'd been here to hear her woes. Never in my life have I heard such grieving. You'd have thought a banshee was burning at the stake. Her mother had the doctor come and help her to the house she was fainting so much."

Benjamin wanted to hear no more about it. There was nothing he could've done. If Piers and his family wanted to be unkind and insipid, so be it. If they couldn't stand for a little embarrassment, they weren't of the character fit for one such as Sally, he told himself. She most probably hated him, however, and he did not look forward to explaining things to her mother.

"Li*f*ten, I need you to do me a favor..." he began.

The next morning, he sent Peggy with a bank note to secure his and his grandson's place on a boat leaving for the Colonies. It would be another week and they would travel under assumed names. Frederick and Michael Baggage – sounded common enough. While Peggy was out, he hid himself in the cellar, and read to pass the time.

Some minutes after she had gone, he heard the floorboards creaking upstairs. Someone was in the house. He hid behind a barrel in the corner and dared not breathe.

As he dreaded, the cellar door unbolted, opened, and the footsteps came down the stairs. Benjamin held his breath. Who could it be? He wanted to see, but dared not move lest he be found.

"Franklin," said a voice. "It's 45." Wilkes had found him.

Benjamin sighed and emerged from the shadows. "How did you find me?"

"This is where you live. You should really take more care. You are in grave danger. Sinister forces brew against you as we speak."

"Who?" asked Benjamin.

"The Hellfire Club. Perhaps you did not realize that eight of the women in the Dog Star Ladies' Lodge were the wives of the Hellfire Club? And the rest - the wives and mistresses of half the blokes in the House of Lords! There has been talk. Scandalous talk! And threats made against you!"

"What haſ been ſaid?"

"Some appalling testimony, I assure you. Lord le Despencer plots against you. He has called us all to the caves to bring about your demise. Unless you leave here immediately and make remedy to protect yourself, you will never leave Britain alive."

"I've bought paſſage already." Benjamin prickled at the thought of them turning on him. He was not susceptible to their black magic anyway—He wouldn't allow himself to be. He had nothing left financially, socially, or professionally for them to destroy. The only way they could harm him was bodily. The thought was not exactly comforting. "I thank you for your concern," he told Wilkes dismissively and inclined his head toward the exit.

"Do not take this lightly." Wilkes turned back, "You have angered them all, *all* the Lords of the House; they feel you have betrayed them over the letters, then doubly so with their wives at that infernal cat house in the midst of town. We've all known about what they do at night, and it wasn't until now that it's been a topic of concern, but now one of the 'ladies' has turned up pregnant and run amok confessing to liaisons with the likes of you - who should be in Newgate!"

Benjamin shuddered. "Who? Who iſ pregnant?"

"De Spencer won't tell me. It will have to be dealt with, I suppose."

Benjamin thanked Wilkes again and bade him farewell.

"Beware, Dr. Franklin. These men are powerful beyond your knowledge, especially Sir Francis, as ridiculous a pomp as he may seem, wields immense ethereal power that manifests in hard material ways." Wilkes' squinty eyes grew bigger than Benjamin had ever seen them get.

"Yeſ, thankſ. Be off and good tidingſ. Let yourſelf out the back." Benjamin closed the door and locked it.

He sat and pondered what Wilkes had said. One of the sister lodge was pregnant? Was it true? And if so, who was it? Desperate for someone rational to talk to, he sent a note to Joseph Priestly, encoded in the Royal Society's favorite cipher, apprising him of his whereabouts and asking for his good counsel.

Priestly arrived the following day wearing a disguise – a rounded pair of eyebrows and rounded mustache that made him look like a monkey. He expressed his regret at Benjamin's fall from grace and even shed a tear at how he had been treated by the Privy Council.

"Now you are utterly def-f-f-famed, after so long a life of p-p-p-p-prestige and accomplishment, you have landed f-f-f-flat. Tis a shame, a sore, sorry shame."

Benjamin stared at him, peeved by his estimation and offered, "I'll make good yet, don't worry."

"It is so l-l-l-late in l-l-life for you, friend. L-l-l-l-like a deflowered virgin with too many summers and n-n-n-n-n-no prospects, you're ruined. N-n-n-no one will receive you. The Royal Society speaks of having your n-n-n-n-name removed from the brass p-p-plate in the v-v-v-v-v-vestibule," said Priestly painfully, getting some slobber on his hand.

"ſo much for fair weather friendſ," sighed Benjamin. He was touched that Priestly was so aggrieved for his loss of face, but reminded how hollow and idiotic many of the intellectuals with whom he fraternized could be. He decided not to reveal to Priestly the depth of his problems and regretted having sought his company. He would keep his own confidence.

After Priestly had gone, Benjamin found the day's mail

at the top of the steps where Peggy left it. There was an encrypted letter from the Sons of Liberty describing Boston's distress at what they were calling the 'Intolerable Acts.' As Parliament had promised, Boston's port was closed. They were literally being starved out and ruined by the measures the King had undertaken to punish them. The Sons of Liberty begged Benjamin to take their case to Parliament.

Benjamin understood clearly that he would be returning to a land in crisis. He was in Britain now, and wouldn't be for much longer. And it was his responsibility to speak on behalf of Boston, but were he to go out in public, he would likely be arrested. As he wondered what to do, he found a card in the mail inviting him back to Mrs. Howe's for dinner to speak with her brother, Lord Howe and their mutual friend William Pitt, Lord Chatham, about Boston. How fortuitous it seemed. He suspected it was probably a trap, however. Mrs. Howe was certainly being held responsible for his untimely liberation and he reasoned he may well be apprehended if he were to permit himself to be entertained by her.

He sat and made a list of the pros and cons and finding pro a weightier choice, sent letters to Chatham and Mrs. Howe confirming his presence at dinner the following night. The worst that could possibly happen would be that he would be captured again, and forced to participate in the sex rites of the Dog Star sisterhood. There were worse fates, really. And it wouldn't have been so objectionable at all were he allowed to come and go on his own clock. It was the imprisonment part that he could not tolerate.

He spent the day in the sitting room peering over the windowsill at two effeminate-looking men that hung round the tree across the street. They seemed to be watching Seven Craven Street with some interest. He called for King to ready his carriage and he quickly escaped out the back. They drove into the country toward

Essex. It took most of the afternoon. King drove fast as he liked to, and for once Benjamin was glad of the pace, for it would be difficult for anyone to catch up to them.

Finally they stopped at an old crumbling ruin of a church at the bottom of a voluminous and verdant hill upon which sheep grazed. Benjamin got out of his carriage and ventured into the ancient sanctuary, laying a hand on the cool, stone archway. The roof was gone, and ivy and long grass grew out of the cracks in the shattered floor. It was dark and quiet underneath the huge trees that canopied the stone walls, and Benjamin felt safe and alone for the first time in quite a while. He lay down on the only remaining marble pew, and crossing his arms and bowing his head, fell asleep.

Sometime later, a cold draft on his ankles awoke him. He opened his eyes and could no longer find the sun, for it had gone behind the hill. He straightened up with a start, feeling that all was not well. He heard the ivy rustling and felt a presence behind him.

"King?" he called out.

He turned and saw a small whirlwind swirling the grass and coming toward him, growing in intensity. In the center of it, there was a shadow - void, black, and unnervingly sinister. He felt a cold chill.

Benjamin did not linger to investigate its make-up, but leapt to his feet, and ran out of the place. "Let'ƒ go, King! Now!" And dove into the carriage as fast as he could.

King looked behind him, concerned. "What's the matter, Dr. Franklin?"

"Quickly, quickly, King! Get uƒ out of thiƒ place!"

He heard the whip crack. As they shot off, Benjamin looked back and saw the whirlwind behind him in the road. It was following them.

He had never been one to heed his emotions, never spooked easily, but this, he *felt* its Saturnine darkness, how it tugged at him, peered into him, but had no eyes.

For the moment, he could not explain its sudden appearance in such an enclosed space, for the ruin was quite sheltered from the wind by trees.

His carriage quickly outpaced it as they raced back over the hill toward London. Benjamin thought about what it could've been and reasoned that it must be what was known as a wind devil, or small tornado. He promised himself he would research it as soon as he was able. He rationalized the experience into natural, scientific terms and brought his mind back from the brink of terror. Whatever he had been dreaming might have set him up to be frightened by such a sudden confrontation of a natural phenomenon. He felt a bit self-conscious for running away from it in such haste. Fortunately, only King had borne witness to his hasty flight, and would, himself, certainly understand.

"It *waf* a little wind devil. It frightened me," he confessed. "I was taking a nap."

"A wind what?" asked King, unable to hear from the front of the carriage.

"A wind devil," Benjamin replied matter-of-factly.

He went to dinner that evening, twirling his trick cane, and vowing to drink no wine. The atmosphere was awkward as Lord Howe regarded him with a sniff of suspicion. Benjamin wondered what, if anything, he knew about his sister's nighttime hobbies.

Mrs. Howe, herself, stared wicked daggers at him over the fruited ham. When the others were out of earshot, she whispered: "Your escape is only temporary. You belong to us, we've made sure of that."

Benjamin was momentarily disarmed by the comment, then remembered his trusty cane-sword. He would use it yet.

As promised, Chatham offered his diplomatic services on Benjamin's behalf and assured him that there was still a

235

chance that Parliament could be reasonable if he and Boston were forthcoming with an abjectly humble apology. Benjamin informed him that such an event would not be occurring.

"The*f*e new law*f* governing Ma*ff*achu*fettf* are referred to a*f* the Intolerable Act*f*," Benjamin notified him. "Intolerable because Bo*f*ton i*f* not going to tolerate them. Hm-hm."

"They have no other choice," smiled the thin and venerable Lord Chatham. "Only time and coin will quell King George's wrath. Until restitution is made, Boston will suffer. I'll try to mediate nonetheless."

Benjamin knew that a sidebar from Chatham in Parliament would be as good as he would be able to do for Boston.

And all night long, Mrs. Howe tempted him with a glass of wine, wine he knew was drugged with some mysterious poison for he could see the undissolved yellowish-white powder settled at the bottom of the glass. He turned it down numerous times, but still she persisted. "Oh it's most delicious," she said moueing her lips and taking delicious, thirsty gulps from her own glassful.

"What i*f* thi*f*... re*f*idue at the bottom of thi*f* gla*ff*?" He pointed at the stuff.

"What residue?" she asked innocently, and seeing it for herself, became extremely embarrassed. "Oh how positively heathen of me, look at the grime in the bottom of the glass! Our housekeeper is really slipping just notches below the worst of standards. Please pardon me, let me go myself and get you another."

Benjamin was sure she tried it again with the next glass, too. This time he took it and almost drank from it, teasing her, as she watched with great anticipation. Surely, what she was trying to push on him was not a deadly elixir, but a sleeping powder. He wondered how she planned to go through with this in front of her brother and Lord

Chatham. After dinner, he let himself be lured out onto the terrace by her.

"Why do you not drink the wine, Benjamin?" She was beautiful in the moonlight.

"I quite enjoyed you the other night, Mrf. Howe," he said with a giddy "hm-hm."

"And I you, Mr. Franklin." Her sumptuous cleavage and perfect skin lured him closer to her. She wanted him, too, wanted him so badly that she was willing to drug and kidnap him. He kissed her then, remembering her soft mouth and sweet licorice breath. He let his hands graze over the bodice of her dress and across her bare skin. He heard her sigh and felt her mouth warm and velvety as his tongue caressed hers inside her mouth. It seemed then, almost as if the thought flowed from her head into his. Were they the ones who had brokered the deal, selling him to the ladies' lodge? Benjamin looked down at her then. This was a trap, and the tension in her body betrayed as much, the way her palms watered – they were about to make their move. He glimpsed a shadow moving on a nearby rooftop.

Just then, Lord Howe summoned them inside to bid Lord Chatham goodnight. As soon as her head was turned, Benjamin slid down the banister to the bottom of the stairs where he hit the ground running. He leapt into his carriage in the alley, and made off into the night. He had accomplished his diplomatic mission and escaped with his breeches, and his life.

Just before he departed for the Colonies, he received a letter from Lord Chatham that his efforts to smooth over relations between the two sides had failed. He had expected as much.

With all that had been going on, and his ship to set sail the next day, Benjamin had forgotten to notify his grandson, Temple Franklin, who had been at boarding school in Kent, that they would be leaving for the Colonies. He couldn't leave him there; it wasn't safe. He whisked him away in the middle of the night and the two of them boarded the ship for the Colonies.

"They say you've turned on our country, grandfather," said Temple when they were alone in their cabin.

"Yeſ. If you conſider England 'our country' I have. What I have done waſ in the intereſt of our colony – where we were born."

"If you were going to cause so much trouble, you could've at least come and gotten me out of school! Where were you?" the boy asked angrily.

It was then he noticed the greenish bruise under Temple's left eye and felt ashamed. He thought of the weeks spent in prison, the month in captivity of the Ladies' Lodge. There was no part of this story that would be appropriate or wise to recount for his grandson even if it did assuage his hurt feelings. It seemed that no one but the Privy Council, Dunning, and the Dog Star Lodge was aware of his stint in Newgate, and Benjamin wanted that kept quiet. Telling a teenager would be contraindicative to that measure.

"I waſ occupied by diplomatic   dutieſ," he said. "If I could've gotten you from ſchool ſooner, I would have. I'm ſorry if I made you ſuffer." Benjamin regretted the consequences of his actions and wondered how Sally and his sister Lydia fared.

It was May fifth that Benjamin and Temple's *Pennsylvania Packet* landed in Portsmouth. Benjamin's son, Temple's father, William, met them at the dock and had few words for his father. William Franklin was a loyalist, the King's appointed British governor of New Jersey. Benjamin had left it up to him, his illegitimate son by another woman to bury his old wife Deborah in his absence, and this no doubt, sat ill with him. William handed his father a printed page from her funeral and her wedding ring, and said simply, "I wish you had chosen to come back sooner."

Benjamin looked at the page. It had an abbreviated version of Psalm 51 and some biographical information about Deborah Read Franklin. He was listed in the "survived by" paragraph. He felt a deep remorse and embarrassment now, not having bid her a proper goodbye.

He was glad to get on his way back to Philadelphia and sent word to his daughter that he had arrived back in the colonies and would like to see her and his grandson, Benny Bache.

He had never met Benny, but he recognized the Franklin in him when the boy opened the door with the housekeeper. The bulbous nose, the fat cheeks that would one day make handsome Franklin jowls, the drooping eyes that begged plaintively without a word.

"You muſt be Benny," Benjamin said with a smile, and handed the boy a glass germinating bubble full of seeds. "ſaſſaſraſſ ſproutſ," he told him. "We'll make ſo m e rootbeer."

"Thank you," said the boy, delighted. "Are you my grandfather? Are you Ben Franklin?"

"I am he," said Benjamin.

CHAPTER XXIII

WEISHAUPT

The Society of Jesus encouraged meditation and taking retreats to do so, and Adam used the secluded retreat houses that belonged to the Church, to study the books and practice the rites they described. Whoever had collected these books was surely no ordinary person, and Adam often pondered to whom they rightfully belonged. Certainly they were his now. He had found them, saved them from ruin, but it often occurred to him that the owner might be some dangerous, vengeful sorcerer, and may at any moment, drop out of the ethers to fight him for the lost books. He did not want to chance losing them again, so in case of such an event, he worked to memorize them.

He learned of the occult virtues of all things; of how inferior things are subjected to superior bodies; what rulerships the planets held; of sorceries; of perfumes; of magickal rings; of divination; of animals; of geomancy; and of dreams. He learned how to influence another by speaking slowly and locking eyes. He learned how to concentrate his mind to bring about the desired results through sheer force of will. He learned how to consult the ancient Hebrew Qabala for the voice of the Universal Ape; how to transmute metals by fire; and how to raise the dead with lightning. He learned to decipher the gematria and qabalistic encryptions that kept secrets from the eyes of the mundane. He found instructions for scrying in water, and for astral walking, the two talents with which he had been born, and congratulated himself on their mastery, for such things were the mark of a mage of the highest learning.

He often wondered if he would be persecuted as his father was for using his talents, for seeking the holy mysteries of life and death through these ancient, blasphemous practices. Adam now concealed himself and his art with the utmost care so that such a fate would not be his. He removed a binding cover from an old Bible and whenever he was reading something esoteric, he simply placed the Bible cover on the outside of the book so that to anyone passing by, it would appear he was simply reading scripture.

With more knowledge at his fingertips than he'd ever dreamed of owning, he required nothing but Eva to fulfill himself. He searched the books in the desperate hope of finding some spell, potion, or prayer that would bring her to him. He found many and tried them all, but the familiar spirits in his employ were useless in this one task. Despite his repeated attempts to have her delivered to him, it simply was not to be. His minions claimed that powerful spirits protected her, and that she was unreachable.

One morning, he awoke in the Jesuit retreat house in the foothills of Alps. He was staying there alone, except for his horse that he had let into the entryway during the night to keep warm, for there was no stable. He often wondered why more people didn't take advantage of the serenity of the place, of the feeling of peace and strength from the mountains out the back door, but was glad they didn't, for he had it all to himself now.

He had translated all the books he had found, except for one Egyptian scroll for which there seemed to be no key for deciphering. The language was dead, spoken and written by no living man – modern Egyptians wrote and spoke Arabic and a mixture of Bedouin languages. From what he could tell, their religion had gone the way of the language as well, as most Egyptians were now Musselmen and probably had little light to shed on the meanings of the texts, or the long-dead rituals Adam thought surely must be contained therein. He kept the old scroll in a hollow gourd in his satchel and brought it to this quiet place to study.

Sitting on the mat on the floor near one of the large windows, he unrolled it across the floor, placed four stones on its corners and pored over it for hours, scanning the beautiful picture language and pondering its meaning. He grasped clearly that it was meant to be read from top to bottom, for there were vertical lines between the symbols. The bird appeared many times and he tried to guess its meaning. Every now and then, the small picture text would break and there were vignettes, depicting a lunar queen with a headdress bearing the full moon. She held various implements crossed in her hands and was always bare-breasted. In some of the drawings, she was worshipped by two men whom Adam suspected might be priests or servants, for they held sacred plants and something that might have been a feather, and they bowed low at her feet. As he inched his way across the floor on his knees, scanning further, there was a pyramid, and inside it, a priest and the goddess looked to be about to fornicate for the priest's member was erect. He wondered if the scroll was a set of directions for some sort of male aphrodisiac. So many of the books that had come to him, were simply cookbooks for potions and charms, spells and medicines, but he suspected this scroll was more significant. He summoned one of the goetic demons who was supposed to bestow knowledge of languages, and it appeared in the form of a hideous, hairy, little creature outside Adam's circle. The tiny monster snorted in acquiescence to his request for understanding, bowed and vanished before Adam had even sent him away.

Adam looked again at the scroll, but had no more an understanding of the strange language than before the evocation. He scried for some answer, but only saw the glittering visage of a beautiful woman, one that reminded him of the vision he had seen in Hamburg when he had called for his Angel. He expected to have a grasp on the language instantly, but it was not delivered. Painstakingly, he studied the scroll letter by letter, then stood at a distance from it, hoping there would be some key visible from a wider perspective. At the week's end, he was more confused about it than he had been before he had studied it so closely.

He returned to the University, and even though he'd vowed to himself to never reveal the books in his possession to anyone, he sought out Dr. Mahler, the head of the foreign language faculty. He showed him the Egyptian scroll and asked for his help. Mahler squinted at it through his spectacles, made some faces, and like the rest of the world, did not know the Egyptian language either.

"I have some clever friends at the University of Vienne. They might know of someone who can help you," he told Adam. "Don't get your hopes up, but we can contact them and see if they know something."

Adam instantly regretted showing Dr. Mahler the scroll. He provided no help, and now Adam may have to fend off questions from other members of the European intellectual community about where he found the thing and what else he had in his possession. His frustration had gotten the better of him and now he risked exposing what may well be a stolen lot of books that could not only get him arrested for their content, but persecuted by the true owner, if ever he were to come forward to claim them. And worst of all, he probably would never have a translation of the thing.

In the summer, Adam was employed by Dean Ickstatt to paint the dingy hallways of the University. He was on this task when he was hailed by Dr. Mahler.

"I have just received a letter back from a professor at the University of Copenhagen. There is an Egyptian translator in Denmark and he can be reached by post through the University," said Mahler. The Danish professor in Copenhagen had chanced to meet this person, Franz Kolmer, in a marketplace when he had visited Cairo, and found his knowledge of all things Egyptian unparalleled.

Franz Kolmer was a merchant in Alexandria and Cairo for many years, during which time he developed a fascination with Egyptian culture and mythology. He just happened to be passing through Ingolstadt on his way back from Egypt, and agreed to stop in at the University to examine the scroll.

Franz Kolmer dressed like some Egyptian hierophant

from the Middle Kingdom, wearing a long robe and sash, with a metal collar that lay on top of his shoulders. Beneath the collar, he wore a leopard skin draped over half his torso. His head was shaved clean, and though he was a fair-skinned Dane, his long beard was dyed jet black and braided into a lanyard. Adam had never seen a man wear charcoal around his eyes before, but Franz had it artfully applied to both lower and upper eyelids then out into a curl at the edges. He was a strange bird, perhaps a decade older than himself.

Adam watched him with skepticism as he sat at Ickstatt's long meeting table, scanning the Egyptian scroll with his finger and writing down the translation with his left hand. Left-handed people were always idiosyncratic.

"This is most intriguing. Do you know what you have here?" Kolmer said in an excited tone.

"What does it say?" asked Adam, who had been waiting for long minutes to learn the meaning of the scroll.

When Adam first laid eyes on Kolmer, he seemed vaguely familiar though he could not place him. He felt chafed by him as if they had had some previous unpleasant run-in, though Adam could not remember ever actually meeting him.

"What is it?" Adam repeated when Kolmer didn't answer.

"This is an evocation, a prayer to Isis to appear before the priest and perform sacred rites. I have never seen anything like it. And I would say it is a translation of something far older. I cannot guess how old."

"But what does it say?" Adam asked, burning with curiosity.

"It calls the goddess down from her sky chamber, to commune with the priest and bestow him with her power," answered Kolmer looking electrified. "But it must be performed in a sacred temple in Egypt. What will you take for this artifact? I can make you a generous offer."

"It's not for sale," said Adam bristling and snatching up the scroll. Kolmer glared at him, during which time Adam felt that he was attempting to pry his resolve, but he was impervious to such a technique, and smiled. "You cannot sway me with your stare, Herr Kolmer. I'm not afraid of you."

Kolmer lit a pipe full of hemp, and after some minutes, responded coolly. "Come with me to Egypt. This rite is a temple rite; it must be performed in Giza at a specific location. We can perform it together. A priest and his attendant. You need me to show you what I know."

"Do I?" asked Adam suspiciously.

"Yes," said Kolmer. "Otherwise, what good is it to you? And how else would you ever get there?"

Adam considered his offer. He had always wanted to go to Egypt and was sure he could coerce Ickstatt to pay his way if Kolmer couldn't foot the bill.

And so it was decided that Adam would finish his studies early that year so that they could leave in early May as soon as the mountain passes were clear. They would join an excursion and drive overland south to the Mediterranean and take a ship to the Nile Delta. The trip would take three months.

Adam wrote to his brother to apprise him of his trip to Egypt. He responded with enthusiasm for the Great Pyramids and said they were perhaps the greatest structures in the world, and lamented that the British Crown was continuing to oppress the Colonies and that export was nearly impossible. No hemp would be coming in the foreseeable future.

Bavaria, as torn as it had been by the Thirty Years War, was now a relatively safe haven for culture and industry, and Adam was glad to be living in such a time and place when he and those around him had the opportunity and inclination to enlighten themselves, rather than scratch at the earth for sheer sustenance, or worse - prepare for war.

He recalled his brother's natal horoscope and remembered that his fighting days were far from over. Adam hated war and all that it entailed, and because of what was happening in the American colonies, and to the Society of Jesus, he was more aware of the forces that could potentially rise against him to thwart his enterprises. It would never be his lot to be too complacent or to place his trust in any governing body. He had read far too much of the politics of the French philosophers, and had had too many political discussions with Ickstatt about the precarious personalities that posed upon thrones ready to strike fear and oppression into the hearts of those who dared to express themselves in ways that might be considered dangerous.

Except for Ickstatt and Dr. Mahler, Adam kept his books a secret. After Kolmer had become enthralled by his Egyptian papyrus, Adam worried that word would spread throughout Christendom about his library, hidden but vulnerable, in the floor of Ickstatt's office. Of all the arts known to man, sorcery was by far the most damnable, and Adam was not about to be recognized as a practitioner of such arts. Ickstatt had made it clear that he would be excommunicated, if not subjected to worse if he were to ever confess to being privy to such knowledge. He had given up the public practice of reading cards and casting charts, and when anyone asked about it, he replied that Jesus had spoken to him and warned him to stop his infernal activities before his immortal soul was corrupted. He would play pious Catholic for as long as it was convenient.

The time came for his departure to Egypt. He had cast a chart for himself for the time of travel, and the stars seemed to bode well for such an undertaking. The position of Venus indicated that he would be influenced strongly by a woman while he was abroad. He wondered whom, but thought little more about it.

Adam and Kolmer traveled in a caravan of several coaches to the Mediterranean shore. Leading them through the mountains were the Steinmahrs, Bavaria's most adventurous couple. Like Kolmer, Herr Steinmahr had made his fortune in importing textiles and art, and had traveled to and fro on the winding mountain roads through the eastern Alps many times. Frau Steinmahr was the only woman traveling with them. She was a sporting type of matron, and a maker of herbal concoctions, he would later have the misfortune to discover. She was cordial enough and Adam wondered if she was the woman who would be of influence upon him during the trip.

Doctors Fehrs and Pattengart were two professors from the University of Konigsburg, and they had been to Egypt before. They, too, sought Kolmer's knowledge of the strange picture language and were always at him to make them a dictionary so that they could read the language themselves, something that Kolmer continually declined to do.

Adam and Kolmer both rode their horses. The trail was precarious at best and Adam fortified his horse with charms for acumen and imperviousness to harm, for the footing was over tumbled rocks against sheer mountain cliffs above deep canyons, and across many a perilous abyss. The Steinmahrs walked their team and wagon over the rocks and Adam wondered how they managed so wide a load on such narrow trails. Indeed the wagon did ride on two wheels at times, but only once did they actually have to stop and lay down pieces of timber to engineer a passable way. Fehrs and Pattengart shared a cart, but often said they'd wished they'd simply ridden on horseback, especially after a wheel broke. It was not an overly long ascent before they crested a green plateau and looked down into the wide expanse of the Italian countryside.

As they broke camp in the evening, Adam listened to

Fehrs recount his previous travels in Egypt. He was an ingenious artist and showed them all the drawings he had copied from the stele on the walls inside the Great Pyramid. Kolmer interpreted the picture language where Fehrs' understanding left wide chasms of inscrutability and Adam realized how learned was Kolmer about all things Egyptian. He was fortunate to be in his company, though many traits still unnerved him about the man.

Once when they washed at a spring, Adam saw him without the charcoal around his eyes. He was stranger looking without it, and whenever Adam met his eye, it was as if he was being watched by not just one pair of eyes, but many, as if Kolmer had a myriad of personalities peering from his pupils, scrutinizing him. He knew that Kolmer had reverence for him, but perhaps it was simply because he was the owner of the coveted scroll. Kolmer had asked him if he had it and where it was, numerous times. Adam assured him it was safe inside the hollow gourd container he carried inside another satchel.

Franz Kolmer himself was heavily burdened with gold pieces and had packed them in all sorts of places on their persons, and on their horses in case they were robbed. He had even stowed away the largest bag of gold beneath the Steinmahr's wagon, of which Adam was sure the couple was unaware.

"What is it that you import from Egypt?" asked Adam of Kolmer as they rode through a winding riverbed.

"Treasure, ancient works of art, beautiful skins and jewelry, things that rich ladies of Paris and Copenhagen will find indispensable," he replied.

"You don't bring anything from abroad to trade with the Egyptians?" Adam asked.

"Indeed, I do ship a great lot from Denmark, but it is too much trouble to drag my wares through this narrow route. My ship will be waiting for us in the harbor, and we can transfer my load to our vessel," he said.

"Why didn't you simply ride aboard the ship with your goods? What if they're stolen or stopped somewhere?" said Adam, mistrustful of the shipping industry.

"It does bear on my mind, but I wanted to travel this way and get acquainted with you," answered Kolmer, his mouth curving into a slight smile. "The ritual that we are going to perform is no small undertaking, but requires ascetic discipline, and clarity of mind. And I'll be frank, I don't know you very well."

Adam was sure he had both attributes, perhaps more so than Kolmer, but he was above boasting all that he knew. Let Kolmer think the least of him, then be blindsided by his power.

One morning when Adam awoke in their camp on the side of a mountain, he found Kolmer absent from his place by the fire. He rose and ventured around the bend to find him, and when he did, he saw him bowing before the morning sun, his arms out as if to embrace the great orb rising before him in the East. He swooped down to touch his hands upon the ground and kicked his feet out in the back, suspending himself on toes and palms like a plank. He curled his body backward in an arch, then leveled out and pushed away with his hands into another strange pose with his arse in the air. Adam watched him for some minutes and envied his flexibility. Mastery of the body was just as important as mastery of the mind, and Adam vowed, if nothing else, to learn from Kolmer this practice of exercise.

"Yoga," replied Kolmer on the trail some hours later. "The lost art of India, a practice that purifies all aspects of a man."

"I want you to teach me," said Adam.

At last the bright green of the Mediterranean Sea sparkled on the horizon.

"Just another day's journey," said Herr Steinmahr.

Adam could feel the humid wind and smell the salt air. He anticipated having some fresh fish when they reached the sea. He appreciated Frau Steinmahr's stews, but he felt that she had become uninspired with nothing but potatoes and dried meat to go in them, and his palate was rather bored.

They arrived in Venice at nightfall. Just as Kolmer had said, his ship was waiting in the harbor. Adam stood by and watched as he boarded the ship via the narrow gangplank and greeted the skipper in Danish. He beckoned Adam, and by the light of the moon, the three of them unloaded the crates belonging to Kolmer and put them on the deck of *The Falcon*, the vessel that would bring them all to Egypt.

The Falcon set sail bright and early the next morning and Adam slept until noon in the gentle rock of his hammock in the tiny, dark cabin where he and Fehrs and Pattengart were quartered. In the evening, they read from Herodotus and Plutarch on the deck of the ship, and Pattengart recounted the myth of Isis and Osiris as *The Falcon* cut through the bright green sea.

"Osiris, lord of the North and his brother Set, lord of the South fought over their sister Isis who loved them both. Osiris and Set fought over everything. Even the land had been divided between them – North and South, for they could not share. Osiris won the heart of Isis and made her his wife, and he ruled the land of the North with a fair and generous hand.

"Meanwhile, Set hatched a diabolical plot to kill Osiris and have Isis and all of Osiris' country as his own. Set had his slaves fashion a beautiful, golden coffin in the perfect size to fit Osiris. He threw a huge banquet in honor of the king, and when Isis had flown off on a ruse, Set tricked Osiris into trying on the coffin for size. Set and his conspiring guests were making a game of it, lying in it to see if it fit them. As soon as Osiris climbed into the coffin, Set's minions slammed it closed, locking Osiris inside. They took Osiris' coffin and dumped it into the Nile.

"When Isis found Osiris absent, Set told her that he had abandoned her for one of the female guests, and he took the forlorn Isis as his wife. It was not overly long until Isis discovered the plot against Osiris. Enraged at Set, she abandoned him, and went searching for Osiris' coffin. After many long years of constant searching along the Nile and in the neighboring lands, she came to Byblos where she found Osiris' coffin built into the roof of the local King's palace. Somehow, a huge tamarisk tree had grown around the golden coffin, enclosing it in its bough, and the bough was built into the local king's roof.

"Until she could devise a way to get the coffin down, Isis disguised herself as a mortal girl and took employment in the palace as the nurse of the King's youngest child, a baby boy. Isis grew to love the baby and decided to give him the gift of immortality. As she held him over the fire in the hearth, suckling him on her finger, saying her incantations, she was interrupted by the child's mother who rushed into the room and broke the spell. This killed the child and enraged Isis who threw off her mundane guise and revealed herself as the goddess.

"The king had the bough and coffin taken down out of the roof for Isis and sent her back to Egypt on one of his ships. Isis planned to use her magic to resurrect Osiris and conceive an heir to his throne. But before she could do this, she was found by Set who cut Osiris' body into twenty-three pieces, and flying over the world, scattered them far and wide."

"Fourteen pieces," interrupted Frau Steinmahr.

"Twenty-three," insisted Fehrs.

Pattengart continued. "Isis searched for Osiris' dismembered parts along the Nile and after much effort, collected them all, except for his phallus, which had been eaten by a fish. That is why you will never see a real Egyptian using cut-up fish as bait."

Adam had read the story before and remembered that Isis put Osiris back together, brought him to life again through sorcery, and fashioned him a phallus out of wax, by which she conceived the child god, Horus. It was the most interesting part of the story but Pattengart must have edited it out for the benefit of Frau Steinmahr who couldn't have cared less.

They passed the days aboard the ship in this pleasant manner, telling the myths and lore of Egypt and harrowing tales of crocodile and hippopotamus attacks, and drinking the claret Pattengart had brought. While Kolmer secluded himself in one of the holds, Adam and a group of them played cards in the galley.

"Why is your friend so antisocial?" asked Fehrs.

"Yes, why has he always locked himself away somewhere? It's most peculiar," said Herr Steinmahr.

Adam shrugged and said he did not know, for indeed he did not. When they had joined up with the other travelers, Adam had assumed that they were all well acquainted with Franz Kolmer, but indeed they were only familiar with his reputation as an Egyptian translator. No one really knew him at all. When Adam had won enough money at the card table, but not too much to arouse suspicion, he stepped out on deck and looked up at the stars.

He thought he had misjudged Kolmer gravely when they were in Ingolstadt, for Kolmer was a riddle in himself. Adam had thought most all of his idiosyncrasies were on the surface, but the more time he spent near this man, the more he realized Kolmer was deeply involved in a world that no one but he knew was even there.

Kolmer's sleeping habits seemed to be inconsistent at best. Once he found Kolmer on deck at four in the morning, sitting upon a pillow naked to the wind. Adam had slipped back inside the cabin and never spoken of it. He thought to himself that such obvious practice of the mystical arts was foolish. No one who did not know Adam would ever suspect him for the mage he had become, for he dressed simply with an attractive panache since his days at the brothel, and he acted humbly whenever he could, for his greatness was sometimes difficult to conceal. But moreover, he never dared speak with authority of such things with mundane people. Kolmer, however, put on a show and continually elicited intrigue from all who came near him with mystical talk and piercing glares from his heavily outlined, hawk-like eyes. But for his merchant business, he seemed to live the life of the mystical Egyptian priest and played the part to tee, so that he believed it of himself within and without, and others had but no choice to do as well. He spent most of the day in isolation, meditating in a hold, yet seemed to be aware of everything that had gone on around him without his having seen it.

It was a dark, moonless night and the fog was thick over the water. Adam and the other men stood on deck smoking their pipes, something for which Kolmer had great distaste. Beneath their jovial voices, the whisper of the water seemed sinister, and a smell like that of a fishing pier wafted into his nostrils. Adam was alerted by the warning signs, but too late to stop what ghastly thing was about to occur. Out of the fog, appeared the battered hull of another ship. It was suddenly alongside *The Falcon*, and no sooner were several scraggly men jumping aboard.
"Pirates! All hands to arms!" shouted the first mate.
Various crewmen rushed onto the scene, and seemed to Adam, sorely unprepared for the encounter with the armed pirates.
Kolmer appeared in the doorway of his favorite hold. He lifted his right hand, and out from it came a beam of

253

blackness like a long, heavy, shadow. It found the captain of the pirates who seized up and fell upon the deck, twitching and vomiting up his own entrails. The others drew swords and pistols and advanced on Kolmer who waved his hand at them. Adam saw the black streak from his hand strike the others down. They lay writhing in pain, vomiting their insides out upon the deck, and were dead in moments. The pirates who had remained on their own ship, watched in wide-eyed horror, and quickly cut the rope that tethered the ships. The pirate ship disappeared into the fog. The captain of *The Falcon* fired his musket after them, but they were gone.

Fehrs, Pattengart, and Herr Steinmahr stood puffing their pipes and gratefully acknowledged Kolmer. Kolmer gave them a hard glare and disappeared into his hold. Adam walked around the bodies of the pirates, inspecting the effects of Kolmer's power, as he made a pretense of searching their pockets. All were dead, and quite gruesomely so. Adam had never seen such power and he guessed from the silence of the other men, they hadn't either.

"What shall we do with them?" he asked of the other gentlemen.

"Feed the crabs," smiled the captain.

As Adam and one of the crewmen shoved each of the dead bandits beneath the rail into the ocean, Adam was suddenly proud of his association with Kolmer. They would have all been killed if it weren't for his strange powers, and Adam vowed to learn all his secrets.

The next day, they stood on deck and he pressed Kolmer for instruction. "How did you make the black shadow come from your hand?"

"You saw the shadow?" asked Kolmer.

"Will you not impart your secret to your apprentice?" Adam begged.

"Since when have you become my apprentice? I thought

you vied with me for the role of priest," said Kolmer defiantly.

"I've gained new respect for you," Adam confessed.
"And I wish to know all that you know."

"The way of the Assassin is already yours, is it not? By different means... I can see the blood in your aura, but it does not plague you, does it? Perhaps you cannot even recall what you have done," said Kolmer, scrutinizing him.

Adam had the feeling again that many souls were looking out of Kolmer's eyes, and he was unnerved.

"How do you propose to know anything about me? I am but a University student of no means," said Adam.

"Anyone who could come by such a scroll as you have, and then find *me* to read it is truly a remarkable person, one aided by divine forces. I am the only one *in the world* who can read the language of the Egyptians. Whoever owned it before you could not have known what he had in his possession. It is destiny that we have met," said Kolmer, his blue eyes becoming singular and translucent again.

"Teach me what you know," repeated Adam. "Please."

In the days that remained aboard the ship, Adam applied himself to learning all that Kolmer would reveal. At times, Kolmer spewed metaphysical knowledge and ancient jargon as fast as he could pronounce it, but at other times, he stared long into Adam's eyes and seemed to wait for him to intuit his meanings. Adam learned yoga and memorized the asanas, and in which order they were to be performed. He felt invigorated, lightened, and purified by the practice and it complemented the strange prayers and channeled forces that Kolmer had him call forth. Through yoga, Adam became sensitized to the subtle and the overwhelmingly powerful energies with which he and Kolmer played. These were dangerous things, and Adam's meticulous nature and rapier memory were called into play almost constantly, for precision, pronunciation, and orders of operations were key to invoking and banishing the entities which Kolmer employed. His league of minions were none that Adam had encountered before. As the Hamburg lot of books had bestowed him with the intellectual information, Kolmer provided him with the application of, and practical knowledge of all that he had read.

As the ship skirted the sandy shores of Egypt on its way toward the Nile Delta, Kolmer became visibly restless and asked Adam to retrieve the scroll that he had brought. They sat together out of the wind, in the doorway of the hold in which the two of them had spent most of their time for the past week. Kolmer again read the scroll to Adam, the very words of which made his hair stand on end. The rite was verily meant to conjure the goddess Isis in the flesh.

"Do you know how long I have searched, how long I have prayed, to make contact with my Lady?" Kolmer asked of Adam, his voice crackling. "This will be a day of reckoning for me. I would not be surprised if my heart gave out and I passed into the Duat."

Adam agreed now to play the role of the priest's attendant. He had learned too much from Kolmer and felt sure that if Kolmer were not placated with the proper respect, he would receive no more instruction from him. Kolmer knew far more than he ever told him, Adam was certain of that, and he was sorry that the ship's voyage was at an end, for he was uncertain if Kolmer's instruction would continue.

When they disembarked in Alexandria, they found the river low, and the land parched and dry. Kolmer explained that the solstice flood was on its way, only days away in fact, for it was June eighteenth when they arrived in Egypt.

Kolmer and Adam unloaded his goods into two donkey carts, and drove them to the marketplace. Adam watched as Kolmer quickly traded all his wares to two merchants in dirty orange turbans. Their shop was the largest in the marketplace and it sold everything from English medicine and exotic birds to Chinese furniture and camels.

Adam was impressed at the ease of the transaction. They drove back to the port and found the others standing by the dock with their trunks and gear. They loaded their possessions and themselves into the wagons, and set out for Cairo and Giza. They rode along the milky, brown river, past camel trains and fishermen.

As the balmy wind ruffled his hair and blew bits of sand in his face and into his tent, Adam made camp with the others beneath the date palms, a stone's throw from the river's edge. In the remains of the daylight, Adam, Fehrs, Pattengart, and the Steinmahrs hiked across the footbridge to the base of the pyramids. As they ambled around the pyramids, the elder scholars proposed their theories of why, how, and when the massive stones were piled into their pyramidal forms. Adam listened with interest and wished that Kolmer was there to give his perspective, for he was raised in Egypt by his merchant father, and certainly his take on the pyramids was more correct than the academic speculations of his present company.

Kolmer had taken the wagon back to the marketplace in Cairo to buy Egyptian whatnot to sell abroad. For two days, he did not come to their camp and Adam wondered what had befallen him.

On June the twentieth, Adam ventured down to the marketplace in search of him and something for their group to cook for dinner. He found some fat chickens for a fair price, and carrying the crate out of the market, spied Kolmer relaxing beneath the awning of a merchant's shop.

He looked surprised to see Adam and called out to him. "Have you been looking for me?" asked Kolmer.

"Yes, but I settled for these chickens instead," quipped Adam without a break in his stride.

"Those are not chickens! You've been swindled," Kolmer gestured to the crate.

Adam looked and there were three young crocodiles inside it. Unflinching, he held fast to the crate, wondering if crocodile meat was palatable. He was not surprised at anything that happened while in Kolmer's company. "Actually, I figured you'd gone to the Duat as you had planned," said Adam.

"I'm sorry, really. I'd expected to be back sooner, but this gentleman has the most exceptional opium." He laughed and gestured to the toothless, black-skinned fellow grinning next to him.

"Tomorrow is the day, and we have made no preparations," said Adam sternly. "I have come all this way and I'm not going to miss this opportunity." He knew that there was only one day a year that the ceremony could be performed correctly, and that day was tomorrow, the day of the flood when the stars were in alignment with Venus, and Venus with the Great Pyramid. His blood boiled at Kolmer's cavalier attitude. If they missed it, Kolmer would be around for it next year, but Adam probably would not.

That night, Adam managed to sleep in his tent despite the sudden influx of mosquitoes and humidity, and the noise of travelers on the road below them. He awoke refreshed and excited. He searched through his things until he found the hollow gourd in which he'd carried the scroll from Bavaria to Egypt. He opened it up, and to his horror, found it empty.

He dug through his tent but could not find the scroll anywhere. Had he gotten it out and then forgotten to return it to its container? He could not recall doing such a thing. He wondered now if he and Kolmer, after they had studied it on the ship, had returned it to the gourd or left it lying somewhere. He dressed quickly, tore open the flaps of his tent and stood peering around the camp at his companions.

"Has anyone seen a scroll lying around?" he asked. But something told him it was Kolmer who was responsible for the theft, for none of the rest of the travelers had even known it existed. Adam and Kolmer had been quite secretive about their ulterior mission.

He walked to the marketplace and combed the shops and avenues for Kolmer, but he was not there. Adam approached his toothless, black friend, "Have you seen Kolmer?" he asked him.

The man only smiled his toothless grin and rolled his bleary eyes toward a small dwelling next door. It was made of limestone covered with mud, as were most of the buildings in the city. Heavy linens curtained the two small windows on either side of the door. Adam smelled a sickening perfume on the air.

He opened the door of the dwelling and found the source of the smell. Thick white smoke curled through the single ray of sunlight that shone through a hole in one of the curtains and back into the dimness of the room. There were several men asleep in bunks along two of the walls. Others lounged upon straw mats on the floor around a giant hookah. Adam followed one of its tentacles to Kolmer's bottom lip. Smoke escaped the slack hole in his head as if he were some lazy dragon.

"Franz!" said Adam, "What did you do with my scroll?"

"I don't know," slurred Kolmer. "Where did you leave it?"

"Today is the solstice! It's our only chance to use it!"

Kolmer looked up at him slowly. "I did it without you..."

"What?" Adam was incredulous and angry. He lifted his fist, thought better of it, and with an exasperated gesture, turned to go.

"It didn't work," said Kolmer at his back. "Nothing happened. Your scroll is useless!"

He looked back, opened his mouth to say one last thing to him, and saw Kolmer's bag hanging on a nail above his head. The scroll was sticking out of it. Adam snatched it up and ducked out.

Adam stormed out of the marketplace. How dare Kolmer perform the ritual without him? How dare he steal from him and lie about it. Why had Kolmer suddenly turned traitor? Had everything been a pretense? As Adam marched across the sands in disillusionment and disgust, he remembered that Kolmer had been absent for several days. Had he been smoking opium the whole time? If so, he would have been out of his mind, and most likely unable to perform even the simplest function. Adam had heard of the waste of opium, of its debilitating effects and fantastic visions, and reckoned Kolmer probably hadn't been outside the opium den since he'd last seen him beneath the awning.

With only minutes of daylight remaining, he ran. He threw open the flaps of his tent and gathered up the objects required in the scroll: The dagger, a waxen image of Isis, two live doves, a jade phallus, some semiprecious stones, some oil, some rosewater, and some incense. All of these, he put into his satchel. He had diligently prepared in the days before, readying himself for the role of the attendant. Now, he would be both priest and attendant.

It was sunset by the time he found himself at the base of the Great Pyramid. He checked Kolmer's translation and scaled the limestone blocks a short way up one side of the great monument. Just as the scroll had indicated, there was an unusual space about an inch high beneath the thirty-third block from the ground, giving the thing the look that it was floating. Adam stood upon the block below and waited for the moon to move into position overhead. When it was perfectly centered above the pyramid's tip, and he felt the power of it, he intoned the incantation to open the passageway. In seconds, the block simply disappeared as if it had never existed, revealing a dark shaft leading into the pyramid. He shuddered in amazement as a chill breeze flowed from the dark cavity.

In his haste, he had failed to bring any means of illumination, and with no other option but forsaking the whole operation, he entered the pitch-blackness.

On hands and knees, satchel slung over his back, he crawled through the dark, up the sloping narrow tunnel, into the inner recesses of the pyramid. The doves inside his bag chirped nervously, sensing their bearer's apprehension, or perhaps the fate that awaited them.

At last, he found himself in a small chamber dimly lit by a purple square of sky coming through a shaft on the other side of the pyramid. The walls in the chamber had been etched with Egyptian stele and writings. Now, Adam sorely wished that Kolmer had found it worthwhile to accompany him.

He knelt on the cool, stone floor, and took in the room. At one end of the chamber, there was an altar, and Adam removed the things he had brought for the ritual from his satchel and spread them out so that he could find them. He opened the scroll and quickly referred to it in the waning light.

With no flint, he could not light the incense he had brought, so he rubbed it on his person and crushing it, sprinkled it around the altar. The myrrh and bergamot wafted up from his chest where he had smeared it, and into his nostrils, as he prepared the waxen figure. This, he stood in the middle, pressing her feet into the altar so that she would not fall over.

He spoke the first section of the Egyptian magic words, and took a small carnelian heart from his pocket and pressed it into the breast of the waxen figure. He intoned the rest of the prayer, and suddenly began feeling strange, perhaps from the sweet smell of the incense. He rolled the jade phallus between his hands to warm it then stuck it between the legs of the figure. "Isis, Isis, daughter of Nuit, I call thee to my side. With my phallus, I invite thee to feast on the delights of my body and my ku."

He stood there waiting, feeling the tremendous and ancient power of the pyramid around him, reinforcing and magnifying his will. After some minutes, he looked again at the scroll for fear of forgetting something. He went on with the next incantation, turning to speak it out the open shaft of the tunnel where he could see the sparkling Evening Star framed perfectly in the azure sky. "Inannaisis, Inannaisis, beloved flower, queen of the heavens, your servant awaits your return with open arms. Come now and join me in the fragrant bower of Egypt where earthly pleasure resides." He made libations of oil and rosewater, and pressed an amethyst into the waxen figure at her midline.

He kissed the waxen doll, then slit the doves' throats with his dagger and let the blood of each one drip upon it.

He closed the ceremony with all the names of Ra and stood waiting for something to happen. The scroll called also for the sacrifice of a lamb, but Adam had been too hurried to find one. And upon entering this place, he had been relieved he had not tried to bring one with him, for it would have been nearly impossible to drag it through the shaft, much less up the side of the pyramid. He vowed, however, to go to the market the following morning and find an animal and sacrifice it near his camp while the others were away. In case anyone was to happen upon him, he would simply say he was cooking. After a long time staring at the Evening Star, he sat down. It was dark now in the chamber, and he resolved to wait there until he had received some sign that it was time to exit. In the dark silence, he fell asleep.

He awoke in the morning, startled at his surroundings

until he remembered his purpose. Excited, he scrutinized the altar for some sign of a presence, but all the elements were as he had laid them.

In the morning light that shone into the chamber from the overhead shaft, he could see the art on the walls and the fine patina of sand over the floor that he had felt underfoot. He wondered briefly if this room were a tomb, but there was no sarcophagus - not that one couldn't have been in there and been pilfered, for certainly a structure as old and conspicuous as the Great Pyramid would have attracted all manner of fortune hunters. Still, he didn't feel it was a burial place at all, but a ceremonial chamber that he had utilized correctly. However, it seemed the efficacy of the ritual was somewhat dubious, and he could not help recalling Kolmer's comment that the scroll was useless.

He made the best of his circumstances nonetheless, for surely only a precious few people had ever set foot in this place. He lingered in the chamber and inspected the stele on the wall, wishing again that Kolmer were there or that he had some sort of quick copying device that would transcribe all the drawings to a small, portable tablet he could take with him. They were scenes of life, of wars, of the cultivation of some grain, of Ra in his boat. The strangest scene perhaps was the largest one that depicted a man inside a square chamber that bore a striking resemblance to the very one in which he stood. Above, there were seven stars, the Pleiades, perhaps, and to either side, there was a lion. He stared at it for nearly an hour and could make little sense of it. He vowed to return another day with quill and ink and copy the stele from the walls. Certainly, he would be able to return, he thought.

Fatigued, he reminded himself of the sacrifice of the lamb he had yet to perform. He gathered up his things and crawled back out of the tunnel the way he had come in. At the end of it, he found the block still absent, but as soon as he had cleared the mouth of the tunnel and scaled down the pyramid a ways, he looked back. He could no longer see the open shaft nor differentiate the stone that had been removed and was now returned, from any other. He puzzled over this, turning back again and again to look, as he made his way across the sands in the mild morning air.

He went into the marketplace and found a plump sheep. It cost him half of his money, and taking it by its lead, he brought it back to his camp across the bridge.

As he had imagined, there was no one about. He tied the animal to a nearby date palm and found his dagger. He had never performed a sacrifice, save for the two little doves on the previous evening, and was unsure of himself. He found two stumps and a large flat stone that needed only crude assembly to form an altar. He started a large fire below the stone. As the smoke swirled about him, he prepared the circle about himself and the sheep, and proceeded as the scroll specified. He said the words of consecration, and slit the lamb's throat with a prayer on his breath, letting its blood spill over the stone. He began to feel intoxicated as he wrote the signs in the blood.

When he had come back to his senses, he hung the animal neatly upside down from a tree to let the rest of it drain into Frau Steinmahr's large cooking pot.

The process was not difficult and when the altar stone was good and hot, and he had eviscerated the lamb and singed off its wool, he laid the animal's body upon it. The tantalizing aroma rose up before him as its skin sizzled and the meat below it began to cook.

Suddenly, he was aware of voices and the sound of rushing water. The inundation of the Nile was not something to be missed, and leaving the lamb to cook, he hurried down the path toward the edge of the river. As he approached, he could hear the Nile's turbulent deluge, feel its wet renewal in the air, and smell the crisp earthy scent of mud. Men with fishing nets were gathering along the shores, and brown-skinned children ran along the banks in excitement. He leaned against one of the date palms and stared at the light, frothy, brown water swirling at its banks below. With the sun reflecting off it, it sparkled like an opalescent fire.

He blinked, and suddenly there she was. Before him was a bronze-skinned and singularly beautiful woman, her black hair piled high upon her crowned head. Twelve turbaned Egyptians formed a guard around her as she sat naked but for her heaps of golden necklaces, upon the back of an elephant, looking out at the river. She met his eye, and he recalled the image of Isis he had visualized in his mind during the ritual. He blinked and she was still there.

"Adam?" she spoke his name.

He thought he was having some sort of unprovoked hallucination, a leak of his aspirations into reality. Her servants lifted her down. He marveled at her unparalleled beauty and reached out to touch her cheek to make sure she was real. He thought that she was even more magnificent than Eva, more beautiful, and more desirable.

"You summoned me," she said simply. Her voice was like the music made by water.

"I…" he stuttered.

"Call me Inanna. Do not speak my Egyptian name unless you *mean* it," she whispered. Her large eyes were unlike any he had ever beheld, and he felt that she could see everything behind his, that he could conceal nothing from her.

He was simply dumbstruck, for he was certain that he was in the presence of the Goddess. He was unprepared, for even as much as he had cerebrated upon this encounter, the reality of it was beyond what his conscious mind could contain. Her presence exceeded anything he had ever before comprehended. She was at once beside him, within him, around him, and above him.

"Come with me. Let's get to know one another," she

265

purred and slipped her arm next to his and grasped his hand. Her touch was pure exhilaration. He felt the cool gold of her armband on the inside of his arm, and the rough-cut amethysts on the girdle about her midriff.

"How is it that you of all men, have called me from my place in heaven? How did you ever find the way to summon me?"

"I came by a scroll," he stammered.

"I would have thought such a thing was lost an aeon ago," she said, looking up at him. "Not to mention, a man's ability to read it."

With her footmen traveling in two straight lines behind them, they took a long walk amid the date palms of the Nile, and Adam boasted to her about the papyrus scroll and all the esoteric things that he had come to know in his young life. She raised her beautiful eyebrow at many of his assertions, and asked him how he knew such things. He told her of the books he'd found, of all that he'd read, of his plans to master himself and all the world.

She laughed then, and he wished he hadn't been so forthcoming with his ambitions.

"Well what is it that *you* dream?" he demanded.

"Am I not dreaming, now?" she stroked his handsome face. "I am here now because you desire me."

At some length, they rested beneath a tree, looking up its trunk, at its spiraling, swaying fronds. As her servants fanned them and they drank cool wine from golden goblets, they spoke of the sacred mysteries of Egypt.

"The gods still lurk in these types of places, though no one recognizes us anymore," she smiled. "A truly wise man would not dare travel alone through Giza. Especially one with magical aspirations. He would be eaten alive in a place like this. All is not what it appears."

She was challenging him, teasing him, he knew it, but something had come over him and he could not escape her charms. Her scent was the most enticing thing he had ever experienced and he could not help kissing her lips. He wanted to devour her and felt his passion mounting as he tasted her delicious skin and felt her smooth thigh pressed against him.

It was then that Adam was transported, for he did not walk. He had the sensation of being lifted suddenly, so fast that he lost consciousness momentarily.

When he opened his eyes again, he found himself in a luxurious room, lying amid silk pillows upon a bed of the softest material.

He rose, naked, though he could not remember how his clothes had been removed. The fine room appeared to be a bedchamber. He walked over to the dressing table and looked at himself in the large looking glass. It was clear and flawless. He looked more handsome than he had ever known himself to appear, but there were strange, dark markings below his eyes and above his brows that pointed like thorns. His cheeks had a fiery glow and when he opened his mouth he saw that his eyeteeth were long and sharp like those of a beast. He reeled back from the mirror, his heart pounding at the sight of himself.

He took in the room, his vision blurred as if he had taken some of Mayer's mushrooms, for the simultaneous beauty and deep empirical reality of his surroundings would certainly be indescribable later. He was already thinking how to explain where he'd been to his companions, and realized it would be extremely difficult, if not impossible. He walked to the only door and opened it. He looked down at the ground and found it made of mist. He dared step out with one foot, but found no solid ground below. Before him there was nothing but blue sky and feathery clouds. He wondered briefly if he was on top of one of the pyramids, and if that wasn't where he was, then where exactly was he? What was this room that seemed to float in the sky? He closed the door and stamped his foot on the floor but then worried that he would bring the whole place down. He walked gingerly across the soft, patterned carpet, and searched through a golden trunk at the foot of the bed. It was full of pretty, silk veils and cords, and smooth oblong crystals of different sizes.

He pulled back the bed covers and found the bed exquisitely, indelibly made, its silk cover expertly bound over what must have been the down of twenty-thousand geese. He reclined upon it and reaching up, touched the wall of the place and wondered at the material, for it was not wood, not metal, not stone, and seemed more like a living thing, like the vine-embraced trunk of a smooth and beautiful tree. He rolled onto his back and looked up. The ceiling was entirely open to the sky.

He stood up and caught his reflection again in her dressing table mirror. His demonic features were still there though they did not detract from his good looks. He admired the pointed curl of hair at his jaw line and the thorn-like accents marked below his eyes and in the apples of his handsome cheeks. He wondered if anyone else had noticed these things about him, if they were actually there to plain sight, and he was the only one who had never noticed them. He began to smell Inanna's sweet, intoxicating scent and became aroused.

She appeared behind him then, gliding her hands around his body. "They say the eyes are the mirror of the soul, but I think my mirror is even more truthful. This is how you look to the gods. You're a very devious boy, Adam Weishaupt," she said putting her finger inside his mouth and touching the point of his tooth. "But it doesn't bother me. I've had much worse than you."

He looked at her reflection and was overawed by the indescribably gorgeous, flowering energies that exuded from her in magnificent, colorful, diaphanous layers, and exalted her looks to the highest heights of beauty. He sighed, overawed, becoming excruciatingly hard. She touched him so gently with her fingertip.

He grabbed her by the wrists and threw her onto the soft bed. She giggled in girlish exuberance and writhed beneath him as he pinned her down, kissing her neck and squeezing her full, round breasts. He teased her hard nipples with his tongue and suckled her. He parted her silky thighs, feeling her wetness with his fingers. He pushed her legs back, holding her ankles, and plunged his manhood into her hot and blissful body. She screamed with pleasure as he thrust into her. And as he invaded her tight core, he was literally captured by it, and transported again, to the place he had seen once before with Eva, the Cathedral made of jewels with its soft, golden radiance.

A sudden intrusion brought him back into his body. She was above him now suddenly, and had placed something warm and hard in his arse. As she pivoted skillfully on him, she controlled the unseen thing that was so divinely penetrating him. He sat up, kissing her deeply, embracing her upon his lap, on the edge of release for many long minutes while she milked the energy of his pleasure from his body with hers and moaned in ecstasy. He caught a glimpse of their reflection in the strange dressing table mirror and saw a pulse of hot, blue light as it traveled up the center lines of their bodies and sparkled and flashed like a huge violet colored crown above their heads.

At last she began slowly withdrawing the thing inside of him, and he was unable to resist his orgasm that quaked through his core and made his every fiber tingle with bliss. He returned briefly to the Cathedral of jewels and when he thought himself done, she withdrew the thing even more. He was again rocked by an even harder orgasm that sent his member deep inside her so that he felt an ecstatic, vulnerable unity with her as she held him fast against her. He called out to her and she spoke to him then, her words a balm for his heart and mind, though it was not in a language he knew. As she kissed him, he felt an exchange of her knowledge into his mind as he allowed his soul to be taken and caressed, for he suddenly saw many unfamiliar sights, ancient and strange, with lights and machines that he did not recognize.

He lay quivering, and exhausted upon her bed, puzzling over the disjointed story he had just witnessed in his mind's eye. She rolled over on her side to graze the sweaty hair from his forehead. She kissed him down the trunk of his body and nuzzled her face against his stomach.

He must have dozed off, for when he awoke the sky overhead had turned to cerulean and the stars glimmered faintly from the deep blue beyond.

"What time is it? I should return to my companions. They will worry if I'm absent in the morning," Adam sat up and looked around, unable to recall precisely where he was or how he had gotten inside this luxurious boudoir.

"You want to go?" Inanna pouted, and her lips were no sooner around his cock, her hot wet tongue stroking his shaft. He felt himself already hard and aching with desire again.

"I should. I'm with a party..." He stammered as she sucked him. He lay back and sighed putting his hands behind his head as she directed all the remaining energy in his body back into his pelvis. Her velvety tongue caressed his testicles and he felt something small and soothing enter his arse. No sooner had it gone in than he wanted to explode. He looked down at her face between his legs and saw the magnificent energies swirling off the tip of his phallus like smoke billowing out of a chimney. She watched, too as she alternately sucked him, building up his energies, and then stopped and teased him with her divine breath, leaving him hanging in the balance between extreme pleasure and excruciating love.

"God, you're beautiful," he whispered. He had barely finished the words when her kiss set him off. He began bucking, releasing uncontrollably in her mouth for minutes, as the light energies of his sex poured out of him into her. Never had he felt so desired. He was lost in the moment and emerged some minutes later, finding himself staring up at the starry sky in a daze of fatigue.

"Tomorrow night would be divine," she was saying in his ear. "If you must go, then go."

Suddenly Adam found himself standing on the warm sand at the foot of the Great Pyramid, his clothes haphazardly buttoned. The night wind blew as he turned silently around looking for Inanna, but he was quite alone now.

He gazed up at the stars. Orion seemed close, much closer here than in Bavaria, for it was mid-heaven and brighter than he could ever recall seeing it.

Fatigued beyond reckoning, he shuffled across the sand and returned to the camp at the water's edge. When he neared, he sensed that Kolmer was there waiting for him. He felt his presence and soon confirmed it by the warm, orange light of the campfire that illuminated his strange, pale face and black, braided beard.

"We've been waiting for you," Kolmer turned to look at him, his eyes inscrutable in the black shadow. "Where have you been?"

"Sorry. I was just wandering around. Lovely country, isn't it?" Adam sat down near the fire where the Steinmahrs were studying a book of maps.

"You left a sheep on the fire. Luckily we came back before it had burned up," said Frau Steinmahr carefully.

"I'm a terrible cook. I went looking for someone to help me," he said. "And then I got lost...and fell asleep."

"You smell of roses and lilies, Adam. Roses and lilies and..." Kolmer didn't finish. "Why do you smell of roses and lilies?"

"I don't know. Why do you smell of opium?" said Adam suddenly, painfully aware of the raw condition of his genitals. "I think I'll turn in now. Good night, everyone."

Fehrs, Pattengart, and the Steinmahrs thanked him for the mutton he'd left them, and said good night. Adam wondered how long they'd been waiting for him and what had been said. It mattered little. If Kolmer had wanted to perform the ritual, he should have put down his hookah and made himself available earlier.

When Adam awoke in the morning, he climbed out of his tent and found Kolmer still tending the campfire. He handed Adam a cup of tea and raised his own cup. "To your success," he said darkly.

Adam said nothing, pretending not to know what success he meant.

"I have worshipped this goddess for many long years, devoted myself to her mysteries and her magic, and you, you come to Egypt and take what I have sought for my whole life," lamented Franz. "I have a weakness for opium. It has always been that way. I lost track of the days. Tell me what happened. You communed with her, didn't you?"

"Nothing happened," answered Adam. "I read over the ritual, realized I wasn't fit to do it, prepared the sheep for our evening meal, and while it cooked I went and sat down to watch the river as it began to flood. I smoked some opium as well. I fell asleep under a tree and then I wandered back here. That's all," said Adam.

"I can tell that you are not truthful with me!" shouted Kolmer. "Don't you remember who I am?"

The Steinmahrs emerged from their tent and quickly gathered up some washing, and departed. Kolmer and Adam sat silently.

At last, Kolmer said to him. "She will use you for your power, till it's gone. She will leave you a dried-out husk, you must know this. It happens to all the men she brings into her giginu," he said.

"What are you talking about?" asked Adam.

"Her giginu is the place where she takes a man to lie with

272

him. You were there, weren't you?"

"You should have come with me as you'd promised,"
Adam got up and walked away. He could take no more of
Kolmer's badgering. If it was so important to him, why
couldn't he have been around to perform the ritual?

Kolmer pursued him, and grabbed him by the arm. "You
don't know what she can do to you."

Adam wrenched away, "You just told me. You made
your choice when you failed to show up at the appropriate
time. You'd rather smoke opium with your toothless
friend."

"Let me tell you something. She will kill you if you let
her. You must learn her sacred names, all of them, so that
you can control her, or you will find yourself like all the
rest – dead, broken, maimed."

Adam chortled. "It was hardly a maiming."

"You think I'm joking, do you?"

"I think you're jealous…" Adam stopped, not wanting to
give away any of the night's events.

"I am. I am jealous. Do you know how long I've wanted
to see her face to face?"

"I really don't care," Adam stormed away.

"Wait!" pleaded Kolmer. "Tell me what happened, and
for that, I will give you an amulet to make her appear and
another magical name for her that will bring her under
your control," Kolmer was sincere, though Adam thought
he could still see the residual opium blearing his coal-
ringed eyes.

Adam thought of all the occult knowledge that Kolmer
had shared with him, how he had expanded his mystical
repertoire more than any book ever could, and he pitied
him. He cared little for this so-called amulet that Kolmer
had or the other magical name for Inanna. Apparently the
name spelled out in the scroll and the sacrifice were
adequate means to make her appear in the flesh. What
more could he ask for? He looked at Kolmer's odd

costume and waxy features. He could hardly imagine Inanna deigning to pleasure Kolmer as she had done him. She would have taken one look at him and refused him.

"All right," Adam agreed at last, and he told Kolmer of the previous day and night's events. When he had finished, Kolmer wiped tears from his eyes and patted Adam on the back. Without a word, he stood and walked away.

Adam rested all day in his tent, for he was quite spent from his encounter with Inanna. He slept peacefully until late afternoon when he heard Kolmer's voice calling him from without. He put on his clothes and emerged into the sunlight. Kolmer was holding a carnelian rose on a string. He put it over Adam's head. "Speak these words and they will bring her under your control." And then he whispered them in his ear.

Adam repeated them in his mind until he was sure he would not forget them.

He worried the carnelian amulet between his fingers as he waited for Kolmer to go on, but he sat silently. He felt Kolmer's jealousy in the form of a hot, abrasive ache that emanated from his side, and he rose, not wanting to know any more of it. Had Kolmer forgone his opium, he very likely could have had what Adam enjoyed. Or perhaps not. Who was to say what caprices the goddess would have? In any case, it was his own fault and Adam reminded himself he was never one to feel any sort of guilt about anything, and he would not start now.

He went back into his tent and slept till late in the evening. He emerged then, and went out into the night. The bright stars shone overhead and the embers of the campfire glowed faintly on the ground. Dinner had long been cooked and he looked in the pot to see if there was any left for him. It seemed that the others had already turned in. Adam found a bit of mutton stew in the bottom of the pot and cleaned it out with the spoon.

He wondered then what the others, what Fehrs,
Pattengart, and the Steinmahrs had done of interest. He
was curious how their studies were going, and he longed
to talk to them, but they were all asleep now. He missed
being in their company and vowed that he would arise
earlier the next day.

At the moment, however, he was wide awake and desired
to take a walk next to the pyramids. He wondered if Isis, if
Inanna, would be about tonight, and he reflected on the
previous night's encounter. It had been real, for his
member still bore the chafe marks of their love as
evidence. Would such a thing ever happen to him again?

He walked across the rope bridge that went over the
rushing Nile. He could just make out the pyramids, three
triangular forms of inky blackness against an otherwise
starry night horizon. He felt a thrill of anticipation and
infatuation for she who had pleasured him, and it dawned
on him suddenly that she was no mortal woman, but a
goddess, a partner fit for a god. He felt his own person
beneath his loose clothes, his fine muscles, and young,
strong frame, and wondered if he had the makings of such.
If he mastered the challenges of this life, would he verily
become a god in the next life? Kolmer had indicated that it
was the goal of the mage – to rule the self and master the
elements of heaven and earth, and all those in between.

He took off his boots and felt the sand still holding the
warmth of the day beneath his feet. Every breath he took,
he felt exhilarated, intoxicated by life. "This will call the
goddess to you," he remembered Kolmer's words about
the amulet that now dangled at his ribs. He touched it and
thought of her. No sooner had he done so than he looked
down and realized he was being escorted by a company of
black cats that formed two long lines on either side of him.
He reached down to pet one, but his hand went through it
to the ground, though he could still see it. It looked up at
him and meowed, and the company of cats led him around

the side of the Pyramid of Khufu.

About half way, the cats turned and began ascending up the side of the pyramid. Adam followed, finding the footing much easier than he would have expected. He knew they were leading him to Inanna for he could smell her flowery scent pervading the night air. A square shaft revealed itself in the side of the pyramid and the cats walked inside, disappearing into the blackness.

As he set foot inside this corridor that was much taller than the one through which he'd crawled before, she appeared in step next to him. The soft shimmer of her gown in the moonlight caught his eye, and he turned toward her, surprised, breathing in her intoxicating scent and feasting on her exquisite beauty.

"What do you have around your neck?" she asked, pointing at the amulet hidden beneath his shirt.

"Something to remind me of you," he answered, producing the carnelian rose.

"That you need to be reminded of me...?" She touched it, transfixed by it for a second, then dropped it back on his chest. "I like it. You must wear it always. How did you come by it?" she asked, her face painted by the shadows.

"It was given me by my friend, the one who was supposed to meet you as well," he said.

"The Dane with the foggy eyes, yes. He called me by my name. He knows much, but he is not half the man you are," she trailed her finger across Adam's full lips. "I would never do with him what I will with you."

Adam could not help smiling at her words and bit her finger, gliding it into his mouth, over his tongue.

She took his hand and put it on her luscious breast, "Come with me into my sky chamber where we can recline together."

He agreed and no sooner   were they inside her beautiful bedchamber in which they had made love on the previous evening. He sat back upon a silken chaise and she began feeding him grapes, putting them one by one into his mouth.

"These are delicious," he commented.

"They are not ordinary grapes," she said.

"What?" he asked, already vaguely aware of a wave of warmth and exhilaration that was coming over his body.

He lay at the ready as she climbed upon his erect cock and rode him exquisitely, holding him in her divine embrace. When her body relaxed in between its waves of rapture, she pleasured him, and the two of them remained in a euphoric state for some days during which time he was not allowed to release, but kept in an excruciatingly heightened state, throbbing and quivering. His will had been diminished by the grapes and by her, and he allowed her to tie him first to a wall where she kept him aroused while all manner of beautiful women, some of them goddesses, appeared one at a time, before him. They eyed him and whispered words he could not understand to Inanna. She was proud and jealous, and careful that none of them look upon him too long, and she banished each one in turn after they had seen her captive.

When all were dismissed, Inanna fastened him into a strange, contraption suspended by cords from above. With a voluptuous kiss, she sat upon his cock and skillfully milked it with her hot, tight core, her feet and silky legs embracing him. He was prone beneath her, burning, aching, penetrating her deeply as the swing moved them together as one, like a pendulum.

Their pleasure was profound, and intensified all the more by the movement of the swing that pressed their bodies together, then pulled them taut and almost apart. When he began to release, he felt it begin from his tailbone, for she had pushed some of the smooth beads from her chest up into his arse. She slowly began withdrawing them one at a time, as his member spurted its white-hot potion. He felt the hot liquid electricity from the base of his tail, moving up his spine and invigorating the sacred places along the centerline of his body, his chakras. They came alive, electrified and set to spin, some for the first time, and united with Inanna's that were ready and waiting to fully engage with his.

As he held her close, their bodies joined as one flesh, one being. Adam closed his eyes as her bright divinity filled him up completely, and they tumbled through space as one consciousness. Where their lips were pressed together, he tasted knowledge, facts and information he would not be able to assimilate for a long time. He saw images of strange lights and mechanical creatures, an entire history that was unknown to him, and he began to piece together a long-forgotten history. Where her heart pressed against his, he felt the pain of a great loss, and saw the needless death of her true love, a great warrior. He tasted the humiliation and rejection of her by a half-mortal man that she had loved. This man resisted her and triumphed against the great killing machine she had sent against him. But she appealed to her grandfather, the greatest of those on High, and he exacted her revenge with powers unimaginable. And Adam saw the great deluge, the greatest flood that ever was, wash away all men and civilization from the face of the Earth. And he was awed by her power, now embraced by his own body, and startled that she could cause such a thing. He felt her half-forgiveness of humanity, her acceptance of her role in the future of this world. He kissed her, then he was enveloped in the sweet black of slumber.

When he awoke, as always, he found himself in some compromised position, either tied up, tied down, and already in a state of arousal with Inanna imbibing her pleasure from his autonomous manhood. She did things to him that left him shaking with pleasure, things he did not understand, that he did not know were possible.

Their divine copulation continued for many days during

which they did not leave her chamber. She fed him fruits, grapes, cherries, pears, pomegranates – each like none he had ever tasted before and each with its own manner and effect of potency for divine lovemaking.

After some time, however, he began to feel imprisoned, for indeed he was, and he grew angry and impatient with her.

"You're insatiable! Please, let us rest for a day. Let me go back to my companions," he said.

His desperation only made her laugh. "But I'm not finished with you, Adam..."

He loved her, could not resist her, but he felt weak, raw, and ill. It was then that he recalled Kolmer's words "She will kill you if you let her. You must learn her sacred name so that you can control her or you will find yourself like all the rest – dead, broken, maimed." He had not listened well enough to Kolmer and could not remember the words of her name. *What was it?* He could see it, a fuzzy script in the forefront of his mind, but the syllables would not come clear.

He wondered if he had been missed at the camp, if there was anyone who was looking for him. He was unsure how long he had been gone. He had watched the dawn brighten the purple night sky so many times now he lost count. Had they left for Europe without him?

"Please, return me to my friends?" he begged her.

She smiled and shook her head no. "You're mine now," she said and kissed him. "Oh perfect Adam."

How he could not resist her, he thought helplessly as she stroked him and shook her hair away from her gorgeous face. No sooner did he find himself in love's embrace again, drinking in her sweet, irresistible essence, and filling her with his own. She bit and clawed him more savagely than she ever had, and blood flowed from the many wounds she inflicted upon his body.

When she had finished with him, he felt ragged, injured,

and weak, and knew that he could not continue in this manner. He could barely recall how his state of being had gotten to this point. She, however, seemed invigorated and empowered by their lovemaking, but he could not even stand. His knees buckled, his legs ached, and his mouth was parched. As she brushed her dark, silky hair at her dressing table, he crawled across the carpet for a pitcher of water that sat upon the table. He reached it and wondered if he should drink it, for all of the food he had shared with her was aphrodisiacal. He sniffed it, and saw his companions about their camp, reflected on the surface of the water inside it. They had not left him behind at all. Kolmer's face appeared then, staring back at him. He mouthed her name again, the name that he had forgotten.

No sooner did Adam pronounce the magical name than Inanna was kneeling beside him, looking up at him. "What wouldst thou have, my lord?" she said. He smiled at the annoyance in her eyes, but dared not question the efficacy of her magical name.

"I must know the secrets of Egypt and the Holy Land. And you must tell me them all," he said to her, stroking her chin with his thumb. He had decided not to return to his camp to rest, but to take advantage of her company and her knowledge while he had the chance to satisfy his curiosity. He would rest while she answered his numerous questions.

"As you wish," she said.

"But first, give me something plain to eat. No more fruits divine. Some meat and some bread," he demanded.

Immediately there was a table set with a roast leg of lamb and two loaves of bread, some wine, and some water. Adam sat and ate it hungrily, keeping a wary eye on her. When he was finished, he reclined again on the chaise and thought of questions she should answer, questions whose explanations would not only buy him the time he needed to recuperate, for he truly did not want to leave her company, but impress the academic world with their revelation once he returned to the University.

"What is the meaning of the pyramids?" he asked her.

Instantly, they were standing on a plateau looking at the pyramids beneath the night sky.

"They are landing beacons for the sky craft that come from my home planet, and other worlds far away. They indicate the Earth's magnetic grid, and they point to the old landing place in Jerusalem. From far above, you would also see how they artfully mirror the stars in Orion's belt," she replied. "The angle of the reflection is navigational for the craft. It would be easier to understand if you, too, had come from a long, long way out there."

Adam looked up and noticed how they did indeed reflect the arrangement of stars in Orion's belt. "What landing place?" he asked intrigued.

"Come. I will show you," she said.

She stepped aside and it was then that he noticed it behind her - a large crystal thing in the shape of a fish. He could just make out one edge of it for it was completely transparent, only a trick of light and the shadows they themselves cast made it discernible from the air, otherwise he never would have seen it at all. Adam looked at it, marveled at the side fins over which he stumbled and the dorsal and caudal tail fins that stood straight up, and at right angles. Silently, Inanna lifted up the door of the vessel that was not much bigger than a small coach, and lay down on her stomach inside it, her head in its head, her feet stretching back into its tail. She beckoned for him to lie down on top of her in the body of the fish.

Carefully, he got in and pressed himself against her back. "What is this?" he asked in her ear.

"This is my sky ship," she whispered. "Let's go for a ride?" She touched something before her and they began lifting up into the air.

He felt a great propulsion skyward and they rose swiftly

above the pyramids, and sped forward through the air without a sound. He lifted his hand and looked at himself and saw only the blur of the ground below, for he and she - except for her green eyes that glanced back at him, had become transparent as well. Though he could not see her, he could feel her, as he let his hands roam over her silky skin.

They followed the Nile river as it wound below, up to the Delta where it fed into the blue sea by a dozen tributaries that watered the lands and crops that grew alongside it. They flew over the bright, choppy waves in the morning light. Adam held her breasts firmly in his hands and slowly began making love to her as they flew over the sea.

He was elated to be up in the air with her in this fantastic bird, en route to the most interesting place in the entire world, the place where the Bible had been authored, and where God had intervened so much in the lives of men.

He looked down and saw the walls of the Holy City and the palm trees that lined the roads around it. He remembered then how emphatically he had prayed for his guardian angel to reveal herself. She had come after all, had answered his prayers, had loved him, and now she had brought him to the place on the earth he most wanted to see, and he was exploding once more with her, inside her blissful confines.

They landed just outside the city wall. He was overcome with excitement and gratitude at being there as he stepped out onto the ground. He felt a lightness of being, a state of exaltation with every breath of the sacred atmosphere. When she reappeared, she was dressed in Bedouin robes and a sand scarf in the fashion of a man. He looked down and saw that he too was wearing a long robe made of fine, light material.

"We are a pair of wealthy Musselmen who have traveled from Arabia," she said as she led him toward the gates of the city.

Adam relished the sights and the sounds of the prayers spoken in so many languages. This was the place where Jesus had walked, lived, and learned the Holy Mysteries from the Rabbis in the Temple, undoubtedly many of the same mysteries that Adam had studied. This was also where he had been crucified. Adam wondered what tangible traces of Christ still lingered.

Upon entering the place where the wall still stood, and seeing the faithful at their prayers, he felt the crisp atmosphere caused by the collective consciousnesses of the high holy ones at prayer. They walked past the Jews and the Christians and the Musselmen, peacefully mingled. He smelled the delicious aroma of flat breads and Turkish coffee as they walked by the long-bearded vendors, to the great Dome of the Rock that had been erected over the Temple Mount - the place where Solomon's Temple had been built and destroyed three times.

Two tall sentinels in turbans guarded the fabulous dome. As they approached, they lifted their scimitars and let Adam and Inanna pass through. They entered, and Adam smelled the camel hair of the prayer rugs and the strong incense.

"This is the ancient landing place, where my people first set down their ship and built a port for the others to come," she whispered, and her breath was like fresh flowers as it brushed his neck.

He was aware of her intoxicating powers. He knew that what little control he held over her by her name she would try to shirk at the earliest possible moment, and he might well find himself in an even more dire predicament than what he had been in only hours ago. He put a cool hand on her shoulder and avoided looking her in the eye. "I don't understand. The sea is miles from here. Was there a sea that dried up?"

"Not a ship for the sea - a ship for the air. Like mine, but much bigger. In the beginning, this is where most of our ships were harbored. Later, they were kept in the Great Cedar Forest where we all lived, guarded by our creations, but it has long since been cut down... to make the Temples."

Adam was out of his realm of understanding, but continued his line of questioning, hoping to have a glimpse of the world from which she had descended. "Who are your people? Where do they come from?"

"We come from a world called Nibiru. It revolves around your sun, but in a longer ellipse."

He regarded her then, in the dimness of the tent. He could see the patterns of energy all around her, emanating in a fountain of colorful flowers. He wondered if she could see herself as he saw her then. As he stood beside her and felt her exquisite presence and smelled her perfumed breath, he felt love for her, and was compelled to listen to her strange story.

"It has been vandalized by men for so many years, you can barely see it for how it was," she said of the enormous Rock.

He looked at the big rectangular slab of granite, tilted and chipped by vandals and tourists over so many long years. Suddenly it appeared as it was when it was new. The smooth surface was suddenly marked with an intricate pattern of raised lines, and at the higher end, there was a spindle protruding from a sturdy, round base. A colorful web of energy filled the space above it, and suddenly the Temple of Solomon stood again as it had and Adam caught his breath at its gilded magnificence overhead and all around him. Outside the open doors, a giant saucer-shaped thing set down upon the spindle on the rock and turned like a top.

"This place was a way for a priest to make contact with us. A small sky ship could land here and the pilot be brought into the temple and sustained. Or a priest could call one of us through the proper ritual, as you called me, and we could materialize here and be sustained in this place without fear of profane men seeing us and harming us. We are inter-dimensional and can move from world to world with or without our sky ships."

He was aware of his heart pounding, and he sat down on the ground. Was all this real? He touched the earth next to him and pinched the grains of sand, so ancient between his thumb and forefinger. They each knew the truth, or their own tiny piece of it.

She knelt down beside him, brushing his thigh. He let his hand slide up her robe and began kissing her neck. Her skin intoxicated him.

"You asked to know the truth," she whispered.

"Yes," he said. "But I'm not sure I understand. Tell me more."

"What do you want to know?" she asked.

"What is 'inter-dimensional?'" he asked.

"It means that I can cross time and distance in the blink of an eye. If you connect to me through the proper ritual or prayer, then I can hear you wherever I am, and if I desire, I can come to your aid. Or send one of my servants to help you."

"So you have no real need of your sky ship?" asked Adam.

"Oh, I do. On earth, it is very necessary, especially if I have a passenger," she said. "I never know when I may see someone I like down here."

Adam fought the pang of jealously her comment aroused, that she would roam about the world seeking sexual partners and picking them up in her sky ship.

She smirked at him. "But I would need a rocket, however, to get here in the first place, then I would be able to make use of the temple, and from there, I could travel back and forth."

"A rocket. Where might one obtain such an object?" he

asked.

"The Knights Templar inherited what we left. They kept them right below our feet, as a matter of fact. Would you like to see?"

He stood and followed her. The sentinels parted their swords and they walked out into the bright morning sunlight, and down the dusty street. At a mercantile stand, she bought a brass lamp and some oil for it. The salesman filled it, lit it, and bowed to her as he handed it back.

She led him further through the winding city streets, lined by ancient stone abodes. At last they ducked into a doorway that led into a house. Unnoticed by the woman who lived there, they stepped into a hearth. At the back of it, a stone door swung open and she showed him into an ancient corridor that descended steeply underground. He heard the soft music of water dripping and smelled the dank scent of wet earth.

"These are Zedekiah's caves and they lead beneath the city. The passageway the Templars maintained was filled with stones when the Temple Mount was taken the last time," her words echoed as they descended. "We could not have gotten beneath the Temple from straight above it."

He followed her through a misshapen corridor of natural caves until they came to a small room where the ceiling ascended upward and the floor ended next to a deep well. Adam peered over into the blackness.

She gestured above them. "The Temple Mount is directly above us. This is the place that held their secret."

"What was it?" Just as Adam asked, he looked again at the open chasm and saw it filled with eight huge, silver, phallic cannons with conical points, stacked upended. "What are they?" he asked incredulous.

"Shems. Rocket ships for the sky. Each one, a way to leave this earth. Each one had enough power to get two people safely through to the dark side of the moon where

286

my people had a working base, a spaceport that no one had vandalized. From there, we could go home."

"Space port," Adam repeated her strange words and looked at the rocket ships again, but they were gone, only the gouged rough stone of the cavernous room remained. "Where did they go? What happened to them?"

"Some were used by my people; the rest were stolen by thieves after the Templars retreated to Cyprus."

"What happened to them? Where did the thieves take them?"

"It's anyone's guess. Certainly they were dismantled for their metals. What matters is that you are aware of our mission."

"What's that?"

"That my people are coming back.   To create a new covenant with yours. The Jews and the other chosen ones who my people created, have not succeeded in taking back this place or building any other safe haven for us to be if we choose to return. If we were to land today anywhere in the world, we would be drug through the streets and annihilated."

Adam stopped her then. " *That your people created* ? Man was created by God."

"Read your Holy Book again.   Man was created by Elohim, in their image. Elohim are the ruling class of Nibiru. I am one of them. *Our* God is Yahweh. *We* are *your* gods."

Adam felt his head begin to ache. He thought of the serpent in the Garden of Eden with its lies and trickery and looked skeptically at this beautiful being beside him. Was she filling his head with nonsense so that he could be corrupted all the more easily and ensnared by Satan?

"Are there other men, other humans, where you come from?"

"Humans are particular to Earth. My great grandmother, who was an ingenious physician, created humans to look

287

like us, but to endure the rigors of working in the mines of Earth, to artfully build our Temple, to procreate, and to die when his days were done. We of Nibiru live many times longer than you. We are not entirely immortal, but suffice it to say, it is extremely hard to kill us."

Adam said nothing and ruminated on all this new information in silence as she led him back through the caves, out of the Templars' sanctum.

They returned to the spot outside the city where her sky ship was waiting for them.

"What am I supposed to do?" he asked compulsively, for he sensed that she, though under his control, had now obligated him by this astounding knowledge.

"You will know when the time comes," she said. "You would not be next to me, calling me by my given name, asking me to tell you the truth, if you weren't to be part of my plan."

He looked at her then, and saw her for the fierce and ruthless warrior that she was. Her beautiful musculature was not simply for lovemaking. Her beauty was not only for the enjoyment of the beholder, but perhaps to entice her enemies in close, so that they could be conquered.

Adam was unsure where to continue his line of questioning. He was in shock, and nuzzled her silky hair as they sped through the air back to Cairo.

She set the sky ship down next to an oasis, and the two of them appeared to their own sight without being noticed by any of the Bedouins who were lingering there, letting their camels drink. They began walking towards his camp.

"Why did your people leave here?" he turned, but she had vanished. He walked back to his camp alone and fell asleep in the shade of his tent.

Each night, she flew him to a different place on earth, some near, some far across the sea where the gods and man had built their magnificent landing places to receive Inanna's people. He saw the Cedar Forest for how it looked thousands of years ago. Inside her sky ship, they dove into the giant crater on the ocean floor. Its corroded and coral-encrusted remains were all that remained of the land that had held man's greatest knowledge and civilization.

Later, they rode over the world at a staggering altitude. Adam saw the uneven coastlines beneath the cover of clouds, the inviting, blue seas and sumptuous sands, then the jagged mountains, and the verdant forests of earth.

"No one remembers us now," she said quietly, looking down at the snow-capped mountains. "The gods appear more often than you would think and no one recognizes us. It has been that way for a long time. But I suppose it is safer not to draw attention to myself."

"What do you mean? You could easily rule the world," he felt her smooth power beneath him as he as flew, looking out at the array of clouds below them.

"There are all manner of others here, too, trying to seize their share of the earth's spoils before someone else takes them. Not just my people have come here. We have many powerful enemies on this planet, hidden below, hidden in plain sight, beings that would do unspeakable things to me if I ever gave them the chance," she said.

He felt her shudder against his hands. "I'll be your protector," he said. He wanted to go on, to assure her he would defend her to the death, but for fear of sounding too dramatic, too in love with her, he held his tongue and made love to her far above the world.

When they had returned to Egypt again, he asked that she bring him to his camp. They lingered by the river, holding each other close in the darkness. He whispered her magical name and kissed her neck. She stiffened in his arms. Adam could tell she was not used to acquiescing to anything that was not her own whim, and bore him no small amount of resentment for using her special name.

Adam returned to his tent at dawn and found it just as he had left it, though one of the poles had begun to lean and the canvas sag. He straightened it up and turned into his sandy bedroll. It was uncomfortable now, for he had grown accustomed to the silken, soft bed that was Inanna's.

He awoke at midmorning to find the camp empty, the rest of his companions already on the day's task, probably unaware that he had returned. He hoped they hadn't worried over him in his absence. He drank some water and set out to find them. He made his way across the rope and plank bridge, to the pyramids. He walked around the monstrous stones, but did not see any of them. It was then he wondered if they had taken a junket up the river to Memphis or Heliopolis or one of the other sites. He was sorry he was not privy to their plans, for he would have liked to be in their company, at least during the day. He had already visited the other sites with Inanna, but knew he would have trouble fabricating the why and wherefore he had taken these tours without them and without the conventional means of travel, and so he resolved not to mention any of it.

He wondered where Kolmer was, and suspected he was looking for treasure among the antique dealers he knew or was looting some graves as he had indicated he was wont to do. "The best things come from the tombs," he had told him.

Adam wondered how he could justify grave robbing. It could only bring the robber the wrath of any restless spirits who had stake in the goods that were taken. Particularly in the Egyptian realm, where grave goods were meant to protect and feed the deceased in the afterlife, Adam could only imagine what negative forces Kolmer would bring upon himself. Adam reasoned that he had undoubtedly set up a powerful system of protection for himself, or banished any entities that would avenge his looting activities.

After Adam had searched the market place for his friends, and found some bean cakes to eat, he returned to his camp and wrote them all a note, saying he was well and had found some academic pursuits that were keeping him occupied. He promised that he would return when the next opportunity availed itself.

He left the note in the Steinmahrs' tent, and wandered away into the desert where he would not be witnessed vanishing or being escorted by cats, or whatever strange means Inanna employed to bring him to her side this time. He had nothing to fear from her, he thought, for he had her magical name on the tip of his tongue if he needed to escape again. He had only a month left in Egypt and there was nothing more he wanted to do than be with her and listen to her reveal to him the mysteries of the Ancient World. He had questions that only she could answer and he yearned to smell her sweet, intoxicating breath, and feel her exquisite bronze form beneath his. He regretted having left her since he'd ultimately found none of his companions. He thought briefly of lingering at the camp till dusk and waiting for them, but his thoughts returned to her and his longing for her had to be satisfied.

He repeated her magical name as he held the carnelian amulet between his fingers. He opened his eyes and the air before him sparkled with an opalescent fire in the shape of a woman. She appeared before him, curtsied mockingly, and said, "What willst thou have me do, lord?"

"I would like to revel in your company all day," he replied.

She smiled at this. "How do you know I am not otherwise occupied?" she asked.

"If you are, you should cancel all other engagements and spend yourself on me," he said.

"Very well," she said, and taking him by the hand, they were instantly inside her bedchamber.

Adam should have known she was angry, that things would not be the same this time. Before he could react, she stuffed his mouth with a plum so he could not speak. The cords on the bed tied themselves around his wrists and ankles, and he suddenly found himself trapped and at her mercy. She straddled him and snatched the amulet from around his neck. She looked down at him intently. "I will not be at the beck and call of anyone. Especially you."

She held him prisoner for many days during which she kept him in a state of heightened arousal, but prevented his release. He realized quickly that she meant to show him no mercy whatsoever, and he worried that Kolmer's warning would come to fruition and he would die by her love. How had he fallen into this trap? The answer was clear as he watched her ride upon him, beautiful and naked and glorious.

Her use of him grew more savage with every passing hour. Whenever he became tired or unresponsive, she let two black snakes out of a basket and let them crawl all over his body. They never bit him, but the fear of them doing so kept him conscious, made him rigid. He realized that she had often played with men in such a way and was used to killing them by her excessive and relentless lovemaking. When he had angered her, she had slipped easily back into her old ways despite the pledges and promises that had been made between them. For an instant, he saw himself reflected in her eyes, a helpless animal.

If only he could speak, then he could reason with her, remind her that he had already pledged himself to helping her and that he was important to her plans for the future.

She smiled, having read his mind, "Of course, but that doesn't mean I shouldn't have my pleasure with you now.

I will not let you die like the others, Adam Weishaupt. We have a long history together. A history that is just beginning..."

He was much relieved that she intended for him to live, and began enjoying the excruciating pleasure she inflicted upon him. At some point, she allowed him to begin a series of fierce climaxes. She watched him with amusement, and taking his member deep in her throat, she drank in his essence as his passion for her rocked his body over and over again.

He awoke suddenly in his tent, sweating profusely inside his bedroll and aching in his stomach. He could smell the musty, canvas tent and the stench of his own, old sweat. He was delirious; his skin felt prickly, crawling hot and cold as if the snakes that had slithered on him were beneath his skin now. He felt weak, too weak to even sit up.

"Hello?" he called. "Is anyone out there?"

Fehrs came into the tent and knelt beside him, trailing in the scent of food. "Adam! How are you? Would you like some stew? Or something to smoke?"

Adam could stomach the idea of neither. "How did I get here?" he asked.

"We all took a ship together and a short trip over land down the Nile. Don't you remember?" Fehrs asked. "Everyone is here now except for your friend. We're all having dinner. The Steinmahrs went to the market and picked out some four-legged creature, something. I'm not sure what it is, frankly. I'll be glad to be home in a few weeks, as I'm sure will you. If you don't improve, Dr. Steinmahr says we're going to take you to the hospital in Cairo. I wish you'd eat. You're nothing but skin and bones." Fehrs looked at him pityingly and went out.

Adam was speechless, now unsure of the past days' events. He laid his head back down, then tried to sit up, but found his muscles too weak and sore to allow him to rise. How had he gotten in this condition?

"Fehrs!" he called to him. "Fehrs!"

Fehrs came inside the tent again, "Yes, my friend? What is it?"

"There was a woman I've been seeing. I must go and find her. Will you help me up?"

"Adam, you've been nowhere outside of this tent for the better part of a month. You've been quite ill. Dr. Steinmahr says it's mosquito fever, malaria. Mrs. Steinmahr has been good enough to nurse you through the night. This is the first and only time you've even been conscious enough to speak. Can you hear me?"

"Mrs. Steinmahr?" Adam stammered, shocked and wondering what had really transpired during his delirium.

She ducked into the tent just then with a bowl of broth. "You're awake! I thought you might sip some broth, Adam," said the rotund, jolly lady, as she sat next to him on his steamer trunk spooning a savory broth into his mouth. It made him feel better, stronger just from the bit she fed him. How had he become so weak? He tried to move his legs, but they ached as if the muscles hadn't been moved in many weeks. His arms felt withered and heavy and a deep sleep washed over him again.

Adam recuperated aboard the ship. He sat out on deck most all day, letting the balmy wind tousle his hair and fill his nostrils, for he had found it quite hard to even breathe the last few weeks. As he wrote down what he remembered of Inanna, of Isis, of the chamber within the pyramid, of her giginu and what had transpired between them, he was baffled at how the single, most extraordinary experience of his life could have been but a mere fantasy. He could still feel the pain and pleasure of her, and almost smell her sensational aroma when he called her face to mind. He had no physical relics of her, for the carnelian amulet given him was gone, and so was Franz Kolmer. Adam had vivid memories of her, however, and relived the details of their lovemaking in his waking and sleeping hours. Despite the accounts by his companions that he had been bedridden, Adam knew that she had been real. At the same time, he could not discount that his own mind was an exceedingly powerful instrument, and perhaps not very well understood. Perhaps the ritual to call her had worked only to his mind's eye. The goddess had been but a figment of the archetypal world extruded from his deepest mind and come to life through the madness and delusion brought on by his debilitating illness.

As the days passed and he neared Bavaria on the back of his horse, this explanation began to seem more real than the extraordinary events he thought that he had experienced. His thoughts drifted back to his studies at the University, to Eva and Mayer, and the Bauers' grand home in Frankfurt am Main. He looked forward to impressing them all with his tales of Egypt and the fantastic places he had seen, albeit perhaps only in his dreams.

CHAPTER XXIV

The crisp, cool air from the Alps restored him, and by the time he had reached the gates of Ingolstadt he was quite recovered from his illness. He was thin, but by no means pale, having stayed out in the sun for the ocean voyage and the ride home. He felt grateful to have endured all that he had in Egypt, and to still be alive to tell the tale.

He tumbled over the story Inanna had told him in his mind, and had written most of it down along the journey home when he was well enough, though bits of it had escaped him, only to return to mind in the middle of the night. Strangely it seemed to fuse with the legends and lore of the Persian heroes of whom Barmoras had told him so much. He would find the notes he took under the man's tutelage and compare them to what he had learned in Egypt.

Again, he searched his possessions and the pockets of his clothes for the amulet Kolmer had given him but could find no trace of it. And as fate would have it, he had misplaced the dagger he had found in Hamburg as well. At times he wondered if the events had been real, or the machinations of his mind under the attack of malaria, as his companions had attested.

He bade the   Steinmahrs farewell where the lane veered off to the University, and they went their separate ways, promising to visit. Bells were ringing in the tower of the Church of Our Lady and when they had gone on past twelve, he wondered at their meaning. He thought surely they were the sound of some alarm, but the warning was not one that he recognized.

Though the foyer and hallways of the University were quite empty, he sensed the presence of a multitude of other people as he walked up the stairs to his uncle's office. There, he found the entire faculty kneeling in two straight lines as if in prayer. None spoke and their looks of pained warning told Adam he should never have set foot inside. His uncle saw him and widened his eyes.

Two monsignors stood before the penitent rows of learned gentlemen. They were obviously emissaries of the Vatican for they were Italian and immaculately clean.

"I confess to my error of faith and to engaging in heretical practices," read the taller monsignor from a scroll.

The faculty parroted him in unison. Baron Ickstatt gave a tilt of his head at Adam, telling him to be gone, but too late.

"Who is he?" asked the other monsignor of Adam as he stepped back from the doorway.

"A student," replied Ickstatt.

"Come in and kneel with the others. We must have everyone, all former Jesuits, in compliance with the bull," said the tall monsignor in a deep Italian accent.

"What's going on?" Adam asked.

"We are formally abdicating ourselves from the Jesuit faith. The Order is extinguished in Bavaria and throughout the world," Ickstatt confirmed quickly.

Adam knelt beside his uncle. The suppression had finally come to pass. Regardless, he had staved it off for his uncle for as long as possible, short of killing the Pope, himself. There was nothing more he could have done, he told himself. If the Jesuits were to come to an end, it was their own fault. The Jesuit priests had annoyed less orthodox Catholics and Protestants alike for as long as the Order had been in existence. They were God's foot soldiers and fervent evangelism was a major part of their work. In Ingolstadt, the population was almost entirely Jesuit Catholic so one almost never saw Jesuit priests harassing anyone in the street, but in Munich they had angered a great many Protestants, he recalled. And in France, Spain and Portugal, he knew that the Jesuits had become unbearable to the liberal nobility, who had for the past decade, been pressuring the Pope to rid the world of the Society of Jesus once and for all.

And what of Lorenzo Ricci, the Black Pope? Adam smiled at the thought of him ousted, burned at the stake, or banished to a cold and miserable prison. Certainly, Father Lorenzo would be suffering just now. Adam was sure of it.

Suddenly something caught his eye. The hidden panel where he had stashed all of his books from the Hamburg lot was lifted up as if it had been plundered! Had the monsignors confiscated his books? He went rigid and cold with anger. If his books were gone, these monsignors would not leave Ingolstadt alive.

"I repent to my Holy Father in Heaven, the Lord

Almighty, for the sins that I have committed. I have forsaken the Holy Covenant, partaken in unclean acts, and denied the Lord's one true representative on earth, His Holiness, Pope Clement the Fourteenth."

The absurd confession went on and on while Adam burned to ask Ickstatt what had happened to his precious books, and imagined a thousand punishments on the Catholic Church. Finally the monsignor gestured for them to rise.

The faculty and Adam signed their names at the bottom of the confession and Adam hoped that no one would ever use such a document against him. He thought it atrocious that someone could force Bavaria's most brilliant minds to confess against their wills and deny their beliefs. And the fact that his most precious possessions had probably been stolen, made him want to go to Rome and assail the Pope himself.

"Where are my books?" Adam whispered to his uncle.

"Safe," said Ickstatt.

Adam sighed with relief.

"Have you been ill?" asked his uncle.

"I caught something in Egypt," said Adam.

"Tell me everything. I want to know about your travels."

Some hours later when the monsignors had left the University, Ickstatt drove Adam to a tall house that was split into two dwellings. One side belonged to a kindly merchant's widow, Ickstatt explained, and the other half would be Adam's. The place had belonged to Ickstatt's mother, and before that, to Adam's own family before they had met their fates in Wurzberg.

It was gray brick and stucco like most of the rest of Ingolstadt, with a small, crooked fence around the front garden to keep out the dogs. Ickstatt opened the Dutch front door on the left side of the house. Inside were two rooms including a kitchen and dining room and a large room with a window onto the back garden. All of Adam's books had been transferred here in haste and covered with a bed linen.

Up a narrow stairway, there was a spacious loft with a window that looked over the lane below. Outside, the garden seemed to be ill kept, and there was quite a lot of dead foliage around the sides and back of the place that Adam promised to clear.

He tried to imagine his parents and himself living there, and searched for any signs of them they may have left. He noticed the old kitchen table with hollows for bowls and thought it surely must have been in the house since it was built, though he could not remember ever sitting down to it. He looked through the kitchen cupboard but it was empty and clean.

He made a comfortable home for himself there, and built cabinets for his library in the big room with the window that he made into his study and bedroom. He used the more private loft for his meditation and practice of sacred magic. He kept a metal bowl of water for scrying, and an old mattress and some candles for reclining and reading.

Since the Jesuit faith had been erased from the University, Ickstatt confided to Adam that there was a gaping hole in the curriculum, for they could not teach the Jesuit doctrines, and they were forbidden from training any more novices. He asked if Adam would mind lecturing on some of the apocryphal books he had in his collection. "The more ecumenical ones that substantiate the scriptures, of course. No alchemy or sorcery," Ickstatt looked at him sternly.

"I would be most proud to be a lecturer," Adam answered.

"Wonderful. This will make the transition into your professorship next year all the smoother," Ickstatt commented.

Adam was relieved that his uncle was going to uphold

his end of their bargain. He prepared himself to lecture, and the next week he found himself standing before a classroom of his peers, discussing the *Book of Enoch* and the angels of the Book of Genesis who called themselves the Elohim.

CHAPTER XXV

HANCOCK

Revere stood breathless in the doorway of the parsonage, "They're coming across the river and then by the East road."

Hancock and Sam and John Adams had hidden out in the parsonage. The Parson and his wife said they could stay there for as long as they liked, and so they had. They had hidden the coach in the great barn at the back of the property and disguised it under a haystack. For two weeks they had let no one save a select few know where they were.

"We must not be found here, brothers. The munitions are one thing, but to capture the leaders of our revolution, that would be the end," Sam began gathering up his clothes and papers from around the house.

"And of course, we'd be hung for treason, let's not forget," quipped John Adams.

"We can't run away," Hancock scoffed. "We can't just incite revolt amongst the people, then run away and leave them to be shot!"

"Our people relish a good fight, believe me," said John Adams.

"Your fate is to lead, friend," Sam patted Hancock on the back, then turned to Hancock's man and told him to ready the coach.

"How did they find our stores?" John Adams asked.

"Tory spy. Daniel Leonard. He was in on everything."

Revere looked at Hancock.

Hancock covered his face with his hand. He couldn't believe what he was hearing, though he half expected it.

Revere looked at him and said in a low voice. "Daniel Leonard said some things, about you."

"Who heard him?" Hancock looked at him, aghast.

"Everyone, sir. Had to be eighty people within earshot, and a hundred more looking on. It was a tarring."

"I see," said John gravely. He did not want to imagine how his reputation had been marred, and what sort of sordid slander would result from Leonard's ravings. "Where is he now?"

"Don't know. Run off tarred and feathered. What would you like me to do?"

"Nothing. There's nothing you can do. Just give me a moment." He went upstairs to the room he had stayed in, and sat at the desk and composed a quick note to Dorothy Quincy.

My Darling Miss Quincy,

I can no longer restrain my heart from its stirrings. Please come to Philadelphia at once to join me forevermore in matrimony. All that I am belongs to you.

Affectionately yours,
John Hancock

He penned another letter to his Aunt Dorothy, apprising her of the marriage proposal and instructing her to accompany Miss Quincy to Philadelphia. He apologized for the haste, but blamed the frivolity of the heart for the situation. "Love is a hard thing to quell once ignited," he wrote. He handed both letters to Paul Revere and sent him back to Boston. If anyone were to inquire of him, Revere had seen a beard-burned, half-dressed Miss Quincy in

Hancock's bedchamber this very night.

The threesome set out for North Salem under cover of night. They rode along in Hancock's long and luxurious carriage pulled by six fine white horses. He hung his head out the window and sniffed the cool bright air. A few stars shone above in the deep blue heaven. He wondered where Leonard was, and thought he should like to have him once more then run him through with a fireplace poker.

Sam Adams clasped his hand and that of John Adams and said, "Let us pray. Bow your head, friend, bow your head cousin, and let us entreat that the Lord take care of us and make our cause His own." Sam began a long, wordy beggance to the Lord that they achieve liberation and justice for the people of Boston.

Hancock rolled his eyes as Sam droned on, and watched as the night passed by outside the carriage.

Just then, a flash of light streaked across the sky.

"By Job, what was that?" Sam's eyes were wide.

"What?" John Adams was facing the opposite way.

"There was a light in the sky."

"Yes, I saw it, too," said Hancock. "Very strange light, streaking."

"A shooting star," assured John Adams.

"Er," said Hancock uncomfortably. "Perhaps it was. A large one."

"Twas a flaming signal from the heavens! A   flashfire of the Almighty!" said Sam.

"A shooting star is just a natural phenomena. It means naught but the earth is traversing through heavenly stones," said John Adams.

Hancock opened his mouth to speak, then thought better of getting in on the argument; there would be enough argument ahead of them in Philadelphia trying to convince the Tory-sympathizers of Boston's dire plight, so he sat back and listened to the cousins berate each other.

"The powers of Heaven *speak*! Twas a warning!"

"It was just a falling star," said John Adams. "Calm yourself."

"Why must everything be naught to you? Is there no great mystery of life, cousin? You make pretense to know it all? You explain everything you are, that is, away so presumptuously by the feeble words of science and you do not see that the indivisible burning power of God is at the heart of all. Call it what you will, cousin, but we and everything that is, was, will ever be - are all in ourselves the makings of God."

"Yes, I believe that, too," said John Adams about to continue.

"That which I just saw, cousin, was peculiar if not portentous," Sam was intense, "Can't you simply have faith that God is with us?"

"Just because you see something, doesn't mean it *means* anything. That's superstition, that's ignorance. You don't know that some star is a sign of anything! It's nature, a natural occurrence."

"What is a 'natural occurrence'? These times are unprecedentedly dire and strange. Do you not see the battle that ragest before us now?"

"I see a very hefty political problem, indeed," said John Adams. "We've stolen tax money, put ourselves at odds with the most powerful nation on earth, jeopardized our lives, our families, our *would-be* fortunes..."

"Because we are God's foot soldiers, waging an eternal war against Satan and his infernal army."

"Don't you realize how insane you sound? You're beginning to talk like poor Otis before he had to be tied up in a feed sack and carted away."

Hancock remembered when James Otis finally lost it completely. They had all watched and listened for months as Boston's greatest orator began making less and less sense until one day, he began barking like a dog. They had all let him go on in hopes that the noise was somehow related to something pertinent, but the barking continued and with increasing fervency and froth until a page was sent to go and notify his next of kin.

"Just try and seem reasonable in front of the other delegates, that's all I ask. Your Puritanical ravings are very off-putting to some people," John Adams scolded him. "Not everyone agrees with your antiquated outlook."

Sam gave him a hard stare. "Do not deny the Lord your efforts lest *ye* be denied at the gates of Heaven!"

"Now, listen here!" began John Adams when their carriage lurched to a stop. Outside, the horses whinnied and bucked against their harnesses. An eerie darkness fell over the night, as if a cloud had blacked out the moon and stars. A delicate vibration permeated the air, tickling the hairs in their ears with its low hum.

John Adams looked out the window. "What the devil is that?"

Then from all around outside, the foliage and ground were illuminated as bright as day. "Mr. Hancock! Mr. Hancock!" called the frantic driver of the coach. "Look!"

The three of them peered out of the windows and looked up. Hovering above them was something immensely huge. From its center, a beam of light shone half way to the ground, just above the frenzied horses.

"Jesus bloody Christ!" exclaimed Hancock. "What is it?"

"A chariot of fire," cried Sam, possessed. "Elijah's wheel!" And he dared get out of the coach. John Adams snatched at the arm of his coat, but he pulled away and climbed outside, staring up at the thing.

The craft hovered silently above them, its lights revolving green and red.

"Come back here!" cried John Adams and tumbled out after him. "Sam, what are you doing?"

"The Lord is come! The Lord is come!" Sam extended his arms in a welcoming gesture. Suddenly, a beam of hard white light shone down upon his forehead and he reeled backward from its jolt of power.

The next morning, the three of them awoke in the carriage to the sound of Sam's congested wheezing. Hancock felt his taut face and saw that his red hands were badly sunburned. The other John's were as well, but the driver and Sam had it worst. Sam looked like a boiled lobster, a very dramatic look for him that made the whites of his eyes stand out. John Adams said he thought he looked like the devil he was always talking about.

At midmorning, they stopped for breakfast at the old stone huts - buildings made of thin, flat pieces of stacked shale. Hancock had heard it said that they were here before the first pilgrims. There was a long, stacked stone fence around the abandoned dwellings, and the place stayed covered with leaves the whole year through. Except for the crackling of the fire and that of the leaves underfoot, the forest was strangely quiet as if it was listening to them.

They spoke of the meeting to come, the quartering of redcoats, their property that was prone and that which was hidden, but never of the previous evening, for it was as if it had never occurred. Hancock was vaguely aware of a strange and otherworldly dream he had had, but nothing more. Surely it had been a dream. Surely that was all it had been.

Hours later after they had gotten back on the road, a rider from Boston named Nelson, caught up with them, and delivered the news of six minute men killed at Concord.

Hancock was beyond distraught, and stormed off into the forest to shed his angst privately, while Sam led his cousin and Nelson in prayer. They were only buoyed by the fact that their Minute Men had inflicted more casualties.

"We are now at war," said Sam.

They arrived in Philadelphia two days later to find the City Tavern overflowing with Sons of Liberty who had answered their call to the second Continental Congress. Benjamin Franklin, whom no one had laid eyes on in years, found them just as they stepped inside the door. He embraced each of them, and invited them to stay at his house. They looked from one to another and politely declined, having heard of his "air baths." They did not care to chance to witness Franklin unclothed.

John Hancock had read much of Franklin's work and found some of it sagacious indeed; some of it was obsequious; and some of it was simply untrue. He admired Franklin's sobriety and quick wit but wondered why he couldn't hammer home to the Crown, Boston's position. Admittedly Franklin seemed genuinely interested in pursuing independence, despite his previous resistance to the idea. He was eager to avenge the six at Lexington and surprisingly, viciously vehement about punishing the King and Parliament. Hancock surmised that his hatred for the British government was probably the reason why he had failed as their ambassador.

At the meeting of the second congress the next day, the Bostonians found they had to say and do very little this time to convince the others that England's oppression was real. They had all felt the effects of His Majesty's persecution up and down the coast. And now with the news of the Lexington ambush and the deaths of the six Minutemen, this Continental Congress was bent on retaliation.

An Anglican Reverend read Psalm 35 to the assembly. "Plead my cause, O Lord, with them that strive with me; fight against them that fight against me ..."

Hancock looked over at Sam and watched his mouth move along with the words of the verse as the preacher read. He had always regarded overly zealous Christians as a bit weird, and more often than not, rather stupid, but what if Sam was right? What if this was not merely a conflict of men, but a war between good and evil embodied by men?

Hancock looked around at the faces from the other colonies, and saw in their eyes an unprecedented excitement. This preacher lit them on fire with his sermon, channeling their nervous energy and anger into the precise words that needed to be spoken. John wished he had before now been able to express what this man was saying about their cause. He could almost hear the cogs and wheels turning in each man's head as he realized that he was born free, that he had God-given rights *not* to be governed, and certainly not by any crooked, arbitrary self-appointed bastards from Britain's corrupt, inbred regime. They were far, far away from English rule in the land of Liberty, and here in this land of verdant fields and clear streams, they could make their paradises on earth.

"Thy oppressor is self-imposed. Slay the beast who will chain ye, and let thy heart shine free under the Eye of God... for only God's Word is Law."

It was what Sam had been saying all along, and Hancock watched as the red-faced man punched himself in the knee with his hard, shaky fist, for the Reverend so aptly, so eloquently put his point into words. And it seemed that everyone present understood it now.

If Hancock had not been so downtrodden by thoughts of Leonard, his heart, too, would have sung out and he would have joined them in their fervent "Amen," their voices crackling with emotion. But still John tasted the bitterness of his broken heart, and the lump in his throat kept him from speaking much.

Their discussion on the floor that morning was a brainstorm of ways to punish Britain and cut ties with her forever. Richard Lee proposed that all trade with Britain should cease. If England was starving out Boston, the other colonies would cut off England's supplies as well.

The motion was about to take the floor when Pennsylvania delegate Joseph Galloway stood up and made a rather plain but momentous case against it, instilling everyone with fear of the wrath of the Almighty Crown. They couldn't survive without the King's governance, without the King's money, without his laws. They would perish by starvation or by the sword. One of the two was inevitable.

Sam Adams watched him with derision and poked Hancock in the ribs with his finger.

"What?" Hancock leaned over to ask him.

"He's asking for it," whispered Sam.

Hancock looked around and saw that some of the other delegates seemed deflated now and were wavering.

"After all, what are we without King and Country? We're no better than the savages whom we found when we arrived here. Our common happiness depends upon compliance. Our government simply wants payment for the vandalized property, and until Boston pays up, we will have this problem, and worse predicaments if we revolt," said Galloway, tapping the podium with his long knobby finger. Sam thought he looked like a woman with his thin face with its high red cheeks and long eyelashes. When Galloway wasn't speaking, he breathed heavily through his nose like a winded horse.

Sam farted loudly in the middle of Galloway's speech and tripped him as he stepped down from the podium. Galloway caught himself on a bench and shot Sam a hateful look.

That evening Sam entertained some of the Southerners in his room at the hotel. Hancock sat by as they drank flip, smoked cigars and thought up cruel ways to intimidate Galloway.

The next few days, Galloway was harassed, teased, and sent various things by messenger including a dead opossum in a sack, and a halter. Galloway said one last bit at the Congress and sat quietly by for the rest of the meetings.

CHAPTER XXVI

WASHINGTON

He left the farm in his foreman's care. He wished that Martha's son, Jack, would have made better and would have taken more interest in the property, but the two of them had never cared much for each other. For her sake, early on, they had made an effort to get along, to do things together as a father and son, but it was never to be. Washington, having lost his own father at a young age and searched in vain for a replacement in Lord Fairfax and others, had tried to sympathize with Jack, and had failed miserably.

"I will never be your father," he said to him one day.

Seeing the sudden hurt in the boy's eyes, Washington immediately regretted his words and tried to soften them, but the day of fishing upon the riverbank was spoilt then, and the relationship that almost was, that perhaps could have been, was ruined. Washington wished he had never opened his mouth, and had simply let the boy view him as a real father, if that was what he wanted to believe. He had meant only that as Jack's stepfather, he could never truly take his real father's place, that he should hold his real father in high honor always, and not forget the man, and nothing more than that. Washington certainly had had the best of intentions, had meant to give his best efforts at raising the boy, but he had said something wrong that could never be retracted or amended, and he wished the day had never happened.

Apparently, there had been a conversation between Jack and his mother regarding the day's events, for Martha had come to Washington that night and asked why he had said such hurtful words to her son. Her involvement in the issue only seemed to rend the situation the more and Jack's close confidence in his sister alienated Washington from Martha's young daughter as well. Soon, Washington felt he was simply tolerated by Martha's children. The civility and small respect that was shown in the house was only exhibited for the sake of Martha, the love for whom was all they held in common.

By the time Jack was in his teens, he was a difficult young man at best. He had a violent temper and would not listen to the advice of his mother, much less Washington. Jack was arrogant, disobedient, headstrong, and his age mates, the affluent-born sons of the neighboring gentry were no good influence on him either, with their nightly gambling and drinking. When Washington would reprimand him for refusing to complete his chores, he threw his own words back in his face, "I don't have to do as you say. You're not my father and you never will be!"

It was a phrase that silenced both Washington and Martha, and Jack used it liberally to quash their opposition to his wild ways. If Washington scolded Jack for his excess, Jack reminded his stepfather often how much property and money had come to him by way of his mother and that whatever he deigned to take, he was more than due.

When Jack was a small boy, Washington had taught him to shoot a rifle and a pistol, for Jack's father had left many guns. Washington sought to make the boy a marksman and a good hunter as he was. He had naively looked forward to hunting with him when he grew old enough, but the damage was done before those days had come, and Washington had only succeeded in teaching the boy to load the guns and shoot them. Jack had an unhealthy love of weapons, and later when he was older, used them to kill all manner of animals on the property. Washington was disturbed by his lack of respect for life, and his callous treatment of the slaves.

By the time Jack was seventeen, Washington had given up on him entirely. He protected Martha from him, for he often assailed her for large sums of money, and when she would not turn it over to him promptly, he threatened her. Martha, however, was always on Jack's side, and no matter what Washington did or said, she would eventually comply with her son's requests.

Because of his knack for disappearing for weeks on end and returning without so much as his horse beneath him, Martha was hesitant to give Jack the bulk of the money left to him by his father. She held off for some sort of proof that he had matured, or had some responsible business plan in mind. This angered Jack and he badgered his mother and stepfather until Washington had had enough. He was much bigger than the boy, and showed him clearly that he was outmatched. After a brief exchange of blows, Jack was hurt and limped away to the stable where he got on one of Washington's best horses. He rode back to the house, and screamed for his mother to come outside. Washington prevented her at the front door, but Martha ran upstairs and opened a window and bade her son farewell. Washington stood by, inside, unseen, angry. He heard Jack's threats.

"You tell that rot-mouthed leach I'll be waiting for him when he least expects me! I'm not done with him! Take care, Mother Dear." And with that, Jack rode away into the night.

In the years that followed, Martha mentioned letters from Jack, that he had gone to New York, or that she had sent him money for such and such. Washington gave it little attention, and was grateful that they had gotten rid of him, if not permanently, then at least temporarily. The respite from him made Washington realize how uncomfortable his presence had made the entire house, how inharmonious his constant, unpredictable behavior had made them all feel. At the same time, he regretted he could not have been a better stepfather to him, and felt ashamed that under his dominion the boy had gone completely and utterly astray. Washington had always considered himself a good leader of men and wondered why he had failed so miserably with Jack. He felt his authority had been undermined by Martha's constant submissions to Jack's demands, and that was why he had not been able to make anything of him.

He thought of young Adam in Bavaria, the young man who wrote to him several times a year requesting hemp for his lodge and asking strange questions that he often thought surely must be mistranslations.

"*I see that your family is in terrible turmoil* ," he wrote to Washington once. "*This will soon pass.*" And indeed, only a few weeks later, Jack left.

He felt strange about the letters from Adam, especially when he could not relate to his own stepson half as well. At the same time, he was proud that he had been able to sway this other boy, a virtual stranger, from wasting his life on the priesthood. Christianity, or rather what it had become, since the establishment of the Church, Washington considered a false avenue at best. The clergymen Washington had chanced to meet seemed to have lived their lives in a bubble and didn't know the least of God's glory or His wrath, and Washington was not the type to bow to the false-made idols of man for the sake of appearing righteous. Therefore, he simply avoided religion altogether, and thought that any wise man should as well, lest his integrity and virtue be compromised.

For a time, Adam seemed to have become fascinated with astrometry, sending him a detailed forecast of the rest of his born days. He thought it a peculiar waste of time and was most relieved when the lodge enabled Adam's reunion with his uncle who led him to the University, and back into more traditional, academic pursuits. Adam kept Washington apprised of his academic successes, of his reunion with his uncle, and hinted at some terrible event that had claimed the lives of both his parents in his early boyhood, thus sadly resolving for him the questions he had about his family.

Washington recalled the fire that had decimated his own house at Ferry Farm when he was just a boy. His father and Lawrence and the slaves rebuilt the house while he, his sister and his mother had gone to his great aunt's home. George's father had become very ill and died not long after the episode, burdening the entire family in untold ways. He felt sincerely sorry for Adam whose situation had so many similarities to his own youth, and hoped he had offered some sort of fatherly guidance to him during his formative years, even if he couldn't be of any help to his own stepson.

He continued to encourage Adam to pursue the higher degrees of the lodge, and wrote that there was much more to be learned from his association with freemasonry that would satisfy his affection for the sacred mysteries. He wished he could reveal what he had so recently learned from his last degree, for it would have made Adam fervently renew his interest in the brotherhood.

In his letters, Adam seemed preoccupied with school, and with a young lady he had met who had married another, and Washington relived through him, the pain of losing Sally Fairfax, Lord Fairfax's charming daughter, who despite his ardent infatuation of her, thought him unsuitable as a mate. Adam's letters became almost incomprehensible when he returned from Egypt where he had fallen ill. Washington regretted not warning him more sternly of the dangers of that uncivilized region.

When the Virginia House of Burgesses was called to assemble, Washington attended. Through the Lodge, he had gotten word from the Sons of Liberty that Boston was in open revolt. He wanted no part in it, and sought to discourage his fellow Virginians from any sort of engagement, for he had seen too many dead men already in the French and Indian war, dead men who haunted his dreams and waking hours, who cast shadows near trees and in the dark places of the barn at twilight. He shut his eyes to them, and did not answer to their calls.

As he sat at the end of the row listening to Peyton Randolph make a motion to send delegates to a Congress of the Continent, he suddenly recalled the tiny, peculiar handwriting of Adam Weishaupt, interpreting the array of star symbols in the strange astrometry drawing he had sent once about five years before. Adam apparently had become adept at this art and lacked a subject on which to practice. Washington had puzzled over the thing, had actually quite agreed with Adam's summation of his past and present life, but tossed the thing in a drawer at the forecast of his future. It had warned he would go to war again, that he would lead an army, but there would be grave challenges, and much strife and misery for many years. It was not exactly a sunny prediction. Washington was satisfied with his role as gentleman planter, happy to bask in the radiance of his green fields and plump wife. Leading men in war was not something he cared to do ever again. But if there was really to be a battle, who else was there? Who of these fat, misshapen gentlemen who sat around him now in the House of Burgesses could even ride well, much less lead men in battle? He did not dwell on the thought and when the opportunity arose, he spoke out against supporting Boston. Armed conflict with the Motherland was not wise.

Peyton Randolph asked if he didn't want to go and be present at the meeting of the colonies, and speak to that point. Washington agreed, and was quickly appointed as one of the delegates, along with Randolph, some overly serious, red-haired, young man named Jefferson, a gangly bird named Patrick Henry who seemed to be his nemesis, and the Lee Brothers, among others.

In Philadelphia, the first Continental Congress listened to the Boston delegates attempt to persuade the rest of the colonies to join them in their opposition to the crown. Washington spoke only once in an effort to cool their anger, reminding them that no one could afford to go along with such an idea. There simply wasn't money, men, or means of enacting a formal opposition. And most of the other Virginia delegates supported his assessment.

But in the time that had passed since, Jack had returned to Mount Vernon with vile talk of the Yankees in New York who tormented his rich Tory friends, and Washington got the idea that most of the colony of New York was loyal to King George. Washington's own crops had been waylaid, seized in transit, and sat in a harbor until they were spoilt. Despite his opposition to the plans of Boston, that small colony had brought the wrath of the King upon the entire continent, and now with six men killed at Lexington defending their stores, there was nothing to do but fight.

Washington sat with Adam's charts and summations before him at his desk by the window and stared at them, reading his words over. Adam had no stake in this situation, had nothing to gain or lose by Washington's involvement in a war, and certainly could have known nothing about the motives or position of Boston at the time he had written it. Washington closed his eyes and sat. He exhaled the other thoughts from his mind, banished the chatter of voices, and when all was dark and quiet, objectively observed what images flowed into that space behind his eyes. That was how he decided things.

Now, great throngs of militiamen rode with him into Philadelphia in the morning sun. He heard his name spoken in reverent terms and was glad that some of them still remembered. Washington spoke little, for he intended to make only one promise. He kept the pace at a canter for most of the six miles outside of town where he had been spotted and joined by volunteers. He knew he had rivals for the position of General of the Army. Benedict Arnold who had also been distinguished in the French and Indian War, and Charles Lee, a talented soldier who reeked of dog urine, vied with him for the position.

He thought of Adam's chart and if it was to be, it would be. He would simply make himself available, make it perfectly clear that he was ready and willing to give himself over to the service of his homeland, and fight this battle that some had declared was a war against Satan.

CHAPTER XXVII

WEISHAUPT

He carried the dirty vessel up out of the ground. The Archbishop, Brother Haster, and several other priests were waiting. He set the vessel on the ground. They took a step back.

"What is it?" they asked.

"Eine kleine *Golem*. It has just expired," Weishaupt replied with a wicked glare.

"Dirty Golem! It was the will of God," said the Archbishop and signaled for the brothers to fling their censers at it.

"Anyone want to touch it?" Weishaupt picked up a shard of an old headstone and smashed the glass container with it. The priests and Archbishop gasped and jumped back, hiding behind the other, as silvery water poured out and ran down through the grass into the earth. Only the pearly, feathery clouds of its swiftly decaying flesh remained in the sludgy bottom. Their eyes were wide with horror as they made signs of the cross, huddled together, and murmured bits of Latin.

"Go and fetch some oil, some wood, and a torch. We shall burn it here so that the evil does not become dispersed through this wretched place," said Weishaupt pushing the empty wheelbarrow at the priests.

The youngest ran off to do his bidding. Weishaupt morosely poked the remains with a stick. The others covered their faces and turned away, sickened.

"It is quite strange for such a creature to simply *appear*. Usually such creatures are created on purpose through the *darkest* of sorcery," Weishaupt glared at them with suspicion. "You must ask yourselves – who among you has made this thing? Who in your midst is a practitioner of the Devil's black art?"

The Archbishop, Haster, and the other priests shifted uneasily and whispered among themselves.

Just then, the young priest returned with a load of wood and kindling. Adam dumped the wood into a pile, and with much enthusiasm and all the oil, set a huge fire rather too close to the church. The flames scorched the old stones as the wind blew the fire against the wall of the Cathedral.

When they were certain there would be no resurrection coming from the golem's burning ashes, the Archbishop pressed a bag of coin into his hand: "Thank you for your assistance. The Pope expects your confidentiality. Now we must put this to rest in accordance with the laws of the Church. Good day, Doktor Weishaupt."

The roof of the church suddenly caught fire. Weishaupt bowed chivalrously, and walked quickly through the courtyard, the fire crackling at his back. The post where he had been beaten was still there.

He untied his horse and galloped away to the millhouse where he stole a bucket and filled it with the cool, clear water of the Isar river. He reached into his satchel and retrieved the shriveled homunculus and plopped him into the bucket of water. "Oh, thank you, master! Thank you!" It cried, "May we never part ways, master!"

Weishaupt had gotten the better of the thing down in the catacombs, and now the little golem was under his dominion, though he had read that such things were capricious servants, and so he vowed to be on his guard for it to misconstrue his intent and so try to foil him.

He asked it again, "How have you come here?"

"I have come to serve you, master," the golem bowed.

"Yes, but how? You are not an animal or a person and yet you have life of your own. Who has given this to you?"

"I am created from the Blessed Host, Master. The Word made Flesh."

"So the priests at St. Michael's who blessed the Host from which you were created gave you life, bit by bit?"

"More or less," it answered. "I am sent from On High to help *you*."

"To help me with what?" snapped Weishaupt. "I need no help from a dirty golem made by the Roman Catholic Church."

It was extraordinarily strange to Adam that it had just precipitated from the ethers and been born of the wasted Host, and with no mage responsible for its creation. He had never heard of such a thing. He was suspicious of it, for it was an odd little creature and a bit too complicit to be trustworthy.

Weishaupt watched the thing slosh silently along in the bucket tied to his saddle as he rode carefully down the highway.

Near dusk, they reached Weishaupt's abode in Ingolstadt. It was not the grand house he had envisioned for himself, but the humble house in which had been born. With all his many gifts and virtues, clairvoyance not the least of them, Adam had not prospered as he had expected, for the simple reason that he was unwilling to bend on principal. He could have taken on any number of legal cases and been paid handsomely, but that would require him to give up his many nocturnal habits, such as staying up all night, having ecstatic relations with young ladies and experimenting with hallucinatory substances. Teaching was the perfect occupation for him. All his classes save one, were late in the afternoon and his students were still young enough to think his wearing a bed robe to class was a novel thing to do.

His house was old, and in disrepair, but the cracks and loose shingles were hard to spot in lieu of the overgrown, over-planted gardens. His neighbor the widow and he vied over the horticulture of the front and back flowerbeds. She had her dianthus and petunias and tulips. And enfolding their dewy stalks and precious petals, he had his deadly nightshade and belladonna, and hidden in a bramble in the corner of the garden, an old stone oven that bore a unfettered amount of Mayer's mushrooms all spring and summer long.

The iron front gate creaked as he stole through, carrying the bucket toward the front door.

"Is this where you live?" it asked, bubbling up from the water.

The widow peeked out the door, startling him and making him slop water all over the stone steps. Her face illuminated in the lamp she held before her, she was thrice his age if she was a day, and she wore rouge that made her look like a garish, old doll. Her chin was huge with a conspicuous mole. Her gray hair she piled high upon her head, and her clothes, though clean, seemed to date from the previous century.

"Doktor Weishaupt…" she growled his name with a gleam in her eye.

Weishaupt cursed under his breath.

319

"I've baked a delicious hare pie," her dry, thin lips curved into a dirty smile, showing her bare gums. "Won't you take a piece for your dinner?"

"Certainly, Dame. You are most kind." He took the dish and bowed his head, holding the bucket behind his back.

The widow curtsied and went in her door.

Weishaupt stepped quickly inside, and sighed with relief that their exchange had been as brief. Sometimes the Dame next door took an hour to avert.

Inside his marvelously furnished abode, the creature poked its head up out of the water and stared in wonder at the various anomalies that were displayed in jars of wood alcohol - great green and orange spotted mushrooms, a two-headed lamb. Skulls of humans and primates were mounted on wooden blocks. Guppies flitted in a great polished cauldron in front of the stained glass window. And above that, there was a grand kaleidoscope for viewing both. Weishaupt cleared the mouse bones and beeswax from a table and set down the golem in its bucket.

The creature looked nervously around the room at his collection of dead things, as he ate his hare pie.

"What sort of occupation have you?"

"I'm a professor," Adam answered him tersely as he pulled out one of the widow's gray hairs and a few of the rabbit's from between his teeth, spit the mouthful out into the bowl and then pushed it aside.

"They only told me your name. I should have perhaps asked more questions." It said.

"Who is *they*?" Adam looked narrowly at him.

"*Ooohh, the road to   Hekatah is long and thin, a thread from paradise she pull me in...*" It sang and sang, and Adam listened for an answer, but it seemed the thing was just singing in lieu of giving any sort of truthful response.

"Hush!" He ordered, letting the thing see the blue blaze of power in his eyes. "Why are you here?"

"I've come to serve you, master," the golem grinned.

"Very well then, get me some bread to eat for supper."

The creature climbed out of the bucket, and fast as a shot, flew out the door. From without, there came screams, the sound of a shattering window, and in moments, the creature returned with a loaf of rye. Adam ran to the door, closed it fast and locked it against the shouts and chaos in the street outside.

"What have you done?" he asked.

"I got you some bread, master," the creature handed him the loaf.

Adam ate the bread, and then put on his coat. "You cannot live in that bucket. It's leaking and it has no lid. I shall go and find you a proper containment vessel. You must obey and stay right there. Do *not* go outside under any circumstances."

He hurried outside to the garden shed but could find nothing suitable to contain the creature. He would need a very large vessel to house the golem. He was still uncertain whether he should keep it alive or knock it in the head and preserve it as a specimen. It certainly merited a glass vessel in either case.

As he walked down the street, he thought what a marvelous creature it was. He had rarely if ever, been so amazed by anything. It had most definitely come from some other realm, one of those usually kept from the eyes of humans. Nonetheless, it seemed to be a pleasant enough consciousness. It was corporeal, unlike most everything he regularly summoned from the ethers, and he was deeply suspicious and mistrustful of it. Who were *"they"*? Had someone else really sent the thing or was it lying, and there of its own diabolical volition? It was nothing he could recall summoning, though it was possible that he could have called it inadvertently. So much about sorcery was an unknown. Who knew what sort of creatures would attach themselves to other energies like those he was always dabbling with. Perhaps things did just appear. Perhaps it had fallen through the filtering mesh into this world like so many living creatures.

He recalled Inanna then. She was most certainly corporeal. He could still taste her on his lips. How strange that affair in Egypt had been. It seemed like a dream, as if it could have been a fantastic hallucination, but in his heart, he knew her to be real, and undeniably so. After calling the demon Andromalius to find the missing object, he had found her amulet in the lining of his vest, but dared not use it. He kept it safe in a special pouch that he hid in a cavity in the fireplace.

The sun was deep in the trees now, and the apothecary's shop was certainly closed. But Weishaupt knew the apothecary well and traded with him often. Ziegler often ordered him special substances from the East, and procured others from the nearby region himself. The apothecary was more of a botanist than an alchemist, and if he had any knowledge of sorcery, he was wise enough never to question or delve too deeply into the business of those who practiced it. Adam hurried through the gray streets of Ingolstadt, past the washerwoman and the fishmonger. Small dogs ran alongside him, their claws clicking on the cobblestones, nipping at his heels. He gave a sudden kick backwards and sent the black and tan one flying into the little white one. They yelped and stopped to lick their wounds.

He rang the bell at Ziegler's. In a moment, the apothecary's young apprentice opened the door.

"Professor? Run out of something?"

"As a matter of fact I've acquired a new curiosity for which I need a large containment vessel."

"Ah, how big would you like?"

"Large." Weishaupt indicated with his arms.

The boy raised an eyebrow. "Master has naught but what's on the shelf."

Weishaupt quickly inspected the vessels containing the apothecary's stock and saw that all of them were smaller than the Host's receptacle he had so foolishly smashed in the Churchyard. The shattering glass had made for good theatre, but the vessel could've been cleaned, and was, in fact, the perfect size to house the golem.

Weishaupt thought of the glass blower in   Amberg and planned to visit him at week's end. "Thank you all the same, and regards to your master." Weishaupt tipped his fine felt hat and strode off through the night.

He was returning home along the straight road that led to the University, and there he saw a group of young people walking toward him, reveling in the warm evening. He recognized one of his former students laughing uproariously at another young man. At his side, a blonde girl of seventeen smiled at their antics. She had the same intense, deep-set eyes, blonde hair, and high straight nose as he. She was, without a doubt, one of the most beautiful girls he'd ever encountered. With a generous bosom like he preferred, and a softness about her that was irresistible, she reminded him of Eva. As they drew closer, they noticed him then and he heard Zwack whisper as if he had been the topic of their conversation, "It's him."

Weishaupt smiled mysteriously and captured the girl's eye, staring into her pupils, and ravaging her in his mind. She blushed scarlet.

"Professor Weishaupt, good evening," said Zwack.

"And a very good evening to you, Herr Zwack," he said.

"Have you heard the news? About an hour ago, just down there, there was a tiny, little, blue man running across the road! He sprang through the grocer's glass window and broke it and stole a loaf of bread!"

They laughed uproariously.

Weishaupt laughed heartily along with them. "Oh, and where is he now, this little man?"

"No one knows, Professor."

323

"Sounds like sheisse to me," quipped Weishaupt.

"It most certainly is," said Zwack apologetically. He noticed Weishaupt's gaze upon his sister beside him. "Have you met my sister, Afra?"

Weishaupt removed his hat and inclined his head. "A pleasure, Fraulein."

"We're going star-gazing," she said, playing her tongue against her lip. "There's a star shower, mid-heaven, in half an hour."

"We'll be right on the top of that hill," said Zwack, pointing to Weishaupt's special hill. Zwack was a short fellow, a fairly good student and Adam had always liked him, though he found his intensity a bit annoying. He had graduated last year and was now a practicing lawyer.

"I'll meet you there." Weishaupt felt the girl's hungry eyes on him as he walked away. She was so pretty. He had remained a bachelor for just such occasions as this beautiful, starry night...

He walked into his house and immediately saw that the golem was in his fish cauldron, busily scraping the algae with its claw. "You're a very neglectful fish-keeper," it said.

"Yes, I know," he snapped, remembering what waited for him at the top of the hill. "I'm going out to meet some friends. Can I get you anything before I go?"

"I prefer to live in holy water. Can you make this water holy?"

It was a peculiar request, for such a rite had never seemed to him to be effective in the least, but it was a harmless request and Weishaupt found his old breviary, and blessed the water, fish, golem and all.

"Thank you, Master," it bowed.

"I demand that you behave yourself while I'm out," scolded Weishaupt. "No mess-making, no rummaging, no pranks of any kind. And *do not* leave this apartment."

"Never, master," it swore solemnly. "I would never."

Adam looked narrowly at it, then poured some vodka into a flask then grabbed a large blanket and threw it on top of one shoulder.

In the stable, his horse looked up at him and whinnied. He opened the door to her stall and she came out and stood there while he put the bit in her mouth and the saddle on her back. He jumped upon her back. He leaned over and whispered his plan in her ear. She started out of the barn just as excited as he.

He rode up the hill, following the goat trail, eating of the sweet night air. As he neared the top, he could hear their voices on the gentle wind. He took a sprig of mint out of his pouch and quickly chewed it up.

The stargazing party sat on blankets with a single candle-lantern burning. In that very spot on the top of the hill, he had conducted so many rituals; he could still feel the residual energies of them. It was his special hill, sanctified, fortified, and consecrated so many times. How fortuitous, he thought. The top of the hill was high enough not to be seen by the town below and perfectly flat and circular on top, with a few old trees here and there around the periphery. There was no moon; it was a night perfect for stargazing and for what Weishaupt had in mind.

She did not look his way as he rode up to them.

Zwack got to his feet as Weishaupt dismounted. "Professor. We saw one just a minute ago."

"It gets better as it gets darker," said Weishaupt, and drawing his hand overhead, commanded the night to fall dark at once.

The girl on the blanket smiled absently as she stared at the sky. Adam lay down beside her.

"Look at that!" said Zwack as a flaming star streaked across the night. He saw that he had lost his place next to his sister, and was about to protest, but then thought better of troubling his favorite teacher, and found a spot in the grass.

Weishaupt felt her next to him, warm, surrendering. She
let her arm brush his. He listened as she sighed. He saw no
reason to wait, and slowly, silently began caressing her
with his fingertip. The others stared at the skies, oblivious
to his hands gliding over her bodice in the dark.
Weishaupt thought of the others falling fast asleep and
they did so, their breaths becoming heavier and heavier till
Zwack and his two other friends were snoring away.

She gave a small laugh in surprise. Weishaupt got to his
feet and pulled her up to hers, and they crept away to the
far edge of the hilltop.

"Where are we going?" she whispered.

They found an oak tree sticking out at an angle to the
side of the hill and sat in its bough, their feet hanging over
the hillside.

"I'm sorry. I can't remember your name." He was upon
her at once, kissing her neck. Stars streaked over their
heads as they necked furiously, taking, sharing the other's
scent. He ripped open her corset and felt the firm softness
of her breast. She tried to resist, but he was an expert at
such maneuvers. His other hand he tore down her
bloomers and found her wet maidenhood. She struggled,
trying to resist him, but didn't dare make a sound for fear
of explaining how she had found herself treed. Adam felt
his breeches unbearably small and wanted to penetrate her
immediately. He reminded himself of her probable
virginity and kissed her tenderly. He removed her
bloomers completely. Her eyes widened in horror. "No,
please," she begged.

He kissed her mouth and murmured to her, how her
beauty shook his soul, he'd never seen a beauty such as
hers. They would be married; she shouldn't fear.

He pulled her skirts over his head and put his lips
between her legs. She spun immediately in his mouth.
Before she had come down, he was in her, filling her
virginity with his massive manhood. She spun again, a

most responsive, if reluctant, partner, and he thought of how his own pleasure was significantly heightened because of hers. Her reluctance gave way to her repeated bouts of ecstasy, an ecstasy like she had never known before, or known herself capable of. He kissed her, devouring her as he exploded into her with possessed immediacy. When they were done, she grabbed her bloomers and left him there.

Smiling and relaxed against the tree, he took out his snuffbox, snorted a bit off the back of his hand, and went to find his horse.

When he returned to his house that night, he remembered with glee, the odd, little golem that he'd left to its own designs.

"Where are you?" he called, and began searching his abode. The windows had been left open, and he worried that the thing had gone. It was then he saw it – a floating orange mass in the fish cauldron. Cautiously, he went closer. He recognized the tabby stripe of the thing, darkened by the water. It was the widow's beloved tabby that was nigh as old as she, dead and afloat in his cauldron full of guppies. But where was the golem?

Suddenly, there was a knock at the door. Weishaupt wondered whom it could be for it was now well after midnight. He opened the door carefully.

It was the widow in her dressing gown and robe, her bed bonnet tied beneath her enormous chin. She held a candle just below it and frowned with worry. "Have you seen Pussy?"

"No, I have not," he lied, hoping that her range of vision did not extend to the cat's floating corpse.

"I saw him climb through your window, Herr. Then I heard a terrible yowl."

"I've just returned home. If I find him, I'll bring him right over."

"Do, please," she said, trying to steal a peek inside.

He closed the door and locked it, then quickly extricated the sopping cat from the water by his tail, and dropped him into the bucket. He thought briefly about placing the corpse on the widow's doorstep, but that seemed too cruel and she might see him do it. He resolved to put the cat in a sack and take it to the garbage heap at the edge of town.

He worried that the golem had come to some harm by the cat and was lying injured somewhere. He searched his house and all its cupboards but could find no trace of the little man. If it had escaped in one piece into the neighborhood, it was in danger of being seen by some fearful person who might put it to death at the end of a shovel.

He scried briefly in his basin and saw the face of the girl with whom he'd copulated, but he could not see the golem or its whereabouts. He put on his coat and slipped out the front door, taking the sack of dead cat with him. He searched the garden, and finding no golem, went out the front gate.

He walked briskly to the end of the lane and slung the dripping cat sack over the fence into the garbage heap. After an hour of searching the neighborhood, he returned home and went to bed.

He awoke in the night with the frightful idea that the golem had been swallowed by the cat and that he had thrown it into the garbage when he had disposed of the cat. Now he feared it was too late to save the creature, and not desiring to go traipsing in the garbage heap at any expense, he fell asleep again.

He rose late the next morning with the vague recollection of the previous day's events. He was certainly in a more solid frame of mind than he had been on the previous morning, but he was weak with hunger. There was no food in his house, so he dressed and went to the market. On the way, he chided himself for failing to keep the unique creature safe. Things such as that were exceedingly rare. It was a shameful loss. He had been negligent and thoughtless.

The market was just closing as he arrived, and he hurriedly bought a few apples and potatoes and some carrots for his horse. He was just leaving when the blonde girl he had made love to last evening came around the corner with her younger sister. She stared up at him, stopped in her tracks, her lips parted.

Now in the light of day, Adam was even more attracted to Zwack's beautiful sister, and as she brushed past him, he thought of following her to her home so that he would know where to find her. He stopped himself and stood watching her go. She whispered to her sister and both of them giggled.

The next day, there was a knock at his door. He knew it was the widow, so he sat quietly grading his students' papers, and pretended not to be home. The knocking persisted for many long minutes until Weishaupt could no longer concentrate on his task, and grew angry. He put down his quill and stormed to the door. He threw it open. There, much to his surprise, stood the girl, Afra.

"Come in," he invited her.

As she moved past him inside, he felt the warmth of her body, smelled her soft feminine scent. She looked around his apartment in wonder and revulsion at his collection. "Is this where you sleep?" she asked.

Weishaupt affirmed that it was indeed. As she perused his curiosities, he watched her soft, blue eyes take in the glistening, yellow wings of the butterflies, widen at the three skulls mounted in a row, follow the flitting guppies in their tank.

Finally she looked bashfully up at him. "I liked what you did to me," she said, coming close to him.

"Perhaps we shall do it again," he answered, aloof.

"And perhaps not," she drew away flirtatiously. "Perhaps

I won't let you touch me ever again unless you marry me like you said."

"You'll be waiting a long time for that," he lit a pipe full of hemp. He felt himself growing aroused by her presence.

"What is it that stinks so in your pipe?" she asked.

"Hemp," smirked Weishaupt.

"Hemp is for ropes and breeches," she said. Her lips were a lovely pink.

"And for smoking." He said, putting the pipe to them.

She inhaled deeply, and coughed terribly. He patted her back, then took her by the hand, and sat her down on his bed. She looked up at him and he thought how easy it would be to ravish her again. Why, she had come here for just that, he told himself, and he was not one to disappoint a young lady. He knelt at her feet and removed her black shoes, then her white stockings. He picked up one of her feet and put her toes in his mouth. She squealed and lay back on his bed as he gently sucked them.

He slid his hands up her smooth thighs that she opened for him, and he began caressing her maidenhood through her bloomers. She made noises of pleasure as he tore them off and put his mouth to her. She spun countless times as he pleasured her. He mounted her then swiftly. At first she tried to resist him, but he made her take him and after a few thrusts, she began to enjoy him vociferously. He kissed her lips and she opened her mouth to taste his as he thrust slowly into her. She was pure pleasure, untainted and sweet.

At some point, Weishaupt noticed the open window to the back garden, and fearful of the nosy widow peering in, he carried her astride him, up the stairs into his loft. He lay her down and undressed her, and himself, and admired her lovely body before ravaging her again. He took her roughly and made her his own.

When they were through and lay entwined together on the upstairs mattress, he wanted nothing more than to have her again and keep her there all day, but she wrenched away from him and put on her dress, saying that she had to accompany her family to Church.

He laughed at her, and raising her skirts again, planned to delay her when she let out an hysterical shriek.

"What? What is it?" he asked.

She pointed and echoed him in terror.

He looked and saw it, too. It was the homunculus, staggering across the floor, shriveled like a prune and lacerated with claw marks. It collapsed, reaching out for them.

"Water..." it rasped.

Afra ran down the stairs and out the front door.

"Afra!" Adam called after her. He wondered if she would say what she had seen there, and bring a mob of rake- and torch-wielding citizens to his doorstep.

Quickly he scooped up the poor, little golem and took it downstairs to the guppy cauldron and dropped it into the water. He watched it hydrate, becoming as invisible as the water, and just when he thought it gone, and had reached into the tank after it, it appeared, glowing a soft blue-white light. The iridescent pink and green peacock feather fins of his guppies flitted through the water around it.

CHAPTER XXIII

It was a cold day just before Candlemas. The kykeon had been frozen solid in its phial in the tin under the steps since late November. At sunset, Adam ducked outside and found it behind the loose stones and brought it into the house. He gently warmed the phial between his palms until it thawed.

Afra put down her book and sat upon his lap. He sipped the rotten tasting stuff, holding it under his tongue, and washed it down with wine. She followed suit and they went to lie down on his bed, watching the room become alive with the energy of the wood with which it was constructed. The knots gnarled out into the air like spiraling fingers. The waves of the wood grain swished like tall grass in a breeze.

He looked at his hands. Energetic pulses of pure light seemed to originate from his capillaries. Purples, pinks, golds, soft blues – he was made of stardust and decorated with jewels. He saw swirling colorful energies moving in beautifully woven patterns about his body. He felt himself lifting, innervated by pure bliss, each breath breathed for him as if inhaled and exhaled by an uberbeing from within and without. For he was beyond breath, beyond this mortal coil.

He was frightened.

Then a rush of love and ecstasy overcame him and he had the sudden urge to love the world with abandon. He could feel the tendrils of his mind reach out into the darkness of the village, wanting to inspire it with his warm, bright, divinity. He found himself at his front door looking out at the snow. His breath seemed to melt it. The whole town was asnooze. He would wake them up; they shouldn't miss this feeling.

"Where are you going?" he heard Afra call.

He responded absently, and stepped into the front garden. He caught his balance on the fence, and that's when he saw them - a field of rolling snowflakes, turned on edge, gigantic like the gear wheels of a enormous mill, but sparkling and translucent like the gossamer wings of a dragonfly. As they turned slowly toward him, he could hear the music that they generated - fantastic, beautiful, alive. He stumbled aside as one came too close. He dodged another behind that one. The sea of turning snowflake wheels rolled by him in waves. He stared into the distance at row after row of them, turning toward him. One of the bigger ones was rolling right through him now, through his body. He felt its overwhelming divinity permeate him, taking his breath away. He looked down and suddenly realized he was naked.

He rushed back inside, bolted and locked the door, stoked up the fire and went about lighting candles. He shivered and decided to dress. He chose some odd things — whatever seemed to call to him from his trunk. A red, knitted, Phrygian cap, a purple smoking jacket and a pair of lederhosen. He had half put them on when he looked at the bed and saw Afra asleep upon it. Her beautiful face so peaceful, her long hair spilling across the pillows. He remembered the beastly things he had done to her and felt a great, awful remorse. He had ruined this perfect girl. Had she never met him, she would have had a good life, the wife of someone wealthy for she was quite beautiful. It dawned on him that he had ruined her life, stolen her virginity and her virtue.

He fell into a fit of staring at his own face in the looking glass when the golem broke his concentration. "What are you doing?"

"Looking into my own soul," he heard himself whisper.

"What do you see?" it asked.

"Snow." He looked up, was drawn to the door, to the openness of the outside world. "I'm going outside again."

Adam opened the door and a blast of cold air filled his mouth and lungs. He walked out into the powdery-soft snow. Somehow, he had gotten on his boots, though he did not remember putting them on, himself.

The moon illuminated the fresh, white snowfall with her cold, blue light. He staggered silently through the village as the snowflakes fell. With snow stacked on their branches, the trees looked like skeletons, and he marveled at the trees' bones, until he stumbled upon some roots. It was as if the tree had tripped him, an unfriendly reminder to be mindful of his environment lest he hurt himself in the dark. He sharpened his senses and strained his eyes to make sure he was not in danger of bodily harm.

He found a large stone and brushed off the snow and sat down to contemplate the icy water that flowed before him, whispering its watery secrets.

Then something beneath the waters shone. He stared hard at the snow-covered floes drifting over it down the stream, and wondered if it wasn't just a play of moonlight off one of these that had glimmered so. But no, there it was again, a pulsing, orange-tinted glow like a firefly under the crystalline water. It did not move, but seemed to cling to the side of a huge rock in the midst of the river. He looked in every direction for the source of the light, but there was nothing that could be making such an illumination or reflection. There was no object he could call to mind that would glow as this thing glowed, and then he wondered if it weren't some fiery salmon, some creature yet to be discovered. He was no stranger to seeing things in the water, of course, but this seemed different than the prophetic pictures that came to him, for it did not change before his eyes, but remained constant.

The longer he looked at it, the stranger he began to feel about it. It was not natural, not logical, and for it to be before him when he was in such a state, was quite perplexing. Was it a hallucination? Adam was just lucid enough to recall that most all the hallucinations he had heretofore experienced stemmed from some basis in temporal reality. This thing seemed to come out of nowhere and seemed, even through the ecstatic veil of imagery superimposed over his eyeballs, to be out of the ordinary.

He recalled King Andvari, the king of the Nibelung elves in the story of Siegfried who had disguised himself as a salmon. Was this he guarding his treasure hidden beneath the river stones? This river was the Danube, not the Rhine, of course, but Adam reasoned the elves would have had ample time to relocate their treasure in all these centuries. He watched closely as the icy waters rippled the orange light making it form a myriad of transitory shapes that he tried to interpret.

Then, before his eyes, appeared a single sector of a web, like a ladder, rising out of the water from where the orange light glowed. He followed its path up, up, and expected to see the moon, but she was not what was there. Up in the sky, was a turning spiral, violet blue, spinning round and round, throwing off sparks. Adam watched it for a long time and looked for some indication that it was burning out, but it spun round interminably until he became quite hypnotized by it.

Suddenly the orange light shot out of the water. Adam felt a freezing droplet splash in his eye and he jumped backwards, tumbling over the rock upon which he'd been sitting. He looked up to see a small, metallic disk about the size of a dinner pot hovering above his head. An orange light blipped around its midline making the same pulsing, glow he had seen underwater.

"What *are* you?" he said to it, crouching behind the rock, terrified.

It was suspended there for a long moment, observing him, he felt. He wanted to run away, but was frozen there, too afraid to lose the cover of the rock between himself and the thing hovering in the air.

"Fear not," he heard a female voice say.

He looked all around but could not see anyone there. "Where are you?" he stuttered.

"Come inside." Her voice was coming from the floating dinner pot. "Enter into my sky chamber and fly with me."

"Let's do it," Adam licked his lips and stood on his feet that felt frozen, for now his boots were gone.

He was suddenly overcome by a bright light that seemed to tug at his throat; it pulled his body through his throat until he could no longer fathom where he was. There was a feeling of being lost in the light, but it lasted only a short time, and then he felt his feet beneath him again, his body warming, weightless.

He looked about and saw that he was inside the dinner pot, only it was not a dinner pot, but a cozy bedchamber with silken couches around the walls, and a sumptuous pit in the middle of the floor where he was laid down and soft, furry tendrils vibrated, massaged, and supported his body in some kind of warm and perfect suspension. The stars in the night sky shone in through the transparent walls of the place.

Suddenly, a form made of opalescent light quivered in front of him and a beautiful woman took shape. She wore a strange, skin-tight suit like an exoskeleton made of ebony bands that covered her body in an intricate pattern, encircling her breasts and flanging up her neck into a bug-eyed helmet. The thick bands extended over the sides of her head, forming knobbed horns that went all the way down her back like two pigtails and ended in some strange insertion box, made of ebony. It was weird, yet at the same time, beautiful.

"Inanna," he said, for he recognized her immediately, and reached out to touch her hand. As he did so, he was filled with information he seemed to glean through his fingertips.

"In the beginning, my grandfather   Enlil and his brother Ea came here to earth with their families. I was born here with my twin brother Utu long before the days of man. There was a great dispute among my family of royals about who would rule this planet. It was finally decided that each of us would take a turn, a cycle of many thousands of earth years. All of us who are waiting to rule again, we wait with bated breath, and can barely keep ourselves from influencing the fate of this planet and its people. It's true we act out of turn whenever we think we can get away with it. It is *not* my turn to rule, but I am preparing the way for my aeon. Each of us has intervened in the lives of humans countless times. And each of us has *legions* of allies, some unwitting, some quite conscious. Until I am in power, there will be many wars to fight. And you, Adam, will be one of my greatest generals. Raise thy army and I will aid you on the battlefield."

Her voice echoed inside his head and he saw the drama of aeons past come to life before him like a play on stage. The Elohim fought amongst themselves for power over the Earth and the right to control the destiny of man and time. They lusted after beautiful humans who had been created in their image and procreated many children who had both human and Elohim traits. When one of them spurned her, Inanna pled with her all-powerful grandfather to exterminate mankind who had become devious and corrupt. And this was Noah's deluge. When the flood subsided, a new covenant was struck between the human survivors who vowed to strive for perfection of the heart, soul, and mind through the worship of Yahweh, and the Elohim, who promised never to destroy the world again. Great favor and the blessings and help of the Elohim were bestowed on those who worshipped Yahweh through prayer and devotion.

The information filled Adam's brain and bridged gaps in his understanding of the world of the past. The scriptures that had made only partial sense, now seemed to fit together into this greater context, though there was so much missing from the Bible. The stories of Moses, Noah, Abraham, and the visitations of Ezekial, Elijah, and Samuel were complete, their meanings clearer, and the Canon Law that he had spent so much time trying to make logical seemed more erroneous, contrived, and arbitrary than ever. And somehow, Inanna's story seemed familiar as if he'd heard some of it before, but he couldn't remember where...

...Barmoras... The stories the dying man had told him of the Mithraic religion were almost identical, though the Elohim, he had referred to them as 'the gods,' and the family who fought for control of the world all had different names, different animal signs.

He suddenly found himself sitting on the rock, looking up at the full moon. In it, the face of Inanna appeared, young, gorgeous and voluptuous. She looked at him, beautiful and glowing, and as she turned her head, her face began to decay, stretching sinew until she was without flesh, the horrifying, skeletal guise of Death herself. He stared into the void black of her hollow orbits and gasped, before she turned away completely. And then from the other side, she turned her face back to look at him again, and there she appeared, born again, beautiful in the dew of youth and shone her virtues down upon him...

He had a vision then of spring and found himself standing in a meadow of blue daisies and buttercups.

"When it is my turn to rule the earth," her voice was all around him, "all life will be renewed. There will peace, harmony, and love. After winter, there is spring, and then summer..."

He opened his eyes a second later, and he was in the warmth of his own house. A fire was built in the hearth, and on the table, was a pile of buttercups and forget-me-nots. He crawled over and touched them, marveling at them. They had come from the field he had seen in the vision, for it was the dead of winter in Bavaria. His fingers trembled as he stroked the fragile petals, twirling one betwixt his thumb and forefinger. The kykeon was still in his system and the flowers began to turn like pinwheels, kaleidoscoping in extraordinary ways, revealing the depths of newness and beauty, and its shocking, heartbreaking cycle of death and decay, then glorious renewal.

"Ewige Blumenkraft," he whispered, barely forming the words. "Ewige Blumenkraft!" he said again more loudly with tears in his eyes. That was it – the same revelation he had had before, on the night before he had found the homunculus, the golem, but now he recalled what had been revealed to him, and had brought the message back to this side of the void. Eternal flower power. The essence of God, the underpinnings of everything in existence manifested in these floral-looking patterns of energy.... And he had it in his grasp, had always had it - this power to *love*, this incredible power of light that could emanate from a pure heart, from the Light of the God of the Elohim. That was the real key to power, not war, not debates, or kings or politics. Love from the heart and mind was the real power, the power of truth, the power of the will to cleanse away all the muck and debris from the soul and let the light of Yahweh shine through it. And if death came, then so be it, for all would be renewed. "After winter, then spring..."

He had to tell someone everything he had seen. He could not focus his thoughts long enough to utilize quill and ink nor did he think he could write the words fast enough to capture them from his rambling mind.

He stumbled to the bed and looked at Afra as she slept. A rainbow corona shone around her head and shoulders. She awoke, looked at him strangely, wondering at the wide black pools of his pupils.

Gently he stroked her hair and whispered in her ear that he had seen a Goddess only a short time ago. She smiled and asked him to explain. He explained with a kiss. She tasted the ethereal sweetness of his saliva and began to understand. They undressed each other. As always, their love was inevitable. A stream of stars was flying by his head.

The next morning, Adam awoke from his dreams. His mouth pasty and sweet, the experience having refined his grosser matter into something godlier. Things still sparkled to his eye so he knew that he was at least still partially divine. He looked over at Afra's gentle beauty, touched her nose and traced her lips and drifted back to sleep. They slept deeply in each other's arms for many hours.

When he awoke, Adam documented the previous nights' events, exactly how he had prepared the kykeon, what time he recalled taking it, and as much of the activity that had transpired. He wondered now if the experience had even been real. He wanted to discount Inanna and her information as part of perhaps the strangest hallucination he had yet to experience, but something about what she said rang true when he heard it. It was a shattering esoteric message. Her story tied together all of the loose ends found in the most ancient texts into a neat little bundle. The people and civilizations of earth originated in some other world, located out there in the smattering of nighttime stars. Genesis, particularly the old Hebrew and Aramaic scrolls he had in his collection and the Books of Enoch and Daniel seemed to make more sense than they ever had with the important role of the Elohim. He pushed himself to record all that he could remember, though admittedly, what he wrote wasn't entirely accurate, but it was as close to the original message as he could manage.

"...becoming all that one has the capacity to become. Each man within himself has the potential to become divine, a *perfect being*, perfectly enlightened, doing perfect things divinely with the Grace of God, for the ultimate good of the universe," he heard himself pontificate as he penned the words.

"Do men aspire to this?" asked the golem, watching him scrawl in his book.

"No," Weishaupt exhaled. "They do not even know it is possible, and usually a man's life is spent in confusion and waste. Men crawl over this place like vermin searching for carrion and crumbs. They are not conscious of what they do."

"That's too bad," answered the golem, closing its eyes.

"It is," replied Weishaupt, and he sank into a deep melancholy about himself and the state of mankind.

In order to be relieved of his depression, he took action and undertook to train his University students to seek perfection in themselves and in their immortal souls. He realigned his curriculum, listing the crux of his favorite philosophy books, each of the systems he had studied, from the most plebian French Naturalist philosophies of the day, to the most ancient and esoteric of the mystery cults. What they all held in common was the fundamental belief in the possibility of the ascendancy of man to a higher state of existence.

This flew in the face of the philosophy of the Church that taught that men were born in sin and had to redeem themselves through Jesus. The Church required only that a soul study the exegesis of the Church and follow blindly its cooked up doctrines, and somehow that would lead one to salvation, but certainly not to any heightened state of mind on this side of Eternity that didn't involve intense suffering and result in stoning to death. And Weishaupt, because of his hallucinatory experiences, knew there were many heightened states, places of exaltation easily attainable by the common sinner. These places of exaltation were paramount to inspiring a man to reach for God in himself, and for a man to know what Eternal splendor lay within and without. Such were the fast paths to illumination. He listed the methods by which one could reach these states and circled "Kykeon," "mushrooms," "meditation," and "hemp."

In the too-obvious name of THE PERFECTION OF MAN SOCIETY, Weishaupt composed several subversive essays that he distributed to the students in his classes. Each paper discussed the methods of various modes of living and the practice of higher ideals, and discussed how each might be implemented in contemporary society. He espoused evangelism of these ideas and sought to make devoted recruits of his readers. There was no contact information, for these circular papers were anonymous, though they mentioned Doktor Weishaupt with the same veneration given Siddhartha Gautama, and with the assistance of the light-footed golem, became widely distributed throughout the land in the wee hours of the night.

Though he never confessed to any of his works as magus or spiritual propagandist, Weishaupt's fame as a metaphysician and intellectual of the first degree, continued to grow, and he was regarded with reverence, deference and circumspection. His professorship at the University of Ingolstadt afforded him more clout than ever and reinforced his position as an expert in religious affairs. He was consulted in every matter of importance at the University, and took on the role of mentor and tutor to many of Ingolstadt's most influential young men.

One of these was Adolphus Knigge, an extremely gregarious grand tourista from Hamburg who had stayed in Ingolstadt to attend the University after reading the Perfectibilis papers, claiming that his life had been forever changed by the words on the page.

Knigge befriended Zwack and the two of them quickly became Weishaupt's most devoted proteges, always angling for occult secrets and putting on airs of having great powers because of their close association with him. They began trailing Weishaupt everywhere, and he soon became annoyed with the lack of privacy they left him, especially because the affair with Zwack's sixteen year-old half-sister, Afra, continued much to his carnal pleasure, and their mutual risk. She snuck out of her parents' house nearly every night to be with him. Some nights he'd devoted to his kykeon or mushrooms and couldn't be bothered, but other nights he was glad to have her. Her brother had no idea that they were lovers, and

Weishaupt wanted to keep it that way. Zwack often spoke of Afra's rich marriage prospects among the gentry, and though Weishaupt had no plans to marry the girl, this annoyed him greatly. As much as he tried to avoid Zwack, the young man pursued him, but proved time and again to be of valuable service. He was an exceedingly clever lawyer and Weishaupt worried about his retribution if ever he discovered the illicit affair with his young sister.

CHAPTER XXIX

It was the first of March in the midst of his third round of Perfectibilis essays, when he received a card from Mayer that Eva's father, Jacob Frank, had been released from exile in Brno during the Russian invasion of Poland and would be received at their estate in Frankfurt am Main for the Vernal Equinox. It was an invitation to join his reception festivities and stay at the Bauers' for a few days.

Adam hadn't seen Mayer in a long time, and was curious to see if Eva would be there. Undoubtedly she would, he told himself. Her father had been in exile and was now returned home a free man. She would certainly be at his side.

According to Mayer, Jacob Frank had been exiled for heresy. There was more to the story, Adam had intuited, but no one had been forthcoming with any further details, and he had not asked nor looked into it. Despite his growing affection for Afra, the prospect of seeing the divine Eva thrilled him more than he cared to admit, and he wrote to Mayer that he would attend. He briefly considered not going and showing Eva that he was callous to her now, but he was anything but, for he burned to see her again, even if it was across a crowded room. And when next might such an opportunity arise?

As fate would have it, he failed to cast a chart, or to even scry, for the time he would be away or he might have seen what was to come and stayed safely in Ingolstadt. The golem also warned him of treachery to come, but he turned a deaf ear on the little thing, and so, he went blindly into a situation that would forever change him.

The ride to Frankfurt was long and uncomfortable and Adam was resentful that Mayer hadn't sent a luxurious coach to pick him up. Of course, the Bauer family certainly had other guests of greater distinction on which their carriages would be employed, so he would have to find his own way. He bought a ticket on the express that took him straightaway to Frankfurt. He was the only gentleman on board, riding with four fat, prim, Franciscan sisters and their emaciated Abbess. The latter was the only one who spoke the entire way, and Adam found them a strange and malodorous lot. They were on their way to perform some good works at a hospice in Frankfurt, said their Abbess. She inquired if Adam was a Catholic, to which he responded in the affirmative, and then she went on to report with grave sorrow that the His Holiness, the Pope had only days ago been murdered – poisoned, it would seem. "By someone *inside* the Vatican," she added with dismay. The discussion provoked a torrent of tears and breathy suffering from the rest of the nuns, and Adam gave them all his handkerchiefs. "Who would do such a thing?" wailed the Abbess.

Adam was immediately struck with the notion that it had been none other than the minions of the Black Pope, Superior General Lorenzo Ricci, and he put he his tongue in his cheek to stifle a laugh. When the Jesuit order was suppressed, Superior General Lorenzo had been banished to Castle San Angelo by the Pope, before his untimely demise, of course. And the Pope's murder, obviously, was an act of revenge from the imprisoned Jesuit leader. Adam had taken much delight in exacting his revenge these past years on the Black Pope, but felt it high time to deliver the world of this vile snake.

Adam gave the nuns a coy smile and closed his eyes. As he dozed the evening away in the coach, he asked to be taken to Lorenzo. He heard the whooshing sound of wind in his ears, then the loud crack of thunder.

Suddenly he was standing in a room made of stone where pigeons perched on the open windowsill. He could hear the sounds of the city and the river far below. He saw Lorenzo lying in his bed, for Adam had left him crippled on one of his previous visits. Above, a silver crucifix hung on the wall. Silently he lifted it off its nail and stabbed Lorenzo in the gut with it. The Black Pope opened his eyes and screamed and spasmed in pain as Adam withdrew the sharp crucifix and brought it down into his throat, then again and again, attempting to decapitate him with it, as he thought of the beheadings of his own parents. Weishaupt watched with satisfaction as Lorenzo gurgled and groaned with his last breaths. "Who is stabbing me?"

"It is I, the Avenging Soul," whispered Adam in his ear, and he began to laugh maniacally, as he continued to sever his head from his body in this vicious and crude manner.

Adam was brought back to his body by his laughter. When he opened his eyes in the coach, he realized the Franciscan sisters were much alarmed by him and squirmed uncomfortably beside and before him.

"Forgive me, I must have dozed off," he explained. He touched his sleeve and felt the wet stain of the Black Pope's blood. He looked at it, rubbed it between his fingers, and saw the sticky, crimson testimony of his crime, and hid his arm beneath his satchel. He had never before brought back any sort of physical trace or memento from his astral travels, and he began to wonder if he could actually remove things from the places that he visited and bring them back to his physical body. It was something he had not before considered.

By the time the coach arrived in Frankfurt am Main, his sleeve was dry again, and Adam cordially helped each of the Franciscan sisters out in front of St. Bartholomew's Kaiser Dom, a tall and wickedly spired Cathedral, the largest building in the area. The nuns politely invited him to mass before setting off to see his friend, but Adam declined, and slinging his satchel over his shoulder, set off for the Judengasse, the Jewish ghetto, where all the Jews in Frankfurt had been forced to reside for the past four hundred years.

South of the Cathedral, he came to the iron gates that cordoned off the Judengasse from Christian Frankfurt. There were no guards posted as Adam slipped through onto the quaint street lined with five and six-story row houses, all side-by-side, brick and timber with not an inch between them.

He could smell the garlic and the rosemary, the delicious aroma of roasted chickens ready before sunset. The neighborhood was astir, for it was the Sabbath eve and the residents were preparing for their day of rest, busily completing any unfinished business in the remaining hour of daylight. The Jews with their heads covered, the men in yamulkes and the women wearing modest scarves and bonnets of black or dark blue - they were his kinsmen, and he wondered if they could tell that he was one of them. He would never have fit in with them of course, for he fit in nowhere, except in his own strange house and lecture room at the University.

Even so, he was drawn to their rich history and his heart secretly longed to be part of this people. There was such a comfortable, simple air about the neighborhood – yes, it was old and some of it could've used a new coat of plaster, but he envied Mayer for growing up in the close comforts of this quaint and beautiful community that should have been his own. He found the ways of Jewry to be pragmatic, true, and the Torah undiluted by time and the caprices of unenlightened priests. No ecumenical debates had marred and tainted their Truths as had happened in the Church.

The Bauers' house was like those tall houses adjacent - plaster and timber, a good five stories tall, six windows across, edged up to the street with no front garden. From the outside, it seemed no different from most of the others in the neighborhood, but the inside belied the wealth of its inhabitants.

The front door was opened automatically by a maid, and Adam stepped across the threshold, eyeing the jewel-encrusted mezuzah inside the doorway. The maid smiled uncomfortably and touched a kiss on it for him.

"Adam Weishaupt," he told her, and she curtsied. He did not know if she would remember his name.

"Mayer will be so glad you're here," she said.

The interior of the Bauers' house was all highly polished dark wood and opulence. The maid led Adam straight back to where a beautiful glass cupola'd solarium opened up into a breathtaking courtyard.

There were Mayer, and several other young men surrounding an older man in a red robe who was reclining on a chaise. His mustache was eccentrically long, an unusual fashion, and Adam surmised correctly that this could be none other than the guest of honor, Jacob Frank. He thought he looked as if he was recovering and wondered how severely he had been maltreated while in exile. He could see his bare thigh and naked chest beneath his loosely fastened robe, and was slightly embarrassed for him. He could not help but notice how thin and sinewy his body seemed, as if he'd been half-starved. He could now see from what stock Eva's slender build and skin tone had come.

He glanced around for her, but he did not see her or her husband.

"She's here," said Mayer suddenly at his side. "Shavuot Shalom, my good friend."

"Who do you mean?" said Adam.

Mayer chuckled at his affected nonchalance. "She's a widow, now. Did I not tell you?"

"What?" Adam was stunned. *A widow?*

"Her husband died in his sleep. His heart simply gave out." Mayer placed his spatula-shaped fingers on his chin and drummed them with a smile, looking up at him and searching his face. "How was your trip?"

Adam caught his breath. She was free. How long, he wanted to ask, but refrained. It mattered little now, for there was nothing to keep them apart.

"So the palace and all the property...?" he asked, recalling the exquisite palace where her wedding had taken place.

"She gets nothing," said Mayer. "She's come back here and will live with her father in one of our houses in the country. Did I tell you I've taken over the bank for father?"

"Oh," replied Adam, feeling sorry that Eva had not made off with what should have been rightfully hers.

"Yes, I've taken over father's operation. On Monday, you'll have to come down there with me and I'll show you my new office. It's really something. And I'm changing our family name."

"What?" Adam asked incredulously. "Why would you ever do such a thing? Your name is your legacy."

"First of all, Bauer means 'peasant,' and I am *not* a peasant," laughed Mayer quietly. "And there's another Bauer from Frankfurt. He runs a store and he's sort of a lowlife. We've been associated with him and it's been everything we could do to dispel the rumors that we were cheating people out of pounds of cheese. I just don't want to have to think about it, and besides, I have a new direction for the bank. It needs a new name to go with it.

Things are going to be entirely different now. ...Don't tell father. If he doesn't know, he can't oppose me till it's all said and done."

Adam was barely listening to Mayer's plan as he stared at Mayer's ring, the golden snake biting its own tail. Its ruby eyes flashed, and it was only then that Adam suddenly remembered what had happened, for it had been blocked to his waking mind.

One night, months ago, he had gone to his bed and lain down. He relaxed and felt the desire for sleep wash over him. "Take me to Eva," he said as he drifted off. He heard the sound of the whooshing wind, felt the numbing vibration in his core, and he floated up above his body. He looked down at himself and pitied the young man who was so handsome, but so alone and growing thinner, sadder. There was a loud snap like the crack of thunder and he was suddenly in Eva's bedroom.

She lounged upon her bed, reading a book. Gently he blew on her cheek. She brushed it away with her elegant hand. Softly he traced a fingertip along her body. She responded then with a moan and rolled onto her back, her satin gown and long hair spilling out around her.

He leaned down beside her to whisper in her ear. "Eva, I love you."

Her eyes grew wide and she sat bolt upright beside him. He put a kiss on her lips and she scrambled away, jumping off the bed. She stepped on the hem of her skirt and fell on the floor.

He pursued her over the bed, and lifting her to her feet, embraced her from behind. "It's Adam," he said, tasting her fine neck.

"Adam?" She turned to look at him, but looked through him. "I can't see you!"

"Shh..." He fondled her breasts through her silken gown. She sighed in ecstasy. "Are you a ghost? Are you dead?"

349

she cried with great grief.

"Yes," he lied in her ear. "I have passed from this life but cannot leave this earth until you give yourself to me again."

She gave a little cry and lay back upon the bed. He took her savagely, for his fury at her betrayal fired his passion. She writhed beneath him as he kissed her deeply. He felt her hot tightness pulling the ecstasy from his pelvis, and with a shudder, he began releasing months of repressed emotion for her. He heard her crying beneath him and he too, shed tears of love and sadness into her soft hair as he kissed her tenderly.

And it was then that Lothar and his man had come into the room. He looked upon his wife with confusion, her back pinned against the headboard, her dress thrown up around her neck. Adam seized her bridegroom's throat and broke his neck. His man retreated in horror as Lothar's body fell upon the floor.

He had completely forgotten the entire incident, as if the whole thing were some foggy, forgotten dream like so many senseless sequences of images that appear to the sleeping mind.

Then came the dim vision of being escorted, dragged actually, by a bunch of flying hags, to a mountain top abode where sat an angry council of white-haired men around a long table. Behind them, out the window was at the great range of fuchsia-lined mountains set against a black sky. He remembered their fearsome guises and the wrathful stares from their purple-black eyes, as they warned him sternly *never* to commit such an act again or he would pay a very severe price. He had been vexed and shamed by them and had pushed the incident to the darkest corner of his mind from where he had just now retrieved it.

"Would you like a drink?" Mayer noticed his friend's sudden change in mood, and vanished inside the house to get them some refreshments.

Adam found himself in the middle of the Bauers' courtyard. He sat down in an empty chair at the Sabbath table and put his head in his hand. He wasn't sure if sitting was the proper thing to do, but reasoned his Catholic upbringing would absolve him of any Judaic faux pas.

"Do not sit until the table is ready!" called a voice.

He turned and Jacob Frank leered at him from where he reclined on his chaise. Adam got up and begged his pardon, and went into the house.

He was a murderer, and though no one else knew it, he felt an unnerving sensation that he had been judged, and was being watched. What was it that the golem had said? He strained to remember. He was irritated at the prospect of being monitored by some self-righteous council, a group unknown to him, and he tried as hard as he could to put it out of his mind. He looked down at the dark red-black stain on his sleeve, and folded his guilty arm across his stomach, hoping that none had seen it.

As he strode through Mayer's opulent house, he searched for some sign of Eva. He remembered her, magnificent in her white dress on her wedding day, and even more so on her wedding night as they had lain together in the beautiful room inside the castle wall. Though he was incapable of feeling guilt, he felt no small amount of remorse that he had stolen the fabulous life of happy leisure she could have enjoyed, and he too, if he had only found some better way of disposing of her husband.

He found an empty room and there changed out of his bloody shirt, washing the traces of his crimes in the basin. He went again and searched for her, hoping to find her at every turn, and when he had thought its corridors and unlocked rooms exhausted, he returned to the courtyard.

Mayer had explained to him before that Jacob Frank, the Bauers, and most of the elite of the neighborhood were all Sabbateans, orthodox Jews who were devotees of Sabbatai

Tzvi, some dead mystic and reputed messiah of the last century, of whom Jacob Frank claimed to be the present incarnation. They were strict observers of the Sabbath and practiced little known rites not found in the Talmud, but extrapolated from other texts, as Adam was to soon discover.

As he stepped into the courtyard, he found Eva in a black dress lighting the candles on the table where the other guests were seated. She looked up at him and gasped audibly, "Adam? You're... here?"

He stopped to take a breath as well, and something electrifying passed between them. Her eyes shone in the candlelight with so much emotion. She had grown even more beautiful and radiant in her widow's grief, he thought, and wanted with every fiber to embrace her. Did she remember the nighttime incident? Was she aware that he was responsible for her widowhood?

Coolly, he greeted her and then the others and took a seat at the table with them. Jacob Frank and Moses Bauer, Mayer's father, sat at the heads of the table. As Eva sat across from him, he could not take his eyes from her beautiful face. He tried not to be obvious with his attentions and did his best to affect interest in Jacob Frank's lecture on *The Zohar*. The others ate quietly and listened. Adam had studied *The Zohar* for several years now, and had found the work to be suspect, though inspirational and veritably a sacred text, but according to Dr. Mahler, not authored at the early date it was purported to have been written. Frank spoke of the Shekinah or divine presence, the materialization of the spiritual wedding of souls. It was a bit of a stretch, but it was interesting, and tied intimately with Qabala, a subject in which Adam considered himself an expert.

Herr Frank had a demanding way of speaking as if one was bound to listen to him and take his words to heart, or else be damned. Adam wanted to interject and argue with several of his assertions, but ate the game hen and turnip greens on his plate, and let the notion pass. He was already on testy ground with the guest of honor, and did not wish to further antagonize the father of Eva.

Adam glanced around at the others as they ate. Eight young couples, none older than thirty, all of them utterly captivated by Frank. They seemed affluent if not extremely wealthy, and all were blessed with vibrant health and good looks. Mayer was certainly the least attractive male at the table, though his petite and lovely bride, Gutle, made up for any shortcomings he may have exhibited.

When the meal ended, Frank gruffly excused himself, and a pair of servants transported him from the courtyard upon his recliner as if it were a litter. Adam refrained from comment, and drank more of the wine, one that he felt was a rather dynamic bouquet. They all sat in the courtyard, laughing and telling stories till late in the evening. Adam could feel Eva's desire for him, the way her eyes lingered upon his face and body – though she would not let herself meet his eye and he wished the others would retire so that he could move close to her and talk to her in private. He was about to effect a sleeping spell when a manservant appeared.

"Herr Frank requests you bathe then come to the ballroom," bowed the manservant.

Adam thought it was an odd request that anyone would ask another person, much less a group of people, to bathe, but he was drunk, and his only thoughts were how he could get close to Eva.

Mayer's wife, Gutle, was feeling ill from the wine and the couple excused themselves for the evening. Adam sensed something amiss in the way they quietly disappeared from the party, but thought little on it.

He returned to his room to find an entire tub of hot water waiting for him. He removed his clothes and sank into the water, letting it relax and bathe him. He thought of soap, for he was still conscious of the residual blood from the Black Pope on his forearm, and searched the dressing table for a cake of it. In one of the drawers, there was a small silver box. He opened it, and to his surprise, found what must have been the remains of the mushrooms that he and Mayer had picked on the way to Eva's wedding so long ago. He picked one of the dried, shriveled stems, and ate it, then another and another. He remembered he was expected in the ballroom and reluctantly climbed out. A satin robe reminiscent of the one Jacob Frank had worn all night was hanging ready on the front of the wardrobe.

Adam put it on and tied its sash around his waist.

He found the ballroom, guarded by two large servants. They opened the doors for him and he walked into the cavernous room that was lit by hundreds of red candles. The others knelt before Jacob Frank who reclined on his chaise longue at the head of the room.

Before Frank, lay thick carpets, silken quilts, and velvet bolsters of various sizes. On the left side of him, the women knelt, and on the right side, the men. The music of a flute came from behind one of the many screens that donned the walls of the ballroom. The women whispered among themselves. At the back of the group, Eva seared Adam with a sultry gaze and he began to feel the surreal effects of the mushrooms.

"Through transgression, the soul is purified," Frank said again. "Tonight, I release you all from your mortal vows of marriage, chastity, morality, and prudence, and invite you to delight in the pure lust that is in each of you. Commune, love, as your passion moves you, for it is the desire of the eyes, the heart, and the loins that we celebrate." He touched himself at each of these points for emphasis.

Adam could not believe what he was hearing. He was no stranger to copulation. He had lived his teenage years in a brothel, not to mention his time with Inanna - whether it had been real or imagined, he had experienced plenty, but for such things to be condoned and ritualized en masse was not something he had yet encountered.

Wasn't this what he, himself, had been espousing of late in his Perfectibilis papers? Free-flowing love from an open, perfect heart, and the light that flows through it shall set a man free, shall make him divine? Verily it was his own philosophy thrown back at him, and he laughed to himself at this strange and beautiful ritual in which he was about to partake. He opened himself up to it, consciously brought down his personal barriers, letting the soft wave of psychedelia open his mind, and stood willing to experience all that was offered him.

"Rise Marie," commanded Frank of someone's buxom wife. He recalled the fine and modest costume the woman had worn at dinner. Now she was nude but for her necklace. She was beautiful in a quiet way, slender but for her large breasts, and she seemed quite intelligent, not the sort of lady Adam imagined who would ever disrobe before a crowd. He did recall that she was one of Eva's bridesmaids who had gone swimming in the nude that fateful evening after Eva's wedding.

"Who will take this woman to the House of the Lord?" asked Jacob Frank of the group of men who knelt at his feet. Another man rose and took her hands, and lay down with her in the midst of the group. They began their foreplay as Jacob Frank selected a beautiful auburn haired woman, and called for a partner for her.

Several men stood. Her husband watched as they all came forward and began kissing her and touching her, dividing her body between them like hungry lions. Her husband was a short fellow, shorter than Mayer with blonde hair, narrow eyes and a pinched face. Adam looked at him and he seemed rather relaxed about the prospect of his wife taking several other men, as did the mate of

Marie, who was now clearly, vociferously enjoying herself on the cock of another.

Jacob Frank presented another woman and pointed at a tall lanky fellow, who stood and removed his robe. "You will be the savior of this woman. Do what thou wilt." And the couple laid themselves down and began making love.

Adam watched as the dark haired man next to him rose and approached the next woman and began to kiss and caress her. He watched the fellow's cock grow long on her hip. He stood there in disbelief, amazed at the sort of sexual theatre that was being acted out before him.

"Will anyone help the Divine Couple on their way?" asked Jacob Frank of the others.

Two women and another man stood and disrobed. They began caressing the first pair. The extra man came up behind the woman and held her breasts, his cock growing erect as it slipped between her buttocks. The other two women let their hands rove over all of the bodies of the others, their lips finding the lips of the Couple.

Eva stared at Adam across the room and he could not help nor hide his excitement though he felt no small amount of revulsion at the audience of her father.

"This is the most sacred communion, the most exalted act in all of Yahweh's creation, and the most debased. Let it be the bringer of light into the darkness, of freedom out of the oppression that has befallen our once noble race. With our love for one another, let the light flow in..."

Adam now recalled Jacob Frank's seemingly pointless banter about divine love, ecstasy in the heart of Yahweh, and suddenly realized he had been speaking of the sexual act all throughout the Sabbath meal.

Certainly sexual rites were not a part of most Jews' practice of their faith. Or were they? No, most certainly not. This group was different, more enlightened than any he had ever met, for they could look past modern society's mores and the confining trappings and desires of their human flesh and use it to be closer to God. He was instantly filled with respect for Jacob Frank who now sat upright on his chaise intently watching the auburn haired girl quake with an orgasm. Her curls shaking, her face glistened with perspiration and flushed as she moaned in staccato beats of ecstasy.

"She is at the Gates of the Palace now. Shhh..." said Frank.

'The gates of the palace.' How familiar a phrase it seemed. It was then Adam recalled his own experiences with Eva and with Inanna, where he had verily risen up into some ethereal cathedral, gilded and jeweled, and been shushed by a strange and divine voice... He had often thought of it, and wondered at its significance now in light of the words of Jacob Frank.

Jacob Frank took the hand of a young, dark-haired girl with keen eyes and a large nose. She knelt before him and began suckling him. Everyone was partnered or involved in the sexual acts of the others until only Adam and Eva were left. The floor writhed with copulating bodies between them and Adam could barely conceal his arousal beneath his robe. Adam wondered if Eva was expected to observe her period of mourning and if his being an outsider precluded him from participating. The first paired partners had joined with others and several mouths feasted on one person, while those feasting were bowed themselves, and taken to the gates by others who came behind them. It seemed that all were joined to each other, through each other, and there was not one pair that was an island unto themselves. Rather, they were part of a great, red, and writhing web of pleasure. Their moans of delight over the sounds of the flute, created a music more lovely than anything Adam had ever heard, and the soft, orange light of the candles blurred with the ecstasy of lovemaking that permeated the air.

"Mistress Matronita," Jacob Frank called his daughter,

and inclined his head at Adam and Eva as if granting approval, and they approached each other. As he gazed at her beautiful face and perfect lips, Adam remembered now why he had strangled her husband.

And now in the stately ballroom on this strange and magical Sabbath night, they were to be together again. No sooner had they neared and stood a breath away from the other then they were cosseted by the nude revelers who pulled off their robes and titillated them as Adam's lips found Eva's. He looked defiantly down at her violet eyes. He saw her gorgeous breasts bared and cupped them as he kissed them. He burned for their perfect union to take place again, and he laid her down and found her virtue. He felt her release on him in a wave of pleasure as the auburn-haired girl kissed her breasts and neck. Adam pulled Eva upon his lap and they were held together in a locked embrace on the verge of some great sensation that he felt might be too large to be endured by one person, for the combined energy of the group was being manifested through them now. The others regrouped around them, creating a matrix of bodies, a sunflower that radiated out from the central point where they were so blessedly joined. Adam and Eva were suspended in their state of ecstasy for many long minutes as their energies mounted, and her hot, wet core pulsed upon his swollen member. He breathed in her scent and feasted on her silky skin as she became a flower before his eyes. He was barely aware of Jacob Frank chanting some incantation in Hebrew. The syllables built in intensity as did the excitement of those around them as Adam's sublime movements brought all of them to orgasmic ecstasy as one.

He heard her voice in his ear, speaking strange, ancient words in unison with the response to Jacob's call. Adam suddenly sensed that Eva was no stranger to this kind of sexual practice and had perhaps been a participant in these rites since a very young age. As he sucked her tender breasts, she leaned back in his embrace and moaned, rolling her eyes back in ecstasy. He thrust deeply into he, joined to her, unable to resist the momentous orgasm that riveted through them, an accumulation of the sexual energies of everyone present that utterly electrified him.

It was in the midst of this ecstasy, that he became of aware of their voices all around him chanting feverishly, breathlessly "Sammael! Sammael!" He saw the strange, frightened look in Eva's eyes and was overcome with dread, for it was the name of a demon. Too late he felt his vision grow dim. He felt an electrifying spike in his stomach, and talons seizing upon his shoulders. Red swirling mist penetrated his body through his navel and opened solar plexus, as he fell back. Spent from his exertion and the assault of the mushrooms on his sensibilities, he could not resist and felt it fill him, overcoming his will and enlivening his cock that swelled to gigantic proportions.

He rose, and towered over the others who knelt around him. Jacob Frank bowed humbly, his own cock extending to the evil like an iron filing to a lodestone. "O Sammael, we welcome you to your hallowed celebration. Take us, men and women, as a holy offering, and give us the earthly boons that you have in your domain, or be not welcome here!"

"I have come to bestow you with the riches and power of the dead Kings," Adam heard a gruff voice come from his throat, but it was not his own. He tried to say something, but his own voice and will were mute and powerless, stifled deep inside him. He stood within himself, witnessing all that was taking place around him, but could not overcome what possessed him.

He took Jacob Frank's place on the chaise and propped up his feet. To his horror, Adam realized they had become black hooves. He felt something beneath him, something that was part of him. His hand reached down to touch it and he found he was now possessed of a long, fleshy tail. Soft black scales adorned it, and on the end, there was rather sharp-looking barb.

One by one, the worshippers bowed before him, sucking his enormous purple member and looking up at him with adoration. His body was overtaken by Sammael, though he was dimly aware of the pleasure given him as the procession sucked him and rode him in turn. Eva straddled him again and came to orgasm on him countless times. Her held her cruelly down upon him, controlling her pleasure and ejaculating repeatedly into her. She tried in vain to resist him, but the excruciating pleasure he wielded with her was more powerful than her will. Her father mounted her from behind and began pumping into her arse with cruel vengeance as the three of them brought each other to climax, and Adam felt his face contorted into a bemused grimace. As the others danced around them in a lewd display, he began vomiting up a viscous black bile.

He lost consciousness for some time and awoke to find himself engaged again in the middle of an orgiastic ring of sodomy and copulation. The orgy lasted until dawn, until the last of them collapsed from exhaustion on the floor.

As the sun broke through the ballroom windows, Adam felt the energies of Sammael dissipate from his body, and the carpet rise up to meet his exhausted form. He awoke sometime later in the haze of the morning light.

He was sick from the night's debauch, and wanted desperately to bathe the shame of it from him. He had lost himself utterly for a few hours and now felt he wanted to hide beneath some stone and never be found. He had opened himself, forsaking his good sense and guardians, and allowed this abomination into himself. He pushed up from the floor and looked around for Eva, for Jacob Frank, but they had removed themselves already from the sleeping fray. It was no wonder Mayer and his wife had bowed out early and not joined the ballroom ritual; they had known what was to come. He remembered now the odd look Mayer gave him as they said good night, and understood that it was a warning that he had not heeded. But he knew that he would not have missed a moment with Eva no matter what Mayer may have said. He banished and cleared the circle that Jacob Frank had opened, but felt intuitively that the entity, Sammael was still in this realm.

He found one of the robes lying on the floor. He put it on, and walked back to his room. He saw himself in the looking glass above the dressing table. There was a demonic expression frozen in his facial muscles, and above and below his eyes, there appeared strange yet somehow familiar, thorn-like markings. He peered at them closely, and they were not shadows, but smudges on his skin, visible even in the light of the morning sun that was streaming in through his window. *Where had he seen them before?* He splashed his face with water, and scrubbed the smudges with his face cloth, but they remained. He felt feverish and his blood felt thick. Was Sammael still within him? He worried that the beast would return against his will, for now that he been a conduit, he was known to Sammael who may try to overtake his body at some future time. He would make every effort to prevent ever being possessed again, recalling the unfortunate Dursmann possessed of the Morgizau. He had done for Dursmann what no one else he knew could do for him, and he would not under any circumstances allow himself to fall into such a dire situation, for there would certainly be no salvation for him. He reviewed the evening's events and realized the opening, amplifying effects of the mushrooms on his sensibilities, combined with Jacob Frank's evocation of Sammael had resulted in this most unsavory situation. It was not the wanton sex acts or even seeing Eva with her father that disturbed him the most, but the loss of control of his own faculties - that was the most unsettling part. Psychedelic substances and demonic evocation, perhaps did not mix well? Adam had never combined the two before, and now had confirmation that he had been wise to enjoy these activities singly.

And why, for what purpose had Sammael been called? He tried to recall all that had been said in Frank's evocation of him, but could not remember.

Adam washed himself as best he could and with some trepidation, fell asleep on the bed. He did not wake until nightfall the following evening. He arose, and to his dismay, recalled the group's lascivious activities, and wondered if he could escape the house without detection and never see any of Jacob Frank's followers again.

There was a knock upon his door. It was a servant summoning him to dinner in one hour.

"Please tell my host that I cannot stay. I must return to Ingolstadt immediately," said Adam.

"You must stay for the close of the Sabbath, and eat the meal," said the servant.

"Why?" asked Adam.

The servant bowed and walked away. Adam closed the door and hurriedly began packing his things.

It was Mayer who next came to the door. He looked weary and worried. "Adam, you must join us to close the Sabbath. Jacob Frank has to perform the last of the rituals. It is very important that you stay. Especially you."

"I don't care. I don't want any more to do with him or his incestuous daughter," said Adam.

"You know she's not really his daughter," said Mayer. "She's actually the daughter of Catherine the Great and her lover. Her birth, had it been widely known, would have caused a great scandal in the Russian empire. Jacob Frank and his late wife adopted Eva. She is *not* his natural daughter, so don't even think that. That would be disgusting."

Adam looked at Mayer narrowly and thought of Eva's

features, so similar to Jacob's. He wanted to believe what Mayer was saying, but could not.

"What did we do last night?" asked Adam. "What did *I* do?"

"You brought the sacred marriage into this realm. You exalted in the divine splendor of *The Zohar*. You, my friend, took on the role that is usually reserved for Jacob Frank. He *is* the Messiah. And I think it may have angered him slightly. Please, just come down to dinner so that he can close the ritual and all go in peace."

With some resistance, Adam finally agreed, and went downstairs with Mayer. The Bauers' dining room was hung with large gilt-framed looking glasses on both sides reflecting the table's bounty and its guests ad infinitum. He was sat next to Eva who did not even look at him. Jacob Frank and Moses Bauer again took the heads of the table. Adam was grateful that the crusty, elder Bauer had not participated in the rite. He undoubtedly had been watching, however. Adam's embarrassment was renewed when he caught the others staring at him over the dinner table as they all joined hands. He felt their energy pass through him from right to left as it circulated around the table. They were all tired, but still desirous of each other, and Adam could not deny his carnal hunger to be united with them all again, but pushed the thought from his mind.

Jacob Frank stood and unrolled *The Zohar* and began reading from it. Adam hated that the sacred book be so heinously misconstrued, but could not find the words to speak his abhorrence of Frank's assertions, particularly in the company of his followers who verily believed him the Messiah. He sat silently, wishing he could whisk Eva away and vanish from the Bauers' and from the minds and memories of all these who had witnessed his transformation and unspeakable conduct the night before. He shuddered, for he had never felt so unclean. If he could have wished it all away, he would have.

Then Frank segued into the book of Revelation that
Adam felt strangely appropriate in light of what had
transpired, and then at last, bound the group together in a
strange ceremony. "These mirrors shall attest to our
existence and our kinship to the other, so we are all bound
to each other for all time. The reflection of the reflection
and its reflection is carried unto the Infinite, to the throne
of God, forging us together as divine brides and
bridegrooms in His Kingdom for all eternity."

Adam thought it strange how refined and beautiful the
opening and closing ceremonies were for such abject
debauchery. When the meal was over, he kissed the others
goodbye as was customary, and politely excused himself.

He planned to buy a horse from the livery down the
street and set out in the dark for Ingolstadt, but Mayer
caught him at the door. "You're not going home?"

"I really feel I should take my leave," Adam insisted.

"In the dark? Now? That's ridiculous. Don't you
remember how we met? You may not be so lucky again.
Please, Adam, I'll send you home in our coach tomorrow.
I want you to come with me to the bank tomorrow. You
have to see what has happened," he said, rubbing his
palms together. "And it's all because of you!"

Adam wondered what he could mean, but figured it was
naught but a ruse to pique his curiosity so that he would
agree to stay the night. Adam unhappily acquiesced, and
returned to his room, locking himself in for the night. Not
once, but three times during the night, there were soft
knocks upon his door.

The third time, he rose and stood listening at the door.
"Who is there?" he asked. No answer came, and when his
curious mind considered opening it, every fiber in his
being warned him against it.

He fell asleep after that and had terrifying dreams that
faceless beings made of fire waited for him on the other
side of the door, and sensing his resistance, tried to draw

364

him through the keyhole to the other side.

He was awakened again when his door opened by itself. He sat bolt upright in bed, and became aware that it must be late in the morning. Mayer's own manservant and chambermaid drew open his curtains, set down a tray of breakfast for him, refilled the basin, and left. He ate in private and tried to shake off the images of his dream that came reeling back into his mind. He washed his face, then cleared his circle, banishing more fiercely and invoking Yahweh more fervently than he had ever in his life.

He went downstairs in a guarded, but better state of mind than in that in which he had spent the night. He could not wait to be back in the safety and comfort of his own little house in Ingolstadt. He would placate Mayer and leave as soon as he could.

Just before noon, Mayer took him down the street and around the corner to his father's bank. It was two-story, built of gray bricks and not nearly so old as the Deutsche Bankhaus in Munich. There was an unusual spring in Mayer's step and Adam thought he seemed excessively enthused about something.

When they had stepped inside, Mayer pointed back up at the place above the heavy, iron front door. "Do you see that sign?" he asked.

Adam saw the red hexagram painted on a yellowed piece of parchment above the door. "What is it?"

"It's our red shield, our *Rothschild*," he answered. "That's going to be my new name. Mayer Amschel Rothschild."

Adam raised an eyebrow at him and said it sounded all right, for indeed it did have a nobler ring to it than Bauer.

"It doesn't sound as Jewish either," Mayer added.

"I don't understand the significance," Adam answered.

"My father put this little red sign up above the door to stop thieves, protect our money, and bring us prosperity. It has worked in spades, my friend, and now, as of this three o'clock this morning, our bank is the richest outside of Italy. The King of Holland has just deposited three million gold pieces with us," Mayer rubbed his hands together.

"Why would he come all the way here to some godforsaken ghetto bank to deposit his money?" asked Adam.

"Precisely, my friend. No one would ever look for it here in my godforsaken ghetto bank. Obviously it's not safe in Amsterdam. So he's hiding it here, out of reach of his greedy relatives I imagine. Would you like to see it?"

"Well, of course," he replied. "Honestly, Mayer, why do you suppose he chose your father's bank?"

"Why not? It's a perfectly good bank. We have a sparkling reputation abroad, I might tell you." Mayer said sharply, and opened a heavy vault door with the set of keys he kept tied to his vest. It was the entrance to yet another small room where there were two seats at a small counting table and two more vault doors. They by-passed those, and Mayer showed him down a set of narrow stairs to a crude basement. In the basement, there was a larger counting table, and another, larger vault door. Mayer opened the large vault. The heavy door groaned on its hinges and Mayer lit the wall lantern. Suddenly, the room was radiant with sparkling gold pieces, stacked waist high, filling the entire floor.

"Sheisse, Mayer, that's a lot of gold!" breathed Adam.

"You don't have to tell me. I was up all night counting it and I still haven't finished. It's going to take weeks."

"Just think if it was really yours. What would you do?"

"I have it. You see it. It's as good as mine," said Mayer, his eyes glittering.

"I think that goes against good banking practices," said Adam.

"Well, I have it to lend and earn me interest," said Mayer. "There's so much here no one would ever miss a little bit. Would you like to borrow some money? My lowest interest for you, of course."

"Doesn't the Talmud warn against usury? Forbid it, rather?" asked Adam, for he had often wondered how the Bauers professed to be good Jews then charged an enormous rate of interest on their money.

Mayer puffed up. "If people could be counted on to pay our money back, then we wouldn't make them pay interest. That's the price the borrower must pay for the risk I'm taking."

"Yes, but what of the risk the King of Holland and your other bank clients are taking by leaving their money in your hands?"

"Pushaw, they're lucky I accept their money and keep it safe for them. My life is in danger – all the time – because of their cursed money!"

Adam clearly saw the inconsistencies in Mayer's thinking, chuckled, and said. "And what of the jubilee year, are you going to forget and forgive all loans every fifty years?"

"Don't be archaic with me, Weishaupt. I have a family to feed." Mayer extinguished the lantern and shut the vault door, locking it thrice.

As they made their way up the stairs, Adam wondered if the demon Sammael had verily delivered this treasure into Mayer's hands. If so, then Mayer owed him an enormous debt, for his body had been the unfortunate channel through which it had come. He would collect his due in good time, and he would not have to borrow it.

It rained on the ride home. Sorrow and worry crept into Adam's tired mind, and he was heartbroken about Eva. She had been so beautiful, so godlily perfect. Should he have stolen her away with him? Or was she too mired in this cult of her father's to ever escape? And did he truly want her now that he had seen her commit such abominable acts? He certainly was as guilty as she, more so for losing control of himself, but he could not forget the sight of her and Jacob Frank. He wanted to believe Mayer that Eva was adopted, an illegitimate daughter of the Russian monarchy. For a while he held that in mind, but doubt hung heavily over it, and he knew in his heart that he had not only been possessed of extreme evil, but a witness to ritual incest.

He wondered how often the group of them practiced this rite. Was it every Sabbath? He thought of asking Mayer, but did not want to bring up the subject again. What they had done was dangerous in innumerable ways. What sort of energy had they brought forth by entertaining and fornicating with Sammael? Did he verily return to the ethers from whence he came, or was he still in this realm? More importantly, was he still within Adam?

He feared that the Frankists' secret would be leaked and his reputation and position harmed by his reckless actions. There were sixteen others who shared culpability in these most sinful of acts. They all knew his name, his title, his city of residence. He knew most of theirs, too, but how long would they keep quiet about his transfiguration? And who knew how many of the Bauers' servants had spied on them. But for the odd blessing before the mirrors at the last meal, there had been no oaths taken whatsoever, and none made for confidentiality. Jacob Frank had gone to prison over this before, and now that he was out, he had taken no precautions so that the same thing did not occur again. How foolish they all were!

If Adam were ever to confess these sins in the Catholic Church, which he certainly would *not*, he would be excommunicated, proclaimed anathema, perhaps even tried and hanged. His sins were beyond the scope of repentance and penance. He would be put to death, and so would the lot of them. They had committed adultery, homosexuality, sodomy, sorcery, and a variety of combined tangential transgressions more grievous than any of these acts alone!

Adam's mind began to reel. How would he protect himself and the rest of them from persecution, for certainly it was inevitable? However odd Jacob Frank's binding ritual before the mirror had seemed at the time, its effect was real and Adam felt an unshakable, familial connection to the rest of the group. The sensation of the bond to them heightened as he rode further and further away from Frankfurt Am Main, and he found himself worrying for their safety as much as he worried for his own. They were Jews, lest he forget, and the favorite target of so many other races.

To protect them all, he would focus on law, not just canon law, but civil and criminal. He would steer Zwack in this direction as well, so that they would all be well-defended when the need arose. In the event that any of them required legal counsel and exoneration from prison, he and Zwack would be ready with an arsenal of arguments and excuses for their behavior.

People were ostracized, exiled, and often killed for their religious practices in this day and age. That was the unfortunate reality. It was a dangerous time for one to be astray from any religion but the Roman Catholic or Protestant churches, much less to be involved in a demonic, ritual orgy.

Adam rationalized that a man was free to believe and practice religion as he so chose, whether it be demonic or angelic, and for Church or state to condemn him was neither righteous nor fair. What if the very God that everyone so sanctimoniously, so piously worshipped, was not a benevolent force after all? What if the God of the Catholic Church was actually Satan himself? It *was* possible, and it explained how Father Lorenzo had risen so close to the Papacy. Adam knew that Yahweh was the one true God of all, but not everyone believed as he did. A man's Truth was entirely dependent on his point of view.

Was it just and right to force everyone to share a common Christian belief? And if not, then who on earth would protect these people from violent mobs like the one that had killed his parents? The same could easily happen to him and his Frankist friends.

As soon as he returned home to Ingolstadt, he sorted through the volumes of his collection that contained grimoires, illustrations and descriptions of demons to see if he could find the entity called Sammael. Indeed several of his books contained entries for him, describing him as hoofed, tailed, bringing money and causing domestic disturbances.

He looked over and found the golem watching him from the aquarium with its large, golden eyes.

"Has all had been well while I've been away?" he asked.

"Your little mistress has come here to amuse herself for the day. She reads your books, you know," said the golem. "Of course, no one's been up to anything as interesting as what you have done," it said.

"What do you know of what I have done?" asked Adam.

"Such transgressions make it difficult for me to help you," answered the golem, looking away.

"If you're here to help me, why don't you *do* something to help me?" Adam yelled at the thing.

"I can give you some sage advice. You have left yourself prone. Look around you, at your home. This is not the abode of someone who's trying to fit nicely into society. Your life does not reflect that either, and you do not hide your avocations very well. If you would do more to conform, you would be less suspect."

Adam thought about what the creature had said. Had he heeded its warning and not gone to see Eva, he would have far less to worry over right now.

That night, he went to Afra's window, and placing a

ladder against her father's house, climbed up to woo her. Her younger sister, Anna Maria came to the window and laughed at him.

"What are you doing?" she asked.

"Windowing," he replied. "Where is Afra?"

"She has gone to mass with Mother," she said. "You can sing to me."

Adam climbed down, deflated. He walked to his uncle's house to tell him that he planned to propose to Afra Sausenhoefer. He was surprised at Ickstatt's response.

"Do not. You will be weighted down by a wife and family. Your studies curtailed, your life abridged. You cannot be effective in your career worrying about a family. What's wrong with your life, now? Are you not happy in your freedom?" Ickstatt was eating dinner alone and reading a book. "Have some stew," he pushed the serving bowl at Adam.

"I just want to be like everyone else, uncle," said Weishaupt. "I want to have a plain, normal life."

"Marrying someone is not the way."

"Why not?"

Ickstatt gulped down a drink of wine and wiped his chin with the napkin that he had tied around his neck, "Not her. I know her mother. Her mother belongs in the nuthouse. Like mother, like daughter."

"Afra's a very sensible girl," said Weishaupt.

"The maladies of the mind often do not come on until later in life, Adam, and you will be the one to have to contend with her. Do you know the whereabouts of her real father? Herr Zwack is only her stepfather, you know."

"I don't know anything about her family, uncle. That's not what's important. I don't even have a family."

"It is certainly important! These people will become your family! And mine... *I* am your family."

"Well, where is her father?"

"No one knows. Some say her mother killed him and

buried him out in the foothills away from town."

"That's nonsense," scoffed Weishaupt.

"Tell me this, have you ever spoken to her mother?"

"No," replied Adam, for he couldn't remember ever seeing her. He had a mental picture of what she should look like, but verily, he had never set eyes on her.

"She's a lunatic, an histrionic, drunken, loud-mouthed, rather stupid, lunatic!"

"I'm not marrying her mother, uncle! I'm going to marry Afra!"

"I am warning you. A marriage to her will be like a prison. It is life-long. Your days of flitting happily to and fro will cease and you will be burdened with cares!"

"You're not married and you don't seem all that well turned out. Maybe it would have done you some good. You wouldn't be so bitter and dull." And with that, Adam left his uncle's house.

He returned to Afra's window after nightfall. She had already dressed for bed and leaned upon her elbows on the windowsill as Adam stood outside on his ladder, reciting verses from the Song of Songs.

She kissed him.

"Marry me, Afra," he whispered.

Some minutes later, he found himself at her family's kitchen table, asking for her hand from the elder Herr Zwack, and Afra's mother, Portia. Portia was missing her front teeth and had the yellowish aura of someone with too much bile, but other than those detractions, she seemed no more a lunatic than other women her age. He thought now that his uncle must have selfish reasons for wanting him to remain a bachelor.

The following week, they were married in the Church of Our Lady by the new Bishop of Ingolstadt. Only the Baron Von Ickstatt stood with Adam, but Afra's entire family, it seemed, came to the wedding. Even Afra's eldest sister, Katja, who had been turned over to the convent since age fourteen, came from the priory in Nuremberg for the ceremony. She, like Afra and her and younger sister Anna Maria, was strikingly beautiful. Despite her beauty and piety, Adam detected a hot streak of madness within the young woman, the way her gaze lingered too long as if she were entranced. Her blue eyes fixated unnaturally on him many times that day, and she would not look away until her mother or some other person distracted her with another subject for her attention. He could not help but wonder what she was thinking. He recalled Ickstatt's warning that their mother was a lunatic, and that such things often manifest in the offspring. Perhaps that was why she had been sent away to the convent. Adam hoped, for his own sake, that Katja had been the recipient of all the madness in the family, and that Afra was spared that blight.

Afra came to live with him in his house next to the widow. Despite his uncle's warnings, Adam felt Afra was perfectly suited to him in every way. She had a keen interest in the arts metaphysical and he held nothing back from her. She was curious about all that he did, and all that he had read, and strove to have the same knowledge and speak with him on the same level as his equal. She read constantly. Weishaupt was glad of her interest but doubted she could fathom much of the material without a working knowledge of Latin, Greek, and Hebrew. He did not concern himself with her education and thought she would glean what was suitable for her, and forego what was clearly beyond her capacities.

Adam, himself, continued to practice sacred rites and partake of kykeon, despite the severe bouts of paranoia that it wrought. He was now guarded and secretive about all that he did, and he banished hourly for fear of astral intruders, particularly the presence of Sammael. Constantly vigilant, he examined everything in his house and surrounding garden for signs of malevolence, decay, and magical treachery, and scrubbed clean almost everything he owned, disposing of many of his more unseemly specimens.

It was the first of May that Adolphus Knigge came by unannounced, to share some hemp he had procured from a brother in France at the Grand Orient. Afra had gone to visit her sister at the convent, leaving Adam alone for the week. He had been waiting to dose his protégés, and began telling Knigge of the strange elixir called kykeon, of Inanna, of the overwhelming beauty of eternal flower power, and the illuminating tale of the extraterrestrial origins of mankind.

"What you're saying is I have to try the kykeon. Please, I must see the Blumenkraft for myself." Knigge held out his hand.

Weishaupt warned him of the pitfalls of the drug, the nakedness, the blithering, the blindingly vivid hallucinations. "But have no fear. I will watch over you and guide you through the abyss," he promised.

That night, he prepared the kykeon exactly as he had done for himself and dosed Knigge and Zwack. He kept a close eye on them, kept them indoors, not allowing them outside until after midnight.

Adam unveiled the oddities and extremities of nature he had collected, and finally the golem. Knigge and Zwack stood open-mouthed and staring at the little luminous creature in the aquarium.

"How do you do?" It said.

"What is it?" Zwack was horrified. "Is it not drowning?"

"No, it must live in solution. Isn't it spectacular?"

Zwack and Knigge stared in amazement while the golem did his best to be impressive, prophesying, turning flips, and singing off-key until Adam had had enough.

"Shall we go outside for a walk? It's late and there will be no one about," he suggested.

The threesome stepped out into the night. Adam looked over and saw the Frau's curtains drop. He often wondered how much she could hear through their common wall, and briefly entertained the idea of strangling her, burying her body in the back garden, and taking over her house himself so that he would not have to keep vigil against her.

The night was warmer than usual and Adam led them down to the Danube where their excited voices would be drowned out by the sounds of the water. While they hallucinated heavily, he told them in detail of the secret doctrines that had fallen into his lap, of the otherworldly origins of humanity, of man's purpose to aspire to a higher state, and finally, of man's obligation to rid the world of evildoers by any means necessary. He spoke of his practice of evoking demons to do his bidding, a thinly veiled threat meant to keep them from ever speaking of what he told them.

When he thought their minds most open and malleable, he took them back to his abode and let them rest on his bed together. It wasn't long before they were kissing and petting. He laughed when they began to fight for dominance, and suddenly they resumed awareness of themselves and became embarrassed.

"You will never tell of my sensitive menagerie and the secrets that I impart to you, and I will never speak of yours!" Weishaupt loomed above them, looking at their fingers on the other's nipples. He'd set them up and now had them for what sins of theirs he had orchestrated and witnessed. They were frozen with that exact realization as they looked at him then back at each other. They were now bound by their confidences and there was no return short of death for the two of them.

When they had come down from their heightened states, the three of them sat together on the floor of Weishaupt's loft and sipped Elderberry wine and smoked hemp without saying much for a long time.

Knigge lay back and sighed. "The ethereal forms were as blooming flowers, changing and growing. Ewige Blumenkraft indeed."

Zwack hung his head, "I never ever would have touched him had it not been for this strange drug. Please don't tell my sister."

Weishaupt shushed him. "We do what we do for reasons known only to the Universe. You have been illuminated and there is no greater gift than that."

"We are the Illuminated Seers of Bavaria," blurted Knigge. "The power of this elixir is indescribably immense. We should invite others to take kykeon and see for themselves these visions we have seen. I know a great number of gentlemen who would give anything to have such illuminating visions. All the grand touristas would come here and pledge our club," Knigge was excited.

"If everyone experienced kykeon, what sort of perfect garden of bliss could this world be?" contemplated Weishaupt.

"Everyone could taste of the illumination, the perfection of the heart, and strive for it in their daily lives. They would all see what was attainable..." Knigge's eyes were alight with inspiration.

"I remembered things, things from my childhood that I had hoped I'd forgotten forever, but they came back to me in grand and horrible proportions, distorted and terrifying. I would never want to take kykeon again or wish it upon anyone else." Zwack put his face in his hands.

"I felt a divine presence all around me and within me. I'm sorry you don't value our exchange. You wish it away as if it was something trifling. It was quite momentous and beautiful for me." Knigge touched his arm.

"Do you not remember what transpired?" Zwack demanded, pulling away from him.

"I was some sort of a succulen, a hothouse flower, a

projectile coming out of the ass of the great pig of the universe and I rode a calliope on the wind. I met you for tea beside a temple for Buddhas and we sat upon frogs and exchanged bolts of ecstatic energy. It was cosmic."

"Well I was someplace entirely different. I could tell you were pleased, but your pleasure seemed only to mock my suffering."

"You must do it again, then," Knigge insisted. "Perhaps when you're in a better mood."

"The more pure and pleasant your thoughts, the more enjoyable a time you will have," said Weishaupt.

"I want to tell everyone I know about this. Everyone needs to drink the kykeon! Everyone in the world!" Knigge sat at Weishaupt's desk and began muttering the names of Europe's most influential persons and writing a list of them.

Adam and Knigge planned how they would begin corresponding with the powerful and influential men they knew and invite them several at a time to a secret ritual where they would take the elixir. As Knigge rattled off the impressive roster of Europe's highest society, Weishaupt's mind spun with ideas of how he would ensnare these throngs of rich, high-minded, aristocrats by making them weak, feeding them mind-blowing esoteric knowledge by which he would ultimately control their actions, and then entrapping them in strange, improper rituals or embarrassing behavior. They would be forced to perfect themselves and their dominions for the good of mankind, or be smote down in innumerable ways. Kykeon would be a double-edged sword, and he knew now exactly how to wield it.

The opportunity to take this drug and experience its hallucinatory effects was a monumental experience, a life-changing event that could wash away a lifetime of negativity and bring one fully into the presence of the Lord, if only for a moment. If properly administered, it could set a man on the path of perfection. But the loss of personal control that came with it, would offer the opportunity to obligate each new member in every possible way. Weishaupt dreamed of the power he could wield over them, and the good he could do with all of them harnessed to follow his plan for the Universal Happiness and the Perfection of Mankind. The union and solidarity of their group would provide him and others like him who practiced unseemly arts, with protection from the Church and from those in power who would condemn a man for his questionable beliefs or experimental religious practices.

Why not even design a standard but damning ritual that they could participate in upon initiation that would make them his just as the Masonic lodges had done to their initiates? If everyone were guilty of the same, then there would be no choice but for each to be tolerant of his brother.

He would have a secret temple within the temple, and there would be degrees bestowed upon the most useful and clever. He would provide them with the answers to life's most pressing questions and if they were worthy, he would lead them to the knowledge they sought. And he would control them all, orchestrate them all, align them like the cogwheels in a finely tuned machine, utilizing and placing them perfectly in accordance with their specific talents and positions.

Though Weishaupt was not so well-connected as Knigge on the Continent, because of Washington, he had been a link in a number of circular letters that came from the Colonies that he forwarded on to central Europe and the East. He would make sure to participate in their every discussion and pepper his replies and commentary with news of his Illuminated Seers and hint at the mystical and esoteric knowledge they possessed. He knew he could elicit some responses from the curious group of minds who read the circulars. He did not know how many there were in the circulary, but he imagined that the chain of readers was quite long.

He responded to all manner of circular writers, including Moses and Novanglus of the colonial Sons of Liberty and forwarded their letters and his Illuminated response to Knigge, writing under the pseudonym Spartacus. He sent copies to Mayer, his richest friend, and back to Washington, care of his lodge number 22.

Knigge wrote to everyone he knew, and Weishaupt was amazed at how quickly their new clubhouse, a rented cottage with a big botanical garden in the midst of town, filled with curious strangers, grand touristas from the wealthiest families in Europe, seeking membership in the Bavarian Illuminated.

Weishaupt wasted no time in organizing them and initiating them into his Perfectibilism Society, meting out bits of ancient knowledge to the worthy and employing their gifts to the benefit of the group. He tested them for psychic gifts and other aptitudes, and found a small number of possible astral assassins. He was verily raising an army.

He traveled to Munich to Lodge Theodore and cleverly provided them with what he called "Sobriety tea," a mixture of Darjeeling and kykeon that laid waste to the entire lodge. After a grand display of his power and some austere words of persuasion, he found them each, even the Right Worshipful Master, loose-lipped and eager to divulge the coveted secrets of his degree. Weishaupt listened to each of them as they gave away all that they had sworn never to speak. Again and again he found them to have only a glimmer of what truly lay at the heart of the mysteries to which they were entrusted. In return for their secrets, he told them some of his, secrets that illuminated their own secrets, but only just enough to make them clamor to be a part of his clandestine group that he assured them would protect them from persecution for all that they had just divulged to him.

Mayer was quick to respond to the invitation to initiation, for Weishaupt had indicated to him that a group of this nature if grown wide enough, could afford him with rich banking clientele and plenty of those touristas who lived far beyond their means and would not protest the exorbitant interest Mayer was charging on his borrowed coin. Most of all, the group would help provide protection for the outlandish group of Frankists to which he and his wife belonged.

Daily, Weishaupt used the private office in the attic of the new clubhouse to scry, meditate and divine with cards so that he would not be caught unawares by any future event. He knew there would be a holy woman, a stranger, who would appear to participate in the sex rites performed by the British Hellfire Clubs, ones that he desired to emulate and improve upon. The unsavory sex rite orchestrated by Herr Frank and the Bauers still haunted him, but he reasoned that such powers were his own to be wielded, and could be used for loftier outcomes, not just monetary gain, but universal peace, freedom, and divine perfection. He had used Afra for similar rites several times without the knowledge or participation of her brother Zwack, and she had enjoyed it, but despite his deep disdain for the sanctity of marriage among most other social customs, he had become extremely jealous when one of Knigge's distinguished guests had enjoyed her overmuch, and so discontinued her participation and the new initiate's.

He had just finished some writing, and went down to tend the flowers in the garden when a hooded figure appeared in the foyer.

"Welcome," said Weishaupt tentatively. "What is your name?" He began the line of questioning he generally used on otherworldly apparitions, for he was not quite sure of the human nature of this one before him. Before he could say another word, Katja, Afra's eldest sister pulled back her hood and stared at him. "I couldn't wait," she said.

"Sister?" Adam asked, perplexed.

"I ran all the way here from the abbey," she declared.

He cautiously helped her remove her cloak. She wore her nun's attire and looked as if she had been sleeping outside, for there was straw in her hair and some stuck to her habit.

"Are you all right?"

"Oh, yes," she said.

To him, it was suddenly obvious that she was the strange, holy woman for whom he was waiting. He drew her a bath and bade her wash, and when she had done so, gave her one of Afra's dresses to wear. She was every bit as beautiful as her sister, if not more so, in her innocence. She reminded him of a wild bird, captured in the hand. He felt that if he did the wrong thing, said the wrong word, entertained the wrong intent, she would fly off in a frenzy.

They sat before the fire and she told him of her escape from the convent, of her dissatisfaction with her life as a nun, and her intentions to fulfill her passion to live a normal life.

He touched her cheek and she turned her face toward his. He kissed her lips, and she let herself be kissed. "We mustn't tell Afra or your family that you're here. You may stay here in our house if you will," Weishaupt invited her delicately.

"Oh thank you. I wouldn't know where to go," a small tear rolled down her cheek. "All my life, they all have been so cruel to me, so vicious to me."

"Why?" he asked, for he couldn't imagine Afra or Zwack or their younger sister Anna tormenting this creature.

"I don't know," she wailed and threw herself into his arms.

When her sorrow had abated some, he took her by her

soft hand, and gave her a tour of the clubhouse and his menagerie, gingerly informing her that theirs was no ordinary group of gentlemen, but an extraordinary legion of enlightened souls who would soon mobilize to put aright thousands of years of oppression, inhumanity, and injustice by annihilating the powers that be by using the most sublime and ingenious of devices. He kissed her hand and laid it on his heart. "I knew you would come to our aid."

She stared at him, wild-eyed, and gushed. "The moment I saw you, I knew... I knew I had to be near you..."

He took her virginity that night in a rite of his own design, invoking Venus and Uranus, and ceremonially raping her. He sensed her reticence and fear and titillated her exquisitely until she had spun upon his member nine times. He held her there in her ecstasy and looked into the deep mystery of her pupils until she began babbling curses and laughing hysterically.

When he had cleared their circle, he told her that the attic room belonged to her. She must not, however, go out in public, or she would be sent back to the convent where she would undoubtedly be imprisoned for the rest of her life. His ritual partner had arrived.

As he predicted with the cards, Franz Kolmer appeared in Ingolstadt two days before the first group was to meet, bearing gifts of incense and wine, as if he had been invited from on High to join the initiation. Adam did not question his timely appearance, only his activities of late. Kolmer revealed that he had been back and forth to Egypt twice since they'd last seen one another. Despite his weakness for opium, Adam still held Kolmer and his occult knowledge in the highest regard, and welcomed him into the uppermost degree and Inner Circle of the club.

Weishaupt grouped the initiates according to their astrological makeup to effect the most harmonious of experiences. The first group contained himself, Rothschild, Kolmer, Bode and Mitten - these latter two he had found to be possessed of tremendous psychic gifts, rivaling, and in some cases, surpassing his own. He planned their night with meticulous precision and prepared for every incidental with care. In case someone got sick, he had salts and a bucket. In case they all wanted to lie down, he had cots. If they wanted to run amok in the streets naked, he had a lock for the door, and posted Knigge and Zwack outside all night to stand guard. He brought some of his favorite curiosities from home to look at. He printed a book in large clear script for when his eyes went buggy and couldn't focus – a list of his own, important ideas and some prayers to ponder while under the influence of kykeon, in case minds wandered to morbid thoughts. He hired a harpist to make dulcet sounds behind a screen, while they relaxed in the confines of the temple.

Weishaupt formed with them a circle in the middle of the room and said a prayer for YVWH to protect them while on their journeys. He had made ready five phials of kykeon. The dosage would prove to be too much for all of them.

They focused on candlelight and music. Weishaupt felt the soft tissue under his tongue tensing and tasting bitter. He saw shadows that formed cats and dots and soon there was an animated play of light upon the floor that had a life of its own. He had seen this lighted floor before, once in the fountain, and he flashed back upon his boyhood for many long minutes, marveling at how far he had come, how fortunate he had been to survive his ordeals, and how exquisite the intertwining patterns of life and fate.

He found himself speaking incoherently of his plans to rule the world and become immortal, but it seemed not to matter. The rest understood and sincerely wanted to be a part of whatever he had to offer. He found no one resistant to going along with him. Each expressed vehement disgust with the ruins to which their governments and religions had declined. All wanted these institutions repaired or done away with. All wanted a better status of life for mankind but knew not where to begin. The Bible seemed to have only partial answers and most knew not where else to look. Weishaupt, even under the spell of the drug, was able to provide them with the esoteric answers they hungered to hear, and he proposed a utopian solution based on this heightened freedom of mind they experienced with the kykeon, where laws and social customs such as marriage and daily toil were no longer necessary.

Mayer and the others fell into fantasies about the future of the enterprise and saw many strange and wonderful things before them. They tried to explain their visions while in the throes of them but soon fell silent again.

Knigge came inside only once to ask if they needed anything and poured them water into their tankards and made them drink. He lit a communal pipe full of hashish and made them smoke. The water and the hashish re-ignited the initial surge of psychedelia and the group found themselves peaking again.

It was around six o'clock in the morning and their hallucinations had not abated, and Weishaupt had not the wherewithal to orchestrate the sexual entrapment he'd had in mind, and simply let the plan go by the wayside, for his mind was in a state of utter fugue. Too late, he wondered if he had not given them all too much kykeon, but there was nothing he could do about it now. He was out of his gourd completely on this batch, catching himself drooling into a puddle on the floor as he stared through the wall at a lavender-colored tiger that hung by its tail. He vowed he would modify the dosage in the future and gathered his faculties enough to attempt to bring them down with a discussion.

Adam explained the ages, the Precession of the aeons, the big astrological cycles found in the rubbings of the Sumerian tablets he had come by. "It is now the age of Pisces, the fish." He explained, and told them what they must do, what role they would have in bringing about a new world order in the Age of Aquarius. He told them of the people who came from a world away from earth and granted Abraham, Noah, and Moses covenants. The Holy Land was key. "And the New World," he explained, "is tantamount to our plan. It is our Promised Land where the Illuminated will flourish and prosper and ring in the light of the New Age."

"But the New World is so far away. And the journey there is exceedingly perilous," added Bode, suddenly lucid.

"Perhaps. But it will be well worth the risk," said Weishaupt.

"How far does it extend to the West?" asked Rothschild.

"There's a river called the Mississippi, and that is its boundary. But the land east of that is vast and rich."

"You make it sound like it's up for grabs," said Mayer.

"It is. It is a land in dispute. The Colonies will soon declare themselves a republic of free and independent states. All we would have to do is buy them," said Weishaupt pointedly to Mayer.

"Or just take them," grinned Mitten.

"And then we could make our own laws," said Bode.

"But we would have to war with the King of England," said Kolmer.

"That is already being done for us," Adam whispered.

CHAPTER XXX

DASHWOOD

Sir Francis Dashwood entered the King's private library and bowed before George III whose manservant was fastening a red cape about his shoulders. "Lord le Despencer, be seated," said the King with an impatient wave of his hand.

"Yes, Your Majesty." Despencer took a velvet chair. He donned his turban and brooch, dressing the part of the Royal Sorcerer, an epithet used only in a whisper by the King himself, and only on the rare occasions when dire circumstances necessitated otherworldly actions. The King sat down upon his throne-like chair, and the manservant bowed and went out, leaving them in private.

"Hickey and that do-nothing governor of New York have failed us!" shouted the King.

"I heard. Some Negro scullery maid or some such nothing servant tipped them off to the plot," sighed Despencer.

"She saw Thomas Hickey putting poison in General Washington's peas! The Irish idiot! How could we have trusted an Irishman to do an Englishman's job?" shouted George.

"Does anyone suspect where his orders came from?" asked Dashwood.

"Dead men tell no tales, Despencer. If they suspected, nothing can be confirmed. Hickey was hanged for treason! *Treason*! How can there be treason if the King's own man is trying to put poison in a usurper's peas?" George seethed. "This has gone too far, with these heathen bastards thirty thousand strong defending Massachusetts Bunker Island, secret meetings of continental congresses! The audacity of these low-breeds!"

"Have no fear, Your Majesty.   I and my legions are at

your service. We will set all this aright once and for all."

"I want General Washington dead! *DEAD!*" The King's eyes bulged, and Despencer recognized the royal madness, the same that had afflicted his father and grandfather as his pupils went from round to slit like a cat's and back to round again. "I don't care who, what sorcery, what devils you have in your service, whomever, whatever darkness you have to employ to get the job done, do it!"

"He will be dead in a fortnight, sire," replied le Despencer coolly. "It will be my sheer pleasure to smite this ignoble imposter down to the lowest depths of hell where he shall conflagrate forevermore."

"And what of *Mister* Franklin?" asked the King.

"I have something a little more personal in mind for him. He has done me a very personal affront, one that I will not let go unpunished."

"What personal affront?" asked the King.

"I'd rather not disclose…"

"What personal affront?!"

"I beg your most discreet confidence, your majesty," Despencer looked at him and wondered if his secret would be safe.

"Tell me, what has he done?" demanded the King.

"He has sired a child by my wife."

"What?" the King was horrified. "The babe just christened?"

"I love her, nonetheless, for we would have none but for her, and I would have no heir. But when I look upon her face, I see him. I see the jowls, the hang-dog look in the eyes."

"Detestable!" shouted the King. "We shall be avenged! And soon! Avail your blackest arts and do not digress from your purpose!"

Dashwood concealed his own seething fury well, out of proper respect for His Majesty, but the truth was, that he was all-consumed by his thoughts of vengeance, and hourly, sent out arrows to find and injure Franklin. Washington was not someone he had thought too much on, for he had assumed, and wrongly so, that the Royal Governor of New York would not fail so miserably in the plot to kill General Washington, so now it was all back on him. He would adopt a strategy more ruthless and black than he had ever conjured, and so deliver it upon Washington and his army.

He returned home to West Wycombe in the middle of the night, and going outside into the midst of his six-sided mausoleum, set to work, calling forth by their barbarous names, those soulless, ancient entities fit for his diabolical purpose.

CHAPTER XXXI

WEISHAUPT

In a matter of weeks, the Order had all but taken over the Masonic Lodges in the region. Lodge Theodore of Munich was but the shell of the succulent and inviting meat inside the Perfectibilism cult Weishaupt had built, the club that had drawn the most conspicuously wealthy and powerful from all parts surrounding. It became the social hub, the only place to be for someone truly in the know and Adam thrived on their newfound popularity.

Daily, Knigge briefed Weishaupt with the background information on the hundreds of men who met in clandestine groups at the lodges on specific evenings. Weishaupt organized a hierarchy quickly, with himself at the top, Rothschild and Knigge on the next tier and Zwack, Mitten, and Kolmer others on the third tier. The pyramid expanded geometrically from there and included the most famous and infamous gentlemen in Europe.

Adam handpicked certain men and trained them to

perform special tasks as he had done with his students, who now came back to him for initiation. Some, he taught to respond to subtle cues, cues and words of which they were quite unaware, and more so of what they would be bound to do when they heard them. Weishaupt was the most powerful force in their lives, though they did not realize it. He saved the sexual rituals for only the upper tiers and only rarely advanced anyone else into the upper echelons.

He continued to use Katja for his rituals at night, and daily, bedded her at every opportunity.

He would linger all afternoon at the clubhouse, dismissing curious members that he must meditate in the attic. Several times a day, they would quickly engage themselves, copulating silently, madly in the upstairs room. He wanted desperately to let his hands roam over her naked skin, but she always insisted on keeping her dress on in case they were interrupted or caught in the act. She wore no bloomers and he would sit her upon his lap and bring her to madness.

He ripped open her bodice, kissing her nipples and plunging his massive manhood into her. He began tearing off her dress and despite her protests, continued to rape her in this way, growing more and more excited as she struggled against him. He picked her up and shoved her up against the wall, raping her madly. They gushed for what seemed like minutes before he withdrew and exploded onto her huge supple breasts.

They stood together wet and tingling when there was a knock at the door. He'd only put on the chain, and the door opened an inch. It was Afra.

"Adam?" she said, her fingernails curling around the edge of the door. "Let me in."

Quickly, he cleared a trunk of books and shoved Katja inside it. He stripped off the rest of his clothes and let Afra inside. "I'm sorry I was meditating." He gave her a kiss.

She found him still erect, smiled, and knelt down to sheath him in her hot mouth. Adam reeled. There was no one who could make him respond so well, and even though he was momentarily spent, he felt himself surging again in her delicious mouth. He knew Katja was watching them from the trunk; he saw her peek up under the lid, but that only aroused him more as Afra's lips and tongue pleasured him.

He removed her clothes and held her close to him, penetrating her, his most familiar lover, making her spin over and over again. The two of them were better practiced than he and Katja and she bore witness to this from the trunk.

Adam wanted nothing more than for her to reveal herself and join them in a party on the bed, but she did not. Adam thrust into Afra slowly and authoritatively, making her moan and scream in ecstasy. They peaked together, kissed each other deeply, as they reveled a final time.

They lay together motionless only a minute before Afra recalled her motive for seeking him out. "Oh, Adam, Katja's run away from the convent."

"Well that's no wonder. Good for her," he replied.

"No, you don't know Katja. She needs the care of the convent. She can't be turned loose. She can't take care of herself. She'll hurt herself," Afra explained.

"Don't worry. I'm sure she's well," he assured her as he pulled up his breeches.

"Please, can you see where she is?" begged Afra.

"Go home and I'll be there in a moment. My best scrying bowl is there."

When she had gone, Adam helped Katja from the trunk. She was angry. Her hair was mussed and her dress badly torn.

"I'm sorry about your dress." Adam said, holding her close and kissing her cheek. "Please forgive me. I'm voracious when it comes to the Sausenhoefer women." He

390

slipped his hand down inside bodice and held up one of her big, round breasts. His hand glided over the other one and down between her legs. She wanted to protest but he pushed her across the trunk and lifted her dress, pleasuring her. "Please, I don't like it anymore..." she cried, shedding tears. He continued with her until her body could not lie and she was close to spinning. He withdrew his fingers and penetrated her arse. Her eyes widened and nipples hardened and he pleasured her with his hand. She began spinning hard, harder than he'd ever seen her spin upon his member. He barely moved and she moaned, screamed and shook, her juices flooding over his hand.

He tasted her, and feeling her master, he pulled her hips down so that he was fully inside her. He teased her again with his fingers and she spun in spite of herself, squeezing the last excruciating drops of pleasure from him.

He watched her try to fix her disheveled hair as she huffed tearfully about her torn dress.

He looked at the clock. "I'm sorry. I've got to go home and help Afra find you."

She looked horrified, then quickly realized he was joking. He dressed hurriedly and opened the door. "I'll be back in an hour."

Katja pulled on her stole and looked at him icily. "This was our place. You did that to her in our place!"

"It's a gentlemen's clubhouse, actually," he quipped, "And she is my wife." And with that, he went out, locking her safely inside.

Once home, Afra watched him anxiously as he carried a jug of water up to the loft to fill his scrying bowl. "Please, you must find my poor sister," she pleaded.

"Yes, yes, yes," he answered and poured the water into the silver cauldron. Immediately he saw George riding through a green meadow at the head of a thousand foot soldiers. He appeared again, dressed in white shirt and

391

buff breeches walking out into the night. Then Adam heard the sound of a shot, smelled the smoke from a musket at close range, felt the fiery burning pain of a musket ball in his neck, smelled the cooked flesh, then saw him laid out in death, his arms crossed over his chest.

"George!" Adam's heart raced. The water filled with a swarm of amorphous shadows, dark, unkind entities flitting, besetting him, assailing the image of his brother.

He flew downstairs to his desk and began penning a letter, warning his brother of extreme, imminent danger.

"Did you see her? Where is she?" begged Afra.

"I didn't see her. I was unable," he said quickly, then crumpled up the parchment. "There's not time to write a letter," he said to himself. "There's not time. It has already happened!" Suddenly he began thinking that if George were lost, then so would be the great New World upon which Adam had every kind of design. All his plans for the perfection of mankind would die if George died. There would be no place for him to enact his Order, nowhere for him to master, to rule, to design the Society that he had so dearly planned all these years. George's victory, his skill, his luck, were key to Adam's deepest fulfillment, he was not ashamed to admit. It all relied on someone else, someone whom he had never met.

He removed the loose brick on the mantle and retrieved the amulet. "Afra, I might be gone for some time this evening," he called back on his way out the door.

He ran to the top of the hill and unwrapped the thing. He remembered the magic words to summon Inanna and spoke them to the sky, holding the amulet close so that she could not snatch it away again.

It seemed as though hours passed. Night fell and the stars shone down as he repeated her magical name to bring her to him. Suddenly he felt a breeze that swept the top of the hill, and there in the sky swirled a spiral, like a swastika. The center of it dilated open and a great, triangular skyship emerged, too big it seemed, to have been born through the orifice of the spiral. It was even greater still as it hovered above him, blocking out the light of the stars in night sky above.

"Inanna!" he called up at it.

CHAPTER XXXII

WASHINGTON

All that day, Washington and his army were on the move. His scouts reported redcoats less than two days' ride to the south, and closing the distance at a great clip. The village they had passed through had seemed strangely deserted, and Washington was certain the place was a Tory nest. They closed their shutters and locked their doors as his men moved down the main road. His men found a well past the center of town and refilled their canteens. Not a soul came out to greet them or tell them to clear off, and Washington found it eerie.

They marched on through the muddy fields under fair, summer skies. He was aware of the woods around them, aware of the birds, the deer, the standing water here and there, and the tracks that led off into the trees from the road at various places. He was keenly aware of it all, the least of which was the feeling he had of being closely pursued, and he did not rest his men once, but allowed them to eat their bread while marching, and break rank to pot in the bushes and run to catch up to the line. They did not stop all day, but kept marching.

Reluctantly Washington halted them late in the evening, long after the summer sun had set and they broke camp far off the main road. He had posted lookouts for the last ten miles, and figured the first of them would ride ahead and warn him when he should be marching again. But for now, they rested. Washington's personal guard quickly threw up their General's tent, and the man himself retired within. He wasted no time writing, but recorded only a few lines about the day's events in his diary. He turned out his lantern and slept.

It was sometime during the night, that he was awakened by the call of a bird. He had been dreaming a strange dream. An angel had appeared to him with a crown and torch of valor and showed him the three great passings of souls. He turned on his lantern and wrote down the dream, for it seemed portentous. His tent flap moved and the bird's voice called gently on the night air.

"Quacius?" he asked, for that was name of his personal slave, a young Negro who'd been in his service since his birth at Mount Vernon.

Washington walked out of his tent into the midst of camp, looked at the soldiers sleeping around the embers of the campfire. Not a one was awake, even the guards he had posted slept the sleep of exhaustion. He turned back and was met by a caped man in shadow. He could see the white wig beneath the tricorne hat, but no features of his face were discernible. He was about to speak when he realized there was a musket between them. He heard the shot, felt the musket ball enter the place at the bottom of his throat, between his collarbones. He felt the scorch of hot smoke infiltrate his lungs, and then the cool, damp earth beneath him where he fell and lay gasping for breath.

CHAPTER XXXIII

WEISHAUPT

He was suddenly standing in a dark, soggy field at the edge of some woods. He heard the sounds of distant gunfire and excited shouts, and knew that he had indeed arrived near the front lines of the American war. He walked swiftly toward the noise and prayed he wasn't too late.

He stole around the camp in the dark, much afraid that he might be mistaken for a spy. He found the largest of the tents and peeked inside. In the lamplight, George lay on his bed, pale, asleep, his breath labored and shallow. A doctor stuffed gauze into his chest wound and covered it over again. The doctor washed his hands in the basin and went out.

Weishaupt crept inside and looked at the man. How much he looked like him, indeed! He was unnerved by their resemblance and Washington's deathly guise. It was as if he was watching himself die.

Adam knelt at his side and whispered in English. "I finally see you at last." He pressed his hands upon Washington's temples and charged him. He recalled Inanna's warning, not to save him, not to resurrect him if he was too late. Washington opened his eyes in the dim lantern light and recognized him. "Brother, you've come to my side as I called you. I would not have believed it, but for the dream that I have had just now."

"You must recover your health now. What do you require? Water?"

"Yes a sip, please," whispered Washington. "I am so thirsty."

Weishaupt found a wooden cup and dipped some water into it. He helped George lift his head and put the cup to his mouth. He swallowed. Weishaupt saw the water mixed with blood trickle out the hole in Washington's chest, and drip pale pink upon the sheet.

Tears welled in Adam's eyes. "Tell me of your dreams, brother, tell me what you will have me do." This was not how he had imagined their meeting.

"Let us have a smoke. Did you bring any hemp? I have run out weeks ago," said Washington.

Adam had the pipe he'd given him. He took it out, lit it,

and put it to Washington's lips.

"Before you came to me, an Angel of the Lord appeared to me and led me by the hand. She was so beautiful, and she showed me three great passings of the souls of mankind. The first was a terrible plague where many perished. The sky was full of the lights of souls flying from this world," said Washington.

Weishaupt was reminded of the Black Plague and the Thirty Years' war, both events had taken a large human toll.

Washington continued, "The second great cataclysm was twice as horrible and many suffered, but nothing has ever been so great as the devastation of the last world. Almost no one was left here. All flew away from this place. I saw the sky as bright as day, so many souls filled it as they departed."

"Why?"

"Wars that should have been stopped. Evil, inhuman men who should have been assassinated were allowed to persevere, opened and paved the pathways for unthinkable crimes. Injustice was tolerated by the common people - too weak and ignorant to fight their oppressors, to use their God-given power. Everyone suffers for the greed of a few. You must continue training the assassins to keep the evil ones at bay. *You* must bell the cat. *You* must ensure that my Order lives on so that the assassins will know their art tomorrow and be not afraid to practice it when the time comes."

"What assassins?" asked Weishaupt, feeling a chill. "What order is this of which you speak?"

Washington choked and his eyes grew wide. Weishaupt grabbed his hands. "Please brother. Stay! Tell me what you mean!" Weishaupt begged.

A dark figure entered the tent. Adam spun around to face a young, Negro servant.

"Who you?" asked Quacius, dropping his bundle of

clothes and brandishing a musket.

"He is my brother..." began Washington.

"Him?" asked Quacius. "He's your brother?"

"...come... to replace me." Washington's voice was barely audible.

This was the first Adam had heard of such a plan. "No. I don't think that's a good idea..."

Washington knew little of Adam's habits or he never would have suggested such a thing. "Please. Or my troops will lose heart. All will be lost. Their commander cannot die. Not now." Washington's eyes penetrated his.

Adam swallowed. He knew nothing of military maneuverings and he hated war. Not to mention, the organization of Europe's foremost secret order was dependent on him and his continued cultivation of it. He had a wife and a home, and a mistress locked in an attic in the middle of town. He could not undertake what Washington was suggesting. It was then he heard Inanna's voice "And you will be one of my greatest generals."

Washington exhaled all that he ever was, and his hand went limp in Adam's.

"Master, no!" Quacius shook him by the shoulder, and wailed pitifully. The great man was dead.

Weishaupt looked around and put a hand over his mouth. "If I am to replace him, you must say nothing. And we must bury him quickly before we are found out."

Quacius nodded, wiping his eyes on his shirttail. "We'll cover him up and take him out to a pretty place."

It was nearing dawn, and every available soldier now combed the woods for Washington's assailant. Adam and Quacius put Washington's body in a wagon and drove it quietly out of the camp.

"Where did you come from? You look just like General Washington," asked Quacius.

"Virginia colony," lied Weishaupt.

"You sho' don't talk like it," said the slave.

They buried Washington on a hill, between two oak trees, and for fear of their plot being discovered, they did not mark his grave.

They returned mid-morning. Adam washed the evidence of having dug a grave off his person, climbed into Washington's bed, and put the dressing on his chest where Washington had been wounded, and fit his wig on his own head. He found Washington's diaries and began reading them. His brother had been a serious and complicated man, but fortunately one who took copious notes and wrote extensively about his military plans. The more Adam read, the more he realized what dire circumstances the army was in. They would run out of food in two weeks, some of the soldiers' tours were expiring, and Washington disliked most of his officers. Intelligence afield had reported that the forces gathering against them numbered in the tens of thousands. In any engagement, they would be outnumbered nearly four to one. The plan for action was speculative at best and Adam was completely unfamiliar with the geography. Once more, Washington had written that they were hotly pursued.

Adam Weishaupt dressed in Washington's buff and blue uniform. Washington was quite a bit taller than Adam and he thought he should stay seated or in the saddle so that it would be difficult for anyone to measure his height, for it would be all too easy to see that he was an imposter. He prayed that Quacius would keep his confidence.

He was already on horseback and riding down the line when the doctor came to tend his wounds. The doctor proclaimed his recovery miraculous and the soldiers were enlivened by Washington's prominent and healthful presence after witnessing him so gravely wounded only the day before. He murmured his commands and Quacius shouted them overhead so that none could detect his newly acquired accent. He wrote notes to his officers and had Quacius or one of his personal guards deliver them.

Weishaupt hoped that he looked enough like Washington that no one would be the wiser.

He rode to the bluff overlooking the army's camp and wondered how his life had come to this. He had lost himself in another man's identity. Another man's mission had become his own. Below him on the field lay the tents and cannon, and the horses and men of war, and they were all under his dominion.

And watching him with acute suspicion from across the field in the cover of the trees was Major Benedict Arnold who wondered at the miraculous recovery of his would-be victim.

****

RITE OF THE REVOLUTION

COMING SOON...

The American Conspiracy

Roquel Rodgers'

Spellbinding Sequel to

RITE OF THE REVOLUTION

RITE OF THE REVOLUTION

Made in the USA
Lexington, KY
18 October 2011